PRAISE FOR

Sleeping in Eden

"Baart expertly unravels the backstory of her intriguing characters, capturing the nuances of both life-tested relationships and the intense passion of first love. Ripe with complex emotion and vivid prose, this story sticks around long after the last page is turned."

—*Publishers Weekly*

"*Sleeping in Eden* is bittersweet and moving, and it will haunt you from page one. Nicole Baart writes with such passion and heart."

—Sarah Jio, author of *Goodnight June*

"Nicole Baart's *Sleeping in Eden* is vivid storytelling with a temporal sweep. In Baart's cleverly woven mystery, the characters' intertwined fates prove that passions transcend time—and secrets will always be unearthed."

—Jenna Blum, author of *The Stormchasers*

"Nicole Baart has written a novel that satisfies on every level. *Sleeping in Eden* is a compelling mystery, a tragic love story, a perceptive consideration of the callous whim of circumstance and, perhaps most important, a beautiful piece of prose. I guarantee this is a book that will haunt you long after you've turned the last page."

—William Kent Krueger, author of *Ordinary Grace*

"*Sleeping in Eden* is intense and absorbing from the very first page. Written in lovely prose, two seemingly different storylines collide in a shocking conclusion."

—Heather Gudenkauf, author of *Little Mercies*

"With lyrical prose and a narrative that kept me turning pages at a breakneck speed, *Sleeping in Eden* delivered everything I yearn for in a novel: evocative plot lines, well-drawn characters, and a heart-stopping conclusion."

—Tracey Garvis Graves, author of the bestselling novel
On the Island

"*Far From Here*, Nicole Baart's tale of the certainties of absolute fear and the uncertainty of love whirls the reader up and never lets go."
—Jacquelyn Mitchard, author of *The Deep End of the Ocean* and
Second Nature: A Love Story

"*Far From Here* was a rare journey to a place that left me healed and renewed by the end of this beautiful, moving novel. A tribute to love in all its forms—between a man and a wife, between sisters, and among mothers and daughters—my heart ached while I read *Far From Here*, but it ached more when I was done and there were no more pages to turn."
—Nicolle Wallace, author of *Eighteen Acres* and *It's Classified*

"Nicole Baart is a writer of immense strength. Her lush, beautiful prose, her finely drawn characters, and especially her quirky women, all made *Far From Here* a book I couldn't put down."
—Sandra Dallas, author of *True Sisters* and *The Quilt Walk*

"Nicole Baart is a huge talent who has both a big voice and something meaningful to say with it. *Far From Here* is a gorgeous book about resilient people living in a broken world, finding ways to restore hope and even beauty in the pieces."
—Joshilyn Jackson, author of *Gods in Alabama* and
A Grown-Up Kind of Pretty

THE BEAUTIFUL
DAUGHTERS

ALSO BY NICOLE BAART

Sleeping in Eden
Far From Here
The Snow Angel
Beneath the Night Tree
The Moment Between
Summer Snow
After the Leaves Fall

THE BEAUTIFUL
DAUGHTERS

A Novel

NICOLE BAART

ATRIA PAPERBACK

New York London Toronto Sydney New Delhi

ATRIA PAPERBACK

An Imprint of Simon & Schuster, Inc.
1230 Avenue of the Americas
New York, NY 10020

First Atria Paperback edition April 2015

ATRIA PAPERBACK and colophon are trademarks of Simon & Schuster, Inc.

For information about special discounts for bulk purchases, please contact Simon & Schuster Special Sales at 1-866-506-1949 or business@simonandschuster.com.

The Simon & Schuster Speakers Bureau can bring authors to your live event. For more information or to book an event, contact the Simon & Schuster Speakers Bureau at 1-866-248-3049 or visit our website at www.simonspeakers.com.

Interior design by Jaime Putorti

Manufactured in the United States of America

10 9 8 7 6 5 4 3 2 1

Library of Congress Cataloging-in-Publication Data

Baart, Nicole.
  The beautiful daughters: a novel / Nicole Baart.
      pages cm
  Summary: "Two best friends—soul sisters—experience a traumatic event and find themselves quite literally flung to opposite corners of the earth. Five years later, they return home to Iowa to confront the secrets that tore them apart and, hopefully, find redemption"—Provided by publisher.
  1. Female friendship—Fiction. 2. Life change events—Fiction. 3. Secrets—Fiction. I. Title.
  PS3602.A22B43 2015
  813'.6—dc23

                                        2014049133

ISBN 978-1-4391-9738-7
ISBN 978-1-4391-9739-4 (ebook)

For all the beautiful daughters.
You know who you are.

"Hope has two daugthers; their names are Anger and Courage. Anger at the way things are, and Courage to see that they do not remain as they are."

ST. AUGUSTINE OF HIPPO

Prologue

He fell forever.

Of course, it was all over in a second or two, a stutter of heartbeats that shivered through her chest. But as she watched, the world paused, and she could feel the earth shift, the wind, fine-edged as a blade. Her life was contained in those spare moments. The first time that David kissed her, and the last. His skin against hers. His hands. Mouth. Breath warm as summer.

She missed him before he was gone.

She wondered if his life passed before his eyes, or if the memories had somehow come undone and were being quietly unraveled in the space between them. Each impression a slender ribbon that scattered in the breeze before she had a chance to collect it and tuck it away, safe.

So he came at her in wisps and sighs, scraps of life that she gathered with greedy fingers and fumbled, lost. His laugh. His arms. His lips.

And then, he was the little boy in all those photographs that graced Piperhall. Slight and tall, handsome even before he could be considered a young man. She felt sometimes that she had loved him before she even knew him. At six and seven and eight, and all the years that came after. Heart and soul, up until the moment her loathing matched her love and she found herself trading places with a woman she didn't recognize. She was two halves of a whole.

But David Galloway was a mystery. Her lover, her best friend, a stranger. He was the beginning.

And his death was what felt like the end.

PART I

ADRIENNE

1

~

It was less a car accident than a struck match.

Adrienne had felt off all day, lopsided and a little dizzy, like the time she had taken the cable car to the top of Gibraltar and nearly fallen off the rock from vertigo. But she had ignored the strange sense of premonition, the feeling that her world was about to change, because Adri didn't like change. And she didn't like the madness exploding around her, each scene a snapshot so smudged and surreal she had to wonder if it was all a bad dream. A nightmare. But it wasn't.

Broken glass. The thick scent of gasoline whipped up by the wind. Two dark slashes on the concrete that marked the place where the truck driver had hit the brakes too late. The road was a menacing swath of sharp edges, and the crowd a riot of colors and fists and dialects Adri didn't understand. She could taste the musky press of hot skin, the sour-sweet tang of the red dust that churned beneath her feet. It was familiar and foreign, home and away.

She wasn't afraid until someone reached into the wreckage of the overturned truck and brandished a single bottle that hadn't been shattered in the rollover. It was an empty Fanta bottle, utterly harmless. Until he smashed it against the up-turned bumper and held it, jagged and glittering, like a blade.

The man wasn't even looking at her. His fist was raised high above his head where the bottle caught the sun and refracted light like fine crystal. But Adri knew that pretty things could be deadly, and whether or not she was a part of the drama that smoldered around her, she had to get off the street. She had to get Caleb off the street. Adri put her hand out for him, but she clutched at air. Spinning around, she scanned the crowd and caught sight of him in the ditch below the compound.

"They're shutting the gate!" Caleb called. He looked back at Adri, frozen amid the African Kristallnacht that roiled around her, and shouted something that she couldn't hear over the sudden rush and roar of the growing mob.

She ran. And thanked the Lord and her father and The North Face for the grace of sturdy boots as glass crunched beneath her feet. Adri had swapped her sandals for boots at the last minute because it was an immunization day, and the children had learned quickly what the needles meant. Sometimes she had to pin them down. She had to scuffle and wrestle and fight. And though it was easily a hundred degrees in the shade, she wore cargo pants, a long-sleeved white shirt, the boots.

The heavy metal gate that guarded the entrance to the compound had been swung into place, but Caleb was already halfway through the pedestrian door. He held it open for Adri, scanning the crowd behind her to see if anyone would try to follow, and when she was close enough to touch, he grabbed her by the elbow and yanked her through. Slammed the gate shut with an iron clang.

Tamba, the security guard, laughed. "It's an election day," he said, offering his hands palm up as if he was gifting them with an easy answer to the madness. "We are a passionate people." His easy smile dispelled the thin fog of her fear, and Adri's cheeks warmed in embarrassment. West Africa had been her home, her place of chosen exile, for nearly five years and Adri liked to consider herself a local. But every once in a while an unexpected encounter reminded her that she was not. She had run like a child, like a foreigner. It was humiliating.

Even worse, Adri suddenly realized that Caleb was still gripping her arm, his shoulders curled around her protectively as if he intended to shield her from the chaos unfolding behind them. She was tiny inside his arms, so small she felt like she could turn her face into his chest and disappear. It was a dangerous feeling, the sort of longing she couldn't let herself give in to. Adri went rigid at the warmth of his breath on her neck, and willed herself to remember who he was. Who she was. Even though she tingled in the places where he touched her. "It's okay," she murmured, forcing herself to pull away. Caleb's hand tightened for just a moment before he let go.

Taking a deliberate step back, Adri tucked an errant strand of hair behind her ear and tightened her ponytail with a tug. She gave the earnest young security guard a wry smile. "A passionate people. I should know that by now, right?"

"You are a wise woman, Miss Vogt." Tamba's eyes sparked like lit coal in the sunlight. "People will get hurt, but it is not . . ." he trailed off, searching. "Intended?"

"Malicious?" Adri offered. "It means they don't mean to do any harm."

"Yes." Tamba grinned. "It is not malicious."

"Looks malicious to me." Caleb stood well away from the gate and surveyed the swarm with a critical eye.

It was a sight to behold. The streets were full of people, and though most of the political parties had advocated for a peaceful election, the air had shimmered with a live charge for days. When the truck that collected empty bottles from the hundreds of roadside stands had crested a hill and found a small knot of people deep in conversation in the middle of his lane, he couldn't stop in time. No one had been hit, and the driver had crawled out of his vehicle with nothing more than a scratch on his arm. Adri knew it wasn't serious, she had examined him herself—though he had only allowed her ministrations after someone recognized her and vouched for her credentials.

Adri wasn't known by name, she was known by title: The

Nurse. It didn't matter that she wasn't their nurse, that she worked for a series of orphanages that spread throughout the capital city and beyond instead of for the tiny local clinic. What mattered was the stethoscope she wore around her neck or tucked in an oversize pocket. The ability to diagnose crypto with a few questions and prescribe boiled water and rest. The Nurse was a miracle worker, whether she believed in her own abilities or not.

The noise and confusion of the accident were still drawing a crowd, and as far as Adri could see in either direction, the highway was completely gridlocked. There were people standing on top of cars, the sharp report of provocative presidential slogans, the sickening knowledge that things could go sideways, whirl out of control in a heartbeat.

Sometimes they did. A slow-burning election battle exploded into violence. A humanitarian crisis ignited global outrage. But, just as often, the flame of revolt burned fast and bright, leaving nothing behind but shards of broken glass on the pavement.

"Stay safe," Adri said, dragging her attention away from the scene. She gave Tamba an abbreviated form of the traditional handshake. It was the way locals said hello, goodbye. It was second nature to her.

"I will." He nodded, but it was obvious that he didn't think there was much to stay safe from. They were, as he said, a passionate people. Loving and loyal and strong. Forgiving. Of themselves and each other. Adri had been the recipient of such small mercies more times than she could ever hope to count. And she knew better than to fear what she didn't understand. Although sometimes, amid shouts and confusion and sharp edges, it was hard to quiet the voice deep inside her that screamed: run.

"He can't defend the gate alone," Caleb said at Adri's shoulder as they started down the hill, toward the houses and the sea.

"Who, Tamba?" Adri was only half listening. Her heart was slowing to a normal rhythm, but in the aftermath of panic her backpack felt unbearably heavy. She was hot and exhausted and covered in a fine film of sticky dust. She longed for a swim.

"They'll storm the compound."

Not breaking stride, Adri glanced toward the gate and took measure of the throng of people beyond the thick bars. She shrugged, choosing to take her cue from Tamba's cool assessment. It was her job to stay calm, collected. She did it well. "It's more like a party than an uprising," she said. "I've seen worse. It'll fizzle out soon enough."

"Come on, Adri. Don't act all tough. You were scared back there."

Adri regretted her earlier lapse of self-control. Weighing her words carefully, she said, "It looks worse than it is. We don't understand the history and emotions that contribute to a day like this. Elections are a big deal."

Caleb just stared at her, his steps quick and sure on the uneven road even as he questioned her judgment.

Adri couldn't quite read him. He wasn't scared, but there was something simmering just beneath the surface. "We probably should have stayed in the compound," Adri admitted. It was almost an apology. "But, no harm done."

"No harm done," Caleb repeated quietly, his expression blank.

"What? It's like, five o'clock, and this is the first indication of disorder we've seen." She tipped her chin as if daring him to disagree. "It was a perfectly normal day until ten minutes ago."

"Normal? Disorder?" He thrust an arm backward and pointed to the melee they had left behind. "You call that disorder?"

Adri stopped abruptly and faced him. Passing the back of her hand across her forehead, she reminded herself that Caleb was new—and an almost-riot in a country fresh from civil war was enough to make her heart skip a beat, too. Caleb had been in West Africa for less than twelve weeks, and the bright-eyed ideology he had carried with him like an oversize suitcase was still being dismantled bit by frustrating bit. She tried to remember her first few months. The spiders and the fire ants, the bites that swelled to the size of small tumors. Malaria medication made her sick and gave her night terrors that transformed her into an insomniac. The food turned her stomach to water. Adri didn't mean to, but she thought about the exact moment that baby had died in her arms, the fraction of a second when the feather-light brush of his tiny limbs became deadweight, and he was so simply, so irrevocably gone.

She swallowed hard. "I'm sorry," she said. "We shouldn't have left the compound today. My mistake. I wanted to administer the second round of the hep B vaccines on schedule."

Caleb softened a little, and Adri was startled by the dark intensity of his gaze as he studied her. He had flirted with her before, suggesting with the slightest graze of his fingertip that they could be more than coworkers, with a look that could be interpreted a hundred different ways. He was tempting. More than that—there was something about him that was undeniably different, compelling. But Adri worked hard to be aloof with him. With everyone. It was just one of the many ways that she hid in plain sight.

"Apology accepted," Caleb said. "But, just so I know? What are we going to do if . . . ?" He let the question dangle and a dozen terrifying possibilities spilled from the hint of his suggestion.

"There are contingency plans." Adri started walking again. "Our night security guard is coming early."

Caleb narrowed his eyes. "He's not a security guard. He's a kid."

"Samaritan's Purse has a helicopter."

"And the UN has Blackhawks," Caleb said abruptly. He seemed to be comforted by the thought. "They know where we are."

Adri laughed. "They have bigger fish to fry."

Caleb didn't respond.

At the bottom of a long hill they entered the compound proper. The dirt road branched off in three different directions, and squat, block houses cropped up among the cotton trees and oil palms. Scarlet rhododendrons flanked small porches clustered with sagging lawn chairs, and here and there residents tried to urbanize the jungle with random attempts at domesticity in the form of potted plants. It struck Adri as downright ridiculous. Wasn't the native flora enough? After five years of living at the very edge of the known world, she still couldn't get over the fact that she could step out of her front door and pluck sweet, ripe plantains off the tree in her yard.

The compound was a haven in the heart of the capital city, a sprawling village where various NGOs and missionary families had congregated after the civil war ended and it was officially declared safe to return. Adri had never known war. She stepped foot on African soil after the last of the rebels were driven from the bush. To her, the collection of homes, guesthouses, and small office buildings that populated the compound were simply neighborhood and community, and the mélange of humanitarian workers and expats were family. More or less. Adri had found that although many of the volunteers and aid workers in her little corner of Africa were sincere and altruistic in their motives, just as many were running away from something. Or someone. She could relate. They didn't pry and neither did she.

Adri's house was a two-bedroom bungalow with a tiny, eat-in kitchen and a bathroom that was perpetually grimy, no matter how much she cleaned it. All inadequacies aside, Adri adored every inch of the six hundred square feet of her home.

She had bunked with other coworkers, board members passing through, friends of friends. It was how things were done when space was at a premium and nothing quite worked out the way you hoped it would. A bigger house was in the works, but funding had dried up, and, for better or worse, Adri's place was forced into service as home base. Once, when she was hosting the founder, his wife, and teenage son for a single night, Adri had slept in her bathtub, a late-nineteenth-century claw-footed monstrosity that had amazingly found its way to the west coast of Africa. But living with Caleb had come with a brand-new set of discomforts. The air was alive. Charged.

He had earned his nursing degree after backpacking through Asia and deciding that life was too short to not make a difference. That's how he introduced himself to her in their first email exchange: "I want to make a difference." So did Adri, but his admission looked especially ingenuous in type. She liked him more than she wanted to, and bristled at the way he made her feel jaded.

"Are you going for a swim?" Adri asked, fitting her key into the front door. Her back was to the ocean, and although the water was across the road and down a wide, orange beach, she could imagine that the spray licked the back of her neck, her bare arms.

"Tonight?" Caleb sounded surprised. "The fence doesn't go down the beach, Adri." They could hear the beat of drums in the distance now, the swell and whoop of voices shouting for something they couldn't make out and wouldn't understand even if they could.

"You think we're safer in the house? They're cement block walls. A hammer would take them down."

"You said we were safe."

"We are."

"But—"

"I'm messing with you," Adri said. She wrenched open the door and held it for him.

Caleb was a year or two older than her twenty-six years, knocking on the door of thirty, but she couldn't help feeling like the more experienced one. She interpreted his optimism as naïveté, and sometimes doubted the wisdom of the board of the nonprofit she worked for in appointing him her second-in-command. He was confident, enthusiastic, gorgeous. He was wreaking havoc in her carefully ordered world. And yet, Adri knew that pickings had to have been slim. Not many people wanted to live halfway around the world in an unstable country for little more than room, board, and the unfamiliar, often slightly rancid food they ate.

Adri hadn't known what she was getting herself into when she signed the contract fresh from college. She just wanted to get away. And Africa was as far away as she could imagine. The plan was to run and keep running—staying hadn't really been an option, but the kids at the orphanages she served turned out to be a pure addiction. Adri loved them simply. Fiercely. They made Africa home.

"Can I say something off the record?" Caleb said. He didn't move to step into the house, but stood in the grass just off the cement slab that served as a front step. He blurted, "Sometimes I hate it here."

She didn't know what to say. He had been her faithful side-kick for weeks, his enthusiasm a veneer that seemed impenetrably thick, slathered on with a heavy hand. Caleb had never once given her the impression that life in Africa struck him as anything other than a grand adventure. But here was something real; the riot had scratched the surface. Beneath was the flush of sincerity, something as heady and masculine as the scent of his skin before a swim. It tested the safe borders of their roommate/coworker relationship. The intimacy of it made Adri white-knuckle the edge of the door.

Caleb ran his hands over his head, his eyes widening at the prickle of the buzz cut Adri had given him only a couple of days before. His hair had been camel-colored and just a little curly, but when he finally begged her to get rid of it for him, the cut had revealed dark roots that accented his jawline and sun-bright blue eyes. He was beautiful in a rugged, unexpected way, and that only made him more likable. Adri didn't want to like him.

"I don't mean that," Caleb said, dropping his hands to his sides. "I don't hate it here."

"Yes, you do. At least, a little." She almost said, We all do. But that was a terrible lie. And also the truth. Adri let the door fall shut behind her and tossed her pack onto the grass. "I shouldn't have teased you. We shouldn't have gone out today, and I shouldn't have teased you."

Caleb looked up at the door frame of the house, the tile roof, and the crumbling breezeway blocks of the two front windows. His jaw hardened almost imperceptibly. "What if I want to go back?"

He certainly wouldn't be the first. "Why?"

"Maybe I can't cut it here. The schedule, the mosquitos, the sickness, the poverty. The kids. They break my heart, Adri. What are we doing? We're not their parents, but that's what they need. I feel like I'm drowning sometimes. It's too much. We can't help everyone, and I wonder if we're helping anyone at all."

It was true, everything he said was true, but it felt like an attack all the same. She bristled, wanting to fight. But just as quickly as her anger had flared, it fizzled out and died. "Fine," Adri sighed. "Whatever. I'm sure the board will want to hear from you before you make any travel arrangements, but this is hardly a prison. You're free to go." She indicated the door with an outstretched hand, inviting him to go inside and pack, to pretend that his third-world hiatus was nothing more than an inkblot on the predictable map of his life.

He was embarrassed when he swept past. His head was down and he wouldn't look at her. But just over the threshold, Caleb stopped and turned back. Stared her straight in the eye, boldly and without an ounce of guile. "You don't have to stay here, either, you know. You're not a prisoner."

The sun was beating against Adri's auburn hair and sending little rivulets of sweat down the side of her face. But his words were a slap of ice water. Cold and so startling that for a moment she couldn't breathe.

He must have sensed that he'd struck a nerve. "You could go home, Adrienne. You could come with me."

Caleb's eyes betrayed him. She had assumed that he was

after nothing more than a tropical fling, a no-strings-attached affair that he'd casually forget the moment he decided to shoulder his backpack and abandon her little corner of Africa in search of the next big thrill. She figured his tattoos lacked meaning and his Médicins Sans Frontières poster-boy persona were affectations. But standing across from him in the slanting light, Adri could almost believe that his offer was something more. Maybe he was something more.

You could come with me.

As if she could just leave it all behind and start over. As if she could be the girl she had been all those years ago, those years before she crossed an ocean and became a person that she didn't recognize when she looked in the mirror. As if he could offer her the sort of new beginning that she had stopped dreaming about long ago. As if.

If there was anything Adri knew, it was that some things could not be undone.

"Go pack your stuff," Adri said, turning away toward the ocean and the sunburned sand and the dark sliver of an impossibly thin fishing boat beyond the breakers. "I'm never going back."

And inside a zippered pocket of her cargo pants, her cell phone began to ring.

2

Adri swung her pack into the back of the Land Rover and slammed the hatch.

"You're not taking much," Caleb said, putting his hand out for the keys.

It had been a point of contention—who would drive to the airport—but in the end, Adri reluctantly conceded that if Caleb was going to stick around, he'd better learn to navigate the streets. If they could be called that. She handed him the key chain with what she hoped was a reproachful smile. But her face felt frozen, numb. *She* felt numb, and had from the moment she answered the phone and heard her father's voice.

She's gone, Adri. I'm sorry, baby, but you need to come home.

Adri didn't fight with her father. She never had. It was pointless to shout at a man who would never raise his voice back. But she had argued for almost an hour, begging him to take care of it for her, to somehow fix things so that she wouldn't have to leave Africa. In the end, there was nothing for it. And if Adri was really honest with herself, there was a certain poetic justice in going back. She deserved it.

Adri felt her heart squeeze to a pinprick. She tried to swallow and made herself focus on Caleb. His comment. "I don't need to take much," she said. "I won't be gone long."

Caleb cocked an eyebrow and disappeared around the side of the Land Rover. "You said you wouldn't be gone at all," he called over the top of the dusty vehicle. "In fact, if I recall correctly, you said, and I quote, 'I'm never going back.'"

Adri wrenched open the door and swung herself inside. "And you said you hated it here. You said you were leaving."

"Yeah, well, things change. And you called it: it was a party, not an uprising." He shrugged off the conversation with a casual lift of his shoulder.

Adri didn't want to let him off the hook that easily, but life here was nothing if not a flash of silver. The shuffle of the everyday was slow, almost tedious, and yet in less than a second the entire world could tip and change. A clear blue sky tore open along a hidden seam and spilled a storm so furious it ripped leaves from trees. A child who had previously refused even to look at Adri tucked himself beneath her arm and fell instantly and peacefully asleep with his cheek pressed tight against her chest. Adri understood the swift flip of emotion, the way it was possible to be tossed like a coin and land, unexpectedly, facedown.

Caleb had watched her eyes, the way her knees buckled at her father's proclamation, and he had fallen exactly where he needed to be. He hadn't gone into the bungalow to pack his things. Instead, he made her a cup of tea and called the airline to search for a flight for Ms. Adrienne Claire Vogt. She couldn't help but admire him for it.

Watching him settle into the bucket seat, Adri wondered for a moment if she should say something, maybe thank you, but Caleb had already turned his attention to other things. He clicked his seat belt on and started the Land Rover with entirely too much relish. His throaty chuckle matched the growl of the SUV as he revved the engine.

"You do know how to drive a standard, right?" Adri grabbed the gearshift as if to stop him from driving out of the compound, but Caleb seized the opportunity and covered her small hand with his own.

"I think I remember," he smirked. "But I suppose we could shift together."

Adri tried to wrench her hand away, but Caleb held on.

"Hey, take a deep breath." He ducked his head a little so that he could catch her eye. Giving her a sympathetic smile, he said, "Everything is going to be okay."

Adri snorted. "Here or there?"

"Both. I've got things covered here, and you'll take care of everything at home."

"This is home."

"This is where you came when you ran away from home." Caleb searched her face for a moment, but he didn't seem to find what he was looking for. He lifted his hand and Adri snatched her arm away. Weaving her fingers together in her lap, she forced herself to look out the passenger window at her bungalow, the turquoise sea beyond.

Her throat tightened at the sudden, shocking reality of leaving this place. Of going back to her provincial hometown in rural Iowa, and all the memories—all the people—she had tried hard to leave behind. She didn't belong there anymore, and just the thought of going back was enough to make her break out in a cold sweat. She hadn't been home in over three years. She hadn't seen her father. Or Victoria. And now it was too late to say the things she had always hoped to say.

But she couldn't face all that just yet. Instead, as Caleb eased the Land Rover into reverse, she focused on the details. The way the sunlight waltzed with the leaves. A handsome little gecko on the side of her house. The plantains that hung heavy on the tree in her front yard.

They would be ripe in a matter of days. She wondered if Caleb would remember to bring them to the cooks at the orphanage, or if they would rot on the branch and slip off the tree to molder on the ground.

"Don't forget—"

"The bananas. I've got this, Adri."

"They're plantains," she muttered.

"For the fufu. I know."

Caleb waved at Tamba and took a left out of the gate onto the only decent road in the entire country. It was relatively smooth black asphalt, an aberration in a city where the rest of the streets were unmapped and nearly impassable. The rainy season washed away gravel and left behind jagged rocks and deep craters where garbage and water collected in a septic soup diabolically perfect for mosquitos. It was the beginning of September, almost the end of the rainy season, but there were still several difficult weeks ahead. Adri glanced at Caleb out of the corner of her eye and hoped that he—and the Land Rover— would survive her absence.

She couldn't stop herself. "The mosquito nets—"

"I'll check them. And I'll make sure Joseph gets his sickle cell meds and I won't forget the community cookstove project meeting tomorrow afternoon." Caleb bumped Adri's elbow with his own. It was a consoling gesture, a reassurance of his dependability. "I promise to hug them every time I leave. Extra squeezes for Hannah and Lucia."

"Because they still cry every night." She held herself rigid, willing the tears to evaporate before she had to wipe them and broadcast her weakness.

Caleb dutifully kept his eyes on the road before them.

It wasn't far to the airport, less than an hour's drive if there were no goats on the highway, but the route was clogged with history that made Adri catch her breath no matter how ordinary the landmarks became. There was the shell of a single ancient tank, vines twisting through the wreckage as if trying to hide the grisly reality of past violence. Here was the corner where a warlord had hid his troops in the jungle and ambushed unsuspecting travelers. There were bombed-out cars in the undergrowth and surely bones in the dirt. Who could forget? And yet there was grace in the lavender snowfall of jacaranda blooms beneath a lone, willowy tree. Pardon in the way a child brushed a petal from his head and sipped water from a plastic bag in the shade of his mother's roadside stand.

Adri gulped it all in, greedy, wanting. It was wild here, but safe. So different from home, where everything that seemed tame had fangs. She didn't hate Blackhawk or the people there. She never had. But she could never quite seem to live gracefully beneath the weight of expectation. Adri had crumbled.

Caleb was driving too fast. There wasn't enough traffic. She'd be gone in a heartbeat. And that terrified her even more than all that waited at home.

"Will you make it for the funeral?" Caleb asked after a while. Adri felt a jolt of annoyance, but he didn't seem to be fishing for lurid details.

"No." It was one whispered word, but it sounded like a guilty admission to Adri's ears. She cleared her throat. "No, Victoria wanted to be buried straightaway. There will be a memorial next week."

"Do you have to arrange that?"

Her head whipped around. "I hope not."

"What exactly are you supposed to do?"

"I don't know. I've never been the executor of a will before."

Caleb tried to give her a reassuring look. "Whatever you have to do, you'll do it right."

"And you know this how?" Adri was too preoccupied to worry if she sounded snappy. But Caleb didn't seem to mind the sharp edge in her voice.

"I've never seen you give anything less than a hundred and ten percent," he said. "You're more than a perfectionist, Adri."

"What's that supposed to mean?"

He thought for a moment, his lips pressed in a tight line. "You're a purist," he finally concluded. "The journey matters to you as much as the end result."

Adri was rattled, but she hoped Caleb didn't realize how much he had unnerved her. He was right. She could hardly brush her teeth without considering the consequences. When every action sent a ripple she couldn't control out into a world she barely understood, it was impossible not to believe that her choices mattered. Adri swallowed. "What makes you think you know me?"

"You wear your heart on your sleeve," Caleb said simply. "You think you're big and tough and untouchable, but you're not."

Adri tried to laugh but only managed a strangled, choking sound. "I guess you have me pegged, don't you?"

"I didn't mean it in a bad way." Caleb flicked his blinker on and turned down the winding road to the only airport in the country. Two sniper towers stood sentry on either side of the intersection, and long rolls of barbed wire unfurled above miles of chain link fencing. "It's just that I've seen you with the kids, Adri. I know how much you love them and how much you're willing to sacrifice for them. I can only assume you'll extend the same care and consideration to settling your friend's estate."

Adri didn't know what to say, so she didn't say anything at all.

The airport parking lot was makeshift at best, and she was grateful when Caleb was forced to drop the disconcerting thread of their one-sided conversation and focus on finding an empty space. There were people everywhere, touching the SUV, rapping the glass with their knuckles and motioning that Caleb should roll down his window and listen to whatever sales pitch they had rehearsed. He ignored them all.

"Was she a good friend?" Caleb finally broke the silence as he eased into an alarmingly narrow space in the midst of a swarming crowd. He tapped a teenage boy with his bumper in the process. The kid threw up his arms and shouted something vile at the Land Rover, but by some small miracle he kept walking. Caleb was unfazed, and Adri added an imaginary check mark to the running list of her coworker's attributes. "Victoria, I mean. Were you two close?"

"Mrs. Galloway was supposed to be my mother-in-law." Adri felt a stab of satisfaction when Caleb was stunned into silence.

She didn't say anything more, didn't offer any resolution to the story that hung untold between them. His curiosity was almost palpable, but she unclicked her seat belt and was out of the vehicle before he had turned off the engine.

In some act of unnecessary loyalty, or maybe misplaced chivalry, Caleb kept Adri company for more than two hours as she waited for entrance into the airport proper. She admired his devotion, even if she wished for the reprieve of solitude. But she reminded herself that the transatlantic trip was well over thirty hours. She'd have plenty of time to steel herself for the culture shock of stepping foot in tiny Blackhawk, Iowa.

When the metal gates before the single check-in counter were finally swung open, Caleb was obliged to stand on the other side of a rope barrier. But though the security guards kept shooting him dark looks, he stayed shoulder to shoulder with Adri, waiting for the moment when she would cross through the crowd and the door and be gone.

"I've never been to Disney World," Caleb said out of the blue. "I grew up in Florida and I've never been to Disney World."

"What?" Adri shot him a funny look, convinced the heat had finally fried his brain.

"It's a game." He smiled. "I've decided I don't know you as well as I think I do—"

"Shocking," she interrupted.

"And I'd like to change that."

Adri did a rough count. "There are less than twenty people ahead of me. I'll be gone in a minute. How much do you think you can learn?"

"Enough," Caleb said. "I've never been to Disney World. Now, tell me something about you that I don't know."

"Victoria Galloway was supposed to be my mother-in-law."

"I already know that." Caleb suddenly sounded serious.

Adri sighed, but she didn't have the energy to argue. Besides, she couldn't help feeling she owed Caleb something. He was staying. He was taking over her job, and even if she came back in a couple of days and he decided to leave, she could never thank him enough for filling in when he was desperately needed. She flipped through a mental file and came up with something more or less innocuous. "I used to barrel race."

"Barrel race? As in horses? Like in the rodeo?"

She nodded. "In high school I had a friend whose dad was a bull rider. One summer we trained on her horse and signed up to barrel ride during the county fair."

"How'd you do?"

Adri shrugged. "There were only three of us. I got second place."

"Okay." Caleb rubbed his chin as he digested this tidbit of information. "My dad designed all of my tattoos. He's an artist."

"Wow." Adri considered the colorful landscape of his arms with new appreciation. There was a ship and a storm cloud so real in cast and hue that she could almost smell the rain. An exquisite bird. A word in a language she didn't recognize. Stretching out a single finger, Adri almost touched the shaft of a sharp-tipped arrow that ran the length of his forearm. When she realized what she was doing, she balled her hand into a fist and crammed it in her pocket. "He's very talented."

"Thanks. Your turn."

She had to think for a moment. "I grew up on a farm."

"I grew up in the city."

"I have a twin brother."

Caleb's eyes widened. "Fraternal or identical?"

"Identical twins can't be a different gender," Adri laughed.

"I mean, does he look like you?"

"We're more like polar opposites."

"Cool," Caleb said with a smile. "I'd like to meet him."

The line was dwindling and the security guards seemed to be increasingly uncomfortable with the tattooed white man who refused to leave Adri's side. "You'd better go," she said, nodding at two armed guards who were talking furiously and motioning to Caleb.

"One more thing," he said. "Tell me one more thing about you and I'll walk away. I promise."

"I'll be back in a week, Caleb. We can continue your ridiculous trivia then."

But he wouldn't give up. "Humor me."

Adri rolled her eyes. Caleb was playing a dangerous game, one that toyed with the stabilizing anchor that Adri had dropped in the sea on the day she first arrived in this country that was so far from everything she had ever known. She didn't want to be moved. She didn't want anything at all to change, because she felt, if not exactly safe here, at least grounded. The borders of her world were solid and comforting. Caleb was wrong. She was a prisoner—but she was exactly where she wanted to be.

It was time to shatter any romantic notions Caleb insisted on harboring. As much as he liked to think that he knew her, he didn't understand the first thing about Adrienne Vogt.

Taking a step toward him, Adri broke all her own rules and laid a hand on his chest. Caleb was taller by a few inches, and she had to stand on her tiptoes to reach his face. He stiffened when she leaned into him, but when her lips grazed past his cheek and lingered against his ear, Adri could feel the tremor that vibrated beneath his warm skin.

"I killed a man," Adri whispered.

Caleb went perfectly still and his heart beat a single, hard thump that Adri could feel in his neck.

She hadn't prepared herself for the wave of disappointment that engulfed her, the unexpected sorrow of understanding that she had done it: she had effectively and permanently succeeded in pushing him away. It broke her heart a little, but grief for what might have been was a luxury she didn't have time for. Adri swallowed it down like a bitter but necessary pill.

"There you go," she murmured in his ear. "That's all you need to know."

Adri pushed away and took a few steps forward to keep

pace with the steadily moving line. Straightening the strap of her backpack where it had slipped off her shoulder, she took a shaky breath and told herself that she had done the right thing. Caleb had to go. She refused to look back at him, but she could imagine his dazed stare, the hurried scrape of his feet as he all but ran from her. By the time she got back from the States, his bags would be packed and Caleb would be ready to join the ranks of all the memories she kept secreting in corners of her soul. At least, she hoped so.

But before she could mentally rearrange the soon-to-be-spare bedroom in her little home, someone caught her by the arm and spun her around. Caleb kissed her once, a sweet but firm weight on her slightly open mouth. Then he put his lips against her ear and whispered, "Then I guess I'm falling for a murderess."

He winked as he walked away, and the gentleman behind Adri in line had to give her a shove to keep her moving. When they took her pack from her and rooted through it, she barely registered the brash invasion of her privacy, and she didn't even blink when a female guard patted her down.

Within minutes she was sequestered in a cramped waiting room, surrounded by strangers who looked like they longed to be anywhere but where they found themselves: caged like cattle awaiting transport. Adri made her way to the farthest wall and a bay of windows that pointed in the direction of the parking lot. She couldn't see the Land Rover, the angle was wrong, and even if she could find the spot where Caleb had parked hours ago, she doubted that he'd still be there.

He had disappeared with a wink and a grin, and Adri was left with nothing more than the lingering impression of his kiss and the harsh understanding that her plan had backfired.

Caleb thought she was lying.

3

~

Adri had nothing but time.

Forty-two hours, to be exact, as her last-minute ticket out of Africa routed her through Brussels to New York, where she had to switch from Newark to JFK and endure an overnight layover. She spent the slow hours of the intercontinental flight wishing for sleep as she flipped through stations on the in-flight TV. The movies and sitcoms were supposed to be a distraction, a way to erase the memory of Caleb. His kiss. But by the time she touched down on American soil, Adri was numb with exhaustion and convinced she could still feel the warmth of Caleb's hand on her arm. He seemed to draw her to her feet as everyone around her began to disembark. To prod her forward with an encouraging squeeze.

Somehow Adri made it through Customs and Immigration and found her way to the bus stop, where she boarded the Newark airport express and prayed she was headed in the right direction. As the shuttle bus wove through New Jersey, Adri closed her eyes against the crush of traffic and fought to keep down the pretzels she had nibbled on the plane. She was accustomed to the chaos of third-world congestion, not the efficient, breakneck hum of taxis, buses, and commuter cars in one of the world's largest and most modern cities.

When the bus pulled into New York's Port Authority Bus

Terminal, it became a hub of quiet activity. Travelers grabbed their carry-ons and moved toward the door single file, some pressing bills into the driver's hand before they hurried down the steps and disappeared. Adri blinked around, surprised by the order, the unfamiliar scent of expensive cologne as it mingled with a perfume, maybe a lotion, that reminded her of blackberries in cream. She had forgotten what blackberries tasted like and it made her unaccountably sad. People stood a respectable distance from each other, careful not to touch. It was so polite. And somehow cold.

"Are you getting off?"

Adri looked up to see a young woman poised at her elbow. She had left a little room between her and the businessman in front of her, and with an outstretched hand was offering Adri a space in the line for the door.

"No," Adri stammered, a little confused. "I'm getting off at JFK."

The girl flicked blond hair over her shoulder and smiled ruefully. "Actually, you have to switch buses to get to JFK. You need the NYC Airporter Express. It leaves every fifteen minutes."

"Oh." Adri fumbled for her backpack. "Are you sure?"

"You came from Brussels, right?" The girl tipped her head toward Adri with a confident arch in her eyebrow. "I think we were on the same plane. I sat a few rows behind you. Anyway, I have to switch airports, too. I'm headed to JFK."

Adri yanked her pack off the floor and shuffled awkwardly past the empty aisle seat to take her place in line. "Thank you," she said. "I probably would have circled New York on the bus all night."

"No prob. It's kind of confusing."

The terminal was alive with people. A light breeze swirled up by all the motion sent a shiver down Adri's spine, and she wrapped her arms against her chest to ward off the chill. She hadn't been out of West Africa in three years, and the sudden rush of the world she had left behind was almost more than she could bear. It was dizzying and inexplicably heartbreaking.

"It's this way," the girl from the bus called over the noise of the engines and the intercom and the crowd. She set off through the swarm of people and Adri followed a step behind, anxious not to lose sight of the one person in a sea of strangers who had shared a smile with her.

But it was more than that and Adri knew it. This girl, this complete stranger, was a reminder.

She was a stride or two in front of Adri, just out of reach, and in those few wordless moments everyone and everything else faded away. Adri was aware of nothing but the swing of the girl's caramel-blond hair and the way she threw her shoulders back, parting the crowd with a self-assured sway that was so familiar Adri felt her eyes burn suddenly hot. Adri had run away from a lot of things when she boarded that very first plane bound for Africa. Her hometown, her memories, the ghost of David Galloway. But in the end, it didn't matter what had happened or how everything had imploded. When the dust settled over the wreckage of her life, she knew she couldn't stay.

She couldn't stay because when everything was said and done, Adri still loved Harper.

But she hated her, too.

～

Harper Penny was a liar.

A storyteller and a dreamer. She was an artist whose medium was the everyday, the people around her. The world. Harper painted it the way she wanted it to be, and reinvented herself to match the landscape. Cropped shirts to tease, stilettos when she wanted to rule. Even sweatpants could be wielded as a weapon. But Harper was practically naked the first time Adri laid eyes on the woman who would become her best friend.

It was the last Saturday in August, the air so thick it was a tangible thing. Adri kept brushing her wrist against her forehead, trying to smooth the sticky breath of summer away, though she only succeeded in further tangling the damp strands of her shaggy, dark bangs. Her arms were full of clothes on hangers, her entire wardrobe transferred from the passenger seat of her dad's truck up the two flights of stairs in the freshman dorm of Anderson Thomas University to her room halfway down the hallway. No air-conditioning.

Thankfully, the building wasn't yet packed with new students. The official move-in date was two days off, but local students and athletes were encouraged to come earlier. Adri had decided at the last minute to live in the dorms instead of at home, even though Maple Acres was less than a ten-minute drive away. Now she was grateful that the first impression her peers would form of her wouldn't be a Polaroid of this moment. A drop of sweat slipped behind her ear and down her neck. She needed a shower. Her formerly clean clothes needed a washing machine. And her door had fallen shut. Locked.

Adri melted against the closed door of Room 212 and let her head tip back to smack the wood.

"I did the same thing. Locked myself out." The voice came from across the hall, and Adri's skin prickled at the realization that she wasn't alone. She didn't bother to open her eyes to address who was talking. She couldn't. "The door locks automatically."

"My keys are inside." Adri was embarrassed to admit it.

"Roommate?"

"She's not coming until Monday."

"No worries."

The sound of movement and Adri looked up to see what was happening. A quick shuffle in the sunny dorm room across the hall, and a girl emerged, beer in one hand, ice pick in the other. Who took an ice pick to college?

"Here." She thrust the sweating bottle of Coors Light into the mountain of clothes that Adri still clutched to her chest. Adri was forced to trap it between her chin and a black cardigan that seemed almost obscene in the hazy heat of the second floor. The bottle was frosty, mostly empty. She must have slammed it. ATU claimed a dry campus, but the girl wasn't even trying to hide her alcohol.

"Thanks," Adri said, remembering her manners as the girl bent at the waist to thrust the ice pick in the lock. She couldn't help staring. The stranger was wearing a pair of boy shorts, striped, and a gray tank top. Bare feet, bare arms, bare legs that were at least a mile long. She was so tall that Adri wondered if she could fit through the door without ducking.

"It's not yours," she laughed.

Adri realized she was talking about the beer.

A faint metallic click and the girl swung the door open with a flourish. "There you go. You can thank me later."

"Um, thank you," Adri said dumbly anyway. She shuffled past her as the girl held the door open. A hand snaked out and snatched the beer bottle, so Adri dropped the clothes in a heap on her unmade bed. "I'm Adri, by the way."

"Harper."

An awkward moment passed where Adri would have normally stretched out her arm to shake hands. But Harper stood there with a fist on her hip, the other wrapped around the dark bottle. One side of her pretty mouth was curled up in a half-smile. Questioning? Playful? Adri couldn't tell. Harper was decidedly gorgeous and just as intimidating. Golden-blond hair swept in a French braid that twisted over her shoulder and eyes the color of wet stones. Gray and green and blue and brown all at once.

Adri wasn't sure what to do next, but then Harper threw the last swallow of her beer down and set the empty bottle on Adri's desk. "You can't just leave your clothes there," she chided, and, separating out a couple of hangers, moved to Adri's closet and began to arrange her wardrobe. By season and color.

When Adri's brother, Will, and his best friend, Jackson, arrived carrying a ratty old recliner between them, Harper was sitting cross-legged on Adri's hard-backed desk chair regaling Adri with stories. The closet was open behind her, the rainbow-colored contents so neat it looked like it had been staged for a photo shoot, but the guys didn't give it a second glance. Will almost dropped his side of the chair when he saw Harper.

"Over there." Adri pointed, giving her twin a look like daggers. She didn't yet know if Harper was her first friend at college or just the girl across the hall, but she wasn't thrilled about the way her brother looked like he wanted to trace the line of her leg from ankle to thigh.

"Who's your friend?" Jackson asked. Adri worried that Harper might be offended by his casual assumption that they were friends.

She either didn't care or didn't notice. "Harper Penny," she said, unfolding herself to stand full height and thrusting an empty hand at Will. He was still settling the recliner, his fingers caught between the floor and the piece of furniture, and was forced to give her nothing more than a wistful look. She shrugged and sat back down.

"You local?" Will asked after introductions, sans handshakes, had been made. It was a stupid question. Of course she wasn't local. Blackhawk was a small town; the population practically doubled when ATU was in session. If Harper were local, they would have known exactly who she was. But Will didn't seem to realize how inane his inquiry sounded. He perched on the arm of the recliner and looked for all the world like a puppy who would love nothing more than to curl up in Harper's lap.

"Nah. I'm a soccer player." Harper raised a shoulder as if it was obvious. She certainly had the body for it.

But Adri found out later that Harper wasn't on the soccer team. Or even a recreational player. She had left home early, sick of summer and sicker of her parents, and figured no one would bother her if she showed up and acted like she was exactly where she was supposed to be. She was right.

"Where you from?" Will asked, trying to be offhand and failing miserably. Adri exchanged a look with Jackson, but he seemed more amused than annoyed.

"DC." Harper pressed her cuticles back with a long, painted fingernail the color of green apples.

"How'd you end up here?"

"It was the farthest place from home I got an acceptance letter from."

"That bad?" Will asked, the slant of his mouth sympathetic. As if he knew what it was like to be so sick of his dad he was willing to fly across the country with no backup plan.

The truth was, Adri and Will had been raised on a small dairy farm, more of an acreage than an actual farm, really, in a corner of the country where one couldn't claim the distinction of "farmer" unless he boasted a couple thousand acres and a combine worth half a million dollars. But Sam Vogt didn't mind that he was a bit of a joke. He was a hippie, a gentle soul who sang to his chickens when he butchered them and taught his children to love little things. Snow peas in June, a warm bath, fresh-baked bread with honey straight from the comb. Adrienne and William grew up without television or Kraft Macaroni & Cheese, and knew a life so sweet and tranquil that the world beyond the borders of their little homestead, Maple Acres, seemed shrill and explosive.

"They're philosophy professors," Harper said, making her parents' profession sound like a synonym for ax murderer. "They've crammed John Locke and his ilk down my throat from the moment I slipped from the womb." She laughed at herself or at them, Adri couldn't tell.

"John Locke?" Adri didn't realize that she said the name out loud until Harper fixed her with those mossy eyes.

"And you thought John Locke was just that bald guy on *Lost*."

It was true. Adri had no idea who John Locke was until Harper explained much later—the famous philosopher and the TV series character—but far more unnerving than her own utter naïveté was the sudden shocking realization that a creature like Harper Penny could exist. She was fierce and bright and attractive in a decidedly handsome way—all angles and lines and broad shoulders that were both beautiful and somehow masculine. With the body of an athlete, the mind of a scholar, and the tongue of a politician, Harper was a force to be reckoned with. And a surprisingly new breed of femininity that Adri couldn't quite get her head around.

Women were a bit novel to Adri. Her mother had died after a short battle with breast cancer when the twins were four, and Adri had a single, precious memory of her. A memory that she couldn't even be sure was real, but that she buried like treasure all the same. She dug it up from time to time—this moment of such inconsequence, a woman's hands in her hair, plaiting the earth-colored waves so gently that Adri's lids fell heavy—and savored it. It made her eyes sting hot every time.

Adri didn't understand women. They were bright pieces of a dozen different puzzles. She tried to fit them together, to make some sense of womanhood and the mother she had only briefly known, but it was no use. There was no pinning them down. But that didn't stop her from loving them in secret. From watching and waiting and gathering fragments of the feminine that she admired and respected and weaving them into the fabric of herself. Adri loved pretty things. Mild, peaceful, gentle things. Until Harper.

"You're like a little fairy," Harper told her after they had been friends for less than a month. "You're so damn cute and sweet. If I didn't love you so much I'd have to hate you."

"Did you just call me a fairy?" Adri tried to sound disgusted. It wasn't her fault that she had perfectly pointed ears, porcelain skin, wrists so narrow she couldn't wear bracelets because they slipped off. She wasn't tiny by any means, but because Harper was Harper, their differences were markedly exaggerated. Adri was lovely and exotic and small. Quiet and bookish and good. And Harper was her counterpart.

"A princess? You could be my little princess." Harper narrowed her eyes at Adri and rubbed her chin as if considering the possibilities.

"Your princess?"

But of course she was Harper's princess. Or Fairy or Adri-Girl or Peanut or Her Highness; the Honorable Queen Adrienne when Harper had had too much to drink. Harper was not just the center of her own universe, she liked to be the center of Adri's too.

Adri didn't mind. Usually.

And she didn't mind that Harper had adopted them all, her and Will and Jackson, and made them her own. Adri loved how Harper made her feel: brave and brilliant and glittering, as if she was more than the sum of her agonizingly ordinary parts. As if she was waking up, memories sparking like fireflies at dusk, and she hadn't even known she was asleep.

"You coming?"

The blond girl was several paces ahead of her, hands on hips like Adri had failed her somehow.

"Yes," Adri sputtered, staggering into the present as a commuter clipped her shoulder. She forced herself to focus on the terminal, on the backpack that was so heavy her neck was starting to ache. Memories had anchored her to the ground. Adri hadn't even realized that she had stopped in the middle of the crowd, forcing travelers to veer past her, clogging up the already congested space. "Sorry about that," she called.

But the girl had already turned away. Adri had no choice but to follow.

~

4

Adri had forgotten about autumn.

The kaleidoscope of colors, the warm brushstrokes of copper trees along the river, flaming against yellowed fields and a ribbon of dark water beneath the wheels of the plane as it banked and came in for a landing. It was so different from the hazy blur of monochrome green she had left behind, so bright and unexpected that she spent the last few minutes of the flight from JFK to Sioux Falls Regional Airport with her nose pressed to the window, fogging the scratched, acrylic surface. Below her, the world was on fire, and Adri with it.

She hadn't checked any luggage, so after shouldering her backpack and collecting her carry-on from the jet bridge, there was nothing for her to do but face her father.

Adri wasn't nervous. She was terrified.

Although she had rehearsed a dozen different apologies, heartfelt pleas of forgiveness for everything from not phoning enough to shutting him out all those years ago, Adri couldn't think of a single suitable thing to say to her dad. They had always had a fantastic relationship, all the way through college and even after David asked her to marry him and she said yes. It was obvious that Sam Vogt never believed that David Galloway was the right man for his daughter, but he acted happy for them anyway, and even gave David his late wife's wedding ring to pass on to Adri. But after the accident, when the lawyers came calling and tipped her world upside down, she simply couldn't face her dad. It was as if a steel door had slammed between them, and Adri wasn't sure that she wanted it to open. How could she possibly face him after all that had happened?

Everyone wanted the truth, but she didn't even know what the truth was. That didn't stop them from asking again and again, from making her repeat those final minutes and hours until the memories blurred together in her mind and on her tongue, and she didn't know if she was telling them what really happened or what they had together made up. A paint-by-numbers masterpiece of who and what and when and where and why. Why? But who could possibly answer that?

Through it all, Sam never questioned Adri's story, never demanded an accounting for things she couldn't begin to explain. And when she ran away, her dad let her go. It was probably the most selfless act of love she had ever experienced. She couldn't repay him for it. Worst of all, she couldn't ask forgiveness for the things that mattered most.

Sam wasn't in the little waiting room just beyond security, but as Adri rode the escalator to the ground floor of the Sioux Falls Regional Airport, he came slowly into view. First his ratty cowboy boots. Gray and crisscrossed with deep scratches that scarred the leather black. Then faded jeans, a belt with a John Deere buckle, a plaid shirt tucked in neatly over his flat stomach. His shirtsleeves were rolled up, and his forearms were ropy and muscled, tan from long hours in the sun. He was wearing a Dekalb baseball cap, but as Adri caught his eye he slipped it from his head and twisted it in his hands, working the bill as if it was brand-new instead of falling apart at the seams.

Sam's hair was still dark, but thinner on the top than Adri remembered, and his temples were more salt than pepper. He was clean-shaven, and yet even from a distance she could see that there was no five-o'clock shadow—his beard, if he chose to grow one like he had when she was a child, would be white.

When had he aged? When had the middle-aged handyman she remembered crossed the fine line from the prime of his life to what she could plainly see were the golden years? For he seemed golden to Adri. Indistinct as a dream. So soft around the edges that she didn't dare blink for fear he'd disappear.

But before she could grieve the years she had lost, Sam took a few hurried steps and swept Adri into his arms. As her toes skimmed the ground, she wondered how she could have imagined, even for a moment, that her father was on the brink of retirement. He was as fit as ever. Wiry and strong as the young man who had carried her on one shoulder and Will on the other. "Look at you," he said against her hair, though of course, he wasn't looking at her at all. "Just look at you."

She could have said the same thing. And honestly, there wasn't much else they could say. How to make up for lost time? How to reconcile the two halves of her life? The woman she had been with the woman she was?

That seemed to work well for Sam Vogt. He was a man of few words. But when he backed away and cupped Adri's face, everything that she needed to know was contained in his eyes. It didn't matter to him what had happened or why. It didn't matter how far she ran or how hard she tried to shut him, and everyone else, out. She was still his little girl. And she was home.

"Thank you," Adri said, though she wasn't entirely sure what she was thankful for. A hundred little things. Everything.

Her father just nodded and reached for her backpack.

Adri relinquished her pack and carry-on, and the two walked out of the airport and into the cool sparkle of a perfect fall day. The sky was sharp and blue, the sun glittering white. It felt fierce to Adri, the clean zest of the air was strangely intimate as it grazed her skin and raised goose bumps. She shivered.

"Are you cold?" Sam smiled at her, but his words were flecked with concern. "It's almost seventy degrees, sweetheart."

"That cold?"

Sam laughed. "Guess that's cold to you."

"The kids wear sweatshirts when the temperature drops to eighty-five," Adri said. "They huddle under blankets and complain about how they're freezing to death."

"I have a jacket in the truck," Sam told her. "You want to run?"

They jogged across the parking lot, and when Adri caught sight of her father's battered pickup truck, she was as surprised to see it as she was to realize that Beckett was still alive. He was lounging with his head on the open tailgate in the bed of the truck, watching them come with what Adri interpreted to be a look of warm but tired welcome.

"Beckett!" She tore up the final yards at a sprint, and was rewarded for her efforts when the ancient Great Dane rose carefully on his front paws and greeted her with a sloppy kiss. Resting on the tailgate, he towered over her, but Adri didn't mind. He was at perfect hugging height, and when she wrapped her arms around his chest he seemed to tremble with contentment.

"How old is he?" Adri asked, roughing Beckett's brindle neck and tugging his ears as her father hoisted her carry-on and backpack into the bed of the truck.

Sam rested his arms on the pickup and took stock of his daughter, his dog. "Nine? You and Will bought him for me your first year of college."

"For Christmas." Adri smiled.

"So I wouldn't be alone."

"We put him in a box and tied it with a red ribbon."

Sam laughed. "And Beckett ate the box."

"Not entirely. He chewed on it a bit." Adri massaged the dog's great, floppy ears as he settled down again in the truck. Her father had never had the heart to dock them, and Beckett's favorite form of affection was a lengthy ear rub. She loved indulging him. "I can't believe he's still around. I thought Danes weren't supposed to live very long."

"He has hyperthyroidism, but we've got pills for that." Sam shrugged. "He won't make it much longer, but we've had a good run. Beckett's a good boy."

Adri pressed her cheek against the dog's head and stifled a shiver. She hadn't cried for Victoria, or about leaving Africa and the impossible situation with Caleb. But she felt like she might cry over Beckett, even though she had assumed that he was long buried in the grove behind the machine shed.

"The jacket," her father said, snapping his fingers. He swung open the door of the truck and grabbed a gravel-colored Carhartt coat off the bench. Walking around the bed, he settled it over Adri's shoulders. "Better?"

She swallowed hard and nodded, suddenly shy. It was unnerving to be here. She felt disoriented and confused, like she was masquerading as a girl she only barely knew. And yet this place was home, the lift of the breeze familiar. Her father was almost exactly as she remembered him. Even Beckett still cocked his head at her like her was listening to her thoughts. She grabbed his muzzle and shook her head, willing him to know that she was not the same Adrienne, the person he thought he knew. But as his whiskers prickled against her palms, Beckett seemed to regard her with bland forbearance, as if he knew better than her how far life had dragged her from home. From herself.

Adri pursed her lips and nudged Beckett off the open tailgate. Swinging it shut, she turned to her dad. "Ready?"

"I was going to ask you the same thing."

They drifted home, each long stretch of road splitting golden fields like the clean cut of a knife. Sam was a deliberate man, careful in everything he did from shaving to driving. The speedometer floated at an even fifty-five, and he kept his window rolled down just enough to slip his hand above the glass and rest it on the top of the pickup as if anchoring the vehicle to the road. Adri was cold, but it was a faraway feeling, an afterthought in the hulking shadow of the almost visceral reaction she felt to the world around her.

When Sam turned down the road that led into the heart of Blackhawk instead of bypassing the town on the way to the farm, Adri didn't complain. He was giving her a tour of sorts, reacquainting his daughter with the place she had called home for the first twenty-one years of her life. It was a bittersweet walk down memory lane.

Blackhawk was a postage stamp of a town, an orderly map of neat streets cutting north and south, east and west. The buildings along Main Street were a hundred years old, stately and restored, almost too pretty for the mundane trades they housed: a flower and gift shop, a small stationery store, a salon called La Rue. And then they were through the heart of the quaint municipality, driving slowly through the scalloped edge of town, where the houses were bigger and the lots sprawling. The hills began to rise toward the east, and on the top of the bluffs the redbrick buildings of Anderson Thomas University stood tall and imposing among the trees. To the west was the road home.

Iowa in September was a Willa Cather novel, windswept by the longing and loss of *My Ántonia*, rich with the bittersweet anthology of the untold stories of poet farmers. Adri had always known that people who work the earth have a certain eternity written on their hearts, an understanding that the ground beneath their feet bears much more than the simple drudgery of a crop that can be measured and valued by an elevator in the nearest town. Her father was one such daydreamer, the kind of man who spoke volumes in silences and heard God whisper in the song of distant stars keeping watch over the land that he plowed.

Even Harper, who had grown up in the city all her life, saw the complex hues of a life lived in rhythm with the land, the very first time she visited the Vogt farm. It was less than a month after classes had started at ATU. Harper had been nagging Adri to take her home—it was just on the other side of Blackhawk, after all—but Adri had demurred. She was afraid that showing Harper where she had come from would somehow tip the balance of their unlikely friendship. What if Harper realized she was a country mouse from a shabby farm with none of the sparkle that Harper seemed to see in her?

But Harper seemed utterly charmed. "It's an upside-down fairy tale," she said, rubbing the smooth curve of the porch banister with an absent, almost awe-filled motion. "It's beautiful, but somehow premonitory."

Harper was given to such melodramatic proclamations, and Adri didn't flinch. Nor did she tell Harper that her father had turned each spindle of the porch on a lathe in the shed behind the milking parlor. It was a detail too rich and provincial to be believed. "It's not a fairy tale, upside down or right side up. It's a farm." She pushed herself up from the porch steps and took off in the direction of the pasture.

Harper jogged to catch up. "Oh, I know. But it's so dissonantly idyllic. I always assumed rural life was harsh and unsentimental, peopled with women wrinkled before their time and men who were downright . . ." she gestured toward the holding pen where Adri's father was getting ready for the afternoon milking, "bovine."

"Bovine? Did you just call farmers stupid?"

"I did. But I was wrong. I like your dad. He's a Renaissance man—and I'm not just using the term casually." She wrinkled her nose. "People don't even know what that means anymore."

"I never pegged you as such a romantic."

Harper laughed. "You know I'm not. But this is deliciously shocking. Your little life isn't at all what I expected it to be, Adri-Girl. You live a fine balance, my friend. You walk the very edge of two worlds."

Adri snorted, but didn't respond.

They wove between the barns without another word, though Adri could practically hear the enthusiastic patter of Harper's thoughts. A cat! An old wagon! A tangle of spent wild rose! Life and love and the aching beauty of our very existence contained in the droop of a wilted flower! It was mildly patronizing, and

Adri wished that there was something that would lend validity, weight to her upbringing. She already battled Harper's blithe assumption that she was innocent, sheltered, untried. Apparently a weekend visit to the family farm wasn't helping matters at all.

At the end of the alley between buildings, Adri climbed over the wide, metal gate at the entrance to the pasture, and leaped deftly over the nearly invisible wire of the electric fence that cackled just on the far side. She stood, arms crossed, and waited for her best friend to navigate the unfamiliar obstacle. It wasn't often that she had the upper hand in their relationship, and it was hard not to take a certain satisfied pleasure in watching Harper flounder out of her element.

But Harper hesitated only for a moment. Then in one fluid motion she raced up the rungs of the fence as if it were a ladder, paused with one hand and both feet on the very top, and launched herself, a free-form dancer sailing over the side and into the tall grass. She nicked the electric fence on her way down.

There was a spark, a sound a little like a whip being cracked, and Harper jerked as if she were being electrocuted.

"Hot damn!" Her legs went out from under her and she landed on her ass in the grass.

Adri couldn't help but laugh.

"Your fence almost killed me!" Harper pouted, rubbing the back of her calf where the fence had slapped her skin.

"It's three thousand volts. On a pulse. My fence did not almost kill you."

"Whatever. I'm suing."

Adri offered Harper her hands and hoisted her to a standing position. "Knock yourself out. You won't get much. You've seen the extent of our fortune and I'm going to let you in on a little secret: we're mortgaged to the hilt."

Harper put her hands on her hips and did a slow survey of the land. The pasture was by far the prettiest corner of the farm. It was sparsely wooded and sloped toward the river, flooded by a waving sea of prairie grasses that bowed to the breeze and sent pollen-like diamond dust to float in the warm autumn air. There was a certain magic here, in the dappled shade of the gnarled trees, their arthritic branches angling low to mingle with the creamy tufts that still clung to slender stalks of switchgrass.

Adri could see that Harper was enchanted by all of it, and she grabbed her friend by the elbow before she could fall too deeply in love. "Watch out for the cow pie."

"Shit!"

"No pun intended," Adri laughed.

"Oh, pun absolutely intended."

They made their way past the few grazing cows—Jerseys, all caramel brown with eyes as wide and damp as a fawn's—and climbed carefully over a second fence, this one barbed wire, at the very edge of the Vogt property. The river was on the other side, and beyond that, the bluffs above Blackhawk. Because the river was serpentine, they couldn't see the long, white bridge that led into town, even though it was less than a mile away as the crow flies. But they could see the peak of the Galloway mansion poking through the treetops in the hills above the river. And as soon as Adri caught sight of the square turret of the tower, she knew that the mansion was exactly why she had led Harper through the pasture in the first place. If Harper wanted a fairy tale, she'd find it in the arched Palladian windows of the Galloways' Italian-style villa.

The corniced roofline stamped an orderly edge against a strip of blue sky, and even from such a distance, they could just make out the ornate corbels that propped up the projecting eaves. Adri had visited the mansion once a year for as long as she could remember, and her memory filled out the silhouette of the sweeping veranda, the high windows, the artful stonework that transported her to another era, another world.

"What is that place?" Harper asked, wonder in her voice.

"Piperhall." Adri grinned. "That is your fantasy. Your happily-ever-after ending."

"Is there a prince?" Harper's lip curled up hawkishly. "Because I think we should seduce him and split the spoils."

"Be my guest." Adri stripped a stalk of volunteer oats and began to husk the grain in her palm. "He goes to ATU."

"Shut up. There really is a prince? And he graces our humble little halls of higher learning?"

"How do you think a small town like Blackhawk supports a college like ATU? The Galloways practically own the university. David's daddy probably bought him a diploma and the A's to go with it."

"David Galloway?" Harper's mind was spinning. Adri could practically see the whirl of her daydreams. "Tall and blond? Kind of hunky? I think he's in my Western Civ class."

"I don't know that I'd call him hunky," Adri snorted. "But he's not blond. More like pale brunet."

Harper threw back her head and laughed. "Pale brunet? What does that even mean? Spill. What do you know about this guy?"

It wasn't like Harper to care, but Adri could tell that she was genuinely interested. Maybe even more than interested. Harper had closed the space between them and was mere inches from Adri's face, searching as if she could find answers hidden in every nuance of expression. "I don't know." Adri shrugged, taking a step back. As much as she adored Harper, she didn't much care for her habit of close talking. "It's mostly gossip and hearsay."

"Ooh! I love gossip."

Adri couldn't help but smile. Harper was an amazing gossip—to the point that Adri suspected her friend of making up rumors when there were none to spread around.

"Fine," Adri sighed, giving in. But even as she feigned reluctance, she was eager to invite Harper into the mystery of her youth. The riddle that was the Galloway family. But she didn't know where to start. "What do you want to know?"

"Everything."

After a moment Adri said, "The Galloways are old money. Liam—that's David's dad—was the descendant of a lumber baron who made his fortune in Michigan and decided to settle as far away from his family as he could, or so the story goes."

"Was?"

"He died a few months ago." Adri raised a shoulder almost imperceptibly. "I saw him once a year, at the Piperhall summer picnic, but we never spoke. He was tall, gray-haired . . . kind of scary."

"You find all men scary," Harper teased.

Adri didn't justify the comment with a response. "The Galloways are new money, too. Biodiesel."

"I don't think that's a thing." Harper raised an eyebrow. "Old money and new money? It's all just money, Adri. Besides, I don't really care about where they got it. I want the juicy stuff: who they sleep with, what skeletons they have buried in the woods, why in the world their estate is called Piperhall."

"It's the stuff legends are made of," Adri said with a sly look. She started walking, and didn't bother to look back and see if Harper was following. "When the house was built over a hundred years ago, Lord Galloway—"

"He was a lord?" Harper interrupted from somewhere behind.

"Who knows? The stuff of legends, remember? Anyway, he had a little daughter—"

"Named Piper," Harper cut in again.

Adri nodded. "Apparently he and his wife were so wrapped up in the construction of the mansion, they didn't pay any attention to the girl. She wandered off one day and was never found. Lord Galloway had wanted to call the estate Galloway Hall, but when Piper was lost, people kept calling it 'Piper's Hall.' I suppose the name just evolved."

"What happened to her?" Harper asked almost reverently.

"I'm guessing she fell into an old well. It happens. Or maybe she made it to the river and drowned."

Harper was silent for a moment. "Sounds fictitious to me," she eventually said.

"Isn't that the point? I told you, it's a legend."

"Piperhall," Harper mused. "I like it. It's musical somehow."

Adri held her tongue.

There was a trail through the underbrush, a mostly overgrown footpath that had suffered neglect in the month that Adri had been away at college. Weaving through the trees, she felt a worming sense of disquiet at the realization that her feet had kept the dirt path clear in the years before she left. What did that say about her? About her interest in the Galloways? In Piperhall? Because now that she was leading Harper to the bridge, to the secret place where she gazed at the tower of their impenetrable mansion, she understood that her interest in the Galloways bordered on addiction. Adri stifled the unsettling thought.

They were a good mile or more from the farmhouse when Adri caught sight of her destination and stopped. The old train bridge was barely visible, poking through the trees as if stealing a peek at the two girls as they stood side by side, polar opposites in almost every way. It was really only half a bridge, because the other half had crumbled into the river long ago. There was a thin tendril of stone that connected one side to the other, but it was uncrossable. At least, Adri considered it so. An almost paralyzing fear of heights prevented her from ever finding out if the narrow walkway would support her weight. But she had managed to scale the footings at the base of the bridge on her side of the river, and had claimed a spot near the top as her own. Sitting with her back against the ancient rampart was an adrenaline rush parallel to none. And it was the perfect spot to sit and daydream about the mansion at the top of the hill—and the family inside it.

"Damn," Harper said, the word leaking out in one long, slow exhalation. "You are completely obsessed, aren't you?"

Adri pushed a hard breath through her lips. "Whatever. It's a great spot."

"A great spot for spying. I see what you're doing here. You can't pull one over on me. Great mansion, family fortune, handsome prince . . . You're angling for a shot at a dream."

"That's absurd. You're being completely ridiculous."

But, of course, Harper wasn't being ridiculous at all. She was slicing through it all to the very heart of the matter. Because a dream was exactly what Adri wanted. It was all that she'd wanted all her life.

Adri shouldn't have been surprised when, just over a week later, Harper poked her head around Adri's open dorm room door and gave her an elated, silent scream. She had her hand linked around none other than David Galloway's arm.

And just like that there were five of them.

Harper was sketchy on the details of how she befriended David, or more accurately, how she hijacked him long enough to make him fall just a little bit in love with her like all the rest of them were. But it didn't really matter.

That first day, sitting backward on Adri's desk chair, David was as cool as a crisp autumn day, reserved and dignified as a prince. Adri could hardly form a single coherent thought. Here he was. Her dream, her David. The small-town luminary, a prep-school demigod from a family so rich they owned a private jet just so that they could fly away from Blackhawk if they wanted to see a Broadway show or enjoy St. Lucia in the spring. It turned out the only reason he had stuck around northwest Iowa for college was because Liam had just passed away, and though he had acceptance letters from Dartmouth and Duke, and probably a handful of other schools, familial duty required he stay close to his mother and transfer out of the Midwest in his sophomore year. Of course, it didn't hurt that ATU was endowed by the Galloway family. Their name was featured on plaques that graced nearly every building of the stately, redbrick campus.

But David wasn't aloof for long. He was well-bred, almost frighteningly self-controlled, but it wasn't who he wanted to be. He'd launch himself onto Adri's bed after classes, tucking his suntanned arms behind his head, and ask, "How are we going to get into trouble today, girls?" Harper always had an idea.

Not too shockingly, David never transferred. Adri liked to believe that was because of her. And Harper and William and Jackson. But she hoped it was mostly her.

Whenever Adri thought of David in the years after, she could never quite remember the cant of his eyes or the exact shade of his brown hair. Was it chestnut? Or umber? Were there dark blond streaks in the summer? Or did her imagination paint them in? Every once in a while Adri could pretend that she caught a whiff of his scent. Horses and leather, and maybe just a hint of Scotch if he'd been drinking a little, or an undertone of Clive Christian X if he'd been drinking a lot and wanted to cover it up. David had admitted to her once that his mother had spent more than 300 dollars on the bottle of cologne when they were in London one winter, simply because she wanted him to be singular—she wanted to be able to pick him out in a crowd, even if she was utterly blind. Which was stupid. Anyone could pick out David in a crowd. Deaf or blind.

But try as she might to conjure up the David she had known, the one she fell in love with all those years ago, the man with the quick smile and beautiful hands and the voice of a jazz singer, the picture that was burned in Adri's mind was a still life of David and Harper. Always Harper. Forever Harper.

Harper with her arms around David, his face turned toward the sky. His eyes open, surprised and wide. Her head bent over his like a lover. They were gorgeous together, cut from stone, a Renaissance masterpiece but for Harper's hair. It fell around them both, swirled up by the water. It was tangled and sticky, a dirty mass of clinging spiderwebs curling against her cheeks.

It was black with the stain of his blood.

"We could stop, you know."

Adri didn't mean to gasp, but as she jerked her attention to her dad, she knew that her shock had unnerved him.

"Sorry," Sam said. He ducked a little, tucking his chin into the curve of his collar before straightening and indicating a road off to the right. It was almost completely hidden by trees, but Adri found herself angling for a better view all the same. "I didn't mean to startle you," Sam apologized. "I know this must be a lot to take in, but I thought you might like to go see how things are at Piperhall."

No, Adri thought. Tomorrow. Maybe tomorrow.

But that's not what she said.

She said yes.

~

5

The road to Piperhall was a narrow, tree-lined drive that felt distinctly antebellum to Adri. Branches of gnarled burr oaks tangled overhead, dappling the sun and creating an emerald cathedral that inspired an unexpected reverence. Passing beneath the hushed nave in a vehicle had always seemed wrong to her, and it wasn't until David had taken her riding that she realized her discomfort was because the estate belonged to a different era. An era of horses and carriages and skirts so wide they required sidesaddles and delicately crossed legs. Of course, Adri didn't ride sidesaddle—no one who frequented the estate did—but that didn't stop Adri from pretending that she had been transported to another time when she visited the sprawling grounds. Something she did with ever-increasing frequency when she fell madly, astonishingly, head over heels in love with David.

Not that she could remember a time when she hadn't been in love with him. Though their land was separated by the river and a couple of miles—the bluffs too sheer to navigate, even if she had dared to try—Adri had felt the pull of Piperhall, of David, even as a child.

"Victoria let her gardeners go," Sam said, almost apologetically. "A couple of years ago. She hired a local landscaping company to come in once a week, but they can't keep up."

Of course they couldn't keep up. Fourteen acres couldn't be tended in a day, even if the Galloways hadn't bothered to commission formal gardens. If rumor could be trusted, the formidable Liam Galloway had insisted that the extensive lawns be kept neat and trim, but Victoria had petitioned for a more organic approach to groundskeeping. She adored the natural prairie grasses. Liam wanted a manicured yard. It was no secret who had won that particular battle, as the pristine lawn around a small forest of trees was fairway short in spite of the unforgiving climate of northwest Iowa.

Or, it had been. Now the lawn was patchy and thin, bared down to the dirt in places and sprouting seed in others. The thin blades of grass that did exist were bushy and limp, hanging to the ground as if in surrender.

Even the gravel drive seemed unkempt, deeply grooved from tire tracks that hadn't been graded in a very long time.

As they neared the house, it struck Adri that Harper had been right all those years ago. Piperhall was a fairy tale tipped crooked, spun off its axis at a disconcerting angle that made Adri feel as if she'd had just a sip too much wine. And yet, as jarringly different as it was from the life she had left behind in Africa, the gorgeous, iconic Galloway estate was also her home.

"It's different," she managed. What she meant was: It's the same. It's exactly the same.

The stables were the first thing that could be glimpsed through the trees, and Adri found herself craning, sitting forward in her seat for the tiniest glimpse of the long, low redbrick building that had become little more than fodder for late-night regrets. And yet, when she saw it, she fought the urge to close her eyes. The stable was a flint that sparked the tinderbox of emotions Adri had successfully buried for years.

"You okay?" Sam knew enough about his daughter to pull up in front of the stables instead of continuing on to the house. He let the engine idle, patient, waiting.

"Fine," Adri said. She wiped her palms on her knees, but it

was a superfluous action. She wasn't sweating, she was cold. Ice cold.

"Are you sure? Because we can come back tomorrow. Or the next day. You don't have to do this right now."

Adri ignored him. "Do you have the keys?"

He did. A fat key ring that jingled cheerfully. As far as Adri knew, the Galloways had never had a butler—gardeners, house-keepers, a cook, yes, but no one who lived on the estate full-time and who made sure that everything continued to function at optimal performance levels. And so, because they were in the middle of nowhere with little to no threat of burglars, and because there simply was no one to hold the keys, the entire set used to hang on a hook in the small, detached carriage house that had been constructed west of the mansion. Adri was happy that Sam held them now.

There were at least twenty keys. Some shiny and newly cut, others so old they were copper colored. There was even an antique skeleton key, though Adri had never discovered what it was for. Briefly, when she and David were first dating, she had fancifully entertained the notion that there was a hidden room somewhere. Perhaps a closet, shut tight with a rusty padlock and harboring secrets like weary prisoners in the dark. She loved the thought of finding such a door and peeking inside. She feared it, too.

"Thanks." Adri took the large key ring from her father, and quickly fingered her way to the one that would fit the padlock on the wide double doors of the stable. They hadn't always locked it, there was no reason to, but she was grateful that the doors were sealed now. She couldn't bear the thought of rebellious local teenagers prowling the horse barn with questionable intent.

When the door swung open, it sighed a low breath of dust and musk, a scent so sweet and long forgotten that Adri grinned in spite of herself. For a moment it was just another September day and David was beside her, Harper and Jackson and Will just behind. The stable echoed with the memory of their laughter and the breezy nicker of Amira, who was always happy to see them.

But the only sound in the dark stable was the muted stomp of curious hooves and the occasional snort of uncertainty. Adri could hear the horses shuffling around in their stalls, kicking up hay that held the sharp tang of old urine and ripened the stale air. The light switch was to her left, and though Adri's eyes were already adjusting to the dimness, she fumbled for it and clicked the dark away.

It seemed like nothing much had changed. Amira, Hasana, and Farah, the sisters, though they weren't really, still occupied the first three stalls on her right. The mares were all lean and lovely, but when Farah dipped her head over the gate and regarded the visitors, Adri could tell that she hadn't been groomed in ages. Her mane was matted and her coat flat and dingy. Though Adri wanted to go to them, to rub their foreheads and tickle their muzzles with her fingertips, her heart was beating fast. She was already turning away.

The tack room was on Adri's left, and then the wash stall. Adri didn't mean to rush down the aisle, but by the time she neared the fourth stall she was jogging.

It was empty.

Bard was gone. The big, black stallion that David had always favored was no longer strutting around his oversize stall, even though the gate still bore a plaque with his name.

"Victoria sold him," Sam said. He had caught up with Adri and put a comforting hand on her shoulder. Squeezed briefly and then let go. "Sheer black like that? He was worth a mint."

Adri struggled to find words. Liam had purchased the horse when David turned sixteen. Bard was bought on auction, a promising colt with a pedigree that could be traced back to a series of Supreme Champion sires and dams in Egypt. His bloodlines guaranteed lucrative breeding options, but Liam hadn't gifted Bard to sire foals. He bought him to teach David a lesson.

"He called me a cheeky sonofabitch and said I needed to learn a thing or two about respect." David had laughed when he shared the story with The Five. "He wouldn't buy me a car until I learned to ride the stallion."

"How hard can it be?" Will had asked, reaching over the gate to tug at Bard's forelock. But the horse threw back his head and bared his teeth, whinnying so loudly that the stable echoed with the sound. He trotted a few circle eights in his stall just to show them the dark ripple of muscle and the arch in his long, aggressive neck.

"Pretty hard," David said. He was the only person who hadn't leaped back from the stall, and he leaned with his arm lightly on the gate. Even so, Adri could see that his back was rigid, his shoulders tight and ready for action. "When you ride a stallion, you have to remember that he's in charge. You don't break a stallion, he breaks you. I figure my dad bought an expensive horse to raise me instead of doing it himself."

"Didn't work very well." Harper curled herself against David, her mouth just grazing the curve of his ear, and mock-whispered, "You're still a cheeky sonofabitch."

"Nah. I just know how to play the person in charge." David winked at her.

Bard was calming down and Will dared to take a few steps back toward the stall in an attempt to reclaim some of his dignity. "I thought poets and playwrights were supposed to be dull and bookish."

David laughed. "Bard isn't named for Shakespeare. His name is Arabic. They all are. Amira is the princess, Hasana, kind, and Farah means happiness."

"What does Bard mean?" Jackson asked.

"Cold. Because he's a coldhearted snake."

But he wasn't. Not really. Big and powerful and intimidating, yes. But not cold. Adri had ridden him once, only because she was so angry she was half hoping one of them would be killed. And when he ran beneath her, the stallion was so hot that it hurt to grip him. Or maybe her legs just burned with the strain of holding on.

It was a harrowing memory. And yet, Adri stared at his empty stall, the molding hay piled in one corner and the scuff marks along the wide planks, and wished that she had saddled him up more than that one awful time.

"I'm sorry," Sam said. "I should have told you. I guess I just figured you would've suspected as much."

"I did," Adri nodded. "I knew he'd be gone."

"That doesn't make it any easier," Sam finished. Then, turning, he motioned in the direction of the far corner stall. "If it helps . . ."

Mateo was the only bastard of the bunch, a gorgeous blue roan that Victoria had purchased because he was the most beautiful gelding she had ever seen. She didn't learn until after she brought him home that the classic roan gene does not appear in her husband's beloved Arabians, and the mottled, silvering effect that she adored was evidence of his disreputable heritage. Liam suspected there was quarter horse in Mateo's blood, or worse, Tennessee Walker. After that disheartening discovery, no one paid Mateo much mind. Until Adri started hanging around the estate.

"Hey." Adri's mouth tilted in a half-smile and she crossed the aisle to take Mateo's face in her hands. His lips flapped at her fingers, and just as she wished that she had brought something for him, Sam handed her a sugar cube.

"I stuck some in my pocket before I left for the airport," he said with an innocent shrug.

"Thanks." Adri offered Mateo the sweet and he snatched it out of her hand instantly. The short whiskers on his muzzle prickled against her palm as he swallowed and searched for more. When Mateo realized there was none, he let out a short, deep whinny, then gave up and contented himself with nuzzling Adri's chest. It was almost as if he remembered her. But that was impossible. Five years had gone by since she had seen him last, because her homecomings had never included a trip to Piperhall. Adri simply couldn't summon the courage. Now, Mateo was middle-aged, nothing like the young adult he had been when Adri first rode him. Back then, he had flowed like water, bubbled up and out and away even as she did everything in her power to control him. Mateo looked like he'd need coaxing to gallop now.

They had stayed on the estate many weekends, The Five, and, in the beginning at least, spent as much time on horseback as they did in the pool or hot tub. On warm days in the fall and spring, they'd do homework on the lawn and then ride before supper. Afterward, a swim to cool off or a dip in the hot tub to relax tired muscles. Early on, Adri had claimed Mateo as her own and no one contested her choice. David, of course, rode Bard and the other three took turns with the sisters. Will had a soft spot for Hasana, but only because she lived up to her name and was endearingly gentle-spirited.

Later, when the others grew tired of horseback riding, Harper began to throw small parties at the estate. Liam was long buried by then—a man who existed only in photographs and in the chill that crept down Adri's spine when she found herself alone in the grand, old mansion—and Victoria was retreating into herself, an odd but elegantly aging woman who deferred to her son as the head of the household even though David wasn't exactly the responsible sort. He had it in him, anyone could see that from a mile away, but in his college years he seemed eager to savor every last morsel of youth, and he lived hard and drove fast and drank altogether too much Scotch from his father's extensive collection of costly, dark bottles.

And so David and Harper threw parties of the Great Gatsby kind, and populated Piperhall with various groups of people who drifted the scant miles from ATU's campus in the heart of Blackhawk to gawk at the Galloway fortune. Harper liked theme parties, beach-styled luaus by the pool when it was hot, and elegant soirees that spilled from the dining room to the loggia and were lit by candlelight when the stars came out. Once, there was even a 1920s-themed murder mystery, and Harper set it up so that she and David played the part of a chic, enviable couple, the hosts of the glitteringly ominous event.

They played house, really, all five of them. Or, all four of them. They adopted David's reality as if it was their own, and Adri had never stopped to wonder what would happen when their games came to an end. None of them did.

"Would you like to go for a ride?" Sam asked, stroking Mateo's neck. "I know it's been a while, but it's kind of like riding a bike. You never forget how."

Adri shook her head, dissolving the haze of her memories. "No, thank you. Not now."

"You must be exhausted. How long have you been traveling?"

"Days," Adri said wryly, and it wasn't a lie. "But I'd like to at least groom them. And maybe muck out the stalls. It looks like it's been a while."

"Sorry about that." Sam said.

"What for?"

"It's my fault they're not groomed."

Adri was stunned. "You're taking care of the horses?"

"Will and Jackson help me when they can, but they're busy." Sam paused. "Jackson's going to be a daddy, you know."

No, Adri didn't know. Throughout college, several boyfriends, girlfriends, and acquaintances had tried to work their way into the tight knot of The Five. It worked, for a season. But inevitably someone got bored, or irritated that no matter how hard they tried to ingratiate themselves, The Five remained impenetrable at their core. Only Nora managed to orbit their circle with any frequency, and Adri hadn't been surprised by the phone call she received a couple of years before to announce Jackson and Nora's wedding. She had been invited, but she hadn't made the trip.

"A daddy," Adri said, a little belatedly. "Jackson will make a great dad."

"He really will." Sam nodded. "Jackson and Nora are a beautiful couple. She's struggling a bit with the pregnancy, but the baby is healthy. Everything will be fine."

Adri probed her emotions as if pressing a bruise. Was she jealous of Jackson and Nora? Of their marriage and baby? No, she decided. It was just strange to imagine that while she was trapped in her own self-inflicted purgatory, life was going on without her. Jackson and Nora were proof that some people were granted the grace of a new beginning.

"Jackson isn't much help," Sam said, reaching out to pat Mateo, "but I don't hold that against him."

"And Will? Is he around much?"

Sam shrugged. "Brothers is doing well. They're very busy."

Several years ago Will and Jackson had claimed their bachelor's degrees were useless and started a small construction company that specialized in home repairs, additions, and remodeling. It had been a rocky start, but apparently business was booming. But that was beside the point. Surely Victoria had hired someone to take care of the horses.

"I volunteered," Sam continued before Adri could formulate a question. "Victoria called me to ask if I could help get Bard ready for sale, and when I realized that no one was looking after the stable, I volunteered."

It was a lot for one person to handle. Caring for a single horse was a big commitment, but tending to all four of them was a part-time job.

"We ride them when we can. Pasture them when we can't." Sam passed a hand over his face and sighed a little. "I'm hoping there's a provision for them in Victoria's will."

Adri did too. "Thanks, Dad." She laid her hand on her father's arm and attempted to convey just how much it meant to her that he had stood in the gap when no one else could or would.

It would take hours to groom all four horses the way they deserved, but Adri found a pair of curry combs and offered one to her father. They could do a preliminary brushing to get rid of the worst of the matting, and focus on hooves, mane, and other details later.

Adri found it oddly calming to work herself into a sweat as she wielded the curry comb on Mateo's rump. The harder she brushed him, the more he leaned into her care, his skin rippling beneath her vigorous ministrations. It reminded her of scrubbing the tile floors in her little beach bungalow, only it was much more satisfying to feel Mateo's obvious delight at her attention than to do battle with a never-ending stream of fire ants that crept through a crack in the wall of her tiny kitchen. And a lot less painful.

"Tell me about it," Sam said suddenly as he worked on Farah's neck. He had tied her in the aisle near Mateo's stall. Adri didn't ask why, she assumed it was because after all the years between them, proximity was a luxury worth indulging.

"About what?" She figured he was talking about the horses, her time with David, the past.

He surprised her by saying, "Africa. Your job. Your life."

Adri didn't know what to say. *There I'm me, and here I'm someone else altogether. There I know who I am and where I am, here I feel like I'm living in the skin of a stranger, an alien in a strange land.* And yet, every remembrance was filling her up, splashing into the quiet, empty spaces and reminding her of a time that had been so rich and full and decadent and lovely her heart hurt to think about it. *How could she say all that? How could he understand?*

"It's hot," she said carefully and stifled another shiver. "Very, very hot."

Sam laughed. "I knew that. You post pictures on Facebook every once in a while. The heat seeps through."

Adri gave him a guilty look. Her father had bought a cheap laptop from Walmart and signed up for a Facebook account several years ago because Will had informed him that Adri occasionally uploaded photos to her timeline. But she was a sporadic user at best, and if she remembered correctly, the last time she had shared anything was when Dawn, her assistant before Caleb, had scraped her knee in a soccer match. In spite of their best efforts, the cut had become violently infected and Dawn was forced to travel stateside for treatment. She never came back. "It's busy," Adri added to her paltry description. "I'm busy." And then, "I'll try to post more pictures."

Sam nodded, but didn't say anything more, and Adri felt a stab of remorse. She was, without a doubt, the world's worst daughter. When she first moved to Africa she had come home regularly. Once a year. But she tired of the excruciatingly long journey, of navigating the life she was desperate to leave behind. She could never bring herself to visit Victoria, even though that was exactly what she should have done. After two short trips home feeling helpless and useless, she decided to stay put for a while. A while had turned into almost three years. Three years of nothing but phone calls, emails, and the occasional Facebook photo. Who did that?

In the beginning of her exile, she had routinely asked her dad to come and visit, but it was a hollow invitation. Adri knew he wouldn't come. He couldn't. The farm was small, but there was no one else to take care of it. And in all of his fifty-eight years he had never been outside of the Midwest. Ever. Sam wasn't about to jump headfirst into international travel, and Adri could hardly blame him.

"Time is different there," she said slowly. Fumbling toward familiarity. "We get up early in the morning and work until midafternoon. You just can't get anything done after that, so we don't even try. I go to bed at nine o'clock."

Sam grinned. "So do I."

"I get up at five."

"Gotcha beat. Four."

Adri tipped her head in acknowledgment of his victory. "Okay. We eat twice a day. Something light in the morning, and then a large meal in the afternoon."

"I forage," Sam admitted.

"But you're an excellent cook!" Adri protested, her mouth watering at the thought of her father's mashed potatoes, glistening with pats of butter and swimming in gravy that he made from the drippings of his roast chicken. When they were kids, she and Will had eaten like royalty. Fat steaks charred on the grill, meat loaf sandwiches with homemade vinegar-and-ketchup glaze, pork roast with caramelized onions and baked apples. Sam also had one go-to cake, a dense, chocolate confection made with sour cream and a can of cherry pie filling, that was best hot from the oven. And even better with a handful of half-burned birthday candles stuck in the gooey frosting.

"It's not easy to cook for one," Sam admitted.

"No," Adri agreed. "It's not." There was a beat or two of silence, but Adri had opened the tap and she was ready, if not eager, to watch the drops accumulate. "I love the kids I work with. They are sweet and funny and smart. They're going to change the world."

"I think you're changing the world."

Adri didn't know what to say, so she stroked Mateo and didn't say anything at all.

"What's the best part?" Sam prompted after a few moments.

"I like evenings best," Adri said slowly. "When I hit the compound and the day is behind me. It's not that I don't love the kids or the clinics or really all the aspects of my job, but everything comes at me so fast sometimes, I feel like I can only experience it in retrospect. I sit on the beach or I go swimming and I think about the details of my day. Who said what and why. Which medications we could really use. Why I don't trust the new community leader appointed to handle the co-op." Adri ducked under Mateo's head and started brushing soft circles just beneath his chin. "I guess it's crazy that I like thinking about my days better than I like living them."

Sam was staring at her. "I understand," he said. "Truly I do."

"But all the self-help books tell you to live in the moment."

Adri peeked over Mateo's neck and offered her dad a shy smile. "Aren't you going to tell me the same thing?"

Sam went back to brushing Farah. "Oh, I don't know. Living in the moment is great, but there's something uniquely powerful about the contemplative life. I think if we slowed down enough to think about what we say, consider the consequences of our actions and reactions, the world would be a better place."

Adri knew he wasn't alluding to past events, but his words felt like an indictment all the same. Her father had inadvertently summed up the halves of her existence: the euphoric Tilt-A-Whirl of her life before, the thoughtful plod of her days after. But she hadn't been quieted by a deep desire to center herself, to abide in the heart of her own story. Instead, Adri had been extinguished. Brought to the very brink of it all and thrust over the side. The hush wasn't so much peaceful as it was ghostly. She could hear the whisper of every lament in the silence.

"Dad?" Adri said.

"Yeah."

"I'm sorry."

Sam didn't ask what for. He just smiled sadly. Said, "So am I, baby. So am I."

6

~

When Sam finally turned his truck down the gravel drive that led to Maple Acres, the sun had already begun to set. Adri's hair smelled of dust and horses, and there were dark crescents of grime beneath her fingernails. Jet lag ringed her head like an ill-fitting hat. She was weary and dehydrated, desperate for a drink of water, or better yet, a swim in a warm ocean. But she was agonizingly landlocked, and it made her feel panicky and claustrophobic. Better to focus on other things. Like the shiny trailer that sat askew on her father's front lawn and the logo splashed across the side that claimed Brothers Construction was "The Best in the Business."

"Will's here?" Adri asked, her voice catching. It had been three years since she had seen her twin, too. A detail that hurt so much she preferred to ignore it.

"Will did the afternoon milking for me," Sam said. "With Jackson. Nora is visiting her parents in Minnesota for a week, so Jackson is a bachelor again. Will's loving it."

Adri detected amusement in her dad's voice and decided not to comment. Back when the world had been a very different place, William and Jackson had been inseparable. Only one person could coax them apart, and only because Will had been in love with her. Of course, his infatuation had never amounted to much. Everyone had been in love with Harper.

But Adri wasn't thinking about Harper. She was thinking about Will. Sitting up a little straighter on the bench seat, Adri reached for the visor and flipped it down. No mirror. Instead she ran her fingers along her hairline, smoothing strays and removing a wayward piece of straw. She wished for a tube of lip gloss, but the only makeup she owned was tucked away in the carry-on that Beckett was currently using as a pillow.

"You look pretty," her dad said. Not fine or nice or good. He had never been the sort to hand out halfhearted praise.

"It's been a long time since someone has called me that," Adri laughed.

"Well, that's a shame. It's true. But even if it wasn't true, it doesn't matter." Sam pulled up beside the trailer and put the truck in park. Switched off the engine. "Will still loves you, honey."

Her father had carved right to the heart of it. That was exactly what she feared: that after all this time, after enduring the sort of unforgivable neglect that she had inflicted on him, her brother, her twin, her Will wouldn't love her the way he used to. Wouldn't grab her knee when she sat down because he knew it would elicit a scream from his insanely ticklish sister or give her that look across a crowded room that said simply, "I know." I know exactly what you're thinking and how you're feeling. I feel the same way. How could she bear it if he was indifferent? Or worse, if William tried to be the brother he had always been and his efforts were stale and insincere?

"It's been a long time, Dad," Adri said.

"Some things never change." Sam wasn't one for platitudes, but this particular cliché was a warm blanket for Adri, something she pulled tight around her shoulders as she opened the truck door and slid out.

Adri stood with her arms across her chest, hugging her shoulders, and watched while Sam dropped the tailgate to grab her bags and let Beckett out. Her back was to the house because she couldn't quite bring herself to look at it straight on, to make note of the places where paint was peeling off of the narrow board siding or how the screen door of her youth had been replaced by a newer, rip-free model. She knew every square inch of that house, from the stair that creaked no matter how many times her father tried to fix it, to the hairline crack in the attic window where Harper had once thrown stones in the middle of the night to wake Adri. Such an exercise in futility. The window didn't even open into Adri's bedroom.

Beckett seemed to sense Adri's discomfort. Stretching lazily, he made his way over to her and pressed his head into the palm of her hand. But before she could settle in for a quick, comforting ear rub, she heard the front door slam.

"Adrienne Claire."

She turned slowly on her heel to see Will leaning up against a porch column, regarding her with the same forced nonchalance that she was attempting to portray. It only took her a second to drink him in: tall, tanned, and slim like her father. But his shoulders had filled out in the years since Brothers Construction bought their first Yellow Pages ad, and his T-shirt was tight against his arms.

"William Jude." Adri laughed suddenly, a bright sound that brimmed from somewhere deep inside and caused her brother's eyes to flash with relief. And then joy. He bounded off the porch, skipping most of the steps, and ran across the lawn to scoop Adri up in a hug.

It felt normal, so perfectly right and good to see Will, to wrap her arms around her brother without any of the hesitation, the reservation that had held her back for so long. But it was a brief moment of peace. There was much between them, and while Adri longed to pretend that everything was as it should be, the delight she felt at their reunion was quickly dampened by the understanding that nothing at all had changed. She kept secrets, so did he. There were ghosts in the spaces between them, whispering over his shoulder and hinting at all the things she had worked hard to hide. Will didn't blame her for what had happened, but he should have.

Adri swallowed hard and pulled away, tried to cling to the moment of elation that had made her believe that maybe everything could be as it had been. "So," she said, and was happy to hear that her voice was calm and even. "When did you go all bodybuilder on me?" Adri squeezed his biceps as he let her go.

"Hey, now." Will slapped her hands away. "Inappropriate touch. I don't let strangers touch me like that."

"Strangers?" The word stung, even if it was obvious Will was teasing her.

"No letters, no phone calls, no visits . . ."

"I write, I call, and I've visited a couple times—just not recently. When are you going to visit me?"

Will gave her a wicked look. "When you invite me and mean it."

"Ouch." But it was true. Adri had asked him to come to Africa many times, but she had always harbored a private hope that he wouldn't accept her invitation. "What makes you think I don't want you to come?"

"Because it's your secret place." Will draped his arm around her shoulders and steered her toward the house. "You might as well string a sign across all of West Africa: Adri's Hideout. No boys allowed."

"I like boys."

"Just not this one."

She shoved him away. "Whatever. Maybe I'm protecting you. Maybe I think you won't like it there."

"Why? Because it's so different?" Will ran a hand through his ginger hair and Adri was struck for the thousandth time by how beautiful it was. How red. Her brother would be a wonder in Africa.

"Well, it is."

"Got a banana tree in your yard?" Will asked.

"You know I do."

"Well, we have an apple tree in ours. And a peach, a plum, and two pears, a boy and a girl. Just like us, little sis. See? Not so different after all. Actually, I think we're more exotic."

"You make it sound simple," Adri said. She was too tired to argue, too awed by her small family to engage in the sort of verbal sparring that Will adored. So she gave in. "Come. Please."

Will studied her for a moment, his dark eyes narrowing to seek out the place where she couldn't hide from him. She didn't know whether to blush or be annoyed. "You know," he said after a long moment. "I think you might actually mean it this time. Can we climb Kilimanjaro?"

"That's on the other side of the continent, you twit."

The porch door slammed a second time and Adri looked up to see Jackson emerge from the house. "Ah," he said, settling his hands on his hips as he observed their reunion. "Sibling love."

"Or rivalry." Sam brushed past Adri and handed her bags to Jackson. "Put those in her room, would you? I'm going to walk through the barns before supper."

"Will do, Sam. I'm just going to give this world traveler a proper hello first." Jackson put Adri's bags by the door, then met her at the bottom of the stairs for yet another hug. But this time, Adri was aware of the phantoms that slid among their tangled arms. "We've missed you," he said into her hair while they embraced. "We're all glad you're home."

Ignoring the knot in her throat, Adri forced a laugh. "Bunch of guys like you, of course you're glad I'm home. You probably expect me to do your cooking and cleaning and—"

"Laundry," Will cut in. "Don't forget the laundry. You know how I hate folding socks. Of course, you'll have to commute between our houses."

"You'd be surprised," Jackson said, ignoring his business partner and friend. "Will's very domesticated. Your dad taught him well."

"Well, isn't that a fine little twist of fate." Adri grinned. "William makes a great housewife and I don't lift a finger."

"What do you mean?"

"Ma Sarah does my laundry and people from the community often bring me meals. I mostly sit on the beach."

Jackson gave her a sideways look, and Adri couldn't help but admire his blue-jean eyes and the way the sun still sprinkled freckles across his nose. He had always been the serious one of the group. Soft-spoken and studious and so very smart. Jackson saw everything. He understood things that the others couldn't, simply because he took the time. Adri had always admired him for it. And in the end, it was Jackson she feared the most. She was afraid that he could see through her with a glance.

"I don't believe you," he said eventually. "You work your fingers to the bone. It's written all over your face."

"Are you saying I have wrinkles?" Adri asked. But she knew that wasn't what he meant.

"No. You're as lovely as always." And he kissed her sweetly on the cheek.

"Hey, congratulations," Adri said, catching his hand before he turned to go back into the house. "On your marriage. And the baby."

"Thanks." Jackson smiled, and something in his eyes flamed a little brighter. "It's been a hard pregnancy, but Nora's strong . . ."

"She's a good girl," Adri said.

"The best."

While Sam checked the barns, Will and Jackson took over the kitchen. After downing a couple glasses of water from the tap, a luxury she certainly wasn't used to, Adri realized that she was famished. She couldn't remember eating much of anything on the planes, though she had vague memories of pretzels and peanuts and some unidentifiable snack mix that reminded her of caraway seed. So Will pried off the cap of a bottle of his latest brew, an amber ale that smelled like heaven to Adri, and sat her down at the kitchen table with a view of the counter where they were working. Jackson cut multicolored peppers and a fat, red onion into bite-size chunks and drizzled them with olive oil, and Will sprinkled their father's homemade rub onto thinly sliced rib eyes that he would later flash on the grill. The Vogts liked their meat medium rare. Or they used to. Adri could hardly remember what a steak tasted like, much less how she liked it cooked.

"I'm ravenous," she admitted after gulping quick swallows of the beer. She could practically feel her heart rate slow.

Almost as soon as the words were out of her mouth, Will tossed her a bag of Cheetos from the cupboard. "A little appetizer for you."

"I'll probably get sick," Adri confessed.

"Nah. You always had a stomach of steel."

Adri didn't remind him that that was a lifetime ago. Long before her first bout of *C. diff* and countless other nameless illnesses that had dropped her average weight a good ten pounds. But in the warmth of the kitchen, with Will and Jackson making entertaining small talk to ease her transition into a life that was so foreign it seemed surreal, none of that seemed to matter. Adri ate Cheetos, drank beer, and looked forward to that first bite of steak with all the anticipation of a girl waking up on Christmas morning. She even let herself forget, if only for an hour or two, that they weren't friends so much as accomplices. That the bond they shared was born of a love spoiled with time, a ripe fruit in the sun.

~~

The house was silent when Adri woke, and it took her a few disoriented minutes to remember where she was and why. Sunlight filtered in through the sheer curtains of her childhood bedroom and danced on the quilt that she had pulled all the way up to her nose. There were yellowing posters on the walls, half-used bottles of perfume on the dresser, a handful of careworn stuffed animals in a basket by the door. Adri looked around slowly, taking everything in as if she was seeing it for the very first time. She tried not to read her youthful excesses in terms of her current life, but it was hard not to see the closet that was still crammed with her clothes as anything other than gluttonous. Though she hated the sanctimonious attitude of some of the aid workers she knew, it was almost impossible not to feel at least a twinge of guilt.

Adri moaned as she got out of bed. "I am that girl," she whispered to herself. "That smug, holier-than-thou prick I've always hated." And then she went straight to the bathroom and threw up.

A shower and a cold drink of water did much to right what was wrong, and by the time Adri realized that it was nearly ten o'clock in the morning, she was at least somewhat ready to face her day. When her dad came into the kitchen smelling of cows and what he affably called money, she was scrambling eggs for him.

"Good morning." He smiled, looking somewhat surprised to see her up and about.

"What's that look for?"

"Will carried you to bed last night, sweetheart. I think his home brew did you in. I guess I didn't expect to see you up. At least, not up and making breakfast."

"Brunch," Adri corrected him. "And you think one beer did me in? A more likely culprit is the steak. I can't remember the last time I ate red meat. Or blame it on jet lag. Not counting last night, I think I slept a grand total of five hours in two days."

"That's unconscionable."

"Tell me about it. Go shower up and we'll have a bite to eat."

The eggs went down much better than her feast the night before, and while they ate, Sam answered all of Adri's questions. He explained how Will was living in a spec house Brothers had built when construction jobs dried up last winter. That the boys, as he liked to call them, routinely helped him out on the farm and looked after Victoria as much as she would let them before she passed away. And Sam shared his great relief that Will's most recent girlfriend had dumped him and moved to Cleveland.

"That bad?"

"I'm not sure the two of you could have existed in the same family," Sam said. "Be very, very grateful that Miss Marietta decided she could do better than your brother."

"She couldn't," Adri said vehemently. But even as she said so, it struck her that it didn't really matter who Will dated and eventually decided to marry. She was hardly a part of her own family anyway.

"Oh, I know that. But I'm glad that she didn't think so."

They washed the dishes side by side at the farmhouse sink, an enormous, porcelain rarity that Sam used to bathe Will and Adri in together when they were still young enough to have rolls of baby fat between their elbows and wrists. "You don't remember that, do you?" Sam asked as Adri plunged her hands into the deep bubbles, but she was sure that she did indeed remember every detail. The scent of baby soap on her skin, the way that Will's red curls formed perfect ringlets on his forehead. But maybe her father had just told the story so many times that Adri had adopted the memory as her own.

"What are you going to haul off today?" Sam asked cheerfully, nestling the final dish into the cupboard. "Any big plans I should know about?"

Adri shook her head. "Nothing major. I need to touch base with Caleb." She glanced at the clock on the wall, and swallowed the tiny butterflies that threatened to flutter up and out of her throat at the mere thought of her coworker. "We're six hours behind, so if I call now, the timing should be perfect. And then I'm heading into town. I want to talk to Clay and get this whole thing cleared up quickly."

Something in Sam's eyes dimmed. "Your appointment isn't until the day after tomorrow."

"I know," Adri said. "But I'm hoping I can talk Clay into letting me off the hook. Victoria didn't know what she was doing when she named me the executor of her will."

"She knew exactly what she was doing."

"I mean, she didn't know how difficult it would be for me to carry out her wishes."

Sam sighed. "I think she did it on purpose, Adri. She wanted you to come home. Take a break. Face whatever it is you ran away from when you left Iowa in the first place."

There was a note of frustration, or maybe even anger in her father's voice, and Adri was stunned into silence. It was one of the only times that he had directly admitted that Adri had run away after David died, and it chilled her to realize that she wasn't fooling anyone—at least, not her father—with her passionate aid worker act. She *was* passionate about what she did, but she sometimes wondered what her life would have been like if she had done things differently all those years ago. If she had taken that job as a traveling nurse instead of submitting an application online for a medical aid job with an obscure organization that was floundering its way through ministry in West Africa. They had been overjoyed to receive her résumé, and in the months after accepting the position, Adri came to suspect that she hadn't been the best applicant, she had been the only applicant.

But none of that changed the fact that her life had evolved into something raw and beautiful, even if she had never dared to hope it would. It was a tenuous peace Adri had made with herself, and one she didn't want to disrupt.

"I'm sorry, Dad, I have to get home as soon as possible."

Sam gave her a long, hard look. "Adrienne Claire, you are home." And then he turned and stormed out of the kitchen, letting the screen door slam behind him.

Adri sank against the sink, and leaned there for a long time, listening to the door rat-a-tat-tat against the warped frame as the morning breeze gusted through the porch rails. Her dad was the definition of calm, and it had been a long, long time since she had seen him visibly upset. She had forgotten how much it stung. How guilty she felt knowing that she was the one who had etched disappointment across his features, even if she felt his reasons were unjustified.

But as she tried to convince herself that his anger was groundless, Adri realized that he wasn't angry at all. He was hurt.

It was the reason why her bedroom had remained untouched for the five years of her exile, T-shirts still folded in her drawer and prom dresses zipped up in plastic bags in the back of her closet. Her antique hairbrush still sat on her little white vanity, a pretty thing that she loved to look at but never used. And though Adri hadn't checked, she was sure that if she opened the chest that sat at the end of her twin bed she'd find all of her old journals still lined up in a row, the desiccated remains of a yellow rose Harper had once given her, and the jewelry box that contained her mother's wedding ring. A ring she wore for less than a year before tucking it away out of sight. But never out of mind.

Of course, there was an entire box devoted to David. A few of the ill-suited gifts he bought her—a gold bangle bracelet that slipped off her wrist, a shell-pink cashmere sweater, perfume that stank of money—and a handful of letters that he had written to her during class. He liked to pepper his notes with thees and thous, shalts, and a pretentious closing that always felt dispassionate to Adri. Truly. Ever devoted. Sincerely yours. She hadn't opened the box in years.

"Go ahead and get rid of that stuff," Adri had told her father the last time she visited home. "You could turn my room into a spare room."

"I already have a spare room."

"But my junk is just taking up space."

"I wouldn't know where to begin," he said, avoiding her gaze.

"Box up the clothes and take them to Goodwill. It's not like I'm ever going to wear them again. And," Adri paused, "throw the rest away."

Sam snorted. "I'm not throwing your stuff away. You can do that yourself."

Of course, she didn't. Because she couldn't. Adri couldn't

help it if she was sentimental. If she could spritz an old perfume and be transported to her first day of high school. She had been terrified. Or brush her fingers along the satin ribbon of the teddy bear that the hospital had given her when her mother had died. She was too little to know what it meant, but that bear slept with her until she was well into her teens. And when it was David who held her to sleep, she secreted away mementos of the life she hoped to have with him. Adri simply couldn't throw them away.

And, apparently, neither could her father.

Standing in the kitchen with his words ringing in her ears—*you are home*—Adri knew that her dad wasn't just sentimental. He was optimistic. Clinging to a hope that no doubt hung like a millstone around his neck.

Her father hoped that someday, for more than a week or two, Adri would come home.

It broke her heart a little to know that she never, ever would.

7

In spite of her father's misgivings, Adri felt she had no choice but to go on with her day as planned. She called Caleb, punching in the fifteen digits of his cell number and the country code, but there was no answer. A ring or two, and then an automated message that insisted the owner of the phone had either switched it off or was out of the coverage area. Adri couldn't help but be annoyed. Towers were infrequent and poorly spaced throughout the jungle, coverage often hit-or-miss, but it seemed like a personal affront that she couldn't get hold of Caleb.

"Never mind," Adri muttered to herself, slamming the antiquated rotary handset onto the hook. She wondered for the millionth time why her dad insisted on keeping a landline when he owned a smartphone. Especially this mustard-colored relic from her youth. It seemed to her like an intended reminder of simpler times, but Sam claimed he was just too lazy to take it off the wall.

Adri loved to complain about the junk that cluttered Maple Acres, but she was thankful for her dad's hoarder tendencies when she lifted the heavy garage door of the old shed and found her car awaiting her eventual return. Really, it was Will's car, too, but the practical, nondescript Buick in a dull granny gray was hardly the sort of vehicle that Will, at eighteen, was eager to claim. When they left for college and needed transportation, Will made a point of finding a friend who had a better set of wheels than he had been strapped with. Jackson fit the bill nicely, and Adri ended up driving the Buick. Well, Adri and Harper. They eventually nicknamed it Betty and decorated the doors by painting little fingernail-polish daisies over the handles and signing their initials in glitter glue.

Their artwork had survived the decade, though the flowers were obscured by a thin layer of dust and faded by time. Adri ran her hand over the tiny pink petals and traced the curlicued *AV* with her fingertips.

When Adri had told Harper that she was engaged to David, Harper hadn't hugged or congratulated her friend. At least, not right away. Instead, her nose crinkled as if she had caught a whiff of something indefinable but pungent, and the first words out of her mouth were, "How the hell are we going to change the *V* to a *G* on Betty?" As if they'd drive the car forever, perpetually young and carefree, sun-kissed arms and legs draped out of open windows.

Best friends forever.

It took Adri two tries and a bit of gas, but the engine turned over without much fuss. Evidence that, despite the grime, Sam regularly took Betty out for a stroll. Pulling out of the garage, Adri scanned the barns for some sign of her father, but he was either working hard and hadn't heard her start the car or he simply didn't want to see her. She guessed the latter.

Blackhawk seemed deserted to Adri as she drove the empty streets. Quiet and oddly bereft of people milling about, loitering near buildings, and weaving through crowds with packs of Chiclets and bags of water. It was so different from her home in Africa; it made her feel hollow. There was no music, no laughter. And there were no cars parked in front of the squat, brick bungalow that Clay Foster had transformed into a law office.

Blackhawk was a small town, but there was a fairly large law firm on the picturesque main street that handled most of the civil and even the few criminal infractions that the community drummed up. The city paper still published every traffic citation and parking violation, and in her college years Adri had noticed that more insidious crimes had crept their way into the community. Trespass, possession, and, every once in a while, assault. An ugly, hidden part of Adri had felt mildly superior in the face of such public failure. Midwesterners kept a tight lid on things. And she was a master of pressing down. Hard.

In the moment before Adri stepped out of the car and walked the path to Clay's office, she did exactly what she had become so adept at: she buried. Every thought and emotion and memory of those days following David's death, of sitting in Clay's conference room, she and Clay on one side of the table, a small contingency of plainclothes cops and top-notch, big-city lawyers on the other. It had been hell.

The first time she had been formally interviewed, Adri hardly said a word. She couldn't. Everything was too new and fresh. So far beyond her understanding. David's blood was still stiffening on her T-shirt, the metallic scent mingled with the cold, mineral smell of the shallow water where he had died. They had taken a trip, The Five, a last hurrah only days after they graduated and stood poised to take on the world. David had died there, in British Columbia, a world away from home. She had irrationally hoped that it was all just a bad, bad dream.

But, of course, it wasn't.

Adri stepped out of the car and made a point of throwing back her shoulders the way her dad had relentlessly encouraged her to so many years ago. He used to walk up behind her and put his fingers on her upper arms, his bony thumbs between her shoulder blades and spine, and pinch until she had the posture of a ballerina en pointe. She hadn't appreciated it then, but she certainly did now, for it was a uniform of sorts and she donned it purposefully.

Clay's secretary was his self-absorbed daughter-in-law who was absent as much as she was around, so Adri wasn't surprised when she stepped into the reception room and found it empty. Since there was no bell, no way to alert anyone to her presence, she stood awkwardly at the counter for a minute before taking a few tentative steps in the direction of Clay's personal office. She didn't have to go far.

"Adrienne Vogt." It was a statement, not a question, and when Adri turned, Clay was standing in the hallway behind her with a look of mild bemusement on his face. "I didn't think you'd come."

"I didn't think I had a choice." Adri gave him a crooked smile. "Sorry to just pop in like this. I was hoping you could squeeze me in."

"As you can see, I'm very busy." Clay grinned and wiped his hands on his khaki pants, a pair of ill-fitting chinos that stopped short of his ankles and were oddly endearing. Paired with an expensive dress shirt and cheap tie decorated with rainbow-colored fishing lures, it completed an ensemble that made him at once lovable and absurd. His clothes and a shock of wild, snow-white hair camouflaged a quick and brilliant mind that was able to siphon the most minuscule, pertinent detail from a sea of useless facts. Adri loved him like an uncle, but she had never once dared to tell him so.

"Sorry," he said, offering her his palms. She noticed for the first time that they were stained a brownish green. "I was yanking out old petunias. I should wash up."

"No need." Adri crossed the narrow room and held out her hand, but after a second of studying her outstretched arm, Clay gave her wrist a tug and pulled her into a clumsy embrace. "We're a little past that, wouldn't you say?" But they couldn't quite figure out where to put their chins, and when Clay finally stepped back, Adri's cheeks were on fire.

She didn't argue when he offered her a drink, and minutes later they were settled in his office. Adri cupped a mug of hot, if bland, Lipton tea in her clammy palms, but she wasn't the least bit interested in drinking it.

"It's good to see you," Clay said, studying her features. There was more to his words than she could discern.

"I'd say the same." Adri smiled wanly.

"But . . . ?"

"But this is hard, Clay." Adri's heart felt like a stone in her chest. It thumped painfully. "None of this is mine. It never was. Not the name, the family, the home. It feels wrong to be in charge of it. Victoria was . . ." But what had Victoria been to her? A friend? Less. An acquaintance? More. She had been the hope of what might have been. But Adri couldn't say that.

From the moment David proposed, Victoria had considered Adri a Galloway. There was something almost regal in the bestowal of her favor. Something binding. Never mind the fact that Adri was a penniless nobody or that Liam, had he been around to grant his own approval, would never have smiled on his son's choice. David had made up his mind, and that appeared to be enough for Victoria.

But it was more than that, too. The older woman seemed almost relieved when everything was official. She dutifully examined the ring and gave Adri a stiff hug, but when she pulled away there was something unhidden in her eyes. Just for a moment, just a flash of raw emotion. Maybe understanding? It felt to Adri like she had unwittingly sealed some sort of covenant with her mother-in-law to be, though she couldn't begin to imagine what they had pledged to one another.

Clay gave her a sympathetic look and dug into a bowl of caramels. He produced a tiny key and fit it into the bottom drawer of his desk. "Shhh." he winked. "Don't tell anyone."

Adri buried her nose in the steam from her tea and inhaled. "I didn't see a thing. Though I can't imagine why you have to lock anything up. This is Blackhawk after all."

"And this"—Clay slapped a nondescript manila envelope on his desk—"is Victoria Galloway's last will and testament."

"So small?" Adri raised an eyebrow. "Shouldn't it be reams of paper long?"

"It was longer," Clay said. "Before Victoria started making changes."

"What's that supposed to mean?"

"Don't worry, she didn't go off the deep end and leave it all to the horses. And Iowa law doesn't allow for holographic wills—nothing handwritten or unwitnessed—so it's not like she scribbled out all of her original provisions and did something crazy. I was the testator and there was also a witness for every revocation and amendment."

"Who was the witness?"

Clay reached for a pair of bifocals and, after he had settled them on his nose, regarded Adri over the top of the lenses. "I don't intend to tell you that until I know if you are willing to carry out your duties as the executor of Victoria's will."

Adri paused. "If I don't . . . ?"

"Your appointment may be revoked by the probate court on the grounds that you've breached your fiduciary duty to the estate. If a hearing determines that there is cause for removal, another administrator will be appointed in your place."

"Who would that be?"

"That's none of your business, young lady." Clay's tone was flinty.

Adri squeezed her eyes shut. She didn't want to stay. To take her place as the counterfeit daughter of a woman she had stolen so much from. It was true that Adri had never intended to hurt Victoria, but isn't that exactly what she had done? And now, this. It felt wrong on many levels.

"She wanted you, Adri." Clay seemed to read her mind. "This is my personal observation, not a legal assessment, but I believe she wanted you to do this for a reason."

"Why?"

"I don't know. But I think you owe it to her."

The tea was lukewarm and no longer enveloping Adri in a cloud of comforting steam. She set the cup on the edge of Clay's desk and shoved down the panic that boiled and foamed its way up her throat. It blistered and singed, but that didn't stop her from nodding, once. "I committed to this the second I got on the plane."

Clay nodded, too. "Then let's get started, shall we?"

Although Adri had half expected a public reading of Victoria's last will and testament, Clay assured her that there would be no such Hollywood theatrics involved in the disbursement of the late Mrs. Galloway's estate.

"Nobody does that," he said, sliding the envelope across the desk to Adri. "Urban legend has it that public readings date back to an era when many people were illiterate and couldn't read the document for themselves. I'm assuming we don't have an issue there?"

Adri managed a wan smile.

"Good. This copy is yours. I have documents ready for distribution to the other beneficiaries, but I wanted to go over everything with you first."

"Other beneficiaries? What do you mean? I'm just the executor."

Clay ignored her. "If you'll open the envelope . . . ?"

Adri stared at him for a second before pulling the slim package toward her and fumbling with the clasp. There were only four sheets of paper inside, all thick, creamy stationery that bore the logo of the Foster Family Law Group and were held together by a small paper clip. She took a deep breath and tried to listen as Clay walked her through the preliminary declarations and the stark notations that told Victoria's sad story in three short lines: I revoke all prior Wills and Codicils. I am not married. I do not have any living children.

Then there was nearly a page of provisions for the Personal Representative. Adri's heart sunk as she realized just what was required of her. Duties ranged from "open or close bank accounts" to "maintain, settle, abandon, sue or defend, or otherwise deal with any lawsuits" against Victoria's estate. Her alarm must have been palpable, because Clay stopped and looked up.

"It sounds worse than it is."

Adri raised an eyebrow.

"Victoria settled many of her affairs before she passed. She didn't qualify for a heart transplant, but she wouldn't have gone on the list if she did. Anyway, Victoria knew she didn't have long and she couldn't stand the thought of leaving any loose ends."

"That's comforting," Adri said, but there was a note of uncertainty in her voice.

"And you don't have to worry about the Galloway's IRAs or 401(k) plans. They're not included in the will."

"What a relief."

For some reason her comment struck Clay funny, and he chuckled. "I'm not sure I've ever worked with such a sour executor. Grieving, yes. Greedy, certainly. But you are quite the sourpuss, my dear."

"It's a bit hard to take in, Clay." Adri put her face in her hands and gave her forehead a quick rub. "Victoria's gone and I'm left to pick up the pieces . . . I never even got to say goodbye." Her voice snagged and tears sprung to her eyes. She had no idea how her emotions had crept so close to the surface, and she struggled to get hold of herself even as Clay passed her the box of tissues.

"Oh, honey. I know." Clay looked as if he wanted to come around the desk and hug her again, but something stopped him. Adri couldn't decide if she was grateful or disappointed. "But there aren't many pieces to pick up. You're kind of window-dressing." He flipped a paper and said, "Why don't we get to the good stuff? Maybe it'll cheer you up."

There was a lot of good stuff. Tens of thousands, hundreds of thousands of dollars donated to some of Victoria's favorite charities. Habitat for Humanity, The Carter Center, and World Vision were represented, as were Doctors Without Borders and the American Red Cross. There was yet another endowment scholarship to be set up at Anderson Thomas University in David's name and even a nice contribution to the nonprofit that Adri had spent the last five years serving.

"This is wonderful," Adri said. She felt calmer now, more in control, and she gave Clay a genuine smile. "Victoria was a very generous woman."

"Indeed she was."

"But what about family? Surely there are nieces and nephews, a sister somewhere who will inherit part of the estate?"

"As you know, Victoria was the youngest of two and her brother died young. She lost contact with her family when she married Liam and moved from Virginia to the Midwest." Clay shrugged. "I'm sure you know the story better than I do. Bad blood from what I understand. She was supposed to marry someone else."

Adri didn't know the story. At least, not well. David had never really talked much about his parents, let alone his relatives. And Victoria, while impeccably polite and adept at small talk, wasn't the type to divulge family secrets over the supper table. Adri realized that she actually knew very little about her ex-fiancé's kin. "What about the Galloways?" she asked. "I'm sure Liam would've wanted to keep the inheritance in the family."

"He did. The retirement funds will all stay in the family. And when Liam died, fifty percent of his biofuel empire reverted temporarily to his brother until David was of age to claim his rightful inheritance. Everything else he left outright to David."

Adri was stunned. "David? But what about Victoria?"

Clay turned back to his papers. "I wouldn't dare to speculate. I'm sure Liam intended David to care for his mother in the event of his passing. As for the biofuel company, it remained in the Galloway family—with Liam's older brother—after David's death. Victoria never contested it. There was no reason to."

Liam must never have imagined his wife would outlive his son. Adri stifled a shiver and wished for another cup of tea, if only to absorb the warmth.

"David's will was a template at his young age, but it left everything to his living heirs." Clay was all business now. "And since you weren't yet married, well . . ."

"Victoria was it."

"And any way you cut it, Victoria Galloway died with a sizable legacy and no one to leave it to."

"Except charities," Adri finished.

"And you."

Adri could not have been more shocked if Clay had struck her. "Pardon me?"

"Page three," Clay said, tapping the papers with his index finger.

She fumbled through the stiff sheets, all thumbs, for she was numb from head to toe. Had he said page three? Her vision was blurry, distorted, and yet suddenly, there it was: I bequeath Piperhall of 1124 Dakota Drive, Blackhawk, Iowa, and all the property and assets therein, to Adrienne Claire Vogt of 480 Goldfinch Avenue, Blackhawk, Iowa, for her own use absolutely.

"And all the residue of her estate," Clay quoted, reaching across the desk and pointing to the next numbered point.

"What does that mean?" Adri barely managed to whisper the question.

"It means you own a great big house and a nice bit of land. Plus any extras that Victoria forgot to provide for in her will." There was a sparkle in Clay's eyes, but it dimmed when he realized Adri wasn't over the moon about this unanticipated inheritance. He seemed confused. "You won the lottery, girl."

But Adri wasn't listening. "No," she said slowly. "No, I'm sorry. I can't accept this. I won't."

"You don't really have a choice." Clay was sober, though the slight upturn of his mouth suggested that he still hoped Adri was kidding. "Victoria left it to you, Adrienne. It's yours. Now, it's a big responsibility and I understand that. She left everything in the house, as far as I know, and the outbuildings could be full of rubbish. But you can hold an estate sale and have a breeder come look at the horses. They're far too much work for one person."

"But . . ."

"And I suppose you could sell the property, though it might be hard to find a buyer around here." Clay wouldn't let Adri get a word in edgewise. "Fourteen acres is a lot of land when you can't cultivate it, and I don't know many people in Blackhawk who could afford the house anyway. What are there? Eight fireplaces? And they're all marble, right?"

"Something like that," Adri mumbled. She had fanned the four scant pages of the will in front of her and was scanning them for some indication that the whole thing was a hoax.

Clay cleared his throat, and when she shot him a hasty glance, there was a deep wrinkle between his eyes. "Victoria set up a small bank account to cover the yearly taxes, insurance, and maintenance fees for the estate. Tax and insurance are in escrow even though the house is paid for, so you don't even have to worry about writing those bills. It's all yours, free and clear." There were a few tense beats of silence before he asked, "Aren't you happy?"

Happy? It was a question no one ever asked Adri. Come to think of it, it was a question she never asked herself. She couldn't help feeling like she had blown her one chance at happiness, and she didn't dare to hope for another. And yet, against all odds, Adri was content. She had found a fragile peace, a place to land, and a deep purpose in life that had taken her completely by surprise.

And she wasn't about to let Victoria take it away.

"I can't stay here, Clay."

"No one said you had to stay."

Adri hadn't expected him to say that. "What do you mean?" she asked, her eyes narrowed.

"There are lots of possibilities." Clay spread his hands as if to encompass the many options available. "Just because you own the title to the land doesn't mean you have to live on it. You could rent it out, let it sit empty while you decide what to do long-term, or lease it to a historical society or nonprofit organization. I'm sure it's a landmark of some sort. There aren't many reproduction Italian villas in Iowa."

Adri's mind tilted wildly as she tried to make sense of Clay's calm advice, but she was beyond listening.

"I guess letting it sit empty would be at the bottom of my suggestion list simply because it's cruel to leave the horses to fend for themselves," Clay continued, apparently oblivious to Adri's shock, "but really, there are many creative options."

He sounded so reasonable, so logical, but Adri couldn't form a coherent thought. Much less decide how she wanted to deal with Piperhall. "I can't do this right now. I need some time," she said suddenly, lurching to her feet.

"Of course." Clay stood, too, and then quickly dropped back into his chair and groped once again in the drawer where he had stowed Victoria's will. "Here," he said, after he found what he was looking for. He handed Adri a small white envelope and a set of two new keys. "I almost forgot."

"What are these for?" Adri reached automatically for the items, though a part of her was loath to entrench herself even deeper in such an impossible situation.

"The letter is from Victoria." Clay waved his hands as if to absolve himself of any involvement in this one aspect of the bequeathal. "I haven't read it. I have no idea what it says. She wrote it for you and told me to burn it if you didn't come. And the keys are for the house."

"My dad has the keys."

"No, he has the old key ring. We had to change the locks when Victoria died and put padlocks on all the doors. This is Blackhawk, but people aren't beyond temptation." Clay noted Adri's shocked look and added, "Don't worry, Alex and the rest of the police force have been patrolling the house for weeks. Since long before she passed."

Adri didn't know what to say. "Thank you" seemed the safest bet.

"You're welcome." Clay's smile was hesitant as he reached across the desk for her hand. He pumped her arm up and down, a handshake so warm and solid it seemed he hoped to infuse her with all the certainty she lacked. It didn't help. "I'll be in touch about some of the specifics. I guess Victoria's news kind of trumped your duties as executor, but there are still things to be done."

"Okay."

"Okay," he echoed, patting his legs as if wiping his hands of the situation. "Well," he sighed. "Let me walk you out."

"I'm fine." Adri forced a smile. "I know the way."

Adri quickly made her way to her car and sunk into the driver's seat. She tore open the letter.

Dear Adrienne,

You were never my daughter so I won't pretend false affection. And yet, I leave this world exactly the way I always feared: alone. I am fond of few things, and even fewer people, but I always liked your face, and I believe that you loved my son. If fate had not intervened we would have been a family, and I like to hope that we could have grown in affection for one another. Is it sentimental to say that I always wanted a daughter? You could have made a lovely Galloway.

Yet here we are. We each hide in our own way I suppose, and though you run to the far corners of the earth I am no less a coward than you. I know more than you think I do and less than the truth. And though I sound exactly like a dramatic old woman, my own death feels like a chance to open every window and see if there is some way to make darkness light. I have no idea how I expect you to do this, or why I feel compelled to leave you a gift that, let's be frank, you haven't earned by name or connection. But I suppose there is some value in being an eccentric old woman, and I can do whatever I please. It's yours, Adrienne. David would have wanted you to have it.

I shall die pretending things were different and you were the daughter of my heart. May God be with you.

I have secrets, too.

Victoria Galloway

8

Adri always felt a bit like Cinderella when she pulled into the circular driveway in front of Piperhall. There was no fountain, though she could close her eyes and picture the arching cherubim, feel the mist of water as it splashed into the shallow pool below. Instead of a sculpture, a trio of elegant cherry trees stood sentry, their canopies entwined and their tiny blossoms a wildfire blaze of fuchsia in the spring. But it really didn't matter what stood before the house, for once the full view of the villa was free and unobscured, it was impossible to look at anything other than the wide, stone staircase and the sharp angle of the three brickwork stories that soared overhead and blazed white in the sun. The four pillars of the loggia framed the double front doors—ten-foot mahogany planks inlaid with wrought iron grills in elegant scrollwork—and tall windows winked on every story of the imposing facade. Over it all, a stately tower kept watch, the ornate iron cresting giving the mansion a decidedly romantic appeal.

The home was, quite literally, a dream come true, and after it had been completely restored in the late 1990s, Liam had framed the original floor plans and hung them in the entrance hall. According to family legend, the cracked linen pages of the design had been hand drawn by an English architect in 1836 for Liam's great-great-great-uncle's country home. They were then carried to the United States, where Liam's lumber baron ancestor reproduced the gorgeous Italian villa in his own little corner of Iowa as a wedding gift for his legendarily beautiful wife.

Adri didn't know if David's skillfully spun anecdote was true, or if it was just another extraordinary gem of Galloway mythology—the family seemed rife with stories that were both dramatic and mildly unbelievable. But she had always loved the faded, subtle lines of the drawings in the grand hall, and admired the quaint calligraphy that marked bedchambers, dressing rooms, and even the servants' quarters. Of course, there was no servants' hall anymore; instead Liam had installed a billiards room in the garden-level basement that boasted a long wet bar with four pull taps and revolving barrels of his favorite microbrews. And what was supposed to be a thirty-six-foot by forty-foot billiards room and picture gallery on the principal story was instead the main living space, with sixteen-foot ceilings and open archways onto the vast, marble-floored kitchen to the west and the formal dining room on the east. When the sun rose, it washed the entire mansion in a pale, yellow glow, and the dark wood floors burned golden as it set.

Everything in the house was light, designed to collect drops of sunshine and splash them back on smooth wood and soft-colored walls and mirrors hung in strategic places. But after Adri had opened the padlock and pulled the chain through the handles of the double door, she stepped into the long shadows of the entrance hall and stifled a shiver.

Piperhall was cold. Never mind the fireplaces or the warm embrace of the sun. The ceilings were high and the walls echoed with the sound of her tentative footsteps.

The library was to Adri's right, the narrow entry cut from beneath the stairs so that it felt appealingly hidden, a not-so-secret room that contained an impressive collection of old encyclopedias. The Galloways hadn't been much for reading, and Adri often wondered why they bothered with a library at all. But it was her favorite room, even if it lacked the books it should have contained.

"You don't have time to read," David chided her, back when they were in love. Before everything changed. "I've never seen you read a book for pleasure."

"I used to do it all the time," she huffed. "And someday I will again. When I'm not killing myself every spare minute of the day trying to complete my degree."

"Well, then. I'll fill it for you," he said. "With whatever you want. Erotica?"

"You wish," Adri's voice was low, coy, and he caught her from behind and eased her to the leather couch. He took her hand and kissed each fingertip in turn, then slowly worked his way across her wrist and up her bare forearm while she tried to maintain her composure. "Books," Adri whispered. "We were talking about books. I like the classics. Hemingway, Austen, Brontë could . . . Piperhall should have the entire collection of Dickens."

"Mm-hmm," David mumbled, and she assumed he hadn't heard. But the next time they came to Piperhall, there was a paper-wrapped package waiting on a low table in the library.

"Open it," he said.

There were five old books inside, their colors faded and bindings worn to string in a few places. Adri slid them through her hands, admiring the delicate artwork and tracing the titles. The prettiest was called *Lucile* and written by someone named Owen Meredith. It was dated 1884, an impressive hardcover in green and gold. But Adri had never heard of *Lucile*. Or of *How They Kept the Faith: A Tale of the Huguenots* or *Anne's Terrible Good Nature*, a children's book. "They're beautiful," Adri said, because she didn't know what else to say.

"This one," David slid out Longfellow's *The Song of Hiawatha* from the stack, "was ninety dollars. For a book." He made it sound like a crime.

Adri took the slim novel from him, and stood on tiptoe to brush a kiss against his cheek. "Thank you."

"The beginning of our library," David said, and gave her a self-satisfied little smile. "You can read them all. Someday."

His gift should have made her heart soar, but Adri battled a twinge of disappointment. The books were certainly antiques, lovely to look at and possibly even valuable collectibles. But David hadn't heard her. She didn't care about the age of the books or how expensive they were. Content was what mattered in her library. Adri should have told him so, right away, but she didn't. And the library still bore witness to David's misguided tokens of affection. Stacks of old books littered end tables and curio cabinets; some were even artfully arranged on the wide windowsills. They were mostly obscure titles with handsome covers. Books that Adri had no desire to actually read. She ran her fingertips along a copy of a book called *Rascal*, and forced herself to leave the library behind.

Directly across the hall was a formal sitting room that went mostly unused, but a quick glance inside stopped Adri cold. Victoria had found a purpose for it in her final days. There was a hospital bed in the very middle of the cavernous space, the sheets clean and tucked so tight around the mattress, a quarter would have bounced like a happy child. Apparently the hospital supply company hadn't yet come to retrieve their rental. Adri made a mental note to track down and call whoever needed to be called. It would be her first act as executor.

But even making a mini to-do list didn't stop Adri from feeling the full brunt of emotion as she confronted the place where Victoria had breathed her last. It wasn't just that the older woman had almost been her mother-in-law. It was that Victoria embodied everything Adri might have been. Everything she had lost. A husband, a home, a name. An inheritance that spanned centuries and was carefully marked in books that were meticulously kept. What would she be if David hadn't died? A wife, certainly. A mother? A daughter? Would she have nursed

Victoria as her fragile heart slowly stopped beating, lifting a glass of cold water to her lips and listening to the confessions she whispered?

It was impossible to face the harsh reality of the years of erosion, the casualties of such a cruel life, and not be moved.

Adri could have spent the rest of the morning there, leaning against the vaulted entrance to the room and agonizing over Victoria's letter and the tide of guilt it had unleashed, but the sound of the chain rattling on the front door spun her around.

"Anyone here?" Will's voice resonated in the empty space, announcing his arrival before he poked his head around the side of the heavy door. "Adri?"

She palmed away tears and tried to sniff discreetly. "Of course I'm here," she called. "Who else would be driving Betty?"

Will gave her a knowing smile and let himself in. Shutting the door quietly behind him, he moved toward Adri as if to give her a hug, but she crossed her arms over her chest and he stopped short. "I figured you'd be here. Dad told me you saw Clay this morning."

"Yeah."

"And?"

"And what, Will?" Adri hated herself a little for being short with her brother, but she didn't have it in her to parry his subtle insinuations. If he wanted to ask her something, he was going to have to just come out with it. "Aren't you supposed to be at work?"

"I wanted to see how you're doing." He looked hurt, and Adri regretted snapping at him.

She sighed. "I need a drink," she said by way of apology. "You coming?"

The main living area was at the very back of the house, and the only way to access the kitchen was to go straight through it. The floor-to-ceiling windows afforded a gorgeous view of the free-form pool and waterfall hot tub that had always struck Adri as a nonsensical feature in a Midwestern home—even one as grand as Piperhall. Because the temperatures dipped so low in winter, the hot tub was completely unusable seven months of the year. Sometimes more.

But the ornamental terrace that swept around the large pool and hot tub was still striking in any season, and large pots of hibiscus bushes and cheerful red geraniums clung to foliage with admirable tenacity. Adri was surprised to see that the pool was full and the surface was glassy and clean. A thin wall of warm water fell from the stone hot tub and was swallowed up by the deep end of the glittering pool. The water would be a comfortable 80 degrees. Adri hadn't expected to see it up and running.

"Who's taking care of the place?" she asked, motioning through the windows.

"She liked the sound of the water." Will pulled out a bar stool and sat down as Adri lifted a pair of glasses out of the cupboard near the sink. "Once the big spring prep work is done, it doesn't take much maintenance to keep the pool clean."

"And I suppose you're the pool boy?" Adri's back was turned to Will as she filled the glasses with water from the tap, but she could feel his eyes boring into her.

"As a matter of fact, I am," Will said. "Do you have a problem with that?"

Adri shrugged as she handed him the water. "You don't find it a little strange?"

"That I helped out someone in need? That Dad and Jackson and I worked hard to fill in the gaps when you ran away?" Will gave her an uncharacteristically hard look. "Someone had to take care of Victoria, Adri, and it sure as hell wasn't going to be you."

"Then why'd she leave me the house?" Adri watched her brother closely, waiting for the shock that would breeze across his features. There was none. "You knew?" she whispered, incredulous.

"Of course, I knew. I was the witness when she changed the will. Didn't you see my signature?"

She hadn't. She had forgotten to look. It had seemed important at the time, but when the full understanding of what Victoria had done hit her, suddenly who had known what didn't seem to matter at all.

"Why didn't you warn me?" Adri asked, too surprised to worry about the tremor in her voice. "Why didn't you talk her out of it? I don't want this. I never asked for this!"

She was half shouting, and Will raised his hands, palms up, as if that would somehow calm her. "Hey. It's okay. I didn't talk her out of it because I thought you would be honored. You're all she had left, Adri."

"Don't make me feel guilty!"

"I'm not trying to make you feel—"

"Well, you are. What am I supposed to do with this? What in the world did she want from me?"

"Take a breath," Will instructed. Adri tried to comply, but the air felt thin and insubstantial in her lungs. "Again." He was silent as she struggled to get her breathing under control, though he covered her hands with his own when she slapped her palms on the countertop and pressed down as if she expected the granite to hold her up. After a few moments he said, "I don't think she wanted anything from you. You're reading too much into it. It's a gift, Adri. You can do with it whatever you want."

But he didn't know everything. He didn't know about the letter. Or about the things that had happened between Adri and David. Will didn't know the truth about the day that David died.

Adri pulled her hands out from under her brother's and gulped down the water that she had poured for herself. "I don't think I can do this."

"Do what?" Will didn't try to hide his irritation as he rolled his eyes. "I love you, little sis, and I'm glad that you're home, but this whole tragic love story is starting to get old."

Adri was speechless, but Will was far from done.

"It's been over five years, Adri. You've run as far away as you possibly can, ignored every responsibility and relationship you left behind, and now you've been given a once-in-a-lifetime opportunity by a woman who owed you nothing, and you're going to act like it's a burden?"

"You don't understand."

Will gave her a gentle smile. "Sure I do. I know you feel guilty—I do, too. I was there, you know."

"No, you weren't. You and Jackson were hiking. You were nowhere near when—"

"Whatever," Will interrupted. "All I'm saying is, we all hate what happened to David, and we all wish that things would have been different. But you have got to stop beating yourself up. I know you loved him and I know you miss him. We all do. But you need to learn to live again. To let it go once and for all."

He made it sound so simple, but when Adri probed each of his confident declarations, she was far from convinced that his words were true. She had loved David, but she wasn't sure that she loved him when he died.

And what in the world was she supposed to do with that?

Adri was a fraud, pure and simple. She had killed him, but she could never, ever admit that to anyone but herself. And Caleb, she realized with a start. She had told Caleb. But he'd be long gone by the time she reclaimed the life she had worked so hard to make for herself. "I never stopped living," she said defensively. "I happen to like my life."

"Your life didn't begin five years ago. You can't keep ignoring everything that came before."

Will was right, but Adri could hardly tell him that. "Victoria should have left the house to you," she finally said. "You and Jackson. Nora and the baby. You could have lived like royalty."

"What if we don't want to live like royalty?"

"And what about me? What if I don't want to live like a queen?"

Will shrugged. "Then you do something about it. Sell it, give it away, write a big, fat donation check to every health clinic you can think of in West Africa."

"It's not about the money."

"You're right," Will said, and there was a note of bitterness in his voice that made her cringe. "It's about you." And then he pushed back from the counter and stalked away.

Adri was sure that he had left, though the front door was so far away from the kitchen, she couldn't hear it slam.

～

The rest of the house was in pristine condition, but Adri hardly noticed as she walked from room to room. Some wings had been closed off entirely, yet when Adri threw open the doors and wandered the abandoned halls, there was barely a speck of dust to mark her haphazard passage through the mansion that was now, impossibly, hers. She avoided Victoria's bedroom on the northeast quarter of what the late Mrs. Galloway had pretentiously designated "the chamber story" (it was actually the third floor), and also David's apartment in the garden level basement (only a couple feet were underground). But everywhere else felt like fair game, including the suite at the opposite corner of Victoria's rooms on the uppermost floor.

The first time David took The Five to Piperhall, he didn't give them a tour. He let them explore. A quick rundown in the vast entryway outlined the bones, and then he disappeared down the steps to his rooms. Adri wanted to follow him, but the allure of the mansion was too much to ignore. They'd find their way downstairs soon enough.

"Have fun," David called over his shoulder, trailing Will and Jackson in his wake. "Get into all the trouble you want."

Harper looked as if she'd love nothing more than to do exactly that. Grabbing Adri's hand, she hurried her through the halls, up stairs and around corners, half running as if they were being pursued. "It's huge," Harper gasped after they had wound through the dining room, the library, and a room that looked like it had once been used for formal balls. "Have you ever been inside?"

"No." Adri was as breathless as Harper, but she tried to suppress her excitement. After all those summers of walking the grounds but being strictly forbidden to enter the mansion, it felt strange to be unchaperoned in Piperhall. And she couldn't forget that somewhere in the recesses of the seemingly endless estate, Victoria Galloway hid.

No, not hid. Victoria was not the sort to hide. Cool and regal at every summer picnic, Victoria had presided over the festivities as the proud matriarch of Piperhall. She was narrow and elegant, always wearing a tailored, sleeveless dress that hung off her body as if it had been made for her. Adri once overheard a woman value one of Victoria's dresses at several hundred dollars. "It's a Vera Wang," she muttered to her frumpy, T-shirted friend. "How would you know?" the other responded. But of course it was. Or another equally expensive label that was nothing short of outrageous in a town as inconsequential as Blackhawk, Iowa. Victoria shone against the backdrop of her peers. But they weren't really her peers at all; they were small-town people, hardworking but ordinary, and Victoria was everything they weren't. Adri didn't necessarily admire her for it. But she was intimidated by her. And she had no desire to bump into her before their intended rendezvous for dinner in the dining hall.

"We're supposed to find a bedroom," Adri reminded Harper. David had told them to avoid the rooms to the east of the central staircase, and Adri fully planned to comply. "Second floor, west wing."

Harper snorted. "West wing. Don't you love it?"

They wound their way back to the main entrance and up the sweeping staircase that opened onto the second floor. Adri led the way left, past half a dozen rooms on each side interspersed with arching windows and serene sitting areas that looked like they had never been used.

The hallway narrowed here, as if the builders had run out of room and were forced to slant the hallway just to fit everything in. It was almost quaint in a house of vast excesses, and Adri had been immediately charmed. A shuttered window opened on the west lawn, and as Adri and Harper dragged their small suitcases and duffels down the corridor, there was something warm and alluring about the pink wash of late-afternoon sun. Best of all, there was a separate staircase that started in a hall behind the kitchen and ended almost at the door of the bedroom that Adri and Harper decided to claim as their own. They didn't care that there was only one queen-size bed. Harper called dibs on the plush couch, and the girls pretended that the reason they wanted to bunk together was companionship and not because the mansion was enormous and filled with eerie sounds with no discernible origin.

Part of the appeal of the room was the close vicinity to a lesser-known exit, but when Adri stepped over the threshold, she also fell in love with the small balcony that overlooked the garage. Victoria insisted on calling it the carriage house, but as far as her son was concerned, it was little more than a place to park his Audi in the rain. And smoke. He loved to smoke tucked beneath the eaves, and from her first visit to the Galloway home until the very last, Adri loved to watch him.

"He's like candy, isn't he?" Harper purred on the inaugural night they spent in the room. She was hanging a purple cocktail dress in the huge, empty closet, and Adri couldn't help but suppress a smile at her friend's ridiculous choice of weekend attire. And her words.

"Candy?"

"I just want to lick him."

"That's disgusting." But David was leaning against the side of the garage, smoking the last inch of a Camel, and Adri's gaze was drawn to him like a moth to the proverbial flame.

"Nothing is disgusting when David Galloway is involved." Harper threw her a wink. "Nothing is off-limits."

Adri tore herself from the window and grabbed her own

duffel bag. The clothes she had stuffed in it were far more casual than Harper's getaway wardrobe, and, truth be told, the contents leaned heavily toward books. There was a thick pharmacology textbook and a slim paperback about the ethics of health care. Adri loved those books with something akin to pie-eyed adoration, and it was no great sacrifice for her to bring them along on what was supposed to be a leisurely excursion to Piperhall. But she had also brought her Western Civ notes and a college comp book that gave her an involuntary tic. When she plopped them all on the desk in the corner, Harper laughed.

"What are you doing? This is supposed to be a fun weekend! We're here to relax and party . . ." She waggled her eyebrows up and down. "And get to know our new friend David better."

"I have a test on Tuesday," Adri confessed. "And a chem lab on Monday that will eat up all my study time."

"You're such a puritan." Harper climbed over the bed and swept Adri's books into one of the desk drawers, ruffling the pages and making Adri cry out. "It won't kill you to take a break."

"It's a tough program!" she complained, trying to rescue her books. Harper snapped the drawer shut and leaned against it.

"I'm sure David would love to spend some time with Nurse Adrienne." Harper spun Adri around by her shoulders and gathered her dark hair into a low, messy bun. Pulling a few strands loose to frame Adri's face, Harper whispered, "I think you should wear your hair like this tonight. After supper. In the hot tub."

David had told them to bring their bathing suits, but Adri had hoped to excuse herself from such public awkwardness by claiming tons of homework. Thus the books. It wasn't that she was a prude, she just wasn't ready to prance around half-naked next to her pinup-girl best friend. Adri had seen Harper's bathing suit—it was white (white!) and stringy. Her own swimming suit was a conservative Speedo two-piece left over from her lifeguarding days. It even said *Lifeguard* across the chest. She needed a new suit, but it was nothing she had ever thought about until David uttered the words *hot tub*.

"I don't think so." Adri pulled away and her hair fell back to her shoulders. "I'm not really a hot tub kind of girl."

"It's the suit, isn't it?" Harper gave her a sympathetic look. "Don't worry, I saw it and I brought a few of my extras for you to try."

From deep in her duffel came an explosion of color, bikini separates sprinkling the duvet like cheerful confetti. And Harper made Adri try them all on. At first Adri disappeared into the private bathroom for every wardrobe change, but Harper wasn't the shy sort and she couldn't stop herself from tightening straps and tugging bottoms so that they accentuated Adri's assets. "Heavy on the ass," Harper laughed. "Not that you aren't perfectly perky in every way," she hastened to add.

When the ideal suit had finally been selected—a robin's egg–blue ensemble with diminutive flowers that was the most conservative of the bunch by far—Adri slipped her clothes back on and flopped on her stomach on the bed. Harper was attaching false eyelashes as she sat on the desk, face turned toward the light and the mirror she had propped against the sash of the double-hung window.

"Why would you do that?" Adri asked.

"Do what?"

"Bring suits for me. I mean, obviously David is interested in you or he never would have invited us all here this weekend. And any man in his right mind would pick you over me. But why try to make me pretty? I don't get it."

Harper turned from the window, one set of false eyelashes in place and the other clinging to the tip of her finger. She looked uneven, maybe even a little mad, and by the way she was staring at Adri, she wasn't very impressed by her friend's casual observations.

"First," she said, holding up the finger with the eyelashes still attached, "David isn't the least bit interested in me. Nor I in him. We could never be lovebirds. Friends, coconspirators, more like."

"Second—" Harper's middle finger popped up and dislodged the clinging row of lashes. Adri watched them flutter to the ground but Harper seemed not to notice. "He invited us over because he's a very lonely young man. Don't tell him I told you so; he'd be pissed."

"Third, never, ever underestimate yourself, my lovely friend. You are a thing of beauty, a slow burn, a heart enflamed and a soul enchanted. Beauty is eternity gazing at itself in the mirror. But you are eternity and you are the mirror."

Adri rolled onto her back so she could clap slowly. "Bravo," she muttered, gazing at her friend upside down. They hadn't known each other long, months not years, but time had felt condensed in the early days of their friendship and Adri already knew the way that Harper's mouth quirked when she was on the verge of laughing. "And who, exactly, are you quoting?"

"Kahlil Gibran. Hell's bells, girl, tell me you've read him!" Harper looked at her finger and realized the eyelash was missing, so she hopped off the desk and went to her knees on the hardwood floor. "Didn't your father teach you anything at all?"

"Nope," Adri said. "Neither Gibran nor how to apply false eyelashes."

"Well, you're missing out." Harper burst upright, slightly mangled lashes once again dangling from her index finger. "I have so much to teach you!"

They dressed for supper, Harper in the cocktail dress and a pair of heels that made her look downright Amazonian. She was stunning, and Adri felt diminished in comparison. Her navy skirt and striped sweater seemed matronly, and any confidence that she'd gained during the bikini fashion show had long faded. But she dutifully followed Harper down the main staircase at seven o'clock sharp, just as David had directed them to do.

A part of Adri couldn't believe that she was actually inside the mansion. It was all she had ever wanted as a little girl at the Piperhall summer picnic—even the smallest peek would have sufficed—but no one had ever been allowed to step foot in the house. But all at once the entire setup seemed inauthentic to Adri, distortedly grandiose, and as they descended the sweeping staircase she felt a stab of annoyance that David would put them through such theatrics. Who did this? Who lived in a twenty-room house with two people? What sort of man expected his college-age guests to get dressed up for supper on what was supposed to be a carefree weekend away from school? The whole thing felt affected to her.

But when they rounded the curve, David, Jackson, and Will were lounging in the entryway, watching them approach. They were all in exactly the same clothes they had on when they left campus hours before—jeans and T-shirts, even though they had expertly feigned irritation at Victoria's dinner dress code and the need to pack a tie. Will and Jackson seemed almost sheepish, but David wore a self-satisfied smirk that should have been unattractive. It was somehow enchanting.

"Told you," Will said, stepping forward and putting a hand on David's shoulder. "She's really not the type."

"Excuse me?" Harper was standing on the bottom step, the heels and the added inches of the stair making her tower over the guys, even though David was far from short.

"We had a little bet going," Jackson smiled, but it was hesitant. "David figured you'd both get all dressed up if he told you to, and Will said Adri wouldn't."

"I'm dressed up," Adri huffed, tugging at the three-quarter-length sleeves of her thin sweater.

Will looked between Harper and Adri, then gave his sister a look as if to say, Seriously?

She would have marched right back upstairs and changed into a pair of jeans, if Harper hadn't thrown back her head and laughed like she was in on their little trick. "Ohhh," Harper said, drawing out the word. She smoothed her hands down the curve of her formfitting dress and sighed. "You are such pathetic little men. It's sad, really, to realize that you wouldn't know what to do with us even if you could catch us. I had expected more of you. Come on, Adri."

And then she took off down the long hall, her heels clicking against the floor in a staccato of reprimand. Adri watched her go, as ruffled as the men, and didn't realize until Harper was halfway gone that she was supposed to follow.

It was one moment, one insignificant occurrence that should have been nothing but chaff against the backdrop of all her consequential memories. But everything mattered, everything, and though it seemed small, the guys treated Adri and Harper as equals after that. By the time they were known as The Five, they were not the sort to prank each other or pull rank, but they existed in a sort of composed balance where each person was respected and admired as both beautifully independent and inextricably fused. And it was all because of Harper.

Sometimes, it felt like everything was because of Harper.

It had been over five years since the first time she slept in the room at the end of the hall, but the bedding was the same. A neutral duvet cover in an elegant floral brocade. Although it was old, it still looked new, and it felt exactly the same when Adri reached out a hand to touch it. Cool and silky, the flowers a subtle silver pattern on fabric that reminded her of smudged charcoal. She sat on the bed, tracing the petals with her fingertips, and before she knew it, she was curled up on her side, cheek against the pillow. Adri could just see the garage from where she lay, the white paint beginning to peel in places and a couple of shingles curled up at the edges, weathered by rain and snow and wind. This was exactly where she had spent so many nights with Harper, dreaming about being David's lover, about becoming the next Mrs. Galloway. And though some things felt like they would never change, everything was different. She was different.

When Adri closed her eyes, she could picture Harper perched on the desk, her face turned toward the sun.

She missed her with an ache so deep it felt bottomless.

She missed Harper more than Blackhawk and the life she almost had. Adri missed Harper more than she missed David.

9

When Sam found Adri later that evening, she was in the horse pasture on the estate, mending the whitewashed fence. An old tool belt from the workbench in the garage was slung low on her hips, and though the light was fading quickly and a nighttime cool was wisping through the air, fine beads of sweat clung to her forehead. Adri knelt on the ground, one knee in the dirt and the other propping up a ten-foot length of fallen board. She was working to pull a bent, rusty nail out of the warped wood. "Need a hand?" Sam asked, leaning his forearms on the fence.

Adri glanced up and saw her father bite back a grin. She would've been angry, but she knew he wasn't laughing at her. He simply loved to watch her work. He always had. When she was little, he would catch her on the floor in her bedroom, the contents of every drawer and closet in her room spread around her. She'd fold, refold, and then carefully organize and arrange everything so that if she wanted her green T-shirt from 4-H, she could find it blindfolded in five seconds flat.

But Adri wasn't just organized. She was a fixer, too. A mender of broken things, a one-stop repair shop of a girl who learned early how to wield any tool like a pro. It was exactly why she had decided to go into nursing—an occupation that David had routinely tried to talk her out of. "You don't need to work," he told her after they were engaged. He nibbled her ear, his warm breath making her shiver. "You'll never need to work another day in your life." It didn't sound like a promise to Adri. It sounded like a threat.

The nail finally gave and skidded out of the wide board with a hollow squeak. Adri plucked it out of the crowbar head of the hammer and added it to a growing pile of rusty nails in the front pocket of her tool belt. "No thanks," she said hefting the board into place and centering it on the post. "I don't need any help." But Sam reached down and secured the wood for her anyway so both of her hands were free to drive the new nails.

They worked in silence for a few minutes, Sam holding the plank steady as Adri expertly hammered three nails in a triangle pattern. When she was done, she stuck the hammer in the loop of her belt and pulled herself up. Her knees were sore and she bent and flexed them until the blood started to flow back into her feet. Only then did she give her dad a small smile of thanks and set off down the fence in search of the next spot that needed patching.

Sam trailed her, a step or two behind. "It's getting late," he said. "You've got to be cold."

Adri hadn't noticed the drop in temperature, but goose bumps rose along her bare arms at the mere mention of the weather. "I want to get just a bit more done."

Sam didn't say anything, but Adri knew what he was thinking. She had chosen an odd job to get started on. A few loose boards on the pasture fence were nothing, really. The horses weren't going anywhere. Even if an entire section fell down, there was still the thin line of electric fencing and the memory of shock that would keep the small herd contained. But this felt to Adri like a step in the right direction. She was doing something quantifiable. All she had to do was glance back the way she had come to see the neat line of white fencing and know that she had accomplished something.

"Let me help you finish, at least."

Adri shrugged and Sam interpreted the gesture as a yes.

They worked until the sun fell behind the trees and the shadows became so deep they couldn't see clearly anymore. The labor was undemanding, but they worked in silence anyway, and when Sam straightened up from the last board he broke the quiet with a jaw-splitting yawn.

"I suppose we missed supper," Adri said as they headed back toward the driveway.

"What day is it?" Sam asked. "Tuesday?"

"I left Africa on Saturday, traveled until Monday . . ." Adri could hardly believe it had been only a couple of days since she left Caleb standing beneath the blaze of a West African sun. Her entire life had tipped upside down in less than a week. She shook her head. "Yeah, I think it's Tuesday."

"I have supper with Will on Tuesdays and Thursdays. Sometimes Jackson and Nora join us. Tuesdays they cook and Thursdays I do."

"Sounds like a nice setup. But didn't Will and Jackson make supper last night?"

"You're home," Sam said, giving her a sidelong look. "I have a feeling we'll have supper together every night if you let us. And you don't need to worry about the time. We eat late."

They always had. The afternoon milking came first, and by the time Sam was done cleaning up the parlor and scraping the holding pen, he was in desperate need of some cleaning up himself. First he had a hot shower in the stall that had been added to the converted sunporch on the back of the house, and then he liked a half hour to just be still. That short span of time was one of Adri's fondest memories of childhood. There was a certain balance to the world, an indisputable peace as her father sat at the table, a Bible open in front of him and a glass of ice water close at hand.

Sometimes he read out loud. He loved the Psalms, and sometimes the cadence of those words washed over Adri as she sliced bread or set the table around him. It was a love song that he sang to her.

They had reached the drive and Sam's truck was parked beside Adri's Buick. The windows were open and Beckett was sprawled out on the front seat, looking for all the world like a rug instead of a dog. Adri slipped her hand in and patted his broad head, and the thought crossed her mind that the humane thing to do would be to put him down. Poor thing was obviously suffering in his own hushed way. Or maybe he was just so old that he was living in slow motion.

She said to her father, "You knew, didn't you?"

"I did." Sam confessed, and there wasn't an ounce of repentance in his voice. "Victoria and I talked about it."

"You were friends?" Adri tried to sound nonchalant, but the thought of her father and Victoria becoming bosom buddies made her heart pinch almost painfully. It felt wrong somehow. Dangerous.

Sam shrugged. "After a fashion. She was a rather isolated woman. When you left I started checking in on her from time to time."

Adri didn't know what to say. "Thank you," she managed, though she didn't know what she was thanking him for.

"She really wanted you to have the estate. She even went so far as to alert her brother-in-law to the change in the will and ensure that he wouldn't fight it at all."

"Why didn't he? Fight it, I mean."

"In the grand scheme of things, Piperhall is only a small fraction of the Galloway fortune. James got what he wanted, and would have sold the house and land if given the chance. His family is in Kansas now—and scattered across the continent, from what I understand. They're not about to move to northwest Iowa. It just seemed better this way."

"Why?"

"It keeps the estate in the family," Sam said.

"Dad"—Adri passed her hand over her eyes and tried not to sigh—"I'm not a Galloway."

Sam reached for the truck door and swung it open, gently

nudging Adri out of the way as he climbed onto the bench seat. "No," he said through the open window, after he had shut the door behind him and started the engine. "You're not a Galloway. But sometimes family is what you make it."

"I know, Dad." Adri nodded, clinging to the decision she had made as if the weight of it could stop her from being swept away. "And I'm going to do good by Victoria. I'm going to make it right. But she's not my family."

Sam didn't say anything.

Adri watched him go, his words as heavy and real as a polished stone that she could worry in the palm of her hand. He was right, and she had spent the last decade collecting a small family around her. One to replace the love she had lost. Substitutes for the people she felt she could never return to, no matter how much she sometimes longed to do exactly that.

It would have hurt Sam to know that Adri had chosen her family a long time ago. They lived halfway around the world and they were her brothers and sisters.

Her children.

~

Adri didn't get hold of Caleb until Friday, and in the interim she ran herself ragged attending to all the details of Victoria's will and trying to ignore the nagging guilt inspired by Victoria's letter. Of course, there were small things to do on the estate itself, but mostly she made phone calls, attended appointments, and wrote checks to tie up the loose ends that, against Victoria's most fervent wishes, were inevitably left dangling. She also fielded calls from the various recipients of Victoria's generosity—it seemed everyone wanted someone to thank for the gifts the matriarch of the Galloway fortune had graciously bestowed. Adri tried to be accommodating, but she felt downright deceitful as strangers thanked her again and again. It didn't matter that she told them she was only the executor. Someone had to hear their gratitude.

When Adri dutifully circled through Caleb's cell phone number on Friday morning, she had merely grabbed the old rotary in her father's kitchen on a whim. After a couple of tries, she had come to the conclusion that Caleb would call her if he needed her, and beyond that there was nothing she could do. She had to let it go, and she was about to force herself to hang up. But after only two fuzzy rings, there was a half-shouted "Hello" that felt like a sucker punch to the gut.

"Hello? Caleb? Caleb, it's Adri. Where have you been?"

More fuzz and static, and then suddenly there was a pop and everything seemed to go flat and clear. "Hey, Adri." There was a smile in Caleb's voice, and Adri was shocked that she could actually hear it. They didn't often get such a good connection. "What's new with you?"

"I asked you a question first." She tried to sound stern, but she was grinning, twisting the curlicued cord of the phone on her finger. "Where have you been? What have you been up to? I've been trying to get ahold of you all week!"

"Calm down." Caleb laughed. "I'm fine. Everything is fine. We went up-country for a few days because one of the outlying churches was experiencing an outbreak of malaria. We've got it under control."

"Thank God," Adri breathed, but she started doing mental calculations almost immediately. The malaria meds were meticulously accounted for and doled out. She wondered where he'd gotten the extras from. Or if he used the medication that had been stockpiled for the kids.

Before she could ask, he put her mind at ease. "A windfall donation. No worries. Your kids are fine."

Your kids. Adri squeezed her eyes shut and fought an ache of homesickness so fierce that it threatened to overwhelm her. She swallowed hard. Then she forced herself to say the words that she had been dreading: "I hate to tell you this, but I won't be back this weekend."

"I figured as much," Caleb said easily. "Might as well stick around a while. We've got everything under control here. Besides, the yearly board trip is coming up in a couple of weeks and our jobs will be rendered rather meaningless for a while. I had planned on talking you into learning to surf and then getting you drunk every night for a week straight, but you might as well stay put. Maybe I'll come to you."

"What?" Adri managed.

"Well, not drunk-drunk, just a little tipsy. You deserve it, don't you think? We both do . . ."

"You're not actually thinking about coming here, are you?"

"Stateside?" Caleb asked. "Of course. Why not? I had planned to go home for Christmas, but it seems to me like you could use a little support."

"I'm fine, really."

"It's not far," Caleb went on, undeterred. "I grew up in Florida, but my family is in La Crosse now and it's hardly home to me. I'm a beach bum, not a farm kid. And La Crosse is like, what? A couple of hours from you?"

"Six, maybe more. A long way," Adri said. She didn't want to encourage him, even though she was almost girlishly breathless at the thought of seeing him. It was ridiculous, and Adri struggled to get a grip of herself. "Just stop, okay? You're not coming here. I'll be back as soon as I can."

"Whatever." Caleb sounded unfazed. "How did the memorial go?"

"It hasn't happened yet." Adri pinched the bridge of her nose, forcing back the headache that came hand in hand with the topic of Victoria's memorial. The impenetrable Mrs. Galloway had been buried in a small, private ceremony only days after she died, but Adri was still working on the particulars of her service. Victoria's wishes were outlined in a second document that she had put in Clay's hands for safekeeping, and after he determined that Adri had gotten over the initial shock of her inheritance, he handed over the instructions. Just another one of her duties.

Victoria wanted a public ceremony on the estate, and had included a number of specific details that were proving to be more work than Adri had expected. A trio of violins on the terrace. Long stems of calla lilies tied with white ribbon. A reading by Adri's father of Kipling (though Adri couldn't begin to imagine why Victoria had been so enamored of "If"). The lady who had always catered meals at the estate was going to provide a veritable banquet of Victoria's favorite finger foods, from petits fours to slivers of artichoke with prosciutto, goat cheese, and mint, and there were two cases of New Zealand sauvignon blanc chilling in the wine cellar for the occasion. It seemed more like a party than a funeral, especially because Victoria had gone so far as to suggest a dress code. Adri suspected that the entire town would show up, if only to see Piperhall one last time.

The only thing Victoria hadn't done was set a time for the event, and her brother-in-law, James Galloway, was difficult to accommodate. After several terse phone calls, he had finally agreed to fly in the following Saturday—and Adri was effectively trapped in Iowa until at least then.

But she didn't feel like explaining all of that to Caleb. "I'll do my job," she said. "You do yours."

"Yes, ma'am. Whatever you say, ma'am."

After that it was all business. Adri asked for updates on specific kids and projects, as well as a review of the medicine cabinet and what supplies they were running short of. When the board visited every fall, she sent a detailed order form outlining exactly what the clinic needed in order to keep running, from Band-Aids to HIV test kits. She was about to launch into a prepared speech about how to cull the list, when Caleb interrupted her.

"It's done," he said happily. "Done and done. Already emailed to the director."

Adri was struck momentarily speechless. "What do you mean, it's done? How could you possibly know what to do?"

"You keep meticulous records, Adri. I saw the past request

forms and spent most of the night last night going through inventory. I couldn't sleep."

She didn't know whether to be happy or put out. "Guess I'm not as irreplaceable as I thought," she joked.

"Just wait till you get back," Caleb said. "You're going to have to fight me for Lucia, too. I think she likes me best."

He was teasing her, but Adri's heart sank anyway. She was used to being second best. Or worse. In elementary school she had always stood in Will's shadow. He was smarter, more athletic. Making friends and getting good grades just came naturally to him, while Adri had to work for everything she got. By the time she graduated from high school, she was a 4.0 student with a small circle of friends, but she'd had to fight for every tenth of a point on her GPA, and the group she hung out with was comprised of the girls who didn't fit anywhere else. They easily drifted apart after graduation.

And, though Harper had chosen Adri that very first day of college to be her confidante, there were times when Adri felt like little more than a generic sidekick in the shadow of her spectacular best friend. Once, at one of their Piperhall parties, Adri overheard someone say, "Who's the dark-haired girl?" He was talking about her, of course. Never mind that she was one of The Five or that it was practically impossible to spot Harper or David on campus without Adri being close by.

"Yeah, well, don't get too used to it." Adri tried to sound lighthearted, but her enthusiasm for the conversation had died. She excused herself quickly after that and hung up.

The house was quiet. Too quiet. Sam was doing chores; Will and Jackson were at work. Adri wasn't used to having so much downtime, and even though there were a dozen small things on her to-do list, it was all busywork that required little skill or even attention. She couldn't stand the thought of picking up the phone for another series of calls to automated services. Canceling cable, disconnecting the landline, putting a halt on Victoria's subscriptions. It felt like an exercise in futility, for even though Adri would do her best to dot every single *i* on her seemingly never-ending list, mail addressed to Mrs. Victoria Galloway would still be delivered to the estate. It was the sort of emotional land mine that would wreck a loving husband or unsuspecting son when he opened the mailbox months later. Except that there was no husband, no son to mourn Victoria's loss. And Adri felt decidedly unqualified for the job. She had admired Victoria in her own, careful way, but there would be no weeping or gnashing of teeth.

Adri needed a break, and, twenty minutes later, Mateo was saddled up. It had been a bit of a chore, and Adri's hands shook as she tried to tighten the cinch, because Mateo was notorious for holding his breath and making the saddle slip sideways halfway through a ride. When she finally straightened up and blew a strand of hair out of her eyes, she surveyed the horse before her with a sort of awe. He was beautiful. And so strong. It had been a very long time since she had surveyed the world from the vantage point of his tall back, and she was so eager to do so now, she could hardly stand it. But there was a vein of fear beneath her excitement. Riding Mateo wasn't exactly like riding a bike. She hoped she remembered how.

He shied a little when she put her foot in the stirrup, but Adri swung up anyway. A few sidesteps, a quick, sinuous turn, and Mateo tossed his head like he was either just as anxious to run as she was, or he hadn't been ridden in a long time. Adri guessed both were true.

"Shhh . . ." She gathered the reins tight in one hand and patted his neck. He fought the bit for a minute, twisting from side to side and nickering softly to his sisters in the pasture. They were all standing against the fence, watching Mateo and Adri like a trio of gossipy neighbors gathered on the front lawn. It made Adri smile in spite of herself and she saluted the mares before turning Mateo's head in the direction of the driveway and the trail that David had cut through the trees so many years ago.

It was overgrown with tall grasses and weeds that had crept over fallen trees and the jagged, slate stones of the prairie woodland. At first Adri tried to lead Mateo, but when she realized that he remembered the way better than she did, she slackened the reins just enough to let him pick his way through the sun-dappled grove.

The path was so thick that Mateo couldn't even trot along the forgotten trail, and Adri tried to relax into the worn saddle and the gentle sway of his gait. Riding was a familiar tune, something that resonated in her soul but that she couldn't quite remember note for note. She gripped the reins too tightly, held herself too rigid, even though the leather creaked pleasantly and birds sang overhead. It was almost idyllic. But something thrummed just beneath her skin, a feeling of impending disaster. Worlds colliding. The promise of a fall. More heartbreak.

She felt sometimes like that afternoon had been an explosion, a bomb that had gone off in the center of her universe and flung everyone from her. David had been killed, but no one escaped unscathed. Will and Jackson wore that day like black bands around their arms. And Harper was never the same. A light had gone out in her eyes, and when Adri finally mustered the courage to look into them in the waiting room of that hospital in Hope, British Columbia, she saw that their friendship had dissipated like smoke. What could they possibly say to each other?

As for Adri, when the debris finally settled, she dragged her thumb through the ashes of her life and stained her own forehead. The rest of her days would be her own unending Ash Wednesday, an unholy offering of repentance and discipline. Of course, no one else could see the mark that she had given herself, but Adri couldn't look in the mirror without being reminded of exactly who she was and what she had done.

And now, in the delicate peace of her disciplined exile, to be given such an unwanted gift. To remember Victoria. To know that her home was neither here nor there. To miss Harper.

To see David in every shifting shadow. To remember all that they had been.

The sound of her sob startled Mateo, and he laid his ears back as if in solidarity. The world felt like a mean, ugly place to Adri, and because she wanted to flee it, when they reached the flatlands at the bottom of the Galloway property, she leaned low over Mateo's neck and hissed. He ran.

For a moment Adri was sorry that she hadn't worn boots. Her foot almost slipped through the stirrup, but she hauled herself up and grabbed the saddle horn. Lifted herself out of her seat slightly and gripped Mateo with her legs. Within seconds her arms ached and her thighs burned, but she didn't care.

There was a service road that wound near the river, and when Mateo reached it he smoothed his gallop into a run. Adri's heart throbbed in her throat as she struggled to maintain her seat. Grasping for purchase, she caught Mateo's mane in one hand and kept a vise grip on the saddle horn with the other. Then it was nothing but the pound of his hooves and the wind in her hair. Her cheeks stung, but she didn't know if it was because of the hot tears or the whip of her ponytail.

Mateo ran for a long time. Adri lost track of where they were and how far they had gone, but the horse eventually tired and slowed to a gallop, a canter, a trot. Then he simply turned and walked back the way they had come, headed toward home and a handful of oats. Adri slumped in the saddle, as exhausted and spent as he was. His coat was damp with sweat and his mouth frothed on the bit, so Adri looped the reins around the saddle horn and gave him all the slack he needed. Adri knew that the gelding needed to cool down after such a rigorous workout, and she forced herself out of the saddle when they were still a good half mile from the stable. It took some serious effort to swing her right leg over his side. She was numb and trembling all over, and when she slid to the ground, her knees almost buckled. Mateo paused and nudged her with his head and she grabbed his halter for support. They walked back like that, Adri with her fingers looped through the cheekpiece, her legs bowed and aching.

When they made it to the stable, Adri removed Mateo's saddle, blanket, and bridle. She slipped on a nylon halter and clipped a short lead shank to the tie ring. She didn't bother coiling a quick release knot around the stall gate. Instead, Adri held the end of the lead rope like a lifeline in both hands and backed up until she felt the wall of the stable behind her. The bricks were cool and rugged against her shoulders, and Adri tipped her head back and closed her eyes.

David had kissed her for the very first time right here.

It was in the middle of one of Harper's parties, though it was really more of a friendly gathering than a true party. A small group of people had been invited for a night of stargazing, and Harper had hunted down blankets from all over the estate and spread them out across the floor of the tower. There was wine and David's father's Scotch, and everyone was well on their way to getting good and drunk.

Except Adri. It was the beginning of their senior year, and though the worst of her classes were behind her, she had two semesters of core requirements, clinicals, and some straightforward ethics and foundations of nursing classes ahead. She felt like she was on the brink of something, the beginning of an era that would be entirely different from the one that had come before, and it wasn't unwelcome. In fact, she fairly hummed with excitement. She didn't know what the real world held, but she was ready for it.

Harper, on the other hand, seemed prepared to strangle her final year of college into submission. It would obey her: nothing would change. And so, constant parties and drinking and fun.

It felt thin to Adri. She loved Harper—she loved them all—but she was starting to wonder if anyone was ever going to take life seriously.

She didn't sneak out of the tower, not really, but she felt almost delinquent as she crept down the stairs. One didn't leave a Harper party. But Adri just had. It struck her as the tiniest bit dangerous. Something small had been severed, but it wasn't a loss that she mourned. It was freeing.

A cool October night, a soft quilt around her shoulders, the stars. Adri hadn't done anything wrong, and yet there was a delicious thrill in the air as she stepped out onto the quiet lawn in front of the Galloway mansion and peered up at the glittering windows of the tower high above her. They couldn't see her beneath a cloak of darkness, but she could just make out their silhouettes as they lounged in the flickering candlelight of a dozen glass lanterns. She wondered if they would miss her. And if they did, who would be the first to sound the alarm. Would they come looking for her? Did she want them to?

Adri found herself at the stable almost by accident. Her feet had followed a well-worn path, and since she hadn't been paying much attention to where she was going, she ended up exactly where she wanted to be. A midnight ride? It was too dangerous, but she heaved open the stable door anyway and wondered what it would feel like to ride sidesaddle in a Western saddle. In a skirt.

Fumbling for the light switch, Adri laughed nervously at herself and the unexpected chill that had crept up her spine. What had been so safe and innocent only seconds before took on the pallor of unease when she couldn't immediately find the switch. It was black in the stable and filled with the muted sounds of animals, a whisper of a breeze in the eaves. And something Adri couldn't quite place.

Footsteps.

She would have gasped, but her throat was cinched tight, and before she could even contemplate running, his hand was on her arm.

"Did I scare you?" David had caught her just above the elbow. His mouth was against her ear, his breath warm and sour-sweet with Scotch.

Adri spun and slapped him on the chest. "Don't do that!" She would have hit him again, but he was still hanging on to her arm through the blanket she had wrapped around herself. It was slipping off her shoulder and David lifted a thumb to graze the place where the creamy fabric of her blouse peeked from beneath the quilt. They were so close she had to lift her chin to look him in the eye, but there was something intimate about his body above her and she took a step back.

"What'd you do that for?" Adri asked, mildly breathless, though she couldn't tell if it was from the shock of David's appearance or his confusing proximity.

He grinned in the darkness and she could see the gleam of his perfectly straight teeth. "I followed you," he said simply. "I saw you creeping away from the party."

"I did not creep. And it's not really a party."

"Not a good one, anyway."

"Hey, party foul." Adri couldn't stop herself from sticking up for her best friend, even if she was the one who had left in the first place. And claimed it wasn't really a party. "Harper throws lovely parties."

"Did you just say that?" David's laugh was rich and genuine. It was one of the things Adri secretly adored about him. "Lovely parties? You sound like you belong in the Hamptons."

"Do I?"

"You're a regular Jackie O."

"Shut up, David." Adri's eyes had gotten used to the dark, at least somewhat, but it seemed strange to her that David didn't just flick the switch. He certainly knew where it was. But maybe he didn't want to draw the attention of the stargazers in the tower.

"Why'd you leave?" David asked after a few breaths.

"I'm kind of over it," she said. David nodded as if he understood completely. But she pressed on all the same. "We're seniors, you know? Aren't we . . . past this?"

"Some of us are."

"You, too?" Adri joked. But David was serious. "I thought you loved this stuff."

"Harper loves this stuff."

"And we love Harper," Adri finished.

"Of course we do."

It was a pinprick, nothing more. The nick of a tiny thorn. Adri had long suspected that David and Harper would one day, when they could stop being part of The Five, be simply The Two. She would be the maid of honor at their wedding and she would cry tears of joy. And just a couple for herself. There was an unwritten rule that they were not supposed to fall in love with each other. But how could they not? Everyone knew that the best kind of love was born of friendship.

"Why aren't you up there?" Adri said, turning David's question on its head. She nodded in the direction of the tower and Harper. There was a certain sad fondness in the asking, but she had come to terms with the inevitable. She almost told him that she knew, and that it was okay. Almost.

But he said something so unexpected, Adri didn't know how to respond.

"I'd rather be here with you."

The silence this time was laced with words unspoken, and questions hung like spirits in the air. Adri tried to blow off David's comment, but it hit too close to the heart of what she wanted. Hope made her tremble.

"Come on, Adri." David moved close to her, and when he reached for her this time his touch was entirely different. He was tentative, as if he expected Adri to slap his hand away. Or laugh and break the sudden spell that had been cast in the darkness of the stable. For there seemed to be magic in the air.

Adri wasn't used to this kind of whimsy. She was a practical girl. And David, though rich and spoiled and perpetually nonchalant, was a practical man. He was very matter-of-fact about his life and the privileges it afforded, and he had no problem admitting that his college degree was nothing more than a formality, a piece of paper that would serve as his ticket into the world of his father's company—a seat that had, technically speaking, been his since the moment he was born. In his personal life he was sensible and composed, able to take up and set aside the mantle of a playboy as easily as donning a coat. To laugh and joke and drink until his imposing mother slipped into the room, a quiet and watchful revenant whose presence instantly sobered and reined in her son.

But this. This hesitancy. This softness. This bewitching veil of darkness between them. Adri didn't recognize this man. But she wanted to.

"It's you," David said quietly. A confession. An almost guilty plea for her to understand. To not turn him away. He bent his head over her, his cheek just grazing the top of her head. "Adri, it's always been you."

Adri felt herself brim, and the fullness of every quiet wish and hidden dream overflowed. Then she found herself pressing up and into David, swept along by something she could not restrain. He was there. Warm and alive and more than she had hoped for. He slid his hands beneath the blanket and pulled her closer still, only fabric between them. Adri didn't stop to wonder how this could possibly work. How he could mean what he said and how they would forge ahead in a world that would wonder how they had fallen together at all. She just fell, and David caught her in his arms and held her against him as if this was what he had intended all along.

When he kissed her, she knew that she would give up everything for him. Her dreams of a life beyond. The perfection of The Five. Harper. And when his mouth found the hollow at the base of her neck, the place where her heart beat fast and uneven, she swore to herself that nothing else mattered. Just this night. This man.

But even then, it wasn't enough. It wasn't anywhere close to enough.

10

Sam talked Adri into going to church with him on Sunday.

It was a ritual she hadn't participated in since she was a child, and she dressed for the occasion as if she was getting ready for a wedding. Her closet was full of churchy fare, but it took her three tries to find the right dress, and she hoped that the jewel-green sheath she settled on wasn't horribly out of date. Adri had never been very chic, but after years in Africa, her sense of fashion was downright nonexistent. Fortunately, she was somewhat more adept with a mascara wand and eyeliner pencil, and her hair had always been wavy and as multidimensional as a calico cat's.

"Well, aren't you just a vision," Sam said when Adri stepped into the kitchen. She smoothed her hair almost shyly—she wasn't used to wearing it down—but Sam wasn't done complimenting her yet. "You look just like your mother."

They didn't talk about Georgia often, because even twenty-some years later, Sam went misty-eyed at the thought of his wife. She had become an angel of sorts, a memory that had somehow taken on every wish and longing that the three remaining Vogts could conjure up. She was their own personal dreamcatcher, and whether or not their carefully chosen mementos of her could be trusted didn't seem to matter anymore. Georgia Vogt was, and always would be, the definition of perfection.

But Adri didn't like being compared to her mother. Not anymore. "Thanks, Dad," she said, avoiding his gaze.

"The boys are coming with us this morning." Sam poured Adri a cup of coffee, seemingly oblivious to her tarnished mood. "We'll pick them up on the way. Nora decided to spend a few more days in Minnesota."

"I think we'd better take two cars," Adri said after a few moments. "I know Saturday seems like a long time away, but the memorial will be here before we know it and I've got lots to do." It wasn't exactly a lie.

"We'll come with you," Sam said. "I was planning on helping you out today. At least, when I can. I have to milk this afternoon, of course. But I know the boys would like to stick around and do what they can."

"Sure," Adri said, trying to think of a way to politely refuse her father's help. The truth was, there really wasn't much to do on the estate, and Adri was hoping to do a bit of exploring on her own. She had already wandered through most of the rooms in the mansion, but she had avoided Victoria's quarters as if they were quarantined. It felt wrong somehow to nose around in the late Mrs. Galloway's rooms. But a bout of insomnia had convinced Adri that nosing around was exactly what Victoria knew she would do. She had to. The estate belonged to her, after all.

And if she knocked off Victoria's rooms, she could avoid going in David's a little longer. She hadn't stepped foot in the garden basement yet, because she couldn't bring herself to confront the memories of all that had happened there. The love and the hope, but the hurt and the loss, too. The way that she had spent most of her life longing for something that didn't exist and never had. Just the thought of opening his door and confronting the ghosts that lingered there was enough to make Adri's heart feel as if it had been dipped in ice water.

"Thanks," Adri said. "But really, I'll be fine. I don't want to interfere with your Sunday afternoon."

Sam laughed. "What do you think I do? Nap? Don't be ridiculous. I'd love to help you. There's nothing I'd like more."

There was no way out of it. Minutes later, Adri climbed dutifully into the front seat of Betty—they couldn't take her dad's truck, there would be no room for the boys—and tried to appreciate the exquisite fall day as her dad drove to Will's house. Apparently Jackson and Nora lived a few streets down, and Jackson was going to walk over and meet them there. Adri hadn't yet seen her brother's home, and she was pleasantly surprised when her father drove through a new development on the south side of Blackhawk and pulled up to a beautiful Craftsman that had wide front pillars and lots of rugged stonework.

"It's gorgeous!" she exclaimed, and would have asked for a tour, but Will and Jackson were already on their way out the front door. Instead, when Will slid into the back, she draped her arm over the seat and said, "Nice work, brother. You make a good-looking house."

"It's well built, too," he said, and though he gave her an "I-told-you-so" wink, there was real pride in his voice.

"Will designed it," Jackson said, slamming the door on the opposite side. "I'm the numbers and details guy. Will is the creative genius."

"Genius," Adri scoffed. "Not sure that's what I'd call it."

The banter felt good, but when they pulled into the parking lot of the church, Adri found herself at a complete loss for words. She was convinced that there was a whole lot of condemnation here, and a bunch of people who knew the girl she had been—not the woman she was. She didn't know how to reconcile the two, or how to face the people who would undoubtedly hate her if they knew the role she had played in the demise of the Galloway family. The Galloways were not exactly beloved in Blackhawk, but they were an integral part of the community, and people were fiercely loyal—even if they weren't exactly affectionate.

In less than a week, these same people would flood the estate, invited by tradition. When someone died in Blackhawk, the community showed up en masse, carrying casseroles and waxy-leafed houseplants, condolences like sweet candy they could dole out as comfort. After Liam passed there had been no such public send-off, but Victoria's wishes had been express: she wanted an open memorial. And Adri had no doubt that the entire town would attend.

"Dad," she whispered as everyone else was piling out of the car. "I don't think I can do this."

He was tucking the car keys into his pocket, though most people in Blackhawk simply left them in the ignition. "What do you mean?" he asked, genuinely confused.

"I really don't want to see a bunch of people. Not right now."

"We'll sneak in the back."

"Dad." Adri gave him a knowing look. Everyone loved her father. It was hard for Sam to go anywhere in Blackhawk without pausing for a lengthy conversation with nearly everyone he met.

"I promise." He lifted his hand in a three-fingered salute. "Scout's honor."

Adri resisted the urge to roll her eyes, but when her dad pulled out the salute, there was simply no arguing. He meant what he said and he said what he meant, and Adri followed him into church like a reluctant puppy.

Every face in the foyer was familiar. A few people stared, their attention a mix of curiosity and greeting, but only one person took the time to address her. It was a poised, older woman with a thin but genuine smile, and though Adri tried to place her, she couldn't.

"Welcome home," the lady said, patting Adri's arm. "We've missed you."

"Thank you." Adri nodded, because she didn't know what else to say.

The rest of the service went off without a hitch, and Sam kept his promise by escorting his entire entourage out before the postlude. Sam wore a satisfied half-grin that exposed his delight at having both of his children with him on a fine Sunday morning. Adri took comfort in knowing she had performed her daughterly duty.

They picked up a paper bag full of carne asada tacos, hot, homemade tortilla chips, and fresh salsa from a motor home that had been converted into a portable restaurant and parked beside the Kum & Go. It hadn't been around the last time Adri was home, but Will assured her that Paco's made the best tacos, even if the name was a bit of a joke.

"The guy who owns it is Ernesto, but Ernesto's Tacos doesn't have quite the same ring to it."

Instead of going back to Maple Acres, Sam drove straight to the Galloway mansion so they could eat poolside. It was a gorgeous day. So pretty, in fact, that Adri seriously contemplated a swim. The free-form pool was hardly comparable to the ocean she was used to, but she missed the sensation of water against her skin, the weightless floating that always made her feel as if she was a natural part of the world around her, nothing more, nothing less.

But by the time they had decimated the bag of chips and Jackson had scooped the last bit of salsa out of the plastic tub, Adri wasn't thinking about church or swimming or even the expectations of the men who surrounded her. She felt unmoored and edgy about the entire morning. Something about the older woman in the church fellowship hall felt distinctly off to her, and it nibbled at the back of her mind like a worried mouse.

"Who was she?" Adri finally asked as they cleaned up their tinfoil taco wrappers and swept crumbs and bits of cilantro from the little round end tables beside the lounge chairs.

"Who was who?" Sam wasn't really paying attention, and Adri was glad her question hadn't piqued his interest. He didn't even look at her; he merely kept collecting remnants of garbage.

"That lady in church. The one who spoke to me before the service."

Sam straightened up and looked confused for a minute. Adri thought it was because he was trying to remember, but it became apparent that he was bewildered for a different reason entirely. "You don't remember her?"

"Should I?"

"Adrienne, that was Katherine Holt."

"Katherine?" Adri was dazed. The last time she had seen Katherine Holt was at David's funeral. She had been weeping softly, bent almost protectively over Victoria, who sat in the front pew of church, seemingly carved from stone. In a way, they had both mothered David. Adri had sat on Victoria's other side, though there was a space between them that could never be bridged. It had been torture for Adri to sit there at all, inhabiting a place that she did not want or deserve.

"She has Hodgkin's lymphoma," Sam said. "She finished up chemo this summer and is undergoing radiation."

That explained the silver pixie cut and the willow whip of her tiny waist. The Katherine Adri had known had been more substantial somehow. Made of more than breath and bones.

Katherine was a brilliant woman, an old maid if one chose to refer to her in such an antiquated way, who dedicated her life to tutoring some of the most elite students in the country. She had spent her younger years crisscrossing the map, going where the pay was good and the children worthy of her time and attention. When she took David on, she was nearing retirement and ready to settle down. She ended up falling in love with both her student and Blackhawk, and she never bothered to leave.

Katherine was also the closest thing to a friend Victoria ever had. At least, as far as Adri could tell. When The Five started hanging out at the estate, the only visitor that Victoria ever received was Katherine. It was obvious that even though she was no longer tutoring David, she had a special place in both their hearts and their home.

"She was with Victoria all the way up until the end," Will

said, joining the conversation even though he was deadheading geraniums halfway around the pool. "You rarely saw one without the other."

"Katherine wasn't mentioned in the will?" She made it a question, even though she knew the answer full well.

"I guess there was no reason to leave anything to her. Victoria took good care of Katherine for years. And in the end Katherine took care of Victoria. I'm sure they settled their own debts. Made their own peace."

"I was rude to her," Adri said quietly, fumbling for something, anything to say.

Sam made a dismissive noise. "No, you weren't. You were perfectly nice. Besides, the service had already started. Everyone was hurrying to their seats."

"I would like to talk to her." Adri realized she was standing stock-still, wrappers and used napkins crushed in her hands. She tried to smile. "It's been a long time. It would be nice to catch up."

"You've got time for a meeting with Katherine? I thought you were busy. I thought you were rushing back."

Adri was busy and she did want to rush back. But Victoria had created a sinkhole for her, a place where she had fallen and was now being continually sucked in by guilt and memories and the conviction that she had failed in many ways. It made her sick to her stomach, but there were certain things that could not be left undone. Not this time. Not if she ever hoped to escape.

They worked for the rest of the afternoon, attending to forgotten details around the estate. Everything looked clean and tidy on the surface, but it was such a huge house, and it had sat all but empty for so long, that there were hidden issues everywhere. All they had to do was look.

Jackson and Will found a suspicious stain on the exterior wall of the pool house, and discovered upon closer inspection that there was some water damage from a small hole in the roof. It looked as if an animal had bored its way inside; the opening was perfectly dark and circular like a tunnel. But it was more likely that a branch had fallen just so, or maybe an extraordinarily large hailstone gouged the unusual gap during that destructive thunderstorm in July. Either way, it was a problem they could solve, and while Jackson went to get their work trailer, Will found a stepladder and climbed onto the roof to start ripping off damaged shingles.

Once Sam left to milk and the boys were busy repairing the pool house, Adri found herself climbing the back staircase to the third floor of the mansion. There was no reason to tiptoe— no one was around to catch her snooping, and even if she was discovered she needn't feel guilty—it was her house, after all. A fact she still couldn't quite get used to.

But creep Adri did, and when she finally laid her hand on the cold knob of the door to Victoria's bedroom, she felt a jolt like electricity surge through her. She had never been in this part of the house before. Never. When David had given The Five the official tour of the sprawling mansion, he had brought them to the very top of the stairs and motioned toward the east wing with a dismissive wave. "My mother lives there," he said. Not "she sleeps there" or "her bedroom is there." She *lives* there. As if the mansion was an apartment complex and Victoria rented out 3B. And when The Five got used to being around the estate, they learned that David's assessment of his mother's patterns was very accurate. She didn't often leave her quarters. It was almost eerie.

The door opened noiselessly and the heavy wood paneling swung inward so smoothly that Adri was tugged inside. She found herself standing in a small, prettily allocated drawing room with another door centered in the wall across from where she stood. One of the mansion's marble fireplaces filled up the west wall, and clustered around it were a plush, saffron-colored couch and a trio of chairs. They were high-backed and ornate, obvious antiques, though they had been reupholstered in a rich tweed that was simply too pristine to be original. It looked as if no one had sat in the chairs. Ever. Light from a floor-to-ceiling window on the opposite wall bathed the room. There were no curtains or shades, and because the sun was shining madly, Adri almost felt like she needed sunglasses. Except for the scant pieces of furniture, the room was empty.

Adri let the door fall shut behind her, and stepped into the center of the room. At first blush, it was a bright and welcoming space. But there was something strange about the bare walls, the utter lack of a personal touch in any aspect of the design or decor. No books, knickknacks, or photographs stood on end tables. There was not even a throw blanket or a pillow out of place.

A slow, disappointed breath leaked from between Adri's lips. She didn't know what she had been expecting, but she was sure now that there would be no miraculous revelation to be had in Victoria's rooms. The austere, self-controlled woman who had reigned with such a sure and careful power would never leave hints like dirty fingerprints betraying the things she had done or felt or believed. It was a mildly depressing revelation.

But when Adri opened the door to the inner sanctum, Victoria's bedroom, she was so taken aback she couldn't immediately enter.

The room was an eruption of color and textures and deep shadows that played off every remarkable angle and surface the space had to offer. There were heavy, crimson curtains that flanked the large window and pooled on the floor, and a four-poster bed with ornately carved columns that reached almost to the ceiling. The bedspread looked like an exotic batik, splashed in reds and blues and greens that would have made a lovely tribal dress. Pictures hung on every available inch of wall space, photographs and original oil paintings on unframed canvases and even a couple of crayon drawings. Adri stepped close to one of them and studied what appeared to be three stick people beneath a purple tree. In the corner, *DAVID* was scrawled in shaky block letters, and then the number 5. His age. His family.

Adri put a hand to her mouth and swallowed a sudden wave of emotion. This place wasn't a bedroom, it was the woman herself. It was Victoria in a way that Adri had never seen her before. Raw and exposed and vibrant. It felt to Adri like she was looking directly into Victoria's soul, and it was abundant in a way that Adri had never suspected.

She lost track of time. At first she investigated with her hands folded behind her back, a museum patron well aware of how even the tiniest trace of oil can ruin a masterpiece. But Victoria's treasures begged to be touched, and before long Adri was running her fingers over a soft, leather-bound copy of a collection of early American poetry and picking up trinkets to try to discern their significance. A jar full of shells. A tiny clay pot that contained what appeared to be sand. There was even a small stuffed duck, his brown beak made from corduroy and his body velveteen.

But what Adri loved best were the pictures. She couldn't stop herself from leaning close, her nose almost against the glass, and studying the people inside. There were black-and-white photographs that Adri assumed showed Victoria as a child, her brother towheaded and serious beside her. And then some of an elegant young woman, her pale hair pulled back at the nape of her neck and her eyes lit by some fire that made them sparkle, even through the faded paper of a yellowed photograph. The woman had to be Victoria, and she was lovely in a way that made Adri unaccountably sad.

Scattered between all the others, in no discernible pattern, there were several photos of David at different points in his young life: chubby-cheeked and grinning toothlessly or sitting on the top of the pasture fence with his skinny little boy legs hooked through the slats. It was a bit disarming to discover such sweet, unedited pictures of her former fiancé—these were not the photos that made it into the family albums showcased in the library downstairs. There was an unvarnished quality to them. A sense that they had been snapped quickly, and then tucked away like a well-kept secret.

Adri was so consumed by her makeshift tour of Victoria's bedroom, it took her a long time to realize that there was something off about the patchwork space. It seemed animated, even alive, with memories and things that Victoria had held dear, but when Adri paused to consider yet another candid photograph, it struck her that something was missing.

Liam.

Stepping quickly around the room, Adri scanned the artifacts that Victoria had accumulated for some sign of the imposing Mr. Galloway. A wedding picture, a piece of expensive jewelry that bore his mark, a bottle of old cologne that would remind her of the way that he had smelled. There was nothing. Not a single scrap of anything that even hinted Victoria had been married at all.

Adri couldn't get her mind around it. Her own mother had been dead for over twenty years and her father still had a small shrine to her on his dresser. A scarf she had loved, a few pictures in old frames. Georgia was alive in their home and in their memories, but it seemed as if Victoria had completely erased every trace of her husband from her life.

Why?

But Adri suspected she knew exactly why.

She found the journal on the bedside stand, the sixth book in a stack of paperback novels and a thin prayer book that was dog-eared and looked much used. Adri took a deep breath and considered sitting on the edge of the bed to crack open the pages, but the room was too personal, too intimate for such an intrusion. Instead, she carried the book back into the sitting room, and sank into one of the hardback chairs. Her heart thumped an uneven rhythm as she smoothed her hand over the fabric cover. But Victoria was dead. There was no one left to grant permission. And hadn't Victoria herself invited this sort of scrutiny? Wasn't her letter an open provocation for Adri to uncover whatever she could?

She opened the book.

The first page was empty. And the second and the third. Adri thumbed quickly through the rest of it, shuffling pages several at a time and then going back more slowly to pry them apart one by one just to make sure she hadn't missed anything. It was a thick book and Adri held her breath as she paged through it all. But there was nothing to be found.

Her disappointment was suffocating. After finding the room and all that it contained, she had such high hopes for the diary. But apparently Victoria expressed herself through the items she stockpiled, not words. If only Adri could read each object, a braille of sorts, a tactile story that would pass beneath her fingers and tell her all she needed to know.

Sighing, Adri stood and went to return the journal to its rightful place on Victoria's nightstand. She had no idea what she would do with the room. If it had been a small garden shed or something else contained, she would've considered burning it. A funeral pyre for a woman who had lived two lives: the one she allowed everyone else to see and the one she lived in private. Adri couldn't help feeling that Victoria would have approved. For now she would simply close the door and lock it. The door latched from the inside and she would probably need a locksmith to open it if she ever cared to enter again. But for now, it was all that Adri could think to do. Somehow, it seemed like her only choice.

She stacked the books back in the order she had found them, the prayer book on the top. The thin, navy cover of the uppermost volume was so curled it looked like a dark wave, the inner edge peeking over the crest of a whitecap. Adri thought to place another book on top, just to force the cover to lie flat, when she realized that there was something written on the inside. Bending it open with her finger, she found a name. A number. But it wasn't Victoria Galloway. Instead, in small, neat letters and numbers was written: This book belongs to Katherine Holt. 756-2235.

~

11

Monday dawned bright and crisp. Adri could feel the autumn chill through the cool boards of her bedroom floor, and brought a step stool out of the hall closet so she could snag a tote of old sweaters down from the top shelf in her armoire. They smelled of fabric softener and time, a scent that anchored her heart in the past. It was a melancholy feeling, so she picked out a subtle weave in a dark, stormy blue, and parted her hair deep on the left side like she had when she was younger. At first she swept it back in a ponytail, but her dad's comment before church still echoed in her ears, and in the end she let it hang down around her shoulders. Adri even went so far as to spritz on an old perfume—not her favorite, but a cheap bottle that she had received for Christmas from Will one year. It reminded her of honeysuckle.

She was probably being sentimental, but staring in the mirror, Adri thought she looked like a twenty-year-old version of herself. After just one week in Iowa, the African sun was already fading from her cheeks, and she was a softer, paler version of the woman who pulled her hair back hard from her face so that it would not stick to her forehead when the temperature soared over 100 degrees. The transformation hadn't been intentional, not at first, but as she drove to Katherine's house she realized that a small part of her was hoping to get the sweet old tutor talking. And she figured the best way to do it was to be the girl she had been. Innocent. Just a little naive.

Thinking about Victoria Galloway always made Adri feel un-sophisticated and immature. Victoria had been unfailingly kind to Adri, as reserved and courteous as a well-bred hostess, but there had been little warmth between them.

Katherine's house was an unassuming brick ranch in the heart of town. Surrounded by elaborate English gardens that had gone to seed, it wasn't hard to decipher the retired tutor's beloved hobby—or her age. Ten years ago, Adri knew every bed would have been trimmed and displayed to their full autumnal advantage, but now she could tell that Katherine was simply too tired or too sick to keep up. She wondered if she should offer to help clean the gardens. And yet, one more thing on her checklist would only prolong her time in Blackhawk. The thought made her shudder.

Adri rang the bell and stepped back on the wide front step, tucking her hair behind her ears as if afraid that Katherine would tsk at the strays that flirted with the breeze. She didn't know what to expect. Would Katherine resent her showing up unannounced? Would she remember her fondly? Or hate her for what she had done?

By the time the door swung open, Adri was a wreck of emo-tions, ready to retreat to Betty and forget that she had ever felt compelled to seek out Katherine at all.

But it was too late. "Adrienne."

Whatever Adri had expected, she hadn't planned on the hug that Katherine enveloped her in. The retired tutor was nearly as elegant as Victoria had been, and though she had to be push-ing seventy, she was still smartly dressed and stylish with small diamond drop earrings that accented the polished sweep of her short hair. There were a pair of tortoiseshell glasses dangling from a pretty beaded chain around her neck, and the frames felt like an extension of Katherine's thin figure as Adri nervously hugged her back.

"I didn't know if I would ever see you again," Katherine said when she stepped back to hold Adri at arm's length. "It's a delight. Truly, Adrienne, it's wonderful to see you."

They had coffee in the front room, the windows spilling such warmth across Adri's shoulders that she was sweating in minutes. Katherine seemed not to notice as she poured half-and-half into her cup and stirred the contents with a tiny, etched spoon that looked like it must have come from somewhere exotic. Thailand. Mumbai.

"Tell me what you've been up to," Katherine said, settling back into a navy-colored couch with sigh. "Are you still in Africa?"

"Yes." Adri forced herself to nod, though small talk was the last thing she was after. "But that's not really why I'm here, Mrs. Holt."

"Katherine."

"Katherine," Adri amended. "I'm sorry, I don't mean to be rude, but I would like to talk about Victoria."

"Of course you would." Katherine's eyes went soft and Adri wondered if she would cry. "God rest her soul."

"Amen," Adri said, but she didn't know where the word or the sentiment came from. She set down her cup of coffee untouched and leaned forward to put her elbows on her knees. "It's just that Victoria wrote me a letter."

"She liked real letters. None of this email nonsense." Katherine gave Adri a conspiratorial smile, a look that communicated that she knew better. And indeed, there was a sleek MacBook on the end table that bore witness to Katherine's technological prowess. It made Adri wonder if Katherine knew more than she let on; if she was on Facebook and had peered at all those photos of another life, another Adri that no one here could claim to know.

"I didn't realize that about her," Adri said. "I guess I didn't know Victoria as well as I would have liked."

"What are you here for, sweetheart?" Katherine's gaze was

shrewd but kind, and Adri found herself wanting to please this woman who seemed to hold the keys to the secret of Victoria Galloway.

"I have a lot of questions," she admitted. "And I don't know who to ask."

"I can't promise you answers."

"You knew Victoria better than anyone."

Katherine dipped her head in assent. "She wasn't exactly an open book."

"Why did she leave me the estate?" Adri blurted. Why did she write that she had secrets? And that she knew mine?

Katherine sipped her coffee, holding Adri's gaze over the rim of her porcelain cup. "I can't claim to understand Victoria's intentions," she said when the cup was once again nestled in her lap. "But I do know that Victoria felt she had failed you somehow. There's a saying about secrets being lies and bad manners besides, but that's not necessarily accurate, is it? Sometimes secrets are the truth. I think Victoria was angry at herself for not telling the truth."

"About Liam?" Adri swallowed. It was such an awkward thing to talk about. Rumors had floated around Piperhall for as long as Adri could remember. Half-truths and gossip that painted Liam Galloway as a monster and his wife as a victim. Weak and helpless, the sort of woman nobody could help because she refused to help herself. Adri had never put much stock in the whispers—Blackhawk was a small town and people like the Galloways would never be allowed to exist without scandal. But loving David had convinced her that it was true. All of it? Some of it? It didn't really matter. She was sure that Victoria had been a broken woman clinging to the only thing she had left: her pride. The careful facade of her austerity, the way that she held herself as stiff as a bronze statue, had been an elaborate defense mechanism. And her son was someone she considered a potential threat. It was obvious in the way that they circled each other, close, but never close enough to touch.

It bothered Adri. She imagined that mother love was as automatic, as inherent as breath. How could you not love the woman who gave you life? But David was aloof with Victoria. Indifferent. Every part of her wished that he would be the man she wanted him to be, the sort of man who would adore his mother instead of disdaining her. But he had grown up at the knee of Liam Galloway. The thought sent a little shiver across Adri's skin.

Once, she had put him on the spot. "Tell me you love her."

He was silent for a heartbeat. Two. His expression was unreadable, his eyes deadpan. But then he smiled a little, indulgently, and closed the space between them with a stride. "Of course I love her," David said tucking Adri into his arms. "She's my mother." It was exactly what Adri wanted to hear, but he'd confessed it into her hair. Somehow that lessened the impact.

Katherine was studying Adri, her head tilted just a little. "Yes, I imagine Victoria regretted all the secrets about Liam. And David. About the entire Galloway family, I suppose."

"Would the truth have changed anything?" Adri mused, more to herself than to Katherine.

But Katherine said, "I've wondered that myself a hundred times. I knew what was going on, everyone did. Why didn't we do anything about it?" For a moment her shoulders caved forward. But then she sighed, gave her head a little shake, and straightened herself so gracefully it was as if someone had pulled invisible marionette strings.

"Why didn't you do anything about it?" Adri asked.

Katherine raised her chin almost imperceptibly. "Air that kind of dirty laundry? It wasn't done. What would people have thought if they knew? It would have ruined the Galloway name."

It came down to keeping up appearances. Adri wanted to be furious, but really, she understood. Admitting abuse was a death of sorts.

She had known who David was, or suspected. There was

something dangerous about him, something savage just below the surface. But in the beginning, at least, she believed that she could tame him. Isn't that what love did? Later, Adri worked hard to convince herself that his little indiscretions—palm against her cheek, fingers dug too-tight into her arm, words flung as ammunition—were just accidents of fate, moments of immaturity. Recklessness. And she was a strong girl. It would take more than a slap to break her spirit. But maybe his temper had been a slow burn that would've only grown in intensity. If she had known that David was his father's son, that whatever was fractured in him was beyond repair,would she have stayed?

Would David have died?

Looking back, Adri wondered if Victoria had tried to tell her on one occasion. It was just after their engagement, and she and David had been searching Piperhall, hoping to find her to relay the good news. Just as they were about to give up and return to campus, Victoria appeared in the grand entrance hall like an illusion. It was as if she already knew their news, and she quickly hugged Adri. The embrace wasn't awkward so much as it was wooden at first, but then Victoria squeezed, once, a burst of passion that literally took Adri's breath away. Even at the time, Adri felt sure that David's stoic mother was sending her a message with that hug. And the look Victoria gave her in the second before David led Adri away was almost covenantal. It bound Adri to something. To what, exactly, she wasn't sure.

"I would do things differently now," Katherine confided. "No one should have to suffer the way Victoria did."

"Victoria wants me to fix things." Adri's mouth tugged into a wry smile, her hands open and helpless on her lap. She wasn't used to feeling helpless.

"Not all broken things can be mended," Katherine said. She set her cup down on the coffee table and reached as if she would take Adri's hands in her own. They were too far apart. Katherine twined her fingers together instead. "Piperhall is a sad place with a sad history, and I'm sorry that you got tangled up in all of that. But you have a lot of life ahead of you, Adrienne. Victoria would have wanted you to live it."

"I don't know that I can move on." Adri was surprised by her own admission. "After everything that happened with David and Harper . . ."

Katherine smiled a secret little smile. "Now, that's a name I haven't heard in a long time. Whatever happened to her?"

"I have no idea," Adri said quietly. "Harper is gone."

"What do you mean gone?" Katherine raised an eyebrow. "Passed away or moved away?"

Adri searched for something to say. "Moved away, I guess. I don't know. I haven't spoken to her in years."

Five years, two months, and a handful of days, to be exact. After they parted ways that July, the summer after they graduated from college, the summer David died, they didn't look back. In fact, they had more or less promised each other not to. They hadn't said much in those final days, there wasn't much to say, but when it was over and they both knew that life could never be the same, Harper had taken her best friend by the shoulders. "I'm never coming back," she said, giving Adri one last, soul-searching look. "I need you to know that."

"Neither am I," Adri said.

Harper hadn't seem pleased by this, but she nodded as if she knew. But then her brave facade crumbled and she crushed Adri in a hug, her tears warm and salty on Adri's cheeks. "I love you," she whispered.

Adri couldn't say it back. It wasn't that she didn't want to, she just couldn't unravel the snarl of thoughts and emotions that had anesthetized her to the point of numbness. She could hardly breathe, much less engage in the sort of gut-wrenching goodbye that their friendship deserved.

Harper swallowed a deep, steadying breath, and backed away. The crooked half-smile was back. Her eyes were hard and inscrutable. The only evidence of her broken heart were the tears that were already beginning to dry. "Later," she said. And she turned and walked away.

Adri had never spoken to Harper again. Not even a phone call or an email.

But Katherine didn't seem to find that terribly strange. "Sometimes the hand you hold is the hand that pulls you down," she said, shaking her head as if that explained everything.

The statement seemed cryptic to Adri, and she couldn't understand if Katherine meant that Harper had pulled her down or the other way around. Maybe both. Instead of responding, she thanked Katherine for her time and excused herself down the front walk. The gardens appeared even sadder than they had when she first approached the house, and she ducked her head and jogged back to the car as if protecting herself from the rain. But it hadn't started yet.

～

Adri drove Betty down a series of twisting gravel roads that wound near Maple Acres, but she couldn't bring herself to drive home. The sky that had looked so blue only hours before had bled out slowly into a dark and threatening slate gray as she wandered the countryside, and when the first drops of rain began to fall, Adri pulled into a field driveway and turned the car off.

It felt good to roll down the windows and listen to the thunder rumbling in the distance. The horizon was already patched with light, the storm would pass in mere minutes, but Adri lost herself beneath the torrential rain all the same. She felt alone in the world, the only person awake to the drumbeat of drops and the way that the water turned the empty fields before her black. It was a quick and startling transformation.

Adri slipped her phone from her pocket after the storm had

softened to a mist. Amazingly, she had good reception and she thumbed her way to an old email account before she could talk herself out of such nonsense. It had been a very long time since she had used this account, but the address book was still intact and Harper's information was still there.

Her username had always made Adri smile. Themistoclea@ gmail.com was more than a mouthful, it was an impossible handle to remember. Adri had laughed when Harper tried to give out her email address and inevitably lost patience as people struggled with the spelling and the reference. "The mist o' Clea," Harper would eventually grumble, parsing the name of a priestess in ancient Delphi into a nonsensical phrase. "She was Pythagoras's teacher. She taught him all his moral doctrines." And when she was met with blank stares: "Behind every great man . . ." Harper would circle her hand impatiently, inviting Adri to finish.

Adri laughed. "Is an even greater woman."

"Don't you know it."

Adri had no idea if the account was even live, but it was the only link she had to her friend. And though she had considered sending Harper an email at least a million times, for the first time ever she felt brave enough to try.

She wrote only two short lines.

I came back. Wish you were here.

PART II

ANGER AND COURAGE

12

~

HARPER

The apartment was quiet. Harper woke to the soft weight of stillness, and felt a smile crease her face before she even opened her eyes.

He was gone.

That was always the best sort of surprise, the mornings she loved the most. He wouldn't be gone for long, but sometimes he got caught up in conversation at the coffee shop down the street, and she had a few luxurious minutes to herself. Minutes to pretend that his second-story apartment in the quaint, trendy Minneapolis neighborhood where they lived together was a safe place to be.

It felt safe enough on mornings like this. The elegant rooms of his two-bedroom apartment overlooking the city were downright pristine. The stainless steel gas range would shine in the morning light like something almost otherworldly. The hand-scraped hardwood floors would gleam rich and smooth as honey, and the leather couch would look as if it had been delivered only minutes ago. She could picture it all in her mind's eye, every throw pillow and tea towel perfectly placed and squared at the corners, and she understood that she slept in the very heart of a dream. The apartment, the order, the new flatscreen TV that she didn't even know how to turn on, they were all stepping-stones on the path to the holy grail of the American ethos: prosperity, success, upward social mobility.

Harper slipped out of bed and padded to the living room on bare feet. The floor was cold, but the sun was streaming through the tall windows and she could already feel the gentle warmth on her cheeks. She crawled onto the window seat beside the tile fireplace and turned her face toward the sun. There was a profusion of fat pillows and she loved to sink into them, to lay her cheek against the cool silk and watch the city from behind the gauzy curtains. She never opened them. It wasn't forbidden—she could have tied them back if she wanted to— but she liked the view better this way. Minneapolis was little more than a carved skyline in the distance, cut off by the river and the long, green stretch of Nicollet Island. It looked like a dream from here, a fantasy that would disappear into the mist if she ever dared to try and reach it. But, of course, she accompanied him into the city almost every day. It was a short walk across the picturesque Third Avenue Bridge. She loved that bridge and the way that it curved coyly and unveiled arches in the piers like a small gift around every bend. She loved that it took her away from the apartment, and every time she crossed it she entertained the hope, if only briefly, that she would never come back.

East Bank was undeniably beautiful, the sort of place that most people would love to call home. In the summer the cobbled streets were sprinkled with runners and bikers like colorful confetti, their track shorts and expensive workout tanks bright and perfectly matched. And in the autumn the trees that lined the narrow boulevard between the river and Southeast Main created a watercolor screen that flecked the city with gold. It seemed there was always something happening on or near the island, farmers' markets and art shows, outdoor film nights or a fund-raiser 5K. He liked to take Harper to the Stone Arch Bridge Festival in mid-June, parading her around in a sundress he had carefully chosen, her hand held tight in his.

They really did make a stunning couple. She, blond and curvy, a woman who turned heads and solicited the sort of attention that made her long for the security of a bottle of pepper spray, or, better yet, a gun. She didn't mean to exude that sort of allure; she just did, even though she often wished she could turn off her sex appeal like a faucet. And he was just as attractive. Tall and broad-shouldered, his sense of style faultless. When he removed his jacket—European and cut narrow—his arms pressed against the expensive fabric of his shirts, tugging at the seams just enough to ensure that anyone who saw him would know he spent hours at the gym. He was a gorgeous man. But what had drawn Harper to him that first night all those years ago were his eyes. They were dark and bottomless, intense and complex even from across a room. She had physically felt his eyes on her, a breath at the base of her neck, at the place where her hair curled against her skin in golden ringlets that she couldn't control. When she looked up, he was there, staring, inviting her with a casual flick of his finger and a smile that plainly said, I want you.

She went. God, how she regretted it.

And yet, in some ways, Harper had to admit that her life had turned out exactly the way she'd wanted it to. What do you do when you can't forgive yourself? Some people try to earn salvation, but Harper had no illusions about who she was and what she deserved. She had decided long ago that she would spend the rest of her life punishing herself for what she had done. Pills. A cold razor against her skin. Alcohol that numbed her senses and blurred together the days. Him. But she didn't have to like it.

A man stepped out from beneath the trees below her, and for a moment Harper's breath caught in her throat. But then he turned toward her building, toward the bank of soaring windows where she sat hidden behind sheer curtains, and revealed a pair of wire-rimmed glasses. It wasn't him. In fact, when Harper tipped forward and looked as far as she could down the street in both directions, he was nowhere to be seen. She shot a quick glance at the clock on the mantel. Seven thirty-two. He usually let her sleep in. He probably wouldn't expect her to be up for another half hour or so.

The thought raced through Harper's veins like a drug. She had time. Not much, but if she was quick she could at least catch a glimpse of the world beyond the walls of her prison.

Of course, he had taken his phone with him. Not that she would dare to hack it anyway. And the expensive, tricked-out laptop was tucked away in his attaché. Harper swore that he sometimes put a hair on the concealed zipper of the leather bag just to be sure that she hadn't tampered with his prized possession. But he liked to read on an iPad, and he kept that in the top drawer of his bedside stand.

Harper hurried to the bedroom and lifted the iPad from the drawer with the corner of her pink nightshirt, taking note of exactly where he had placed it the night before. Normally she would handle the sleek pad with a fresh towel, but she didn't have time this morning. She'd just have to clean up well after herself.

Tiptoeing back to the window seat as if he could hear her betrayal from blocks away, Harper clicked on the device and fingered her way to the Settings icon. Though he loved the elaborate photo-editing software on his laptop, he was no computer geek, and the privacy settings on his iPad were embarrassingly simple to overcome. The only thing that had held Harper up was the Wi-Fi password. He changed it every couple of days, but she had learned long ago that he used an algorithm to generate a one-way hash. All she had to do was access it on the server and then use the algorithm to generate her own hash until she got a match. The first time she hacked his password, it had taken her stolen moments over the course of a couple of weeks, but now that she had the algorithm, it was a matter of seconds before she was online. Harper was more resourceful than computer-savvy. The truth was, she had flirted her way into some basic information years ago—a dangerous endeavor that almost ended very badly—and now it was just enough to get her by.

Snatching one last furtive glance at the street below, Harper perched on the end of the window seat and opened Safari. Facebook seemed like an almost frivolous way to keep tabs on people, but it was all she had. She had set up a fake account with no profile picture and no information, but it was enough to allow her to check in on the few people she cared about. Her parents were divorced, and while her dad didn't keep a Facebook account, her mom did. And one with wide-open privacy settings. Anything Julianna Penny posted was available for public consumption. Harper was grateful.

Photos of Julianna and her new boyfriend in Brussels. A status update that included the phrase *to die for*. A couple of new friends with unfamiliar last names and references to the garden party that Julianna had thrown several weeks ago. Harper didn't know whether to smile or cry. Her mother was apparently going through some sort of midlife, post-messy-divorce crisis. Not that Harper could blame her. The years of her youth had been peppered with arguments that started out perfectly civil and then escalated into the sort of frenzy that involved smashed wineglasses and vicious name-calling usually reserved for reality TV. Her philosopher parents were not so philosophical when it came to marital disagreements.

It took Harper just a couple of minutes to catch up on Julianna's life, and even less time to feel the familiar stab of sorrow that pierced her every time she reached out a tentative finger to touch her mother. If Facebook status updates and Instagram photos could be believed, Harper was so far from Julianna's thoughts as to be nothing more than a hazy memory. Did her parents ever think about her? Did they miss her? It seemed obvious that they didn't.

Once, Harper had told herself that if her mother ever indicated she felt her daughter's absence, she would get out. She'd do whatever she had to do. But, as far as Harper could tell, Julianna acted as if she didn't have a daughter at all.

In some strange, twisted way, Harper was grateful. She couldn't just leave him. Nothing was that easy.

Harper had never intended things to end up the way that they did. No one would choose this life, this sterilized imprisonment, where instead of inhabiting a godforsaken cell she slept on Egyptian cotton sheets and wore designer labels. But it had happened when she wasn't looking, one bad decision leading to another until she had anesthetized herself with so many things and so many people. And he had swept in to save her. Poor baby, poor sweet Harper. He was the proverbial wolf in sheep's clothing, but by the time she realized her mistake it was too late. Harper had been with him almost three years. Three years of lies and lust and greed that masqueraded as a relationship of sorts. But Harper wasn't fooled anymore.

Last year, on a summer night so hot and still that Harper felt like she had been trapped inside the vacuum of a pressure cooker, she had been approached by a young man wearing a T-shirt that had read simply, *The Bridge*. Harper noticed because it seemed out of place in a crowd of theatergoers in more formal wear.

"Hey," the stranger said, smiling at her.

The street was packed with people, it was the final day of Fringe Festival, and he had dressed Harper up and taken her out for a night on the town. He liked to pretend he was cultured, and the eclectic performing arts festival was exactly the right venue for his brand of self-satisfied posturing. They had watched a one-act on a makeshift stage in a piano bar and he hadn't understood a second of it. Harper could tell by the way he started to tip back the bourbon like it was water. Afterward the crowd leaked slowly onto the street and puddled there, hot and sticky and pressing sweaty bottles of beer to their temples as if the cold glass alone could drop their core body temperature. There were people everywhere, disheveled and weary in the stifling heat of the night, and Harper had used the crowd to her advantage. She slipped away from him and stood, not too far away, but far enough that she felt, for just a moment, alone.

And within seconds, the stranger. "Hey," he said again, stepping closer. She could see now that he was wearing a small black backpack, and his eyes were unusually clear. "Great night, huh?"

"I guess," Harper said, glancing over her shoulder. He wasn't looking at her, but he would be. Soon.

The man with the T-shirt came closer still. "We can walk away," he said so quietly she had to strain to hear him. "Turn around and go straight to the corner of the block. Take a left. About three blocks down we have an office. We can help you. We can get you out."

Harper felt as if the ground was giving way beneath her, and when she tilted, the stranger put out a hand to steady her.

"Harper!" There were several people between them, but he pinned Harper in place with a glance. Parting the crowd with one hand and holding his bourbon high with the other, he made his way to her. A calculating half-moon smile sliced his handsome face, but Harper knew that smile. She knew what it meant.

In the second before he was upon them, the stranger in the T-shirt pressed a slip of paper into her palm and disappeared in the crowd. When she looked, he was gone. It was as if he had never been there at all.

"What are you doing?" he asked, sliding his arm protectively around her waist. "You know I don't like it when you wander off."

"I didn't wander off." She put her hand on his chest and stood on tiptoe to drop a kiss in the hollow beneath his chin. His skin was impossibly smooth. Like a child's. It unnerved her. "There are hundreds of people here," she protested. "We got separated."

If he had seen the man in the T-shirt, he didn't say anything. In fact, he appeared to be in a remarkably good mood, and when he took her by the hand and started to lead her out of the crowd toward home, his grip was light. "Let's go," he said, as if she had a choice in the matter.

"Home?" Harper let him pull her along, but she put a bit of tease in her voice. "Already?"

He stopped at the edge of the crowd, beneath a squat tree that had been planted on the sidewalk between buildings. "You don't want to go back?" Pulling her close, he lifted her so that she had no choice but to lean against him. If he backed away, she would fall.

"No," she whispered. "I want to go dancing." Of course, she didn't want to go dancing at all, but it was the only thing she could think to say that might convince him the apartment could wait. And then, because she knew exactly how to get what she wanted—sometimes—she laced her fingers together behind his neck and kissed him so deeply that she could feel his immediate, visceral response.

"No," he moaned, catching her bottom lip between his teeth.

"Yes."

"No."

"Please?" She didn't often plead, but she couldn't stand the thought of going back to the apartment with him. Not now. Not with the stranger's words like hot steam in the pit of her stomach. Making her consider possibilities that she had never thought to consider before.

He bent his head and ran his tongue along the line of her collarbone, his breath so warm and insistent that it made her shiver. "Fine," he said. "Dancing. But then I'm taking you home."

Harper didn't look at the paper she had crushed in her palm until nearly an hour later. She excused herself to go to the bathroom and escaped the strobe light of the dance club for a handful of guarded minutes. And in the dim light of the first stall she peeled open the sweaty, makeshift business card and read the short, printed lines. *The Bridge Outreach. We can help.*

That was it. Well, that and an address. Just the number and

street, because the outreach didn't need any further identifica-
tion. It hadn't hit her when the man walked up with his subtle
T-shirt, but Harper had heard of them. She had read a newspa-
per article that described an organization working with the FBI
to help victims of human trafficking. This stranger must have
thought she was one of them.

Harper almost laughed. A victim? She didn't think of herself
as such. Not when she had entered her own sordid existence,
eyes wide open. She didn't have to stay with him. At least, not
in the beginning. And Harper was no delicate flower—she had
always felt that she could walk away if she really, truly wanted
to. But somehow, like an alcoholic who doesn't realize her own
addiction, Harper was beginning to fear that she didn't see
herself and her situation as clearly as she thought she did. The
scrap of paper and the zealous look in the stranger's eyes were
a mirror that cast back a woman in a situation that she simply
didn't want to acknowledge.

What did the man from The Bridge see in her? How had he
picked her out in a street full of people?

Harper wasn't sure she wanted to know the answers to those
questions.

Since that night, when she was able to snag a couple of minutes online, she went to the organization's website. It wasn't a
fancy site and it didn't seem to get much traffic, but maybe it
was better that way. They flew under the radar. Maybe that's
how they did what they did—they were as shrewd as snakes, as
innocent and quiet as doves.

Today Harper was on edge, even though she had woken in
an apartment that all but oozed peace. A few minutes on her
mother's Facebook page was nearly all that she could handle in
the face of risking discovery. She was about to put the iPad to
sleep and give it a thorough wipe-down before returning it to
the bedside table, when she was gripped by a sudden desire
to check her email.

Harper didn't check her email often; there was no reason

to. It had been several years since she sent anyone a message, and just as many since she received a note. Every day she faded just a little more, her presence bleaching so slowly out of the world she had known that sometimes she surprised herself by how disconnected she had become. Harper hardly recognized the girl she once was. But that didn't stop her from needing to gaze at the old Harper from time to time. It was a bittersweet experience.

A quick peek over her shoulder told her that the street was still empty. But that didn't mean he hadn't entered the apartment building when she wasn't looking. Harper slid out of the window seat and tapped in her password as she walked to the bedroom. She wasn't expecting any new messages, and she figured she'd have just enough time to erase the history and put the iPad away before he came back. But when the home screen launched, she was stunned to find that there was one new message in her inbox.

Spam filtered to her junk mail and she cleared out those messages a hundred at a time when she had the chance. It wasn't likely that something had slipped through to her high-security in-box.

Harper's heart skipped a beat when she clicked on the message icon, and it seized completely when she saw who it was from.

Adrienne.

It had been sent four days ago—four, and not fourteen, and that filled Harper with a sense of urgency that made her hands tremble. Why, after all these years? What could she possibly want?

Harper heard his key in the door as she opened Adri's message.

He would not be forgiving if he found her online, but she couldn't walk away from Adri. Not even after all this time. A prayer stuck in her throat and Harper rushed to the bedside stand, her eyes glued to the screen as the note loaded.

Behind her, she could hear the doorknob turning and his footsteps in the foyer of the apartment. He would take off his shoes, hang up his coat, loop his scarf over a second, smaller hook. They were separated by a wall, but she could practically see him go through the motions. If she was lucky he would have coffee cups for both of them, one in each hand, and he would pause in the kitchen to grab a pair of flawlessly blushed apples for them to savor in bed. Coffee, breakfast, sometimes more.

Harper could feel him coming, but she couldn't tear her eyes away from the screen.

Two lines.

She read them once. Again. Committed them to memory. It wasn't hard.

Then, fingers flying, she closed windows, erased history, powered down.

The drawer slid shut on her finger. Harper almost cried out; bit her lip to stop herself from doing so. Shit. She had forgotten to wipe off her fingerprints, but there was no time to do that now.

He was behind her.

"What are you doing?" he whispered, his mouth against her ear, his body molded to hers in a way that would have been sensual if it wasn't so damn terrifying.

"Waking up," she purred. Harper turned slowly against him and dropped her shoulder a little. She was wearing one of his shirts for pajamas, and it slid off her collarbone just as she knew it would, exposing the curve of her arm, the long length of neck he claimed to love. For a moment, she couldn't tell if he had seen her or not. She couldn't tell if he was angry.

He reached around her waist and deposited two coffee cups on the table where she had just secreted the iPad. Hands free, he took her by the hips, palms against the sharp ridge of her bones, and pushed her down on the bed. He stood over her like he was trying to decide what to do. After a few seconds, a deliberate smile crossed his face. He leaned down and fanned her hair out on the white duvet where she had fallen, ran his fingertip over the exposed arc of her décolletage.

"Perfect," he said. "Let me get the camera."

"Whatever you want, Sawyer." Her voice sounded almost normal.

13

ADRIENNE

Harper didn't respond to Adri's email. Not that she expected her to. Hoped, yes. Expected? Of course not. For all Adri knew, Harper had actually moved on with her life instead of being stuck in some self-inflicted purgatory. Not that Harper had anything to atone for. The fault was Adri's alone. And she didn't blame Harper for finding it impossible to forgive.

Maybe Harper was married. Adri tried to picture the man that Harper would marry. Handsome. Quiet. The kind of guy who would gaze at Harper when she wasn't looking, his eyes filled with irrepressible adoration that would make people feel as if they were witnessing an intimate moment when he was doing something as mundane as admiring the way she tucked her hair behind her ear. Harper deserved a man like that. And he'd have to be steady. Laid-back. Someone to counter Harper so she didn't spin out of orbit entirely.

Adri loved to think of Harper in the imaginary world she created for her. One afternoon, as she was wandering around the mansion, replacing all the lightbulbs that had burned out, Adri saw Harper with a baby. It stopped her cold. Harper with a child? It was certainly a possibility, but Adri had a hard time reconciling the woman she was carefully creating with the impulsive girl that she had known. It had been a fun game up until that moment, but as soon as a nameless baby appeared in

Harper's arms, Adri resolved to stop wishing her former best friend's perfect life into existence. It was too painful. Too hard to imagine that she didn't even know the woman who had been a sister to her. They had once been connected by a bond thicker than blood. And now they were strangers.

It cut Adri to the quick every time she opened her email account and found it empty.

Because she hadn't heard from Harper, and because she felt trapped by the days that seemed to collapse upon her until Adri could hardly take a breath for the weight against her chest, she dedicated herself to planning Victoria's memorial. It was much more work than she ever imagined a memorial could be. But it was a welcome diversion, a seemingly never-ending job that she could throw herself into with an almost reckless abandon. Adri stayed up late and worked her hands until blisters formed and tore open and formed again.

By the time Friday rolled around, Piperhall was nothing less than a vision. The windows gleamed (Adri had hired a company to make them sparkle) and the gardens tucked inside the circular drive were trimmed and resplendent in autumn hues from the fat, round mums that a local landscaping company had transplanted in the dry soil. Inside, the entire mansion was lightly scented with Murphy's Oil Soap (Adri had polished the wood floors herself) and the warm, floral fragrance of gardenia candles (the only white candles that Adri could find in Blackhawk).

"You're amazing," Will told her when she took him on a tour of the estate the day before the memorial. "The whole place feels different."

"It's clean," Adri smiled faintly. "The drapes are open."

"Whatever it is, it feels like an entirely different place."

It did. There was an anticipation in the air, a sense that the entire estate was holding its breath. Adri knew she was being ridiculous, but there was a small part of her that wanted very much to believe that the breeze she felt from the open patio doors was nothing less than the winds of change.

Home, she told herself. The change is that I'm going home and I'm going to escape this place once and for all. I broke my promise to Harper and to myself, but I won't make that mistake again.

Will walked slowly to the front door, continuing to admire the house and its beauty, stunningly revived. Following him, Adri shut the door behind her and locked it with the keys that she now carried in her pocket.

Will was standing against one of the pillars of the loggia, taking in the sunset over the stable. The red brick loomed black against the glow of a tangerine sun. It was halved against the horizon, bleeding light between the branches of the trees like honey. Adri wanted to taste it. To reach out a finger and dip it in the ethereal glow. She would take it with her when she left. A memory. Evidence that the place she had come from could be beautiful, too.

"When are you going back?" Will asked, reading her thoughts.

"I couldn't get a ticket out until Monday."

He didn't say anything. Neither did she. After hoping that she could find some sort of peace in the midst of such an unwanted journey, Adri had come to accept that there was none to be had. There never would be. The most she could wish for was more of the same. A watchful measure of every day. The hope that there would be some small, inherent grace left in her life, even though she could not forgive herself. Or ask anyone else to.

"Maybe I'll come with you," Will said. He gave her a sideways smile that bordered on wistful.

"I'd like that." Adri meant it, really she did. But she didn't think he'd come.

They were quiet for a few moments, and Adri thought of a dozen things she would like to say to her brother. An apology, a confession, the truth. He didn't press her, he never had, but if he had, Adri knew in that moment that she would have told him everything.

～

Adri and David dated for only three months before they got engaged. It was a whirlwind romance, to be sure, but it didn't feel unexpected to them. From the moment he kissed her in the stable, they adhered to an unspoken belief that everything that came before could be grandfathered into the covenant they were creating with one another. The years of friendship and fights, the secrets they had told and the moments they had turned away when all they really wanted to do was give in to the pull of each other, all of it could count as time that they had loved. After all, they had loved one another. And well.

The proposal was nothing fancy. Certainly not the world-class event that Adri would have expected from David when she first met him. But that boy, that spoiled, selfish man-child with the fancy car and the affected ways, wasn't the same lover she was falling for in one wild-water rush. Adri careened over the side of love, grasping at bits and pieces of David as if he could save her from drowning. And in quiet moments alone, her cheek against his chest as he stroked the place where her temple curved like a divot in the earth, she gave herself to him in ways that she had never shared with anyone before. Even Harper.

"I want to leave this place," she confessed one night.

"Me, too," David murmured. "Where should we go? Paris is a cliché. I'm thinking Prague."

Adri pushed herself up on her elbow. Her hair fell over their shoulders, tickling David's neck so that he brushed it away and caught it in his fist. Tugging, he pulled her down. Kissed her so hard she almost forgot what they were talking about.

"Okay," he said against her lips, muffling the word so it echoed in her mouth. He spoke for her. "Not Prague. Bali?"

"No," Adri shook her head, pulled away a little, even though it physically ached to do so. "Not a vacation. Let's leave."

"Blackhawk?"

"Yes. Your mother, my father."

"Will?"

Adri bit the inside of her cheek. But David's eyes were so blue, his expression so perfectly serene, that she ended up blurting out the one thing she had never admitted to anyone before. "I'm not the person everyone thinks I am."

The corners of David's eyes creased in the sweetest of smiles. "Nobody is, Adrienne. We are, at best, a thin projection of our true selves." He sat up and took her by the shoulders, threw her down on the bed, and hovered over her. "I'm a monster," he said. "We all are." And he began nipping at her skin, taking bites of her shoulders, her neck, the soft rise of her breasts.

"Shut up." Adri pushed him off and David willingly flipped onto his back. She straddled him. "If we're such monsters, tell me the truth."

"Truth or dare? You know I love truth or dare."

"No dare." Adri put her hands on his upper arms, holding him down. It did no good whatsoever and she knew it. If David wanted to throw her off, he could do it in a second flat. But the question she longed to ask him was a living, breathing, hurtful thing. It was a birth of sorts to utter it at all. Her heart was thrumming high and fast and she had to breathe in subtle little gasps. She hoped he didn't realize how much his answer meant.

"No dare? Just truth?" David lifted his head for a kiss, but Adri ignored him.

"Just truth."

David fell back onto the pillow and gave a heavy sigh. "Fine. Truth. Lay it on me."

Adri didn't stop to think about the implications or what she would do if he said anything other than what she longed to hear. She just said it. "Why aren't you with Harper?"

For a moment David stared at her. His expression was inscrutable, his eyes dark and calculating as he considered her words, her impossible question. But then he blinked and everything about him seemed to give way. He said the last thing Adri expected. "I remember you, you know. Skinny legs and buck teeth and that Americana dress that you ripped climbing over the pasture fence."

Adri's heart puddled at the thought that David had even known who she was as a child. It wasn't something they discussed, all the years that had come before they were suddenly, inexplicably friends. And then so much more. How did they exist all that time apart? A couple of scant miles separated the Galloway Estate from Maple Acres, but it might as well have been an ocean. David didn't attend Blackhawk's elementary or high school. Instead, he was privately tutored and followed his dad around the world. And it wasn't like Adri ever bumped into him at the grocery store or at the little Blackhawk Public Library. The thought almost made her snort. But once a year, the gate was thrown open and Piperhall was as populated as a county fair. Once a year she was allowed a glimpse into his world. Everyone was. How had she stood out from the summer picnic crowd? It seemed impossible.

"I don't remember that," Adri said, clinging to the detail, the dress. But she did remember it. It was a red, white, and blue plaid with spaghetti straps and a bow at the waist. She'd loved it.

"We must have been eight or nine," David told her. "You were this little ponytailed thing with more guts than any of the guys. You intended to ride one of the horses. Bareback."

She remembered. Will had dared her. And she had wanted to glitter. To rise above the blurred canvas of the people around her, the way they all ran together like smudged paint.

"You looked like an illustration from one of the children's books my mother kept in my room when I was a kid."

"You read books?" Adri teased.

"I looked at the pictures." David's mouth quirked the way Adri loved, and she bent to kiss it. Once. Sweetly. "There was a story about a Spanish princess," David continued. "The Infanta.

You stepped off the pages of that book, Adrienne. When I was a kid I was convinced you were her. The princess."

Adri gave him a skeptical look. David wasn't prone to melodrama. Or overly romantic gestures.

"Okay, fine." He grinned. "I thought you were pretty. Even then. You were different from the other kids, Adrienne. It's always been you."

"No," she persisted. "It hasn't always been me. You fell for Harper the second you laid eyes on her. Beautiful Harper. Brilliant Harper. Vivacious Harper."

"Did you just say vivacious?"

"Don't make fun of me." Adri didn't realize that she was pinching his arms until her fingers began to tingle. David hadn't given any indication that she was hurting him, but Adri suddenly sat back and massaged her knuckles. "This is great, David. And you know that I'm loving every minute of it. But if we're going to end badly, I need us to end now."

"What makes you think we have to end?"

"You're in love with Harper."

David slid out from underneath Adri, his hands on her waist, and set her on the bed in front of him. They sat cross-legged, knee to knee, and because Adri couldn't quite endure it, because she couldn't face him like this, she pulled the sheet against her chest and held it close like a child with a blanket.

"Adrienne Claire Vogt." David said her name as if he meant it, as if each syllable held a weight so dear it deserved his attention. "I am not in love with Harper and I never have been."

"You spent three years flirting with her, David."

"Harper's an incurable flirt."

"So are you."

"Yeah, well, I don't flirt with her anymore now, do I?"

"No, but—"

"But nothing, Adri." David took her hand and kissed the knuckles that she had rubbed only seconds before. "What do I have to do to convince you? Harper is a good friend. But I am madly in love with you."

He had never said it before, not like that, and Adri found herself at a loss for words.

"I love you, Adrienne." David repeated himself, and this time when he said it there was a note of surprise in the declaration.

"I love you, too."

David cupped her face, his thumbs tracing Adri's jaw as if he was trying to commit every inch to memory. "What do we do with that?"

"We run away," Adri whispered. She didn't believe him, not entirely, but for now it was enough to savor the moment and hope that someday, when they had been together for longer than this, he would mean what he said. "Remember?" she asked, hopeful that he did, that he wanted it, too. "I want to leave this place."

"Because you aren't who everyone thinks you are."

"Sometimes I hate the farm," Adri blurted out. "I can't stand the cows and the smell of manure. And the way my dad has such high hopes for me."

David laughed. "How dare he have high hopes for you."

"It's too heavy," Adri admitted, shaking her head. Her words began tumbling out, one after the other, as if she couldn't say them fast enough to capture all the things that she wanted to express. "He wants the world for me and I'm afraid I'm going to let him down. I hate it that he sees my mother when he looks at me. It kills me that no matter how much he loves me, I'll never quite measure up."

"Sam doesn't feel that way about you."

"Yes," Adri said. "He does."

"You're being a brat." David gave her arm a flick.

"Excuse me?"

"I used to watch you." He ducked his head almost guiltily. It was so endearing, and so uncharacteristic, that Adri reached out to brush his hair back from his forehead. But the motion was somehow maternal and Adri let her hand fall into her lap, embarrassed.

"What do you mean?" she asked, clearing her throat.

"When I figured out who you were and where you lived, I used to ride Bard to the bluffs and try to catch a glimpse of you on the farm."

Adri punched him lightly on the shoulder. "Shut up. You did not."

"I did. I was a total stalker." David fanned his fingers like claws. "I only saw you once or twice. At least, I think it was you. Unless Will was partial to pink shirts."

"I wasn't partial to pink shirts."

David ignored her. "I was jealous of you," he said. "Everything looked simple from the hills. Your neat little farm, a dad who loved you, a brother who watched out for you. Maple Acres was everything Piperhall was not."

"I think you might be idealizing my life a bit."

"You mean like you idealize mine?"

Adri sighed. "So this is what we do. We posture and pretend."

"We expect too much of each other." David said it quietly, and Adri knew that he was thinking of his own mother. Her expectations. And his father, the man she had never known but who had left his mark on David like a scar. The man who terrified her as a child because he was larger than life, so formidable that one of her picnic games was to never allow less than a stone's throw between herself and Liam Galloway. It made her feel unaccountably sorry for David.

They didn't really need to say anything else. Adri didn't have to tell David how much she loved her father, in spite of the pressure she felt, or that while she loved Will, too, it was hard to live in the shadow of a twin—particularly a boy as irresistible and charismatic as her brother. For a moment they just understood each other, as completely as one person can fathom the soul of another.

"Let's leave," Adri said again. "Just the two of us. We could run away."

"Where would we go?" This time, there was an edge of adventure in David's voice. A sense that maybe they could do exactly what Adri proposed.

"Somewhere off the map," Adri said. "Southeast Asia."

"Brazil."

"New Zealand."

David grinned. "Africa."

"Absolutely." Adri grinned back.

And then David said the last thing that Adri ever expected. "Marry me."

There was nothing for Adri to choke on, but that's exactly what she did. Her throat collapsed and she felt herself go hot and panicky. But David meant what he said and he pulled her close, tipping her sideways so that she could sit on his lap, her head tucked underneath his chin. He said it again, "Marry me, Adrienne. Let's do it."

Adri said yes.

There was no ring, at least, not at first. And then, when they decided to make the engagement public, Adri refused to let David buy her a ring. "I want my mother's ring," she told him.

Either because their arrangement was so far from what he had always expected or because he loved her and wanted to give her what she wanted, David complied. He officially asked Sam for his daughter's hand in marriage a couple of weeks after the spur-of-the-moment proposal, and though her father was skeptical, he granted it. David slid the ring on Adri's finger as she sat at the table in the farmhouse kitchen, with Sam across from them.

When she showed it to Harper later that night, she realized that two weeks was the longest time that she had ever kept anything from her best friend. She hadn't breathed a word about David's proposal. It didn't feel exactly like a secret. It felt like a lie.

The sun was a stain on the horizon when Will finally turned to go. They hadn't said much of anything for the long minutes while they watched the sun set, and when darkness began to descend from the eastern sky like a fog, Will broke the silence by slapping the pillar where he leaned. "I can't believe you're leaving this place," he said.

"Blackhawk?" Adri said.

Will gave her a cynical look. "Everyone knows you always wanted out of Blackhawk. I'm talking about Piperhall. David's home. Your home."

Adri shrugged. "I don't know that it would have been our home."

"Oh, come on. You think Victoria would've let David leave?"

"You think David would have let Victoria tell him what to do?" Adri countered.

"Touché." Will descended a few steps, but Adri could tell that for some reason he was hesitant to go. She thought at first that he was simply reluctant to leave her when they had so few days left, but before she could speculate further, he said, "We were pretty messed up, weren't we?"

"Who?"

"The five of us. All of us pretending to be something we weren't." Will glanced over his shoulder at Adri, and the look in his eyes was so raw that it caught her by surprise. She wasn't sure what he was looking for, but she walked down a few of the stairs so that she could be beside him. "We tried to be like David, and he pretended to be like us." He shook his head. "We all would have followed Harper off the edge of a cliff. And there were times I think she would've loved nothing more than to lead us there."

"I don't know, Will. Sometimes I think it's our fault. Me and David. We ruined everything."

"No," Will said. "We were ruined long before you ever fell in love."

His smile was self-deprecating, wry, and he bumped her

shoulder with his own as if to smooth over the offense of his words. But Adri was already scoffing, the harsh sound surprising her, even though she was the one who made it.

The tears were there, so close to the surface they almost spilled, but Adri controlled herself. "I don't know if I was ever in love with him, Will. I look back and it all seems like pure fantasy. I think I knew it then, too." She let her words hang in the dusk.

Will put his arm around her shoulders, and gave her a brotherly hug. She felt herself melting into him, folding into the comfort of his embrace more eagerly than she would have liked. There were many things she wanted to confess to him. So much she wanted to say.

And she almost said it. Almost.

But she couldn't.

14

HARPER

"We're going in to the city tonight," Sawyer said, not bothering to turn from his computer.

Harper could just see over his shoulder, and what she glimpsed on the screen of his laptop made her stomach pitch. He was editing one of the series he had taken just that morning, the morning she received Adri's email.

In her mind it would forever be That Morning, capital *T* and *M*, because it marked the exact moment that her world cracked open like an egg. She hadn't realized that it was so fragile, or that she would welcome the hairline fracture that threatened everything she knew. Nor could she have predicted how much it would pain her after the fact to watch what Sawyer was doing. The way he shaded the sweep of her hair just so or added depth and detail to features made her skin crawl. Of course, Harper had never enjoyed what Sawyer was doing, but she tolerated it because she figured she had no other choice. Now, only hours after reading Adri's unexpected message, the very sight of him manipulating photographs of her body made her feel unhinged. Violent. She wanted to walk up behind him where he sat at his walnut slab desk and take him by the throat, her fingernails digging into the soft skin beneath his jaw. Her hands unforgiving.

Not that she would ever do that.

Not that it would actually work. Sawyer was much stronger than her.

"Did you hear me?" he called, this time looking over his shoulder.

"The city," Harper parroted, swallowing her disgust like bad medicine. "Of course."

Sawyer turned away. "Wear that yellow dress I like. The backless one with the long sleeves. And the heels with the ankle straps."

"The gladiator heels?"

"Yes."

"I can't walk in them."

She could hear the smile in his voice. "It doesn't matter."

Harper crossed the room behind him and closed the door to the bedroom they shared as noiselessly as possible. She was used to obeying Sawyer's every command, but something about Adri's email made his orders chafe. Of course, the note was only two lines, it didn't really mean anything at all, but to Harper it was an invitation. A summons. A cry for help. Harper ached to go. But it wasn't that easy and she knew it.

Harper didn't dare to lock the bedroom door, but she knew that if she dressed quickly she could probably get out of the apartment without another of Sawyer's photo shoots.

It hadn't always been like this. In the beginning they were just a couple, and though Sawyer's appetites shocked Harper, it didn't cross her mind to deny him. He was too handsome. Too charismatic. In her darkest, most self-loathing moments, she figured she deserved everything she got. And later, when he told her that he knew a guy who knew a guy who would pay good money for a couple of classy boudoir shots, she didn't really think twice. It was her modus operandi; she was the party girl, the wild child, the sexy minx who would try anything once. But Sawyer set the hook deep, and before Harper had a chance to realize what was happening, what he had done to her, it was too late.

Boudoir photos were a happy memory.

Officially, Sawyer Donovan was the founder and president of a small but wildly successful advertising agency and marketing firm that specialized in interactive campaigns. At least, that's how he introduced himself. "I guess you could call me the Don Draper of Minneapolis—and the twenty-first century." It was a well-rehearsed line that somehow came off as spur-of-the-moment, and even a little diffident, as if he was still baffled by the extent of his success. Humility was particularly charming on Sawyer, though Harper knew that he didn't have a meek bone in his body. And she found it disingenuous that he claimed to know so much about the industry when he was so disconnected from his own company. Agency 21 was run by Sawyer's employees.

Sawyer's real passion was his photography. He was a self-proclaimed artist, a shutterbug who had taken his hobby to a whole new level when Agency 21 took off and he could step back to supervise rather than make each and every business decision. When Harper first met him, he had glossed over the details of his second job, disappearing from time to time for photo shoots that he didn't bother to explain. And she didn't ask. What had she thought Sawyer Donovan was doing? Posing some high school senior with a basketball on the tip of his finger? Cracking jokes to make a grumpy kid laugh in a family photo? Sometimes she hated herself for being so thick. For not walking away when she had the chance, when they were still just a couple instead of whatever they were now.

After he took those first few pictures, everything had changed. To Harper, the sound of the digital shutter on his camera was the click of handcuffs snapping shut.

For reasons she couldn't quite ascertain, Sawyer had chosen to keep her close. Harper didn't know whether to be comforted or horrified that she was "the one." There were others, there had to be, for Sawyer still locked her in the apartment when he went to other photo shoots. Harper didn't have to clean; a cleaning service took care of the apartment and Sawyer made sure they were out for those weekly visits. And he would never allow her to get a job. But Harper had to fill her days somehow, and since Sawyer tolerated her cooking, she spent long hours in the kitchen. She pored over gourmet cookbooks and then tried her hand at the complicated recipes. What else was there to do? Once in a while she would pick up a pen, but the words that she scrawled were too angry, too raw to be trusted. They made the walls of her prison echo, and Harper feared she'd lose her mind.

She was so alone. No one else lived with him. No one else penetrated the inner sanctum of his so-called intimacy. How many were there? Women? Men? God forbid, children? What else was Sawyer up to? Film? These were thoughts Harper couldn't focus on for more than a second or two. They made her suddenly and violently sick and she broke out in a cold, panicked sweat.

"I'll tell everyone what you've done," Sawyer said when she fought. And even though there was no such thing as an "everyone" to Harper, there were several someones. Her mother, her father, Adri. To a lesser extent, Jackson. And Will, the boy she sometimes dreamed about when her subconscious was so heartsick for someone safe that she trembled in her sleep. Harper couldn't stand the thought of disappointing them, even if she didn't really know them anymore. She died a little at the thought of the looks on their faces if they knew who she truly was. What she had become.

And when Harper cried—a rare but not unheard-of occurrence—Sawyer told her, "It's because I love you so much, baby. It's because you're so beautiful, so incomparable. It just feels wrong to keep you to myself. We're making art. The most beautiful kind of art."

Change quickly. The yellow dress was hanging in the very back of Harper's closet, but as she reached for it, her hand passed over a little black cocktail dress. And as she brushed the silky fabric, the thought bolted through her like a flash of lightning: Black is better for hiding.

Harper froze, her fingers clinging to the black dress like a lifeline. Sawyer wouldn't stand for it. He had already picked out her dress, her shoes. He wouldn't tolerate a change in costume so late in the game. But suddenly the black dress felt like her only, immediate hope. She had to wear the black dress. Black could disappear into the shadows. Black could sink into nothingness, into a place where she could stop being the girl that Sawyer Donovan used. If that was even his real name. She doubted that it was.

Yellow? Yellow was the siren call of neon. Police tape. A beacon calling him to her.

Yanking her T-shirt over her head, Harper grabbed the black dress. It was thinner than the yellow one, sewn from a sheer material with tiny spaghetti straps that required a strapless bra. And it was cold outside, or, at least, cool. She would need a sweater. Better yet, some sort of a shrug or shawl that she could drape around her bare shoulders.

Sawyer wouldn't understand why she was wearing the black dress, and as she unzipped her jeans and let them fall to her ankles, she realized there was only one way to get away with it and not pique his attention.

Unhooking her bra in the back, Harper slid the straps off her shoulders and yanked it out of the top of her dress. She tossed it on the floor of her closet. Then she snagged a pair of red peep-toe heels from the shelf and stuck her feet in them. A wide, charcoal wrap completed the ensemble, a long, finely woven piece with silver thread shot through the soft pattern. Harper could kick off the shoes easily enough. Ditch the scarf. It would be easier to run in bare feet, to flee with her shoulders free from the burden of tangled fabric. She would be cold, but it didn't matter.

Fully dressed, Harper stood for a moment in front of the closet and considered the jagged pieces of her life. There wasn't an article of clothing that Sawyer hadn't bought for her, and each item felt like a bribe. She should have said no. All those years ago, when she was still fierce and alive and just enough crazy to be stunningly, truly beautiful, she should have thrown it all in his face and walked away. How had she let this all happen? How had she become the woman that she was?

There wasn't a single thing she wanted to take with her.

Spinning on her heel, Harper walked out of the bedroom. She didn't look back.

In the living room, she waltzed up to Sawyer as he sat hunched over his computer. His back was rounded through his shoulders, and it crossed Harper's mind that he looked like an old man. A dirty old man.

She wanted to hit him, but she didn't. Instead, Harper sucked in a silent, steadying breath. And then she draped herself over his arm and took the lobe of his ear between her teeth. "I'm not wearing a bra," she whispered.

Sawyer never asked her about the yellow dress.

～

They went to La Belle Vie, and the irony of the restaurant's name was not lost on Harper. Sawyer was treating a table of friends, men who appreciated his hateful brand of professed art, but like Sawyer, had legitimate, respectable jobs. They were admirers and investors who sometimes commissioned pieces, curators eager to add to their collections. But as far as Harper could tell, they kept their hands clean while Sawyer did the dirty work.

Harper was, as usual, the only woman. There were four men at the table, all wearing Armani suits and devouring poached sturgeon with morcilla, beets, and toasted buckwheat as if they were eating burgers accompanied by Big Grab bags of Doritos. Aside from the occasional, unwelcome ogle from across the table, they more or less ignored her.

"Do you like the morcilla?" one of the men asked, leaning

toward Harper. He was trying to catch a glimpse down the front of her dress and she chose that exact moment to lift a napkin to her lips. She patted her mouth delicately as the cloth serviette draped down the bodice of her dress.

Harper was eager to discourage his unmistakable advances, but it took a strong measure of her patience to be what Sawyer wanted her to be. Sexy, available, coy. "And what, exactly, is the morcilla?" she asked, trying to keep her tone neutral, her expression mild.

"Blood sausage." He speared a thin disk of the dark meat and lifted it to his mouth, enjoying what he apparently believed was a seductive act.

Harper tried not to gag.

They knew who she was. How he used her. All of Sawyer's friends did. It was both a point of pride for him and a way to mark his territory. Harper's mother had been known to deride men who felt the need to engage in a pissing contest with their peers, and sometimes it struck Harper as ironic that she had ended up with a man who loved nothing more than to show the world just what a big, important boy he was. Sawyer loved it that his friends paid for a glimpse of his girlfriend, and he put a big, fat tally mark on some invisible scorecard every time they flirted with Harper. He knew that it couldn't go anywhere unless he wanted it to. And that's what scared Harper the most. That one day Sawyer would let it happen. No, that someday he would orchestrate it. He had already betrayed her in so many ways, it was just a matter of time until he sold her.

Sold her.

Harper felt as if someone had struck a match in her belly, and the fire that began to glow there was white-flame hot. He had no right. No right. And though she had let it happen for years—had welcomed it, even, because she believed heart and soul that she was getting exactly what she always deserved—if Adri could write those words, *Wish you were here*, maybe there was hope for her after all. Not redemption, never that. But something at least a little better than this.

Better than slavery.

The tables at La Belle Vie were perfectly apportioned so that conversation from neighboring tables was nothing but a low buzz against the soft, creamy walls of the award-winning restaurant. Harper's gaze flicked around the room, lighting on couples and small parties, groups of people lifting wineglasses to their lips and spearing bites of tiny portions of food from the tasting menu. Everyone seemed to order the tasting menu, and everyone left hungry. But it wasn't the food, or lack thereof, that made Harper suddenly sick to her stomach. It was the fact that she was sitting among them, beautifully dressed and smiling at all the right times, and no one knew that she was as trapped as a bird in a cage.

Or maybe they did, and they just didn't care.

And maybe tonight was the night. The man with the blood sausage was practically drooling on her, and Sawyer weighed every glance. Harper could tell by the way that her so-called boyfriend watched her, proprietary and cool. But there was something else in his eyes, too. Something calculating.

The dark dress, the dream of running, they were really just a warm-up. A little exercise to stretch her independent muscles, her resolve. But all at once Harper was leveled by the knowledge that *not now* could very easily become *not ever*. What if she waited too long? Sawyer's grip strangled tighter every day, and Harper finally knew that she was suffocating.

The slimeball beside her was still openly staring at her all but bare chest, and Harper stifled a gasp when she felt his hand snake onto her thigh. The tablecloth was long, nearly touching the floor, and it was easy enough for him to hide what he was doing. But when Harper shot a desperate look at Sawyer, she realized that he knew exactly what was happening. He gave the man a half-smile. Looked away.

"Excuse me," Harper said, pushing back her chair to stand.

The man's hand was still grasping at her slinky dress, causing a strap to slip off her shoulder. Harper righted it, heart pounding.

Sawyer was mid-sentence, but he stopped and gave her a black look. She was to be seen and not heard at these sorts of functions. And she was certainly not supposed to interrupt him in the middle of a monologue.

"I'll be right back." She could feel the blood surging through her veins, but there was a heavy dose of fear mixed in with her fury. The men at the table were all staring at her, watching the subtle exchange between Harper and Sawyer with the interest of compulsive gamblers steeply invested in an underground dogfight. Harper knew without even looking at them that they were keen to see how Sawyer would handle his girl. And because she couldn't risk his fighting her, because she was shaking so hard that it was nearly impossible to keep her voice steady, she bent over and kissed him on the mouth. He tasted of wine and foie gras. "I'll be right back," she said again.

This time, he settled back into his seat and flicked his fingers at her as if he had directed her to go.

The bathroom was beyond the main dining room and down a small hallway, and as Harper walked away she felt every eye on her. Not just the men at Sawyer's table, but every eye in the place. She didn't want the attention, in fact, she longed to escape it, so she wrapped her arms across her chest and hurried the last few steps on heels that clicked loudly against the tile floor.

Harper shouldn't have rushed and she knew it the minute she pushed through the bathroom door. It attracted too much attention. But she couldn't change that now. Fortunately, there was no attendant in the bathroom, and Harper didn't have to go through the motions of entering a stall and flushing the toilet. Instead, she thrust her wrists under a stream of cold water in the sink and let the shock of it numb her nerves. Drinking in fast little sips of air, Harper studied her own face in the mirror. The woman that looked back at her was clearly petrified, an emotion that she didn't recognize in herself. And yet, hadn't she been scared for years? Fearful of Sawyer and her imprisonment, yes, but also of herself and the stranger she had become?

But Harper didn't have time for such thoughts. She only had a few seconds, maybe a minute, before she had to slip past the doors to the dining room and down the steps to the street. Any longer than that and Sawyer would wonder where she was and come looking.

Grabbing a towel from the stack next to the sink, Harper abruptly dried her hands. Then she bent down and pulled off her shoes, looping her finger through the straps of both heels so that she could carry them one-handed. She looked ridiculous, she knew. The cocktail dress, the red shoes clutched like a talisman. Her eyes were wild, and there were goose bumps on her naked arms. She had forgotten her wrap on the back of the chair where she had been sandwiched between Sawyer and the man with the blood sausage.

Harper tried to take a deep breath, but there was a boulder on her chest and she only managed a small mouthful. Hardly enough to get her out the door, much less away from Sawyer.

But she couldn't worry about that.

Harper slipped out of the bathroom like a ghost, her tiny footsteps swallowed up by the immense, icy floor. The stairs looked like they were a mile away, and the broad entrance to the dining room loomed between her and freedom. For a moment, Harper couldn't decide if she should tiptoe or run, but before she could worry about her choice, she felt something settle lightly over her shoulders.

Stifling a scream, Harper spun and found herself crushed against Sawyer's chest. His expression was inscrutable, but he wore a hard, thin smile. "I thought you seemed cold," he said. "You were trembling. I brought you your wrap."

Harper almost vomited on him. Terror and something that felt a lot like rage whirled inside her chest like quicksilver. But she couldn't indulge such emotions now. Not with Sawyer above her, his hands holding her up so that she wouldn't collapse on the floor in a heap.

"I am cold," she stuttered, and the tremor in her voice substantiated her claim.

"But apparently your feet aren't?" Sawyer stuck a finger through the peep toe of one red shoe and lifted it slightly.

"My feet are sore," Harper managed. "I told you I can't walk in these shoes."

"You said you can't walk in the gladiator shoes."

"These, too." It was weak and Harper knew it, but her nerves were too frayed from her pathetic attempt at escape.

Sawyer considered her, his gaze glacial and shrewd. "Put your shoes on, Harper."

She didn't think. She just crouched down and did as he said, and when she stood up again, he took her jaw in his hand.

"I don't know what you think you're playing at." He leaned so close their foreheads touched. Anyone watching them would think that they were in love, enjoying an intimate moment. But Harper could feel the hate coming off him in waves as he said, "If you cross me, I'll kill you."

She didn't think he meant it. Not really.

But she didn't ever want to find out.

They walked back to the table with Sawyer's arm around her waist, and before they approached his party, they both clipped smiles to their faces like ornaments. Harper's felt lopsided and funny on her mouth, but Sawyer looked just like he always did: gorgeous. And dangerous.

The rest of the supper was a blur to Harper, and though the wrath she felt toward Sawyer threatened to bubble up and over, she tamped down such hazardous emotions. Kept her face blank. Her hands folded in her lap.

There was something off about Sawyer, something broken and fierce. Harper hadn't noticed it before, or if she had, she had done her best to ignore it. But watching him after her first and only attempt at escape, she could see it as clearly as the perfect nose on his face. That same nose that had struck her as so masculine, so faultless in the beginning, now reminded her of a pig. Nothing was as it seemed, and in a rush Harper could see that the so-called home she had allowed Sawyer to create for her was about to reveal itself for the madhouse it really was. She had no idea what he would do with her now that she had broken his trust.

The night was crisp and clear when Sawyer's small group descended the stairs from La Belle Vie and stood on the sidewalk beneath the streetlights. The bill had been nearly $900 for five people, but Harper knew that the outrageous expense didn't affect Sawyer. It was her perceived betrayal, the understanding that she had tried to do something—even if he didn't know what that something was—that made him clench and unclench his fists like he wanted to hit someone.

But as Harper watched Sawyer say his goodbyes, she realized that his outrage also made him erratic. He stood next to her, shoulder to shoulder and hip to hip, but his eyes hopped around. He couldn't focus on anything for more than a split second at a time. He shifted on his feet, unable to stand still. Harper could tell that Sawyer was distracted and overeager, ready to be alone with her but too arrogant to let his anger dictate the evening he had planned.

It was her only chance.

Ducking down, Harper put her hand casually on Sawyer's wrist as if she needed to hang on to him for balance. She made a show of fussing with her shoes, slipping her heels out of the backs as if the straps were giving her a blister. For a moment she could feel Sawyer's attention, and then just as quickly he relaxed a little. Her hand was on his arm. What could she possibly do?

Stealing a peek to her right, Harper assessed the street. She couldn't go left, past Sawyer, so her only option was the small parking lot. Thankfully, it was filled with dark corners, and old trees cast shadows that quivered on the pavement in the autumn breeze. She didn't have a choice. Not really. She could run. She could hide. It was the most she could ask for. And if he caught her . . . Well, she'd have to deal with that if it happened. Harper couldn't think past the next minute of her life.

Heart thumping wildly in her throat, Harper took her hand off Sawyer's arm and straightened up. He still wasn't paying attention; he was lost in conversation with the blood sausage man. It was now or never.

Harper stepped out of her shoes and bolted.

She wasn't a fast runner, but adrenaline made her careen down the sidewalk and leap off the curb into the parking lot before Sawyer and his companions even realized what was happening. Unfortunately, when they did catch on, Sawyer didn't have to tell them to chase her. They just did. All four of them, racing toward Harper with the intensity of a pack of wolves. She saw their eyes reflected in the lamplight when she chanced one furtive glance over her shoulder.

Harper didn't dare to look back again.

She had a head start, but she was barefoot and they were wearing shoes. Sharp pavement. A bitter wind. The knowledge that Sawyer probably meant what he said. That he would kill her. Or at least, make her wish that she was dead.

Weaving between parked cars, Harper thought to head toward the road, but it was too far away. She could hide, but they would find her. The parking lot was small and they would take their time. Leave no stone unturned.

Panic hit Harper when she realized that there was nowhere to go. A building loomed before her, but Harper couldn't tell what it was in the dark. The men were behind her. She was stuck.

But Harper wasn't the sort to give up.

A small, iron fence cordoned off the vast building, and Harper leaped over it before she could think about how she was cornering herself. They had lost her momentarily, but the fence gave a metal creak when she vaulted it, and it was enough to alert them to her general vicinity. Harper didn't have much time.

The building was sprawling and taller than Harper had first perceived. It towered over her, but there were unexpected corners and small alleyways that belied its massive size. With a start, Harper realized that she knew exactly where she was. She had seen the building a hundred times, maybe more, but in the dark and in her confusion she hadn't remembered.

The cathedral.

Harper had never attended a service at the church—she didn't even know what kind of church it was—though she had often admired its elegant spire and unique architecture. But she didn't have time to ponder the design now.

She could think of only one thing.

For all she knew, the doors were locked tight and no one was around and she would be left in the darkness and the cold to wait for the moment when Sawyer found her. But that didn't stop her from twisting through the paths of the small garden she discovered. It didn't stop her from trying every door she stumbled across. From tucking herself in each alcove and grasping at the handles with hope so high in her chest she feared it would suffocate her.

Harper's entire being wished for it with a longing like nothing she had ever known.

Sanctuary.

15

~

ADRIENNE

Friday night, the night before Victoria's memorial, it froze. Adri wasn't sure how the weather forecasters could have missed such a sudden, devastating frost, but miss it they did. When she woke on Saturday morning, the world outside her bedroom window glinted like crystal in the cold, late-September sun. It would have been lovely, except that she knew exactly what it would do to the baskets of pumpkins and squashes she had strategically placed beneath the arches of the loggia. The mums would be fine, they could withstand a dip in temperature, but the gourds would be mush. Adri hadn't planned on returning to the estate until an hour before the afternoon service, but she would have to now. She was on cleanup duty.

"I'll go with you," Sam said after breakfast.

"Thanks, Dad, but it won't take me long. Everything else is ready to go."

"Chairs set up?"

"Check. One hundred fifty of them in the main living space. I had to push the rest of the furniture against the walls, but it looks okay."

"I don't think a hundred fifty chairs will be enough." Sam shook his head, a thin line in his forehead betraying the fact that he was mentally calculating how to fit more in.

"It's fine, Dad. People can stand if more show up."

He nodded. "What about afterwards?"

"The buffet will be in the library, and people will have to file there after the service."

"Everyone will want to peek around anyway." Sam rubbed his jaw as if the thought bothered him. "Should we cordon off the stairs?"

Adri shrugged. "I already locked Victoria's bedroom. There's really not much else for anyone to get into. The guest bedrooms are exactly that: neutral, kind of boring. They don't contain anything of value."

"What about David's room?"

Adri hadn't spent much time in the rooms that made up David's bachelor apartment in the garden-level basement, but she had been there. She had forced herself to go, even though it took her days to work up the courage.

At first blush, it wasn't as devastating as Adri expected it to be. The bedroom was exactly how she remembered it. Spare and masculine with expensive paintings on the walls that Liam had picked out long before David was old enough to make those sorts of decisions on his own. It was the gentleman's version of a man cave, and it lacked both personality and a sense of David himself. The taps in the billiards room were long dry, and a quick peek in the bureau drawers of David's bedroom assured Adri that Victoria had gotten rid of his clothes before she died.

It was a courtesy that Adri hadn't even realized she'd hoped for. What would it have felt like to hold the shirts of the man she should have married? Would she have pressed her face to the fabric, strained for the faintest scent of the man she had once loved? There were thick layers of emotions beneath the thought, and Adri didn't have the heart to mine them. She silently thanked Victoria for doing the job for her, and tried to leave it at that.

But before she could shut the door on the rooms her fiancé had once called his own, Adri found herself tilting. The world was off-axis, and though she had felt okay only seconds before, everything was suddenly very, very far from fine.

Adri was on her knees before she knew what was happening, fingers in the carpet as if she needed something to hold on to. Something to keep her anchored.

Here, she thought. And she could feel the carpet against her naked back, the blunt pain of David's knee against her hip before he fell against her and stole the air from her chest. She remembered what she felt, the confusion of his body above her, and the truth that she tried to tell herself again and again: He loves me. But as often as she claimed his love, she had to counter herself. He loves me not.

Adri had crawled out of the room, wounded. Pulled the door shut behind her as if sealing a crypt.

"The basement is clean," Adri said in response to her father's question. Her mouth was dry, and she swallowed hard.

Adri could tell that her father was fishing for more information, that he wanted to know if even the hint of David wrecked her just a little. But she couldn't bring herself to go down that road even a short distance. The last week had rubbed the veneer of her resolve thin, and memories were popping up all around her. She had spent years in Africa demonizing this place and the past that dragged her down with the weight of an anchor, but she had to admit that there were moments of beauty, too. Kindnesses that still took her breath away after all this time. And though she remembered the carpet burns on her shoulder blades, the bruises on her arms, there were things about David that made her smile, bright and sudden; things he had said or done that were gifts she could still unwrap and admire all these years later.

That's what hurt the most: knowing that nothing ever was exactly black-and-white.

"Really," Adri said, forcing herself to give her dad's arm a re-assuring squeeze, "I've got it taken care of."

But Sam wouldn't be deterred. "If you won't have me, I'll

take my own car and check on the horses. It is my job, after all." He paused. "Is it still my job?"

Adri sighed. She had spoken to the State Historical Society of Iowa about Piperhall, and though they were interested in getting it listed on the registry of historical places, the woman she talked to didn't seem excited about the prospect of taking on the care and maintenance of the estate. And when she discussed putting it up for sale with Clay, his palpable disappointment cut the conversation short. Adri couldn't tell if he was daunted by the thought of selling such an albatross, or if he was secretly hoping she'd keep it. Either way, she was stuck. Will wasn't interested in it. Neither were Jackson and Nora. Or Sam. Adri felt like she had been shackled with a 25,000-square-foot lemon. Nobody wanted it. Least of all Adri herself.

As for the horses . . . "I don't know, Dad. Would you like them?" she asked.

Sam looked up. "What would I do with four horses?"

"One of them then? Mateo?" Adri tried not to sound too hopeful. What did it matter to her if her father kept Mateo? If she waited as long to come back to Iowa as she had the last time, he would probably be gone before she ever had the chance to see him again.

But Sam nodded. "I'll take Mateo. And maybe Amira."

"I'll sell the other two."

"You mean *I'll* sell the other two. You're going back to Africa, remember?"

Adri tried not to let the comment cut. She didn't like even the implication that she wouldn't take care of her own business. "I'll sell them online. The only thing you'll have to do is show them if a buyer wants to come and look."

"Fine." Sam stuck out his hand to seal the deal.

It felt strange to shake her father's hand, but there was something gratifying about coming to a conclusion concerning one small aspect of the disbursement of the estate. Something definitive in their handshake. She had made a decision. Now all she had to do was make a dozen more.

For a moment, Sam seemed as if he was on the verge of saying something else. He held Adri's hand just a second longer than necessary, but then he shook his head and gave her a lopsided little smile. Adri assumed he was just thinking about her upcoming departure.

They went to the estate, and Sam checked on the horses while Adri hauled the frost-softened outdoor decor to the grove. On any other acreage, there would be a blackened spot far from the house that indicated the burn pile, but Victoria didn't like the thought of incinerating things on her own property. So, long ago, David had taken to dragging refuse to the grove, and there was still a small hill of organic garbage that had endured the test of time.

An old pallet that had been ripped in half, nails sticking out of the gray boards and a piece of burlap snagged on one like a makeshift flag. A rusty wire basket. A wood-slat box that had a sticker proclaiming *Washington Cherries* on the side. Adri added the pumpkins to the pile, and when she accidentally dropped one and discovered that they exploded with a satisfying burst, she started to throw them.

At first she just lobbed them, but by the time she had made it to the last wicker basket, there was something vicious in the snap of her arm. It felt so good to throw something—if there had been a punching bag nearby, she probably would've landed a couple of blows, too—and she began to take an almost perverse pleasure in rocketing smaller gourds at the trunks of nearby trees. Adri didn't even realize she was taking aim at people until she uttered Victoria's name.

And then it was a waterfall. Will and Jackson and her dad. For calling her home. For making her miss them when she wanted to forget. David. For everything. Harper, because she abandoned Adri when she needed her most.

Adri was stubborn and she knew it, a little idealistic, and a firm believer that anything could be fixed with a bit of grit and some hard work. But the truth was, she hadn't been able to fix a single thing that was wrong in her life since the moment that she had said yes to David's precipitous proposal. Everything had spun out of control. And it was making her crazy.

When the last pumpkin had erupted against the trunk of a burr oak and spilled orange pulp down the bark, Adri put her hands on her hips and fought a wave of despondency. "Oh, God," she muttered. "What am I doing here?"

"You still talk to him?" Sam said from somewhere behind her.

Adri spun. "How long have you been there?"

"Long enough." Sam took a few hesitant steps toward her, and when she didn't yell at him, he kept coming. "Look, Adri, I've been trying to muster up enough courage to talk to you since the minute you stepped off that plane."

"We have talked," Adri said, rubbing her forehead. Trying to forget that her father had just seen her lose it. Or get as close to losing it as she got. "We've talked lots."

"But not about the stuff that mattered."

"Dad—"

"Nope," Sam interrupted. "I'm going to say what I came to say, and if you don't want to hear it, I'm sorry. But life's too short, sweetheart, and when you hop on that plane in a couple of days, I'm afraid I'm never going to see you again."

Adri was shaking her head, but Sam wasn't about to be deterred. There was a flinty determination in his eyes, and when he held up his hands as if to ward off any and every argument she could come up with, she bit her lip and let him speak.

"I know that Victoria wrote you a letter."

"You do?" Adri was so shocked, she was surprised that she could speak at all. She crossed her arms against her chest so her dad wouldn't see her hands tremble. "What . . . ?" she couldn't get the question out. Tried again. "What do you . . . ?"

"What do I know? Not much. I don't know exactly what she wrote, but I do know that she was consumed in her final days.

Gripped by the belief that she had failed you somehow. Failed David."

Adri didn't have words for this. She had no idea how to respond.

Sam passed his hand over his eyes and Adri could see him try to gather his thoughts. "Look, I'm not doing this right. I suppose what I should be saying is, I know. First of all, I know what happened to Victoria. Everyone did, I guess, but no one knew how to stop it."

"Dad, I—"

Sam took a shuddering breath. "I know I should have asked this question long ago. That I failed you by not asking. Did David ever mistreat you?"

There were so many things that Adri could have said. Secrets and lies and bad manners besides. But the truth about David hitting her was just the beginning. If she admitted what really happened between them, how they had begun to unravel in the end, she didn't know if she'd ever be able to stop. She didn't recognize herself by the time she knew who David was—who they were together. And Adri wasn't about to admit any of that to her dad. One of the only people in the world who still loved her. Even if he didn't really know her.

Adri didn't pause. "No," she said, holding her father's wounded gaze.

Sam believed her. Adri could tell.

It was one of the only times in her life that she had lied to his face. But somehow it fit.

Harper had taught her well.

Not everybody was happy about their engagement. Least of all Harper.

"You're jealous," Adri accused one afternoon. They were fighting, and though it rankled to admit that their friendship wasn't perfect, fighting was something that they did really well. Harper had taught Adri the fine art of the knock-down, drag-out, and they were known to engage in glorious shouting matches that invariably ended with one or both of them storming out of the campus apartment that they shared at ATU. Often, when they had cooled down enough to handle being near each other without throwing things, Harper would take Adri by the chin like a fond aunt. "How could I ever be mad at you! Just look at you. You're the cutest damn thing I've ever seen."

It was beyond patronizing, but then Harper would redeem herself by making scrambled eggs with cream cheese or offering to give Adri a back rub while they watched old episodes of *Seinfeld* on DVD. It was impossible for Adri to stay mad.

But the engagement had tipped the careful balance of their complicated world. It seemed to Adri that the ring she wore was an unspoken point of contention between them, and the harder she tried to act as if everything was normal, the more Harper set out to prove that it was not.

"I am not jealous!" Harper shrieked in the face of Adri's accusation. "I am the farthest thing from jealous. I feel sorry for you. I think you're making a huge mistake."

There were a dozen things that Adri could have said, but she chose "Marrying the man I love is a mistake?"

Harper didn't even have to answer. The look on her face was enough of a reply.

"You can be a real bitch, Harper. You know that?" Adri regretted the words the second they were out of her mouth, but it was too late to take them back.

Harper blinked at her for a moment, completely stunned. And then she burst out laughing and enveloped Adri in a hug that squeezed the air right out of her.

"I am a bitch sometimes," she said, almost gleefully. "And you need a little bit of that in you, Adri-Girl. Really, you do. The world is a scary place, my sweet friend. You gotta fight back."

Adri didn't agree with her. Either that the world was a scary place or that you had to fight back. And she didn't understand how they had gone from arguing to hugging, but she was too interested in peace at any price to argue.

"She's a little loco," Adri told David, a couple of days later. They were at the estate because Victoria had invited them over, just the two of them. It was one of the few times that they left ATU unaccompanied by the rest of The Five, and although David was acting moody and strange, Adri savored the hours alone. Supper with Victoria had gone okay, and now the two of them were sitting on the edge of the hot tub, dangling their feet into the all but boiling water as a light snow fell around them. The air was unusually warm for January.

"Who, Harper?"

"Of course, Harper."

David gave her a sideways look. "That's cold, Adrienne. She's your best friend."

"Since when do you call me Adrienne?"

"Since when do you call your best friend crazy?" David pushed himself up from the edge of the hot tub and grabbed a towel off one of the snow-dusted lawn chairs. He wrenched open the French door and slammed it behind him.

Adri was dumbfounded. "Are we fighting?" she shouted over her shoulder. Yanking her own feet out of the scalding water she spun on the concrete edge of the hot tub and took off after him.

Adri hated fighting, or she thought she did, but something about the exchange exacerbated the fears that she already nursed when it came to her relationship with David. She might be wearing his ring—or rather, her mother's ring—but she had doubted the veracity of their relationship from the very beginning. Following David, she took the steps to the basement two at a time and whipped around the door of his bedroom, still trickling chlorinated water from the hot tub.

"Use a towel," David said, tossing the beach towel that he had already used at her. "You're dripping all over the hardwood."

"Excuse me," Adri huffed. "What do you expect? You just sided with Harper."

"I did not side with Harper." David was pulling on a pair of jeans, though only minutes ago Adri had imagined that there would be no need to get dressed again that night.

"You did! You know how I feel about . . ." she faltered. "You and Harper."

"Me and Harper?" David barely glanced at her, but Adri was eager to engage, to spar with him like she had sparred with Harper. And then make up in the heady glow of the aftermath.

"Yes, you and Harper." Adri hadn't meant to go in this direction, she didn't really even believe the things that she was saying. But all at once she understood that she had gotten it all wrong when she fought with Harper. Harper wasn't the jealous one, Adri was. She was jealous because she couldn't bring herself to believe that maybe David really did love her. That maybe he really would—and had—chosen her over her exquisite best friend.

Once the thought entered her head, it spread, as fast and vicious as a wildfire. David didn't really love her, he couldn't. But Adri was a safer choice in a wife than Harper, a choice that his mother might actually allow, even if she didn't entirely approve. Maybe David had chosen Adri because it was a way to keep Harper close. A way to have the best of both worlds: the temperate, decent wife and the tempestuous, desirable lover.

Adri told him as much. She didn't mean to shout, to be so shrill and angry and unreasonable, but it was a living, breathing fear inside of her. A desperation she couldn't control. She was ruthless and ripe with accusations that had no bearing and no proof. She was out of control.

He slapped her.

It came out of nowhere. His hand. The bite of his fingers on her fury-blushed cheek. It was open-palmed, not the brutal, backhand blow that, somehow, Adri had always imagined a man would use to hit a woman. Yet the pain exploded in her cheekbone, along her jaw, and for a split second, she was too hurt, and too surprised, to respond at all. But then, before she realized what she was doing, before she could consider the implications of her impossible, impulsive action, Adri cocked her arm and hit him right back.

She put every ounce of the fury she felt into her swing, and when her palm made contact with his face, it whipped his chin to his shoulder. He didn't even try to look up at her.

The room echoed with silence.

"Oh, David." Adri groaned. Her hands were on her mouth, trying to shove the words down, to swallow the awful thing she had just done, and take his sin with it. But she couldn't do it. It was too much, too big, and she couldn't undo what had happened between them. As much as she wanted to smooth it all over, make it go away and pretend that it had never happened at all, she couldn't. It was done. And her fiancé couldn't even bring himself to look at her.

The snow was falling harder when she fled to the stables. Her hair was still wet, but common sense had prodded her to throw on dry clothes and grab a coat. Adri was grateful for those small mercies as the cold air stung her ears, but it never crossed her mind to turn back. She couldn't face David and all the things that had broken between them.

Bard was pacing his stall, his restless energy ricocheting off the walls and making the air inside the dusty building feel malevolent. Alive. Adri's hands shook as she tacked him up, but Bard stayed remarkably still in spite of her clumsy ministrations. It was almost as if he could sense her angst. More likely, he knew what the bridle meant—he could run, and that's exactly what he wanted to do.

It was what Adri wanted, too. To run so fast she flew. Or fell. In the moment she swung herself into the saddle, it didn't matter how the ride ended. She just wanted it to end.

~

Adri swept through the house in her understated charcoal dress. Her dark hair was in a neat chignon; her makeup was perfect. And the memorial had been perfect, too. A tasteful mix of bitter and sweet, melancholy and hopeful, though Adri wasn't feeling very hopeful at all.

Her father had read "If," and her heart twisted on the lines that Victoria had chosen: "If you can bear to hear the truth you've spoken / twisted . . . Or watch the things you gave your life to, broken, / And stoop to build them up with worn-out tools . . ."

And she wondered if they had been picked expressly for her. Adri's heart changed the final phrase ("You'll be a woman, my daughter!") and knew that in her own inexplicable way Victoria had meant it for all of them. An anthem that allowed for all the broken promises and all the ways that they had tried. Failed, but tried.

People wandered Piperhall like it was an open house, and in a way, Adri supposed, it was. Maybe one of the guests would remember the summer picnics, be gripped with nostalgia, and approach her with a purchase price. She hoped that would be the case. And yet, there was a part of her that dreaded it, too. For, as much as she longed to be rid of the burden that was the home that housed her memories and her former dreams, at the moment of letting go she found that her fingers held fast.

"It's beautiful. All of it. You've done a remarkable job."

Adri turned to see Mrs. Holt dressed in a cream tailored suit, a fluted glass of wine raised in a toast. To her? "Thank you," she said. "It was nothing."

"Certainly not nothing," Katherine disagreed. "Piperhall hasn't looked this good in years."

"Agreed." Clay caught Adri's elbow from behind and brushed a light kiss against her cheek. Reaching out to Mrs. Holt, he took her hand and pressed his lips briefly to her wrist. "The only things that outshine the floor are the lovely ladies before me."

Katherine gave Clay a censorious look and drew back her hand, but Adri could tell it was lighthearted. She hadn't real-ized that her lawyer and David's former tutor knew each other, but then, it seemed everyone in Blackhawk was acquainted.

"Victoria would have been pleased," Katherine said, diverting attention back to the memorial. "Very pleased."

"I'm glad to hear it." Adri sighed, and found herself blinking back unexpected tears. It *was* beautiful—the mansion, Victoria's legacy, the evening itself—but it was a fractured kind of beauty, and no amount of cleaning or waxing or maintenance could repair what she longed to fix. If Clay and Mrs. Holt noticed her sudden emotion, they were kind enough not to comment, and before she could be drawn into unwanted conversations about the past or the future of the estate, Adri quietly excused herself.

When dusk settled over the estate, Will lit the gardenia candles that were scattered throughout the mansion. Though Victoria's only real family—the intimidating James Galloway and his equally impressive wife—had left almost immediately after the service, many people were still wandering around, taking in the majesty of the place as if they couldn't get enough. They lapped it up, nibbling on petits fours and thin slices of cucumber soaked in lime juice and sprinkled with sesame seeds and some herb that Adri couldn't place. There were still bottles of wine to open, and though they had all just mourned the loss and commemorated the life of a pillar in their community, there was a definite celebratory vibe in the air. Adri didn't quite know what to do with it.

Wandering outside to the loggia, she leaned with her forearms on the stone railing. It was a cool autumn night, but for once Adri didn't feel the cold. She closed her eyes for a moment and allowed herself the luxury of a dream, a moment inhabited by the life she should have had, a life with David and the airy wishes that she had held for herself in the days before she realized that they would never be quite the people they were supposed to be.

Maybe he would come up behind her, settle a sweater over her shoulders, and pull her close. Better yet, his suit coat. Arms around her waist, mouth against her temple. He'd tell her how beautiful she looked. How lovely the night, in spite of the sad slant of the occasion, the woman that they loved in their own fumbling ways and would always miss. They'd talk about Victoria, and for just a heartbeat Adri caught the faintest glimpse of the mother she could have had. The life she imagined for herself wasn't a flawless world—so very far from it—but Adri's heart rose all the same.

And then a breeze lifted and the night grazed her arm. She wrapped her arms around herself, painfully aware that David would never walk through the doors behind her. And equally grateful that he wouldn't.

Maybe she was drunk. Adri had lost track of how many glasses of wine she had consumed. She wasn't the sort to take it too far, but she felt tipsy as she clung to the edge of the grand porch and watched the shadows that flirted with the dozens of gleaming cars in the makeshift parking lot of the circular drive.

The night was utterly dark and still, the memorial going strong behind her. Adri was utterly alone in the dark. Alone with her memories and regrets. But as she stared into the blackness, a car came down the winding drive. The headlights were thin and indistinct in the distance, and Adri blinked several times to clear her foggy head of the vision that played tricks on her eyes. The light didn't dissipate.

Adri watched as the car came, an expensive SUV with tinted windows and a pitted paint job, as if the vehicle had been left out in a hailstorm. She could see it clear as a stop-frame movie as it crawled around the circle, and she marveled at the unexpectedness of such a late guest. The South Dakota license plate. At the way this sorry visitor had arrived hours too late.

Something inside her stirred.

The car rounded the corner and came to a stop almost directly below Adri. She watched as the back door opened.

It was a woman, tall and leggy, dressed in a short, black skirt and a grey hoodie sweatshirt zipped up to her chin. Her hair was yellow in the lamplight, loose around her shoulders and so long it fell halfway down her narrow back. She wasn't wearing any shoes.

Adri almost called to her, almost alerted the stranger to her presence and offered directions to wherever she was going. But then the woman pulled back her hair with one hand and pony-tailed it at the base of her neck in a gesture so familiar it made Adri feel as if she was being hollowed out. One movement and she was undone, her very heart carved out of her chest, and in its place there was a void that echoed with a thousand might have beens.

When the woman turned her face up, her name was on Adri's lips.

Harper.

PART III

HARPER

16

∼

Harper was barefoot, and she hated that.

She couldn't complain, though, not really, because angels had saved her the night before, and who could argue with the fickle grace of God? She had felt a strong, benign presence with her, leading her to a hidden entrance to the church that would allow her to escape the night and the men who pursued her. And another angel must have stood guard at the gate, for how else could she explain the fact that one moment Sawyer was at her heels and the next he was gone? Harper had crouched in the vast darkness of the cathedral for hours, and when something inside her said, *Now*, she slipped back into the night and ran, stumbling all the way, to the address she had unintentionally memorized so many months ago.

It was a different man who helped her—not the same guy from the Fringe Festival who had taken one look at Harper and plumbed her darkest secret—but he had a kind face, and she liked the soft curls of his short, hippie ponytail.

"We can get you anywhere you want to go," he told her, his eyes rich with concern. "Where will you be safe?"

Harper didn't feel safe anywhere, not really, but Adri had told her: Wish you were here. So Harper went back.

The Bridge bought Harper a ticket on the Jefferson Lines bus that left Minneapolis at a quarter to noon on Saturday and was scheduled to arrive in Sioux Falls, South Dakota, at 6:10 p.m. Harper had to swallow her pride to allow the purchase, but she didn't have a choice. She had no money, no wallet. She didn't even have the little clutch Sawyer sometimes allowed her to carry in case she needed lipstick or a tampon.

The bus was an hour late, and when Harper finally peeled herself out of her seat, she felt like she had been traveling forever instead of only half a day. She was stiff and disoriented, disappointed to emerge from the stinky, run-down bus and find herself in the creepiest depot she had ever seen. Not that Harper had seen many bus depots.

There was a woman who was supposed to pick her up, a friend of The Bridge who liked to do what she could, and the arrangement put Harper in mind of the underground railroad. A cab ride, a bus ride, a stranger in a strange car. It was almost disconcerting how well the imagery fit. Harper was on her way to a freedom of sorts, and she had escaped a situation that felt like someone else's horror story. It was all so blurry and surreal. In fact, Harper couldn't even bring herself to think about Sawyer and the night before. Or, even more troubling, what he would be doing today.

While she waited on a bench in the depot for the next conductor to pick her up and transport her the final leg of her journey, Harper fought the familiar, almost irrepressible urge to run. She had escaped, but she didn't want to stop, not even for a minute. She wasn't safe yet. Maybe she never would be.

She was cold, though one of the volunteers at The Bridge had given her a sweatshirt from the little storage room in their offices that was set up like a mini Goodwill store. He had also found her a pair of shoes, but the only ones in her size were plaid Skechers slip-ons lined with faux fur. They looked simply divine with her cocktail dress and the heather-gray sweatshirt. Stretching out her legs before her as she sat in the dumpy bus depot, Harper decided she looked exactly like a homeless person. The thought made her smile.

"I like your shoes."

The girl was sitting a few feet down from Harper. Her skin was the gorgeous shade of coffee with cream, and while she was startlingly pretty, her eyes were thin and guarded.

"Thanks." Harper smiled. She intended to leave it at that, but there was something about the girl that plucked a note inside her soul. It was an odd offering, but Harper didn't stop to think. She just slipped off the shoes and handed them to the girl. "You may have them."

Harper was almost grateful that she didn't get to see the girl's reaction, because at that moment a forty-something soccer mom with a razor-edge bob and chandelier earrings approached her with a 100-watt smile. "You must be Harper."

She crawled into the backseat of the SUV and slept the rest of the way to Blackhawk.

Just over an hour later, Harper emerged in the middle of what looked to be a party.

The circular drive in front of the mansion was full of cars. They were spilling out onto the lawns, parked at odd angles all down the long road that was lined with old trees. And the house itself was resplendent with light, casting cheerful shadows on the brown grass like pools of bright water where sunshine danced.

Harper was seized with dismay. She wanted to keep driving and never come back. What had she been thinking? She couldn't just show up at the Galloway mansion and expect a warm reception. Email or no, she wasn't welcome here. It would have been easier, maybe, to knock on the door at Maple Acres. Sam had always acted like a father to her. Or she could have wandered the ATU campus. But Adri's email had said, *I came back.* And that could only mean one thing: here.

Harper stepped out of the SUV because she didn't know what else to do. The woman who had taken her this far, Carol, she believed, had parked the vehicle at the base of the sweeping double staircase and enthusiastically announced, "We're here!"

Harper didn't even remember that she was shoeless until she opened the door and slid to the ground, where gravel bit into the sensitive pads of her feet and yanked her into a reality that left her breathless. And terrified.

What if Adri hadn't meant what she wrote? What if she didn't wish that Harper had come at all? Or worse, what if she changed her mind when she saw the woman that her best friend had become?

Fear anchored Harper to the ground. She couldn't get back in the SUV. Carol was already wishing her a good night, a friendly smile conveying that she hoped Harper's homecoming would be a warm one. And the party was before her, the windows filled with silhouettes and the mansion itself thick with all the memories that she had tried so hard to forget.

But Harper didn't have time to entertain dread. In the moment she lifted her face toward the loggia and the doors just beyond, she realized that there was someone on the terrace.

"Harper?"

Her voice was familiar, even after all these years. But the woman who leaned over the edge of the wide railing wasn't anyone that Harper recognized.

"Harper, is that you?"

As Harper watched, the woman hurried to the east-facing staircase and skipped down the steps on heels that sang a snappy welcome. Or a ballad of reproach. She rushed across the gravel, and even in the dark, Harper could see that her mouth was parted in disbelief and her eyes wide, bottomless pools of something that looked a lot like longing. A short distance from Harper she stopped so abruptly that it appeared as if she had hit an invisible wall. But she pressed through. An uncertain step forward. Another.

"Oh, my God. Harper."

Adri folded her in a hug, the sort of layered, uninhibited embrace that contained all their history in the circle of her arms. But Harper's own arms were pinned to her sides, and she was so muddled by exhaustion and the unreality of the situation, she found herself incapable of responding at all. She almost burst into tears. She almost laughed. She almost screamed at the wind. Instead, Harper did nothing at all.

When Adri realized the hug was one-sided, she backed up. Pressed her palms together in front of her chest as if she was praying. The expression on her face was a damaged thing. Crooked hope, a splintered expectation. She looked like she wanted to cry, but there was a lopsided smile on her face.

"What are you doing here?" Adri asked, whispering as if Harper might disappear in a wisp of smoke.

Harper just stared. She couldn't believe that after all this time they were here. Together. Standing in the shadow of the mansion where their lives began to slowly unravel. Adri was real. And so very lovely in a chic dress that managed to be modest and sexy at once. She was as cool and welcoming as a lake in summer, and Harper could hardly breathe for the feeling that she had been thrust underwater.

Harper grabbed the edge of her soul and gave it a good, hard shake. Somewhere deep inside life stirred, and she grasped at the first thing that floated to the surface. A playful wink. It didn't make any sense at all, but words followed it as if she had planned to act like this all along.

"I got your email!" Harper said. Her voice was shiny and fake in her own ears. "It sounded like an invitation, so I came."

Adri knotted her hands together. "It was an invitation," she said. But Harper could tell by the way she worried her fingers that Adri hadn't expected Harper to show up quite like this. Shoeless and wild-eyed. Glassy bright and hard like a polished stone.

"Excuse me." Harper spun on her heel, a painful experience in the jagged gravel, and stuck her head inside the SUV. "Thanks for the ride," she said, trying to appear unruffled. "I really appreciate it."

Carol gave her a serious look, the sort of question in her eyes that made Harper realize that the woman was willing to take her wherever she wanted to go. But there was nowhere else for her to go. "Thank you," she said again, and meant it.

Harper slammed the door and slapped the window twice to signal it was safe to drive away. A puff of exhaust, the glow of taillights, and then Harper and Adri were alone.

"Who was that?" Adri managed.

"A friend."

Adri didn't question her further, but doubt hung heavy in the air around them. Harper couldn't stand the thought of telling Adri more, so she pulled a strand of story from the night and began to weave it into something that sounded almost believable. "I look ridiculous, don't I?" she laughed, bending one leg at a ninety-degree angle so that her bare foot dangled off the ground. "Bit of a crazy party," she said conspiratorially.

"Would you like a pair of shoes?" Adri sounded completely bewildered, but she motioned over her shoulder like a good hostess.

Hostess? Harper realized that she had no idea what the situation was at Piperhall. When she left Adri that summer over five years ago, she never looked back. She forced herself not to. And she had no idea who this woman before her was. What she did, where she lived, who she loved. But she looked as if she belonged at the estate.

Adri was nothing short of elegant.

Harper couldn't tell how long her hair was because it was pulled back in a sophisticated bun. But that didn't stop little ringlets from escaping and framing the fine angles of her face. Adri's skin glowed gold in the reflected light between shadows, and her eyes were so dark they seemed endless. She was stunning, willowy and classic in her gray dress and understated heels. Harper loved her in a stab of emotion so overwhelming that she stumbled forward a little.

"Yes, actually," Harper said, reining herself in. "Shoes would be great. I don't have any with me. In fact, I don't have anything with me."

"You didn't bring a bag, or a suitcase?" Adri's mouth formed a little O of disbelief.

For a moment Harper considered abandoning the charade before it grew out of control, but she couldn't bring herself to tell the truth. Where would she begin? How could she explain what had happened in the last twenty-four hours, and, before that, in the last five years? It was too much. Her heart and mind couldn't hold the coiling mess of loose ends and frayed strands of stories that made up the sordid tale of who she was. Of how she had become a stranger even to herself. Harper came up with the easiest and most likely scenario, a tale of a wild party, a reckless girl, and an email that prompted her to do exactly what the old Harper would have done: abandon everything in an absentminded, impetuous act.

"Nada," Harper said in response to Adri's question. "I guess some things never change."

"Well"—Adri turned a bit and motioned that Harper should follow—"I'm sure we can find something in the house."

"Do you . . ." Harper could hardly get the question out. "Do you live here?"

Adri gave her a sideways glance. "No. I haven't been back here since . . ." She didn't have to finish. But she seemed to struggle with something anyway. She opened her mouth, closed it. Shook her head. "It's complicated," she said. "It'll take some time to explain."

They fell into step beside each other, walking slowly toward the staircase and the people enjoying the party inside the mansion. Harper didn't know if she could face them. "Are we celebrating something?" she asked, trying not to sound too invested in the answer.

Adri stopped. Turned to look her full in the face. "No. Victoria is dead, Harper. This is her memorial service."

For a moment, Harper was speechless. She recovered quickly. "You're kidding. Adri, I'm so sorry. I know you really cared about her."

It was a half-truth and they both knew it. But it was the right thing to say. The appropriate social nicety.

They had made it to the steps and Harper climbed onto the first one gratefully. The concrete was cold, but it was better than the gravel. She towered over Adri from here, but Adri didn't make any move to follow her. She just stood looking up at Harper, her expression inscrutable and her hands on her hips.

Shaking her head slowly, Adri laughed. It was a dry, humorless sound, and there was a note of desperation in it. "I don't know what to do with this."

"With what?" Harper asked, but she already knew.

"With us. What are we doing here?"

"Remembering Victoria, I guess," Harper said, because it was exactly the sort of thing she would have said before everything exploded around them. It was her job. Simplify. Deflect. Remind everyone that life is fun and frothy and worth the cost of admission.

"You know that's not what I mean."

"What do you want, Adri?" Harper shrugged as if none of it mattered. "It's been a long time. But you emailed, and I came."

"I'm glad you came," Adri said softly.

"But you're not happy."

"Of course I'm not happy. Have you been happy the last five years?"

The drop of acid in Adri's voice took Harper by surprise. She answered honestly. "No. But what are we supposed to do about that? What are we supposed to say to one another?"

"I don't know."

"Neither do I."

Adri sighed heavily and smoothed the fabric of her wool dress over the flat line of her stomach. "Who? What? When? Where? Why?"

"What are you talking about?"

"Maybe that's what we're supposed to say to each other. We have to start somewhere."

Harper nodded. "I suppose we do."

"But not right now. You need shoes." And then Adri swept up the steps past Harper, her back straight and the clean line of her shoulders betraying that she belonged in the role she was currently filling: lady of Piperhall.

Harper followed, but before she passed through the double doors and into the spectacular foyer with its sweeping staircase and glittering chandelier, she shoved everything that had come before—Sawyer, her race out of Minneapolis, the humbling journey to Blackhawk—into some cobwebbed corner of her mind. Then she unzipped the sweatshirt and tossed it out of the way. She tugged at the edges of her cocktail dress, hoping to erase some of the wrinkles from her long trek and grateful that she'd at least partially fit in. Finally, she smoothed her hair with her hands and tucked it behind her ears in an effort to pull off the same polished look as Adri. Of course, she knew nothing could quite round off the ragged edges, but she had surprise on her side. Maybe people would see the whole picture and ignore the details.

Harper had been wrong about the glow of the estate and the event that was taking place there. It wasn't a party, not quite, and she knew that the second she stepped through the doors. There was a hush in the grand rooms, even though people milled about with glasses of wine. It struck Harper as wrong somehow that all these people were here supposedly to mourn Victoria, but as long as Harper had known David's mother, she had been a recluse. Or close enough. But she also knew from her time with The Five that this is how small towns did things. They were all interconnected, even if the connections were tenuous at best.

Nobody paid Adri and Harper much mind as they wove through the wide hallway from the entrance to the back of the house. There was no music playing, not much noise at all except for the quiet murmur of halting conversation. People were starting to leave, and when they saw Adri they reached out to squeeze her arm and assure her that the service had been lovely. Absolutely perfect. Adri smiled and thanked them, but she was a woman on a mission and she extracted herself from what could have been quicksand conversations with admirable grace.

The main living space of the grand house had been transformed into a chapel, and there were white chairs set up in narrow rows. A podium stood at the front, and there were vases of calla lilies everywhere. Harper thought it looked more like a wedding than a funeral service, but she held her tongue. Perhaps Adri had been working with a very specific set of instructions.

This part of the house was mostly empty, but clustered in the kitchen behind the expansive marble countertop Harper saw a trio of men, their heads tipped together in quiet conversation. She didn't have to study them to confirm what her heart knew in a glance: Sam, Jackson, Will.

Harper didn't mean to thrill at the sight of them, but goose bumps rose along the curve of her spine. She had loved Sam like a father, Jackson like a brother.

And Will.

The truth was, Harper couldn't even begin to grasp what she felt for Will. They had been friends, best friends, just like the rest of them. And if Harper had been in love with anyone, it had been David. Always David. But there had been times when she felt Will's attention like a fingertip brush against her shoulder. It was faint, undemanding, and she had never experienced anything like that before. Everything with Harper was all or nothing, a passionate free fall that made her feel vibrant, alive. Will was a whisper. And she hadn't been listening hard enough to hear what he had to say. But that didn't stop her from wondering. All these years later, wondering.

The men looked up when Adri clicked her way into the room, and what happened after that was a whirlwind that Harper couldn't really even begin to describe. There was a shout, a scattering of words that evidenced their shock. And then she was in the midst of them all. Enveloped in hugs that lifted her right off of her bare feet. Someone even spun her around. She wasn't sure who.

A glass of white wine was thrust into her hand, and there was a string of merry toasts, all of which seemed mildly out of place with the memorial chairs still set up behind them and the mourners in the library. But Harper sipped and laughed along with them, and when Will swiped his thumb across her cheek, Harper was surprised to realize that she was crying.

"I can't believe you're here," he said, grinning at her with a joy so pure it almost took her breath away. "Seriously, what are you doing here?"

"Adri emailed me," Harper said, trying to stagger her way back to the nonchalance of the image she was trying to portray. "I had to come."

"But . . ." Sam looked between Adri and Harper. "But you're too late," he said. "Adri is going back to Africa on Monday."

"Africa?" Harper exclaimed.

But Adri was already shaking her head. "Not yet," she said. "I can't go back now."

～

17

When Harper woke in the morning, Beckett was standing next to her bed, his graying muzzle resting on the faded quilt, his eyes trained on her face. It would have scared Harper, but for the fact that there wasn't an ounce of malice in the dog. The second she saw him, she felt comfort like a balm.

"Well, look at you," she said, reaching out a hand to tousle his ears. "Good morning, gorgeous." It had been so long since she had seen him, she could hardly believe he was still alive. Of course, he must have been around when they returned to Maple Acres the night before, but she barely remembered a moment past the toasts and champagne. Exhaustion had hit her hard, and Harper feared that she had let her careful facade crumble a little. Will had slipped an arm around her waist as they headed toward the car, and she knew it was out of necessity, not affection. She had been teetering.

"Have you been here all night?" Harper pushed herself up on her elbow and gave Beckett a one-armed hug. He seemed pleased, and, backing away, turned a few circles before settling down on the rug beside the bed. "It's morning," she chided. "Shouldn't you be waking up instead of getting ready for a nap?" Harper squinted at the alarm clock on the nightstand. She had never needed glasses, but in the last several months she had started to wonder if she needed them. The fuzzy numbers seemed affirmation of her poor eyesight. Ten after eleven? It couldn't be. Harper leaned closer. It was.

"Shit," she breathed, struggling out from under the sheets. They were tangled around her legs and the quilt had slipped halfway off the bed. It must have been a wild night. Not that Harper could recall any of her restless dreams. She never did.

Finally free, Harper scrambled to the small closet in the spare room. Back in the day, she had kept a change of clothes there. Not that she stayed at Maple Acres very often. A handful of times. Maybe more. But it felt like a second home to Harper all the same. Definitely more of a home than the apartment that she had shared with her parents in DC.

Unfortunately, the closet was empty save a handful of old winter coats and a zipped garment bag. Putting her hands on her hips, Harper spun to survey the room and spied a small bundle on the chair next to the bureau. Adri must have snuck in at some point and put it there—a thick sweater and a white cotton skirt with a wide elastic waistband. Harper lifted the pile and discovered also a pair of underwear and a lightweight, wireless bra, a cross between a sports bra and a halfcami. Adri must have scrounged for items that would fit her. The two women were so far from the same size, it must have been a difficult task. But the clothes were certainly better than nothing, and Harper was grateful for the mismatched outfit as she slipped on the skirt and tugged the sweater over her head. Her cocktail dress would have been absurdly inappropriate.

Catching a glimpse of herself in the bureau mirror, Harper stopped. The outfit wasn't her style—wasn't any style, to be honest—but she wasn't sure what her style was anymore. Sawyer had been dressing her for so long, Harper didn't really even know what she would pick out if given the chance. The skirt was pretty. Full and soft. Just a little short because her legs were so long. And the sweater was a well-worn cable knit, old enough to be comfy without being ratty. Harper decided she liked it, even if she felt a bit like she was stepping into a new identity.

Sawyer would hate it.

The thought made Harper go clammy all over. She put a hand to her throat as if to shove down the panic and tried to focus on the minutes before her, not the hours and days and weeks that she couldn't control. For now, she was okay. She was dressed and passably presentable—now that she was staring at her own reflection, she could see that her hair was washed and her face scrubbed clean of the makeup that had looked caked the night before. Harper remembered in flashbulb bursts: Adri handing her a towel and an oversized T-shirt to sleep in, and leading her to the bathroom. The hot water and soap that smelled tart like rhubarb. And then, the bed. Spare, but warm and empty. Harper loved sleeping alone.

Now the tiny room. Sunshine on the wall. The old dog. It was a little slice of heaven, and Harper had to blink hard against the tears suddenly threatening to spill down her cheeks. She felt like she had woken up in a whole new world.

The house wasn't big, and Harper strained to hear movement as she opened her bedroom door. Surely Will and Jackson were long gone—she knew somehow that they didn't live here, that Jackson was now married to Nora Engbers, even though she couldn't place the conversation—but Adri had told her that she'd be across the hall if Harper needed anything, and, of course, this was Sam's home. Her sister, her father. At least, that's how she thought of them. And while she thrilled at the knowledge that they were likely only a floor away, at the hope of spending time with them and tying together the threads of story that she was just beginning to unravel, Harper was petrified, too. What if they walked away? What if the place where she once tried to put down roots had eroded, and she had washed away from their lives as easily as a half-grown weed?

The very first time Harper ever stepped foot in little

Blackhawk, Iowa, was the day she arrived as an enrolled freshman at Anderson Thomas University. She hadn't gone on a campus visit or even popped in during a happy cross-country family trip. The truth was, her parents were too busy fighting with each other to invest much attention into their daughter's choice of school, and happy vacations were such a far-fetched concept in the Penny family narrative they seemed downright fanciful.

So Harper started her life in Iowa alone. It was a perfect late-summer day, and when she got out of the cab she had taken from the Omaha airport, she breathed deep and turned her face toward the sun. She was surrounded by redbrick buildings, some so old that the ivy twining up their sides boasted woody vines the size of her wrist. The campus was pedestrian-only, and lush green belts stretched between crisscrossing sidewalks that led to places Harper longed to go. It was simple and stately, not grand, but appealing in its own understated way. Harper was enthralled.

The website hadn't captured any of this. How the sun glinted off the clock tower or the way the breeze cooled the sweat on the back of her neck. If Harper had known, she would have come in July. June even. A year ago. This was nothing less than a haven.

Terms like *diversity*, *self-governance*, and *personal responsibility* had prompted Harper to apply to ATU in the first place, but if she was really honest with herself, there were only two things that contributed to her decision to go halfway across the country for college: proximity to the Iowa Writers' Workshop and distance from her parents. Any worries about the wisdom of her decision were erased completely when she arrived at ATU. She was exactly where she was supposed to be.

That knowledge released something inside her, and Harper found herself shouting. Whooping, really. She kicked off her sandals and did a cartwheel in the grass, her shirt pooling around her neck as the world spun upside down.

"I should charge you for the peek," Harper said later, laughing, as the cabdriver unloaded her suitcases and piled them on the lawn in front of the campus center.

He didn't respond, but put out his hand for the money and then left her standing in the middle of everything she owned in the world.

Harper's life fit into three oversize relics she had purchased from a rummage sale for two dollars apiece. It took Harper weeks to decide what to take with her in the suitcases. She wasn't the sentimental sort, and even if she had been, there was little in her life that she would have wanted to take with her. In the end, she separated her luggage into clothing categories: formal, informal, and miscellaneous. Makeup, curling and flat irons, hair dryers, and a collection of expensive, scented lotions rounded out her belongings, but at the last minute Harper threw in a plush, robin's egg–blue blanket that she took off the back of the couch in the apartment where she had grown up. She told herself she just needed something to keep the lotion bottles from cracking against one another.

But the blanket was the only memento she took with her.

Harper grew up in a tumultuous household. The Pennys fought all the time, and on one particular night when Harper was still young enough to play with dolls and wear Hello Kitty pajamas, it hadn't ended well. It never did, but this time a window was broken in the chaos. Julianna and Arthur never hit each other, but they liked to hit things and throw things and destroy things. And that night, when the glass shattered and the shock of it stunned them into silence, Arthur grabbed his coat and swept out the apartment door without a backward glance. Not to be outdone, Julianna raced toward the door herself.

Harper had been in the kitchen, sitting with her back against the cupboard and peeking from between her laced fingers as if she was a small child watching a horror film. And in a way, the situation was exactly that.

"No!" Harper shouted when Julianna reached for her own

coat. She hadn't meant to scream, but her voice echoed in the still apartment like a gunshot.

Julianna barely glanced toward the kitchen. "I'll be back."

"No! Don't go!" Harper peeled herself up from the ground and stumbled the short distance to her mother. She grabbed her by the coat sleeve. "Please, don't go!"

"I said I'd be back. You're old enough to take care of yourself, Harper." Julianna wouldn't look at her daughter, and in that moment Harper grasped that her parents wished they had never had her. Maybe she was an accident. Maybe she was an experiment. Or maybe she was the product of a love that had fizzled and burned out and extinguished their daughter with it. Of course, she couldn't articulate any of that until much later, but it was that moment, the distant look in her mother's eyes, that planted the seed which eventually grew into Harper's twisted understanding of herself.

"Please . . ." But her supplication was useless.

Julianna yanked her sleeve out of her daughter's grip and left.

Harper shook as she locked the apartment door behind them. It was well past her bedtime, but she couldn't stand the thought of going to back to her bedroom alone. So she wrapped herself in every blanket she could find and sat down on the couch across from the door to wait for their eventual return. Snow drifted in the broken window, collecting on the sill in little piles that began to melt and drip slush on the floor. Harper drew her neck deeper into the blankets and clutched the cordless phone in her hands, her index finger poised over the 9 so she could dial 911 in a heartbeat if she needed to. They were gone for hours, but Harper never once fell asleep, and she never cried.

She was eight years old.

Harper took the blanket with her not because she wanted to remember but because she had to remember. It was who she was. Forsaken. Harper Penny had to take care of herself.

What could she expect now, from the Vogt family? From these people who were almost strangers? If they had loved her once, it had been a long time ago. In a different life. Any romantic daydreams she had about loving reunions and intimate connections were exactly that: daydreams.

The kitchen was empty when Harper made it to the bottom of the stairs. But there were voices outside, and through the gingham curtains beyond the oval-shaped table, Harper could just make out the silhouettes of people on the porch. She took a deep breath and walked over to the door.

"Good morning!" Sam said brightly, before she had fully emerged into the cool September day.

"I'm not sure that it's morning anymore," Harper replied, working a glint into her eye even though she felt sheepish. She let the door fall shut behind her.

Sam consulted his watch. "You've got just over half an hour before we have to say good afternoon. You may certainly go back to bed if you'd like."

"I think I'll be okay." Harper forced herself to grin at him before glancing around the porch to find Adri. Her unfamiliar friend was sitting on a low stool in front of several boxes of dusty, red fruit, sorting them into a series of containers ranging from an old-fashioned turkey roaster to a five-gallon bucket. It seemed that her hands knew what to do without the added benefit of eyesight, for Adri continued to grade and arrange the pears as she stared openly at Harper.

"Good morning," Adri said after a few seconds. She plucked another flushed pear from the box, turned it over in her hands, and set it in a large, white colander. "Did you sleep okay?"

"Like the dead." Harper smiled. "I always sleep well in that bed. It's good and firm." The comment came off cheeky and laced with innuendo, but she didn't mean it to. "What are you doing?" she asked, stupidly. It was obvious what Adri was doing.

"Sorting pears." Adri hovered a hand over each receptacle.

"The colander is for fresh eating, the turkey roaster for canning, and the bucket for Mr. McAlister's hogs."

"There's a lot in the bucket," Harper muttered.

"Dad forgot to spray." Adri gave her father a mild look. "There are a lot of worms in the Red Bartletts this year."

"I don't like chemicals."

"The spray is organic."

Suddenly, Sam threw up his arms. "Where are my manners? Have a seat, Harper." He offered her the rocking chair he'd been sitting on, and when she shook her head, he took her by the elbow and gently lowered her into it. "Are you a coffee drinker? I mean, you were, but now? Do you still like your coffee with cream and sugar?"

Harper nodded, completely charmed. "Yes. I can't believe you remembered."

"I can't believe you thought I'd forget." Sam backed toward the door, arms outstretched as if taking orders. "And something to eat? A slice of toast? A banana muffin or two? I could scramble you a couple fresh eggs."

"A pear," Harper demurred. "I would love one of your pears."

"Don't stop at one," Sam laughed, and he disappeared into the house.

A few beats later, Adri said, "He's giving us time alone." She was holding a pear in her hand, and after studying it from every possible angle, she lobbed it to Harper.

Harper caught it, just barely. She wasn't the athletic sort. And this strange, new Adri, this woman who was all clean lines and self-assurance, baffled Harper. But she just smiled and turned her eyes to the pear before she could blush or burst into tears or do something else mortifying. The pear was a masterpiece, all hues of pink and red. It was absolutely perfect. "Thanks," Harper said.

"There's more where that came from."

"And where did you come from?" Harper asked, trying to regain some of the confidence she was so good at faking. "We were going to ask each other twenty questions or something like that. Remember? Your dad said Africa?"

"Yup. I've been there since . . ." She didn't have to finish.

Since then. Or, almost.

"Wow," Harper mused. "Where? What exactly are you doing?"

Adri raised an eyebrow at Harper. "I'm a nurse."

"Well, I know that," Harper blurted out. She remembered all too well the late-night study sessions and pretest hysteria. Her own English classes were nothing compared to the rigors of the nursing program.

Harper took a bite of the pear. It was ripe and juicy. She wiped her chin with the back of her hand and was grateful that Adri had turned away for a moment to toss an empty cardboard box over the porch rail behind her.

"West Africa," Adri finally offered. And then it all tumbled out in a well-rehearsed monologue. "I'm the head nurse and medical care provider for a series of orphanages and churches. I hold monthly clinics and assist when emergencies arise. My home base is in the city, but I do a lot of traveling. I live in the bush a good portion of the year."

It was almost inconceivable. Adri had wanted to travel, but David wasn't the backpack Europe type of guy, and he certainly wasn't into roughing it. The way Adri made it sound, she lived off the edge of the map, and Harper had a hard time reconciling the girl she had known with the woman who sat before her. The Adri she knew—the Adri who loved David and who was poised to be the perfect Galloway—would never live in the bush. Whatever that meant. Realizing that the silence had dragged on a bit too long, Harper made herself say, "That sounds really exciting." And when Adri didn't seem prepared to offer more, she asked, "How many people work with you?"

"One."

"One?" Harper exclaimed around the pear she was chewing. "Sounds like a big job for two people."

"I guess it is."

Harper tried to understand why Adri was being so short, why she was more or less playing hard to get, when she was the one who had sent the email in the first place and set off the chain of events that included her quite literally running for her life. Harper experienced a quick, characteristic flare of anger, and nursed it until she found herself on familiar ground. She had woken up feeling off-kilter, but frustration helped. It was much easier to be proud when she had a chip on her shoulder.

"I guess you're a regular Mother Teresa," Harper said, pushing herself up from the rocking chair and going to lean on the porch railing. Adri would have to turn to see her now, and even if she did, Harper's back would be to her.

"Don't be like that." Adri gave a heavy sigh. "I'm sorry I'm making this harder than it needs to be. I just . . . I don't know how to act." Harper glanced over her shoulder and caught a glimpse of the old Adri. For just a moment she shone through, wide-eyed and curious, eager to please. But there was a wisdom in her eyes that made her look so much older than she was. Adri was right. This whole thing was way harder than Harper had imagined it would be.

Harper looked away. She wanted to be standoffish, but she couldn't. It had been too long. She hadn't known how she would feel about her former best friend, but seeing her face-to-face, hearing her voice even though she was acting like a jerk, was enough to put Harper over the edge. She still loved Adri as if she was bound to her by an unbreakable covenant. And in a way, Harper supposed, she was.

"I don't know how to act either," she said, not turning around. "This isn't quite how I thought it would be."

"What did you expect?" Adri asked.

"I don't know. More hugging?"

"We were never huggers." Adri rose and came to stand beside Harper. They both looked out over the farm, over the outbuildings and the pasture where Harper had caught her very first glimpse of Piperhall. Back then David had been nothing more than a dream, and there were many days afterward when Harper secretly wished he would have stayed that way. It was true that she sought him out. And, God help her, it was true that she loved him when it was the last thing that she ever should have done. But in moments of perceived clarity, times when she was just a shade from drunk, or maybe waking up in the morning, when her mind was as soft and malleable as clay, she realized that she had opened up Pandora's box. Meeting David had been the beginning of the end.

"This wasn't the way it was supposed to be," Harper said, more to herself than anything. But Adri was at her shoulder and she gave a dry, little laugh. She didn't sound bitter, just sad, and Harper had to stop herself from giving her old friend a one-armed hug. "So," she said, taking a tiny bite of the pear. "Africa. Nursing. Anything else new and noteworthy? Is there a who?"

Adri paused.

"Are you married?" Harper breathed. She hadn't thought to look for a ring. It hadn't crossed her mind to imagine that Adri might have found love again. Weren't they too broken for that?

"No," Adri said, a split second too late. Her tell was a quick drumming of her fingers, and she did that now, playing an imaginary piano on the porch railing.

"Liar." Harper hadn't meant to say it, but it slipped out before she could stop herself.

Adri looked at her full-on, and Harper found herself peering back, searching for the girl she had known, deep inside her friend's hazel eyes. She wasn't there, but Adri was the first to smile, and there was something hopeful in the slant of her pretty mouth. "I'm not in love with him," Adri said.

Harper's heart brimmed. "But you could be?"

"No, I don't think so. It's just . . ."

The possibility. Just the possibility of something more was enough to undo Harper, and she could see that Adri was the same sort of wistful. She loved it that they had something in common.

Adri shook her head. "Enough about me. Your turn. Where have you been? What have you been doing? Are you writing?"

Writing? Harper's appetite disappeared at the sudden reversal in conversation. She dropped the pear over the edge of the porch and watched it disappear, half-eaten, into the bushes. "No," she managed. "I'm not writing." Harper had almost forgotten that about herself, the volumes of poems, the raw explorations of her soul that compelled her to scrawl barely discernible hieroglyphics across a blank page. The way she could take a pen and make it bleed emotion she hadn't even known she felt. There was one poem that she had burned over a candle in their apartment sink because she couldn't discern who it was about: *I love you, and I hate you for obvious reasons.* It had been a very long time since she had picked up a pen.

"That's too bad." Adri ducked her head, admitted something with a shy smile. "I watched for you. Online, I mean. For a book contract or a volume of poetry. You never showed up."

Harper screwed up her mouth as if to say, "You're joking, right?" But Adri wasn't joking, and there was a time when Harper had longed for exactly that. Had believed it could be true.

"So, no writing. What have you been doing? Where have you been?"

These were questions Harper couldn't answer. So simple, and yet so very complicated. "Minneapolis," she said, as if it didn't matter at all. She stood up tall and stretched her arms up over her head, yawned to prove that she was bored with herself. There was no story here. "Lots of little jobs. I was a teacher's aide in an ESL classroom." True. "A secretary for about a day." Also true. "A clerk in a used bookstore." A lie, but a plausible one.

So many lies. And Adri believed them.

But there was something in the way Adri held herself that

made Harper wonder just how much she did believe. Maybe the years had stripped it all away. Maybe time had bent the edges of all the pretty little lies that Harper had hung. Maybe the truth was one small act of violence away. A plunge over the side into the gaping hole between them.

A fall headlong.

18

~

After the pears were sorted and Harper had chugged down not one but three cups of Sam's dark coffee, a sort of lull fell over the farm. It was Sunday, a fact that Harper had forgotten in the mayhem of the days leading up to her quaint breakfast on the porch, and a realization that made her feel downright terrible.

"I'm so sorry," she said to Sam. "I know that you like to attend church on Sunday mornings. I must have messed that all up."

"Nah," Sam said, waving her apology away. "I spent a lot of time in prayer this morning. I had to watch Adri climb the pear trees." He gave Harper a worried look and drew his finger across his throat to show her just how confident he was in Adri's tree-climbing abilities.

"Please," Adri scoffed. "I've been doing that since I was six."

"You've been getting stuck in them since you were six," Sam corrected.

"Whatever."

"Either way, I'm sorry for disrupting your routine." Harper's guilt would not be assuaged.

"Bah." Sam patted her on the arm. "Routines should be routinely disrupted. Keeps things interesting. But now, a little downtime before I have to milk this afternoon."

"Thank you," Harper said. "For everything." She caught herself a split second before she made a complete idiot of herself by reaching out to cup the softening curve of Sam's jaw. It was a startling impulse, but one championed by the deep and latent love she felt for the kind man before her. She forgot sometimes that he wasn't actually family. Harper tucked her hands behind her back and turned to Adri. "You?" she asked. "What are you up to?"

"I have to make a call," she said.

"Okay, I think I'll grab a book off your shelf and read for a bit, if you don't mind." It was the first thing that popped into Harper's mind, but she was surprised at how wonderful, how luxurious it sounded. A book. At her leisure. It was unheard of.

She followed Adri upstairs and closed herself in the bedroom across the hall. The little bookshelf was exactly where she knew it would be, and it still had the books Harper remembered: old Nancy Drew hardcovers, a few dime store paperbacks, and a collection of moldy classics that ranged from *The Swiss Family Robinson* to *Wuthering Heights*. She ran her fingers over the spines, but the choices overwhelmed her and she curled up on the bed instead.

Harper didn't mean to eavesdrop, but the farmhouse was small and she really couldn't help it that she overheard Adri on the phone with Caleb. Adri hadn't told Harper her coworker's name, or even that he was the second half of her medical missions duo, but it was easy enough to piece together from the few lines that filtered across the narrow hallway. Harper imagined Adri sitting cross-legged on her bed, tracing the neat stitches of the patchwork quilt back and forth, her fingertip a tiny train that couldn't jump the rails. Harper could picture her doing it, though the Adri she saw had skin so pale it was almost translucent, hair pulled back at the crown by a clip that was missing a rhinestone.

It was uncanny to hear Adri's voice after all this time, and even more incomprehensible to know that she loved the man on the other end of the line. And it wasn't David.

But maybe Harper was being melodramatic. She was prone to it, she knew, and she could be imagining the way Adri lengthened her words just a little, drawing them out as if she had to concentrate on each syllable or else they would tumble from her lips in a tangled thrill of emotion. Harper had seen Adri in love before. In fact, she had never known Adri not to be in love, and she caught the same lilt in her friend's voice now. It made Harper want to run across the hall and jump on the bed to ply Adri for details.

Of course, she didn't do that. She couldn't.

Harper crossed her arms behind her head and leaned back to stare at the ceiling. But only minutes later, a knock on her bedroom door startled her, and she sat upright so quickly she felt dizzy. "Come in," she called, much too loudly for the small space.

Adri opened the door a crack and considered Harper through a wedge that opened onto the hallway beyond. "I don't know how to ask this . . " she said, holding the edge of the door as if it were a lifeline.

"Ask away," Harper assured her, breathless.

"I mean, it's totally up to you."

"Okay."

"And I don't want you to think that I have any expectations."

"But?"

"But . . ." Adri paused. "How long do you plan to stay?"

Harper almost laughed. Adri's buildup had prepared her for a much more weighty question. But then, just as quickly as she relaxed, a tide of fear swept over her and she realized that it was one of the most baffling questions Adri could possibly have posed. Harper had no idea how long she planned to stay. Or where she would go when she left. And no idea whether she would leave on her own two feet, or if Sawyer would come knocking one day and drag her back.

Kicking and screaming, she decided, turning aside the fear with fury. She was no fool. She knew all about Stockholm syndrome and how some hostages defended their captors. But she felt no love for Sawyer, no bond that lashed her to him in a mangled parody of affection. At least, not anymore. Their relationship had been based on practicality. And exploitation. But she had exploited him, too. Harper had wanted to be punished, and Sawyer was more than willing to take advantage of that.

Adri was giving her a quizzical look, and Harper forced herself to don a casual smile. "I don't know," she said. "How long are you staying here?"

Sighing, Adri pushed the door open a little farther and leaned against the frame. "I don't know. The annual board trip is coming up, and Caleb is scheduled to fly home while the team is in-country. We have the week off."

"Caleb?" Harper asked, feigning ignorance.

"The guy I work with. He told me to stay put. Said he's coming to see me."

"Here?" Harper didn't have to fake the surprise in her voice.

"It's stupid"—Adri shook her head—"I told him not to come. He won't come. But I don't know when I'm going back." There was something guarded in her eyes, and Harper realized that she wasn't the only one keeping secrets. "We have a lot to talk about," Adri finally said.

Harper bit her lip. "Yeah. I suppose we do."

"But that's not why I'm asking." Adri seemed to get a grip on herself. She angled the cordless phone at Harper and said, "If you're going to stick around, we should get you some clothes. There's not much open in Blackhawk on Sunday, but there's a Goodwill in Fairfield. I mean, it's Goodwill, but . . ."

"As if I could forget our Goodwill." Harper pushed herself off the bed, feigning enthusiasm. "Come on, Adri. You know me."

It was the only place they shopped in college, and Harper had been known for her fabulous finds on the used racks. Dresses that somehow seemed tailored to fit her, relics from the seventies, the perfect mix of hipster and sexy, and once, a pleather jacket that was the very definition of cool. But that was so long ago. Harper watched as Adri's eyes flicked to the dress that she had abandoned in a pile at the foot of her bed. Adri's gaze wasn't accusatory, but it was almost painfully obvious that the cocktail dress hadn't come from a secondhand store. Far from it.

"We have the most amazing thrift store north of the city," Harper said. It wasn't a lie, though she hadn't been there in years. "You wouldn't believe the things that rich people are happy to part with."

Adri shrugged as if it didn't matter. Then she turned from the room and started down the stairs. Harper hurried to follow.

In the kitchen, Adri dropped the cordless phone into its cradle on the counter. Sitting directly beside it was the mustard-yellow rotary that Harper remembered from their college days. It had been unhooked from the wall, and the phone cable from the cordless had been plugged in its place. Harper almost asked about it, but decided for once to hold her tongue.

The only shoes they found to fit Harper were a pair of old flip-flops that had mysteriously appeared in the deacon's bench in the mudroom. Harper's feet were almost embarrassingly large next to Adri's tiny ones, and she had been about to slip on a pair of Sam's work boots when she spied the edge of a neon-green sandal that looked like it might work. They had to dig through a couple dozen mismatched pairs to find the flip-flop's mate, but when Harper emerged from the box triumphant, she was glad she had persisted. The sandals looked silly with her skirt and sweater, but they fit. They were better than the alternative.

"Where in the world did these come from?" Harper asked, admiring her new shoes.

"I have absolutely no idea."

Harper spent the next half hour feeling like she was watching her life in slow motion. Whether she wanted to or not, she was forced to confront every detail as it crept past at a pace so slow and unhurried that it was almost painful. There was Betty, and their fingernail-polish signatures on the door. Then the long road that wound from Maple Acres to town—a route she had taken more often than not with her head hanging out the window and the wind whipping her hair into unmanageable knots. Adri had combed them out with detangling spray that smelled of watermelons. Even Blackhawk itself was a trip down memory lane, though Adri avoided campus. There was the gas station where they used to stop for Slurpees. Or, rather, the cheap knock-off of Slurpees that the family-owned gas station sold. Harper always got blue. As if blue was a flavor.

And here was the church where Harper had attended services with the Vogt family every once in a while. At first she thought it wasn't really her thing, religion. Her parents had never been religious, and had even dismissed people who clung to belief like a child clutching a well-worn blanket. But Harper was soothed by the feeling in the room. She stilled when the pastor spoke, mellow and warm when she had expected hellfire and brimstone. God himself seemed to live in the spaces between people, in the moments when someone held a door open for her or shared a smile that was too real to be forced.

Harper would never have admitted it to Julianna or Arthur, but she was glad for the opportunity to hedge her bets. What harm could it possibly do if she prayed now and then? At best, the God of the universe heard. At worst, she was whispering sweet nothings to the air, something she often did anyway. Harper unabashedly talked to herself.

By the time Adri pulled into the parking lot at the Goodwill in Fairfield, Harper was buried beneath an avalanche of memories that had taken her completely by surprise. A small part of her understood that she should be chattering away, making conversation a mile a minute like the girl that Adri knew, but she couldn't bring herself to do it. Thankfully, Adri didn't seem to be much in the mood for small talk, either, and she waited for Harper to get out of the car before opening her own door.

They followed each other around the crowded store, wandering from aisle to aisle and amassing a cockeyed collection of garments that Adri slung over her arm. Harper was astonished to realize that she didn't really know her own size anymore. Six? Eight? Four? She grabbed things she liked, or thought she liked, and when she finally began to try on clothes in the dressing room, she hardly knew how to judge what she had picked.

"Are you finding anything?" Adri asked.

Harper put her hand on the door of the dressing room. Almost opened it. But what was she supposed to do? Parade around in front of Adri like the runway model she used to pretend to be? They had tried on formal gowns and stomped to the front of the store as if it was their stage. They had laughed and let spaghetti straps slip off their shoulders and fantasized that they were breathtaking, the most beautiful women alive.

"I am," Harper called through the door instead. "I'm finding a few things."

She picked out two pairs of nondescript jeans and some camouflage cargo pants that would have sent Sawyer into convulsions. A handful of long-sleeved T-shirts, a thick sweatshirt, and a couple of sweaters rounded out her purchases. Harper knew they weren't fashionable, not even close, but she couldn't bear the thought of trying to put together some sort of trendy outfit. The truth was, she wanted to wrap herself in a thick blanket and wear nothing but flannel for weeks. The small collection that she had picked out was the best she could do.

"Shoes," Adri reminded her as she was about to pile her purchases on the counter.

Harper lucked into a pair of faded red Chucks and added them to the stack. Socks and underwear would have to come from Walmart.

Feeling pretty confident about her purchases, Harper smiled when the clerk told her she owed thirty-two dollars and forty-seven cents. Such a trivial amount. She had just bought the beginnings of a wardrobe for less than the price of the manicure that Sawyer insisted she have every week.

But the clerk was looking at her expectantly, and Harper blanched as she understood why.

She didn't have a purse. No cash, no credit or debit card. The Bridge had given her a crisp twenty-dollar bill, but Harper couldn't even think of where that was right now. It had probably fluttered to the floor of Carol's car when she fell asleep.

Harper didn't know where to turn, or what to say. But Adri was already pulling her wallet out of her purse.

"I've got this," she said. There wasn't an ounce of condemnation in her voice, and while the clerk counted out change from the till, Adri smiled and made conversation as if she had planned to pay all along.

"You didn't have to do that," Harper said when they were in the car. Her shame was using up the air between them. "I misplaced my purse. I could have called my credit card company."

She didn't have a credit card company. Sawyer had long ago combined their earnings, or rather, pocketed hers so that he could better "support her," as he liked to say. Harper hadn't collected a paycheck in years. It chilled her to realize that she didn't have a penny to her name.

Adri wasn't buying it. She sat still for a few moments in the driver's seat, her right hand on the keys and her left hand on the steering wheel. Then she took a deep breath and turned to face Harper.

"I know it's been a while," she said, "and I know that there is a lifetime between us. But you don't have to lie to me like that. I won't presume to know where you came from, or what you've been doing for the last five years, but this has to stop."

"What has to stop?" Harper whispered.

"This lying. The way we dance around one another but never really touch." Adri's voice broke over a sob, but she pressed her hand to her mouth and held it in. "Harper," she said, and it was a plea, "look at us. What are we doing? Who are we?"

Harper tasted the words on her tongue. She tried. For the span of a few ragged heartbeats, she tried.

She wanted to tell Adri about the long string of dead-end jobs. The way she once attempted to return home, only to find that there was no home for her to return to. Julianna and Arthur were in the midst of their sticky divorce, and Julianna's lover made her new apartment an impossible place to be. Harper survived for a couple of years living from paycheck to paycheck and renting apartments that could only be described as the nastiest of tenements. But when Sawyer selected her from across a crowded bar, joked that he was making her an indecent proposal, a respite with a man like him sounded like a break. A place to rest her head for a while.

Yet how could she possibly begin to accurately describe her life to Adrienne? To the girl who had become the next Mother Teresa?

I've done unimaginable things. Harper tried to envision herself saying the words. If you google Stacey Hawk, you'll find me. She shuddered at the very thought of her pseudonym, the name that Sawyer called her when he photographed her in ways that made her want to curl up in a corner and die.

Harper knew that leaving him was just the beginning. Not the end.

Adri's cheeks were damp. She looked so sweet and trusting and innocent, Harper couldn't bring herself to say the words. What would Adri do if she knew the truth? Not just the truth about Sawyer and the life that Harper had led in the past few nightmarish years, but everything that came before?

What would Adri do if she knew about David?

"I'm Harper Marie Penny," Harper said. It was the only thing she could say. She took Adri's hand in her own, pressed it between her palms as if she could love the hurt out of her very skin. "You're Adrienne Claire Vogt. We were best friends once."

"More than that."

"Yeah," Harper nodded. "More than that."

"And it got all messed up."

"Life is messy," Harper agreed.

"And now . . . ?"

"Now what?" Harper urged, because she was sick just wondering what came next. Where were they supposed to go from here?

Adri took a shaky breath. "I'm going to tell you the truth. I want you to do the same."

"Okay," Harper lied.

"Me first." Adri pulled her hand away from Harper and brushed the tears from her face. She turned the car on and threw it into reverse.

"Where are we going?"

Adri's mouth was a slim, wavering line. "I have to show you something."

～

19

Adri took Harper to Piperhall and stepped out of the car with her jaw set. Harper didn't ask, she just followed.

They mounted the stairs to the loggia, but instead of taking Harper into the mansion, Adri turned to lean against the railing that overlooked the circular drive. They were almost an entire story off the ground, and from this vantage point they could see much of the estate. The stable cut a red slash against a bank of trees to their right, and the pasture unfolded beyond that. If she turned, Harper could just make out the edge of the so-called carriage house, its white paint starting to peel after too many years of sun and wind and snow. The rest of the grounds had been recently manicured, and though the lawns were washed-out green and the leaves were starting to brown at the edges, the view was impressive. Harper had always loved it here.

The estate felt safe. Permanent somehow. And David himself, though unruly and spoiled and proud, had been the embodiment of everything that was dependable and sure. One day, he would have become *the* Galloway of the Galloway fortune, and he would never have left. Harper had longed for that sort of security. In many ways, she still did.

David was a gift from Harper to Adri. At least, he was supposed to be.

Harper had fallen into friendship headlong, and she was dizzy with the possibility that someone—three someones, in fact—could like her for who she was instead of who she had for so long pretended to be. It was a drug of sorts, the sweetest kind of intoxication, and she wanted desperately to thank Adri for the simple act of being a friend. It was pathetic, Harper knew that, and she would never go so far as to admit such nonsense to anyone. But she had seen light in Adri's eyes at the mention of David Galloway, and she decided that if she could do anything to make that sparkle stay, she would.

It wasn't hard to figure out who David Galloway was. He was exactly the person Harper would have sought out if she hadn't bumped into Adri first. And though Harper intended him for Adri, she reveled in the serendipity of the chance to have it both ways: a true friend and a trophy.

Harper suspected that a man like David Galloway wouldn't have many, if any, real friends of his own, and when she sought him out after class in the middle of a routine Monday morning, she was putting that theory to the test.

David was in Harper's Western Civilization class. And though there were more than a hundred students in their block, she'd singled David out on almost the very first day. She hadn't yet managed to snag a seat near him, but that morning, she slipped out early and positioned herself next to the drinking fountain. David always stopped for a drink. It looked innocent enough, but Harper had pulled that sort of move too many times herself to see it for anything other than what it was: an out. David left Western Civ with a small flock of people around him. But when he paused to drink, they all stood around awkwardly for a second or two before realizing how desperate they looked and drifting away.

Harper had spent most of the class practicing and discarding various introductions. She flirted with cute and sexy, available and coy, but when David finally straightened up from the fountain, she decided to just stick out her hand. "I'm Harper," she said. And because she oozed nonchalance, or because she was wearing a pair of cutoffs with one-inch inseams, David smiled and took her hand.

He was attractive from a distance, but he was even better close up. Broad-shouldered and handsome in a classic, well-bred way, David Galloway looked like he had just stepped off the set of a Ralph Lauren photo shoot. His hair was longish but expertly cut, and he held an expensive pair of aviators loosely in his hand. The cuffs of his shirt were rolled to reveal tan forearms, and the hem was wrinkled, half untucked. He even smelled amazing. Best of all, he had a dimple in his left cheek when he smiled at her. The most perfect imperfection Harper had ever seen. David was a stranger, but Harper couldn't shake the feeling that she knew him. Surely they had met before and this was a reunion of sorts. Surely she could throw her arms around him and laugh like he was a sight for sore eyes.

"Do I know you?" David asked after Harper had stared for just a moment too long. He was smirking a bit, enjoying the fact that she was tongue-tied.

But Harper was no simpering idiot. "You should," she said, shifting her weight, and the full glare of her attention, away from him. She swept long, blond hair off her shoulder, revealing what she considered one of her very best features: the long swath of honey-colored skin from her neck to the stylishly frayed top of her low-cut shirt.

It was David's turn to stare. "Excuse me?"

"I can stop them from harassing you."

"Who?" He glanced around as if Harper saw something he didn't. Students were filtering through the hall, moving from one class to the next, or heading out the wide, glass doors toward the campus center or their dorm rooms. Most passed Harper and David without notice, but there were a pair of girls near a bulletin board who watched them with hasty, furtive glances. When David caught sight of them he sighed.

Harper smiled sympathetically but didn't say anything.

"How can you stop them?" David folded his arms across his chest and gave her a skeptical look. "You offering to be my bodyguard?"

Harper laughed, a low, rich sound in the back of her throat, and took a step toward David. "You don't need a bodyguard," she murmured when there was only a thin layer of air between them. She could feel the warmth of his body. The scent of cologne mingled with something that was distinctly David made her momentarily dizzy.

But this was for Adri, Harper reminded herself with a jolt of conscience. She was orchestrating a meeting—maybe more?—for the girl who melted a little at the sound of his name. Harper sucked a breath of air, got hold of herself, then leaned in further still and whispered in David's ear: "Follow me."

He did. Close behind, his hand hovering just shy of the small of her back. Anyone who watched them would assume they were a couple, even though David never touched her. It was the simplest of ruses, but Harper guessed it would be effective enough to sprinkle the first few rumors around campus that David Galloway was taken. And by Harper Penny. She already knew that no one would mess with her.

The rest was simple. They talked like old friends, and in many ways they were. Kindred spirits at least, the kind of people set apart by looks and personality and the fickle hand of fate that had planted them in circumstances that forced them to grow differently than everyone else. They were orchids in a sea of daisies, and not at all afraid to admit it.

In the beginning, Harper wondered if David kept coming around in spite of Adri, Will, and Jackson rather than because of them. But affection is sometimes a slow boil, and by the time she nicknamed their little group The Five, she believed that David was as invested as she was. They were, against all odds, friends.

And Harper loved it all.

Her people. Maple Acres. The way that she felt for the first time in her life like she belonged inside her own skin.

Piperhall. Especially Piperhall. Harper never wanted to leave.

Once, a couple of years after they became friends, Harper had almost told David as much. "I love it here," she whispered. It was a Sunday night and they should have been heading back to campus, but it wasn't far and they couldn't tear themselves away from the stars. They had gone riding that afternoon, even Harper, and after the horses had been brushed and put to pasture, they wandered the grounds because the reality of the week ahead felt like too much to bear. Will and Adri were arguing about something in the sort of fond, sibling way that made Harper long for a brother, and Jackson was hand in hand with Nora, a new girlfriend who didn't quite fit. Harper couldn't help resenting her. When Nora was around, they were quick to pair up, but when it was just the five of them, they were a unit. A fist clenched tight.

Harper walked beside David, the others a few steps ahead as they wandered toward the orchard and the last of the autumn apples. Adri had gotten it in her head to make a pie. As if Adri had time to bake anything.

"Everyone loves it here," David responded belatedly. He sounded bored, and Harper jerked her head to study his profile in the moonlight. She hadn't realized that he had heard her quiet reflection. "You really should stick around some summer instead of going back east to work in that coffee shop. You could come to the Piperhall summer picnic and watch the gawkers. It's quite entertaining."

"I thought your mother stopped doing that."

"I'd reinvent it for you." David had a way of making Harper feel like she was the only person in the world during those rare moments. She slowed a bit to let the others pull even farther ahead, and stared up at the man she pretended not to love. Harper knew her charade was thin, but it didn't seem to matter much. Everyone loved David. Or envied him, longed to be with him, longed to be him. He was inescapable.

"How generous of you." Harper couldn't smooth the lust

from her voice, and she sounded warm and inviting, even in her own ears. "But I'm afraid if I stay, I may never leave."

David stopped and turned to her. They were close, closer than Harper had realized as they walked shoulder to shoulder in the near-dark. Because everyone else was ahead of them, and because of the gauzy veil of twilight, it felt for a moment like they were utterly alone. Harper had held David at bay, had pressed him away by the predictable standard of her own flirtatiousness. How was he, or anyone, to know where she had pinned her heart? Harper liked it that way. But as he stood over her, his head inclined as if he might bend a little more and kiss her, she found herself faint with desire.

"Never leave?" David repeated. And then he did the impossible. He lifted a finger and traced a line from the arch of her forehead over her upturned nose and stopped against the fullness of her lips. He parted them slightly.

Harper tried not to gasp when David leaned in a little, his fingertip still against her mouth. But he didn't kiss her. Instead, he brushed past her mouth and whispered in her ear, "I guess I'd have to redo the servants' quarters, wouldn't I?"

It was exactly the sort of thing David would say, and Harper should have expected as much. But his words stabbed all the same. Harper might have fallen to pieces, but she wouldn't let him have the satisfaction. Steeling herself against the ache in her chest, she laughed and tickled his ear with her whisper, "I'd own the place in a year, Mr. Galloway. They'd have to call it Harperhall."

David either didn't realize that he had hurt her or didn't care.

Suddenly Harper was aware of Adri's eyes on her. She had been silent, lost in her own thoughts for far too long. "Piperhall is gorgeous," she managed. "It always has been."

"It's mine," Adri said.

Harper's throat squeezed shut. "What?" Realizing that she probably sounded like she was jealous or upset or worse, she swallowed and tried again. "Victoria left you the estate?"

"Yup. I'm the executor of her will and the new owner of the Galloway mansion. Lock, stock, and barrel."

"Well"—Harper forced herself to smile—"Victoria loved you very much."

Adri snorted. "I don't think she would have said that, exactly. But I would have been her only family, had David and I married. Based on what I've learned about her these last few days, that meant something to her."

"Of course it did."

"If Victoria had known what I did to David, that I was responsible for her son's death, I don't think she would have left all of this to me."

"Don't be ridiculous." Harper grabbed Adri's hand and held it tight. "It was an accident."

"I know, but—"

"But nothing," Harper interrupted. "If anyone is to blame, it's me. If I recall correctly, and I do, the backpacking trip was my idea. I booked the flights and I convinced everyone to go."

"Yes, but—"

"I talked him into cliff jumping."

It was all too much and too soon. A reminder of what had happened and how. Of blood in the water and his vacant, unseeing eyes. Adri and Harper were standing beneath the shadow of the Galloway mansion, but suddenly they could both smell the earthy, elemental tang of mountain and river and rain forest. Adri's hand trembled in Harper's tight grip.

"I don't want to talk about this," Harper whispered. It was a black hole. It was just the beginning. She couldn't stand the thought of tipping over the edge and into the bottomless void.

"I do want to talk about this. You're the only person I can talk to." Adri sounded desperate. "Please, Harper, let me talk about this . . ."

The sound of an engine on the long drive to the mansion made them both look up, and within seconds a truck came into view.

"Will," Adri said, sounding defeated.

They watched as he pulled up next to Betty and cut the engine. He emerged wearing a pair of jeans and a heather-gray T-shirt that hugged his chest appealingly. When he caught sight of the girls between the arches of the loggia he gave a cheerful wave. Harper waved back.

"Hey!" Will called. He stood for a moment beneath them, hands on his hips. "I feel like I should quote something. Isn't there a balcony scene in *Romeo and Juliet*? 'But, soft! What light through yonder window breaks?' "

"There's no window," Adri said. "And no light." She was right. The sun had sunk behind a bank of thick clouds and the world was filled with the slanting shadows of an early dusk. Adri rubbed her face with her hands for a moment, and then turned to Harper. "We're not finished," she whispered, only for Harper's ears.

"I know," Harper said.

And then Will was taking the steps two at a time, apparently eager to reach them. When he got to the top of the stairs, he jogged the last few feet and caught Harper in one arm and Adri in the other. Pulling them close, he said, "It's good to hug my girls again. Are you both really here?"

He sounded so happy, Harper couldn't help but grin. She let her head fall onto his chest, but when she caught sight of Adri's grim look, she straightened up and backed away.

"I suppose we are," Harper said. "Though I can't imagine why you seem so delighted. We were nothing but trouble."

"*You* were nothing but trouble," Will assured her. He still had Adri under one arm and couldn't see the serious furrow in her brow. "Adri here has always been a good girl. Haven't you, Adrienne?"

She extricated herself from his one-armed embrace and stood back to give him a halfhearted smile. It was a weak attempt, and Harper could see that Will finally felt the tension between them.

"Sorry," he said, looking between Harper and Adri. "I didn't mean to interrupt anything."

"You're not," Adri assured him. She didn't sound very convinced. "How did you find us?"

"I went to the farm, and when you weren't there, I guessed." Will shrugged. "It's not like there are a million places you could be."

"Harper and I are just catching up," Adri said.

"That's what I was hoping to do." Will ducked his head almost shyly. "I thought maybe I could talk you ladies into a ride."

"A ride?" Harper honestly had no idea what he was talking about.

"On horseback?" Will's smirk was good-natured. "Remember when we used to do that?"

Harper laughed. "Oh, no. No way. I haven't been on a horse in more years than I care to count. And I didn't particularly like it when I did ride."

"You're joking." Will seemed genuinely surprised. "We used to love riding together."

"I tolerated it," Harper admitted.

"I guess you were a good actor." Will said, smiling but clearly disappointed.

"I'm tired," Adri said finally. "I'm going to head back to the farm." She hooked her thumb over her shoulder in the general direction of Maple Acres, and fixed Harper with a look that indicated she hoped Harper would follow. But Harper didn't want to continue the conversation they had begun, so she pretended not to notice.

"No to the ride," she told Will. "But I'd love to take a walk. You up for it?"

"Sounds great." Will smiled. "Sure you don't want to join us, Adri?"

"Yes." She was already on her way to the stairs. "Have fun," she called over her shoulder, but her voice caught at the end.

Harper and Will headed down the estate drive, following the

dissipating cloud of dust that Adri kicked up on her departure. The old riding trail seemed like the most obvious choice for their path, and Harper was glad that she had changed into a pair of jeans in the car between Fairfield and Blackhawk and slid her feet into the Chucks. She wasn't wearing socks, but the shoes were soft and worn and she didn't think it would be a problem. The warm sweater Adri had loaned her would be perfect for an early-evening hike.

Will didn't appear anxious to break the ice or start in on the catching up that brought him to the estate in the first place. Harper didn't care. She was content to walk and listen to the rustle of the breeze lifting dry leaves from a million crooked branches.

It struck Harper as they walked that she had rarely, if ever, been alone with Will. There had never been time or reason to. Of course, they had all suffered their fair share of crushes on one another, and friendships blossomed and deepened, then paled and ran shallow as the seasons of their college days changed. When Adri was busy with classes, it was easy for Harper to spend more time with the guys, especially David. And while Jackson was the ubiquitous calm of the group, the tranquil center, Will was fun-loving and perpetually ready for anything. It always seemed that there was someone around to match her mood. But Harper had sometimes avoided Will, because she felt that he watched her just a little too intently. Every once in a while she caught a longing in his gaze that made her feel breathless and almost timid. But he was Will. Her best friend's brother. The russet-haired boy-next-door who didn't make her fingertips tingle the way David always did.

And Will was unsettled. He played basketball for a year, then soccer the following. He quit both. Halfway through his freshman year he changed his major from business to preveterinary. Halfway through his sophomore year he changed it back. When he finally graduated, it was with an agribusiness degree, something that he assured her married his two loves, but she didn't really understand what he hoped to do with his diploma. Take over his dad's dairy, she supposed.

Apparently even that wasn't quite right. Adri had told Harper that Will wasn't a farmer. He was a general contractor who built beautiful homes and remodeled old ones. Though Harper couldn't claim to know him anymore, the idea that Will spent his time building things and fixing things felt right to Harper. She told him so.

"Thanks," he said, giving her a sidelong glance. "I'm assuming that was a compliment."

Harper laughed. "A bad one, but yes. It feels right somehow that you're doing what you're doing."

"Brothers Construction has been a good fit," he agreed. "Jackson and I make a good team. He's the brains, I'm the brawn. Or something like that."

"Brothers?"

"Come on, Harper." Will bumped her with his elbow. "Jackson and I are practically twins. And besides, weren't we all a bunch of rowdy siblings back in college?"

"Something like that," she said, borrowing his phrase.

"Jackson and I are like you and Adri."

Harper didn't bother correcting his use of the present tense. She and Adri were about as far apart as two people could possibly be. And while it seemed like Adri wanted to change that, to dredge up past events and uncover the truth behind the lives they now led, Harper was eager to hold her old friend at a safe distance. There was simply too much at stake. So she said, "What about David? Where did he fit into the mix?"

The second the pair of questions were out of her mouth, she realized that she never should have uttered them at all. A pall fell over the path before them, and though it was likely only the dimming shadows of the now ominous clouds, the woods suddenly felt haunted.

Where had David fit? He hadn't. It was as simple as that.

"So," Will said, trying to steer the conversation back onto more solid ground. "What have you been up to these days?"

Harper gave him the same story that she had told Adri—a string of jobs, a crap apartment, nothing to write home about—but her mind was elsewhere. It was on David and where he had fit. How he had played into the five points of the star that had been their impossible, entwined group.

"Are you okay?"

Harper had stopped on the trail and when she blinked and realized that Will was before her, she almost burst into tears. But she stood her ground, screamed silently at the David in her mind. At the stupid, careless, wicked girl she had been.

"I'm fine," Harper said. But she didn't sound fine.

Will took a step for her. Reached for her hand. "I turned around and you were gone," he said. "I thought I lost you."

Harper smiled, but her heart wrenched. You never had me. She thought. No one has ever had me.

20

~

Three days later, the entire Vogt household was ripped from sleep when the telephone rang at 3:20 in the morning. The house was small, the insulation poor, and when the shrill chime split the night, Harper sat up straight in bed as if she had been shot. A second ring, and then the sound of footsteps on the floorboards, a door being yanked open. Adri seemed to take the stairs much too swiftly for someone who had been so rudely woken, and if Harper could trust the voices that filtered from the kitchen, Sam had been roused, too.

It wasn't her home, but the adrenaline buzz of an anticipated emergency was already humming beneath Harper's skin. The last couple of days had been a careful balancing act, an intricate game of memory that required her to keep her story straight. If that wasn't hard enough, everything was complicated by another, even more labyrinthine set of related riddles demanding every last shred of her energy and concentration: What was she supposed to do with Adri? Will? David? Sawyer? Harper had run to Adri when she called, but now she battled the urge to run away. If only she had somewhere to go. But even if Harper had other options, she didn't know if she would be able to leave the woman she had thought about day and night for the past five years.

Because she was awake, and because she was already high-strung and predisposed to fear the worst, Harper pulled a sweater over the T-shirt that she had been sleeping in and yanked on a pair of jeans. She crept down the stairs on bare feet, and paused a few steps from the bottom so she could listen to the conversation in the kitchen.

"No one was there?" Sam asked. "Are you sure?"

"Of course I'm sure. Breathing, I think. And then they hung up." There was a note of exhaustion in Adri's voice. Or maybe frustration. "It was probably Caleb. It's hard to get the timing of calls right."

"Are you going to call him back?"

"No. He'll try again if he needs me."

"So you'll wait up?"

"I'm up now, Dad. Could you go back to sleep?"

He chuckled. "Sweetie, my alarm is about to go off. Well, almost."

Harper could hear the sound of a cupboard opening, and then Adri poked her head around the corner and caught Harper in the stairwell. "You want a cup of coffee?" she asked. Her eyes were tired, but as warm as Harper could hope for in the middle of the night.

"I'd take a cup," Harper shrugged. "I'm up now, too."

"Good morning, Harper," Sam called from where he stood at the counter. He slid her a tired smile and nodded in greeting.

"Morning." Harper stifled a yawn. She tripped down the last few steps and pulled out a chair at the table, but before she could sink into it, the phone rang again. A chill went through the kitchen. Nobody called at such an ungodly hour—twice—unless something was wrong. Harper froze with her hand on the back of the chair.

Adri was still holding the phone and she anxiously clicked it on and pressed it to her ear. "Hello? Hello, Caleb?" She waited for a moment before trying again. "Hello?" After a few more seconds, she held the phone out in front of her and studied it as if there was something wrong with it.

"Nothing?" Sam asked. A fresh coffee filter was cradled in his palm.

"I can hear somebody breathing," Adri said. "But I don't know if they can hear me. Maybe Caleb accidentally switched his phone to mute."

"What makes you so sure it's Caleb?" Sam asked. "It could be Will."

"Will wouldn't be out at three o'clock on a Wednesday morning," Adri reasoned. "But if you had caller ID we wouldn't have to guess. We'd know who was phoning."

"It's not something I've ever needed." Sam dropped the filter into the top of the machine and reached for the container of ground coffee. "I pick up the phone and say hello if I want to know who's calling. Try the other phone."

"The rotary?"

"It's worked forever and a day," Sam said. "I don't know what makes you think the new one is better."

Adri tucked the cordless phone under her arm so that she could take the carafe from her father's outstretched hand and fill it with water from the tap. But Harper wasn't paying attention to them or their good-natured bickering.

Sam's and Adri's backs were turned to the little desk that housed the two phones, and when they weren't looking, Harper moved around the dining room table and reached for the phone jack. Popping the cord from the base of the handheld, she plugged the rotary into its place.

When the phone rang a third time, she answered it. "Hello?" She forced herself to say the innocuous greeting, even though what she wanted to do was scream into the mouthpiece. Or unplug both phones and pretend that their middle-of-the-night wake-up call was nothing more than a bad dream. But she knew that it wasn't. And she knew that the phone would only keep ringing and ringing and ringing. Unless she stopped it.

Sam and Adri spun around at the sound of Harper's voice, and she made herself shrug dispassionately. Then she rolled her eyes as if she was experiencing the same thing that Adri had: a weighted hush, nothing more.

But it wasn't nothing.

Sawyer was on the other end of the line.

They breathed together in silence for a few moments, and Harper hoped that maybe Sawyer hadn't recognized her voice. She had said just one word. But just as she was about to hang up, he whispered through the line: "As if I wouldn't find you."

The phone went dead.

Harper didn't stay in the kitchen for a cup of coffee, and the phone didn't ring again. She feigned exhaustion and mounted the stairs for the spare bedroom, but the adrenaline flushing through her system was so potent that she felt like she could crawl right out of her skin. Fly away. It was exactly what she needed to do.

Dressing in layers, Harper yanked on a pair of new socks and wished for a scarf and some gloves. It was cold outside. She could feel the icy air seeping through the warped frame of the window, and when she squinted at the yard below, she could see the grass glow white with frost. At least, she assumed it was frost. September snow wasn't entirely unheard of.

Though Harper wanted to leave immediately, she didn't dare. Adri was likely still in the kitchen, and while Sam would be heading out to the barns soon enough, Harper wanted to be sure that he was installed in the milking parlor before she made her escape. Escape? Did she really feel like she needed to escape Maple Acres and the Vogt family and the reminders of the life she had once led? No, she wanted to wrap them all up, tuck them away where they would be protected always. But if she had learned anything in the last several days, it was that she couldn't go back. No matter how much she wanted to, she couldn't undo the things she had done.

It was Sawyer she wanted to escape. And the sickening knowledge that he had found her. That he might come here.

Harper had been stupid. Her knowledge of computers was

limited, but she had been too careless—scrubbing the history after her forays onto the internet wasn't enough. Of course there were other markers that pointed to her online activity, a veritable trail of bread crumbs that would lead Sawyer to her fake Facebook account. Her email. A message from one Adrienne Vogt, who could be easily traced to Blackhawk, Iowa, and the little farm at the end of a long gravel road. Information wasn't a commodity these days, it was an inalienable right. Of course, Sawyer couldn't have done it on his own, but his resources were virtually unlimited.

Harper perched on the end of her bed, picking at the fabric of her jeans, bunching it in her hands as if she was holding on for dear life. She needed a plan.

She'd have to steal Betty.

It tore her up to know that she was going to hurt Adri again. And it killed her to think that Sam and Will and Jackson, and even Nora, would think less of her. That the loving welcome she had received from them less than a week ago would be tarnished by the knowledge that she was a thief. But it was better than letting them know what she had really become. It was her only real option when she considered that Sawyer could destroy the one pure thing she still held dear.

Harper wondered if Adri would try to follow her.

And then she was seized with another thought. How would Sawyer know that she had gone?

If she stayed, Sawyer would come for her. If she left, he'd still come—he'd just find her gone, and use the people she cared for as leverage. Harper didn't dare to guess at what Sawyer was capable of, but at best he'd expose her in front of the only real family she had ever known. At worst . . . Harper didn't even want to think about that.

Sawyer knew her. He knew who she was and who she had been and what she had done. Once, she had loved him, or thought she did, and when she admitted the things that lovers admit, he had tucked each confession like a weapon into an arsenal to use against her. Love and lies and jealousy and secrets, but nothing so damning as the truth of what happened that day with David Galloway.

Sawyer knew that Harper was a murderer.

Her only option, the only solution that her frozen mind could conjure, was to go back.

Harper was shaking so hard that her teeth started to chatter. She wrapped her arms around herself and clenched her jaw, furious that he could affect her so much. That she let him. She was stronger than this. Harper Penny was made of tougher stuff, and she wasn't about to let a man like Sawyer write the story of her life. But try as she might, she couldn't see a way out. He was as vast as the sea, and she was drowning.

It was still pitch black outside when the alarm clock on the nightstand read 5:00 a.m. The house was quiet. A couple of hours had passed since she'd thrown on her clothes and formu-lated a half-baked plan, but it felt like minutes. She must have fallen asleep.

The light was still on in the kitchen, and there were two empty coffee cups beside the sink. But as far as Harper could tell, no one was around. She crept through the bright space, pausing at the door to grab her shoes and stuff her feet into them. Then she was on the porch, the morning stars glittering madly overhead. She had read once that stars shine the bright-est in the moments before dawn, but it had always sounded like a myth to her. A bit of convenient fairy-tale fluff. But she could believe it now. The world was so resplendent with starlight, it seemed the air itself shimmered.

Hurrying across the frosted lawn, Harper tried to keep her footfalls soft. The grass fractured beneath her rubber soles, leav-ing a trail so obvious that it was as if she was walking in sand. Sam and Adri wouldn't have to puzzle over where she had gone.

It was harder to heave open the garage door than Harper had thought it would be, and she struggled for a minute before she realized she had to lift back instead of up. But once she got the feel of it, the heavy door swung up quickly, almost lifting her off the ground. Harper righted herself and said a little prayer that the keys were in the ignition. That's where Adri usually left them, and if they weren't where Harper expected them to be, she had no idea what she would do. The truth was, she had no idea what she would do once she started Betty and drove away, but she figured one step at a time was forethought enough. She reached for the door.

"Going for a drive?"

Harper whirled and saw Adri framed in the rectangle of the open garage door. Her hands were stuffed in the pockets of a heavy coat, and her face was completely obscured by shadows. But there were stars in her hair, and the silhouette she cut against the blackness was strong and lovely. Harper almost burst into tears.

Instead, she wrestled her emotions to the ground. "Yeah," she said lightly. "I couldn't go back to sleep. I would have asked you, but I didn't want to wake you up. You don't mind, do you?"

Adri ignored the question. "I couldn't sleep, either."

They stood there for a few heartbeats, studying each other in the darkness. It felt intense, almost calculating, through there was no way that Adri could see Harper any better than Harper could see her.

"Can I go with you?" Adri finally asked. Harper was too surprised by the timidity of the request to worry that her friend was foiling her pathetic plan.

"Sure."

"Keys are in the ignition," Adri said. "You want to drive?"

Harper tingled with the understanding that time was ticking away, that every moment she was out joyriding with Adri was a moment that should be spent making her way back to Sawyer so that he wouldn't come looking for her. Minneapolis was only a five-hour drive, and if he had left the moment he hung up the phone, he could pull up at Maple Acres in a couple of hours.

Would he do that? Harper didn't think so. She had a sneaking suspicion that he was playing with her. A handful of creepy phone calls in the middle of the night were probably just the beginning of an elaborate scheme to unnerve her. Well, she was sufficiently unnerved. No need to torture her any further. And no need to plague Sam and Adri with whatever else Sawyer had in store.

With Adri in her getaway car, Sawyer was just one of Harper's many problems. She half expected Adri to bring up the conversation that they had abandoned the other day at Piperhall, especially since they were alone, and Harper had done everything in her power to avoid time alone with Adri in the last few days. But Adri didn't mention David now or the estate. In fact, she didn't say anything at all for a very long time. She just stared out the windshield and let Harper wander at will. When they skirted the city limits of Black-hawk, Adri finally pointed at an upcoming intersection and instructed Harper to turn.

"Why?" Harper asked, but she had already turned on her blinker.

"Don't you remember?"

"Remember what?"

"The fire escape slide."

It had been ages since Harper had thought about the fire slide, but it didn't fail to bring a faint smile to her lips. Black-hawk didn't have much by way of parks, but the fire slide was legendary, an old, metal slide that was completely enclosed in a silo and nearly two stories tall. It had been around for decades, since long before people started worrying about safety hazards in playgrounds. Wicked fast, it boasted three sharp, steep turns before spitting breathless riders out onto the gravel. It had been a tradition for The Five, a necessary pit stop on the way back to ATU after weekends spent at Piperhall. For Harper, it was a way to leave everything behind, if only for the seconds that she was spinning, the centrifugal force pushing her shoulder blades against the cool metal of the slide, her hair whipped back from her face.

"You want to go down the slide?" Harper asked, pulling into the small parking lot and putting the car in park. She was incredulous that as her life turned to ashes, Adri was ready to play.

Adri shrugged. "I always thought you loved it."

More than the thrill, Harper had loved the attention. David once carried her up the three twisting flights of stairs to the platform at the top of the fire slide. And when she whooshed out at the bottom, someone was always ready to catch her, to pick her up from the gravel and dust her off.

"I like the slide," Harper said. "But it's kind of cold outside, don't you think?"

"I didn't exactly expect us to go down it." Adri turned in her seat to face Harper. "I just wanted you to stop driving so I could look you in the face."

Harper stifled a sigh. "I don't want to talk about it, Adri. I know you don't want the estate, but Victoria left it to you and—"

"I don't care about the estate. You can have it." It was a throwaway statement, Harper doubted that Adri meant it at all. But it was shocking all the same. "I'm serious," Adri said, disregarding the look in Harper's eyes. "It's yours. Turn it into a bed-and-breakfast. Sell it and pocket the cash. Give ghost tours for all I care."

Harper didn't know what to say.

"I want to talk about you. About why you're here and what you're running from."

"Nothing," Harper protested. But the word was weak and ineffectual.

"Okay, who you're running from." Adri threw up her hands. "How stupid do you think we are? You showed up in the back-seat of a strange vehicle, half-naked and without a penny on you."

"I was not half-naked."

"You were half-naked. You didn't have shoes, Harper. Shoes."

"I gave them away."

Adri was breathing hard. She sounded angry, but in the flickering light of the streetlamp, Harper could see desperation in her eyes. "No money, no purse, no clothes. Seriously, Harper, you don't even have a phone. You haven't called anyone since you got here, and the only person who's called for you did so in the middle of the night."

Harper blanched. "I don't know what you mean."

The look Adri gave her was cynical and searching, but she seemed to decide not to press the issue. "You can't even give me a straight answer when I ask you where you work."

"I'm a waitress." But Harper's mind was foggy. She couldn't remember if she had claimed to be a waitress.

Adri ignored her. "What have you done, Harper?"

"I haven't done anything."

"Then what happened to you?"

Harper didn't know where to begin. But maybe the question was rhetorical. Maybe Adri didn't want an answer at all.

They sat for a few minutes in relative silence, the car engine idling and Adri's ragged breathing the only sound in the early-morning stillness. Then she reached past Harper, turned off the car, and yanked the keys out of the ignition.

"What are you doing?"

"I'm going down the slide, and I want to make sure that you don't drive away while I'm gone."

Harper made a sound of indignation, but Adri wasn't buying it. "You weren't going for a joyride, were you? You were leaving." She swung out of the car without waiting for a response.

It was still dark, but there was a smudge of light on the horizon, and the stars were beginning to fade. Harper watched as Adri made her way across the park, her footprints cutting a perfectly straight path from the car to the base of the slide. Harper didn't know what to do. Adri was right to take the keys—if she had left them, Harper might very well have driven away. She didn't know if she could just leave Adri in the dark, but Blackhawk was small and it would be easy enough for Adri to find her way home. A quick phone call to Sam or Will, even Jackson and Nora, and her world would be set right. No Harper in it.

Harper wrenched the car door open and followed in Adri's footprints. It was cold, and she hugged herself, grateful for the long-sleeved T-shirt she had tucked under her sweater.

Adri was already at the top of the slide, and as Harper stepped on the first stair, she could hear Adri pitch herself over the edge and into the tunnel. Harper went up as Adri went down, and by the time she peered into the gaping mouth of the tall slide, the park had been shrouded in silence. She didn't know if Adri was waiting for her, or if she had already headed back to the car. It was a ridiculous hope, but Harper prayed that Adri had stayed. She didn't want to be alone.

There was a thick bar at the entrance to the slide, and sometimes Harper used to hold it and whip herself into the darkness. The cold metal was fast enough on its own, but with a little extra force, she could send herself twining through the tunnel like madness itself. Often, when she crashed to the bottom, the world had been tipped sideways, and the off-kilter tilt was enough to make everything seem fresh again.

It was stupid to be afraid, but Harper was. She sat shivering at the top of the slide, and when the coldness seeped into her jeans she forced herself to scoot forward the single inch that would send her down. Sometimes it felt like her life was decided by an inch. A detail. A secret told.

When Adri came back to their apartment the day after David hit her, Harper knew that something was wrong. They had breathed the same air for over three and a half years, and it was almost impossible for them to keep secrets from each other. Even when they wanted to. And the second Adri stepped into the apartment and shot Harper a flimsy smile as she sat curled in the shabby La-Z-Boy, Harper could tell that something monumental had happened. Maybe it was the tightness in Adri's eyes, the way she held herself so carefully it seemed she was clinging to composure like a threadbare blanket. Maybe it was just that Harper loved her more than she had ever loved another person, and she could feel the pain radiate off her friend in waves.

Harper flew out of the chair and grabbed Adri by the arms. Adri still had her backpack slung over her shoulder, her smile fixed all warped and crooked to her face, but she started to cry almost instantly. Big, anguished tears that spilled off her chin as she began to gasp for air.

"We. Are. So. Fucked. Up."

Harper had to stifle a smile at that. Adri never swore, and the proclamation sounded downright comical from her lips. But in the next moment the story came tumbling out, and suddenly Harper wasn't smiling anymore.

David hit her.

It was the only thing that Harper's fury-clouded brain could think. David hit her.

Something fierce and almost maternal reared up in Harper. She wanted to strangle David, to throttle him for what he had done. Hurt him. Make him regret he'd ever laid a finger on Adrienne.

It was unforgivable.

And yet, while Harper was angry, she wasn't entirely surprised. She had experienced enough life to know that a woman like Victoria didn't become so hollow-eyed and solitary without strong provocation. Though she was quiet and withdrawn, Mrs. Galloway had always been straight-backed and proud, the angle of her delicate chin a kind of regal. Even though her dark eyes told a story all their own, Harper couldn't begin to imagine Victoria with a hair out of place or a note of impropriety in her tone. She exuded composure and good breeding. Perfection. A woman like that didn't roll over and play dead. She was beaten down.

Piperhall, as much as Harper adored it, was a burdened place that harbored many dark mysteries. Only they weren't so mysterious to Harper. How could a child grow up in such an environment and not be affected? How could David endure the iron fist of his father and not boast threads of steel in his own bones? Everyone knew that Liam had abused Victoria, but had he bent his hand toward David, too? Or was David just a good pupil?

Harper knew who David was. She always had. And she had believed that she could control him, that she could keep the monster inside at bay. Weren't they the perfect pair? Beautiful. Dysfunctional. Fire and water and earth and air. Caught forever in a feverish dance, circling each other, near enough to touch but never close enough to wound. At least, not lethally.

But David chose Adri and screwed everything up.

Harper hated him for it. And she hated him for hurting Adri.

It was after midnight when she slid out of the apartment like a shadow. Adri had been asleep for hours, traumatized and exhausted and anxious for the respite of a deep and dreamless sleep. Harper had given her sleeping pills and kissed her forehead as she closed her eyes. But Harper couldn't sleep. Her blood seethed beneath her skin, licking at her heart like a tongue. A hot and living thing that surged through her and begged her to move.

She didn't know where she was going, but she could hardly wander around in the dark all night. The weather had turned and it was starting to sleet; already a fine sheet of ice crusted the sidewalk and splintered beneath the wedges of her boot heels. The sound was cathartic somehow, sharp but incomplete, for even as she walked away the ice continued to crack and moan along invisible seams. A path split before her, the glow of each perfectly spaced streetlamp highlighting a spiderweb map, a broken atlas of her uncharted life.

It took her to David's door.

He was living alone in an off-campus apartment. Jackson

and Will were roommates, and there would have been room for David, but he had elected to rent the second story of a converted farmhouse on the edge of ATU's small campus. Slumming it like the other college students, instead of commuting from his mansion on the hill. The apartment was a place to gather, a place to drink. During the week it was both common room and community center for The Five, a sort of home base that was as much theirs as his. Harper had always wondered why Will and Jackson didn't just join him in the apartment instead of living on campus, but Will had once let it slip that they hadn't been invited. He didn't seem put out. David was just David.

The front door of the farmhouse opened on a short hallway, and it was never locked. To the right was the door to the ground-floor apartment. A simple #1 had been painted onto the faded wood, but David's neighbors kept to themselves. Harper didn't even know who they were. On the left was the narrow staircase to apartment 2, each step so shallow Harper had to tiptoe up the stairs. It had been murder moving David's furniture in. Though Harper and Adri mostly watched from the front lawn, laughing at the guys and offering suggestions in the form of thinly veiled insults. "Lift with your backs, boys. Lift with your backs."

She took the steps now two at a time, propelling herself forward with one hand on the rail. David rarely locked his door, and he was a legendary night owl—Adri often mused that she worried he was a vampire, he slept so little—but, as incensed as Harper was, she couldn't bring herself to just walk in. A wall had been erected between them, and it was more than she could surmount, even in the midst of her fury.

Harper would have pounded on the door, but some small part of her registered the hour and the scene that she would make. Taking a moment to get hold of herself, Harper balled her fists and exhaled. Then she knocked quickly, softly, four times, and waited. Nothing. Four more. She could hear footsteps deep in the apartment, and something being shuffled around. Harper could picture David stumbling from the bedroom in the back, throwing a T-shirt on over his bare chest and cursing whoever had woken him up.

But when David opened the door, it was obvious he hadn't been sleeping.

His hair was so fingered through that it stuck up straight from his forehead, and his eyes were bloodshot and wild. Harper wasn't used to seeing him disheveled, for even when they partied he kept himself tightly reined. He was a slow burn, a quiet fury, and Harper hardly recognized him with his shirt half untucked from his designer jeans, his feet bare on the old hardwood floor of his tiny living room. David looked lost, empty, but his hands were full. In one hand he held a bottle of his father's vintage Scotch, and in the other he balanced an empty glass between his fingers and the round door handle. He smelled of alcohol and cologne and sweat.

"What have you done?" she said. Her anger flared and fizzled and flared again, and she couldn't decide if she should hit him or hug him, he looked so wrecked. Instead, Harper elbowed her way into the apartment and closed the door with her hip. Taking the bottle from David, she glanced at the label and wondered just how much a 1985 Macallan would cost a mere mortal like herself. It was mostly empty, but she lifted the bottle to her lips and took a swig that burned all the way down. She put the Macallan on the nearest end table and stifled a cough.

David didn't seem to notice or care. His free hand was once again in his hair, yanking fistfuls of blond waves as if he intended to pluck himself bald.

"I asked you a question." Harper took the glass from him, too, and when she discovered it was empty, set it beside the bottle. "What the hell do you think you're doing?"

David seemed not to hear her. He dropped his hands to his sides and stood there staring off into middle distance, his lips slightly parted. "I'm a bastard," he said.

"Yes, you are."

"No, really." He looked at her suddenly, and his eyes seemed to carve right through her.

Harper groaned. "I know you are, David. We all do. And we love you in spite of it. Don't ask me why. But this . . ." She couldn't finish.

"What, Harper? What do you want to say to me?"

"This is unforgivable."

His laugh was brittle and unexpected. "You really have no idea."

"Don't play with me, David Galloway." Harper couldn't believe that she had thought to hug him only a moment ago. He was being impossible. She didn't feel sorry for him, not one bit, and though she had come to talk some sense into him, or hit him or something, she found that the only thing she really wanted to do was leave. The room was filled with sparks of every unspoken word and inexpressible hurt, each unthinkable wish and longing that she had felt about David since the moment she first saw him. The apartment was a tinderbox. A dangerous place to be.

Harper tore her eyes from the intensity of David's gaze and hurried toward the door. In a couple of seconds she would have wrenched it open and been gone, but David caught her from behind and yanked her close. She couldn't tell if he was drunk or not, but it didn't matter. His arms were locked around her, his body pressed along the length of her back. And though she didn't want to feel what she was feeling, his breath on her neck made her weak.

They stood like that for what felt like hours, and when Harper finally relaxed the tiniest bit in the coil of his embrace, David's lips brushed against her ear. "It was supposed to be you," he said.

She had no idea what he meant. The relationship? The engagement? The fight? But in a way it didn't matter. Harper would have taken it from him. All of it. They were one and the same. They were meant to be, and she knew it the moment he told her so.

David's fingers fumbled on the buttons of her coat and the zipper of her jeans, and she let him struggle. She was too busy damning herself, her fingers trembling so hard on the hindrances of his own clothes that she ripped a seam.

Then lies and regrets and a love so skinny it hardly existed at all. Bones and lust. A wisp of nothingness.

A sigh.

The knowledge that everything she loved had shattered around her. And it was all her fault.

He never even kissed her. Not really.

Harper let go of the bar at the top of the slide. A matter of seconds. Her life upended. And then she shot out of the bottom and landed on her back in the gravel. But the drunken feeling didn't stop, and when Adri knelt down and laid her hand on Harper's arm, she still felt like she was whirling out of control.

"You promised me the truth," Adri said. "We're not leaving until you tell me one true thing. Just one. That's all I want."

When Harper opened her mouth, she had no idea what she was going to say. And when she heard her own words, it was as if someone else had spoken them.

"I hate him."

It was the truest thing she could think to say.

21

Adri took a deep breath and held it. Softly, she said, "Sometimes I hate him, too."

But Harper didn't want to talk about David. Of course, she could have steered the conversation to different ground. She hated her father. And Sawyer, too. But she couldn't say any of that. Sawyer's name was an incantation, an illicit spell to conjure demons.

"We shouldn't speak ill of the dead," Harper said, pushing herself up from the ground.

"You said it," Adri's voice sounded hollow, far away.

"I shouldn't have."

Harper started to walk back to the car, but it was a struggle to hold herself upright. It made her feel old.

When Harper reached the car, she climbed into the passenger seat and pulled her knees up to her chest. Wrapped her arms tight around her shins. She was freezing, and grateful when Adri slid into the driver's seat and started the engine. Turned the heat on high.

Harper forced herself to say, "Sometimes I think that everything I've done, every moment of my life from the day that David died until now, has been determined by that one event."

"Me, too," Adri admitted.

"I've made a lot of bad choices."

Adri thought for a minute. "I've made a lot of careful choices. I live a very rigid life, Harper."

"I couldn't tell."

"Tease away," Adri said, and she didn't sound at all upset. "It's worked for me."

"Has it?" Harper turned and looked right at her friend, at the sharp angles of her lovely face and the deliberate way that she held her expression so tight and neutral. She didn't look happy. But then again, she wasn't scared either. She hadn't messed up her life to the point of sheer lunacy. If Adri had taken careful, meticulous steps for the last five years, Harper had flung herself out of a plane. Without a parachute. Neither coping method seemed to be working very well.

Adri was still waiting for an answer to all of her questions. Harper knew that she had strained her welcome. Her silence wasn't arch anymore, it was reticent. She had to share something.

"I was in a bad situation," Harper said.

"What do you mean, a bad situation?" The concern in Adri's eyes was difficult to see; instead of watching her, Harper looked out the window at the pink glow of dawn. Traced her finger in the thin film of condensation and wrote her own name in block letters.

"Seriously, Adri. Don't make me say it." Not that Harper would have said it anyway. She couldn't.

A pause. "Okay. So. You left."

As if it was that easy. "Yeah."

"And that woman in the SUV? The one who dropped you off?"

"A friend." Harper palmed away the letters, leaving a trail of droplets on the window. She couldn't bring herself to tell Adri about The Bridge or her escape from Minneapolis. It was too sordid, too much like a bad soap opera. People didn't live like that. Not really. And yet, Harper knew all too well that they did.

"Okay."

"Look, Adri, I got your email and I came. It seemed like the right thing to do at the time. But I didn't mean to burden you with any of this. That was never my intention."

"You think you're burdening me?" Adri sounded incredulous. "Harper, you're my best friend. I wrote you because I wanted to see you, I wanted to talk about what happened in BC, what happened to David. But now that you're here I feel like we're playing some sort of game. Except I don't know the rules."

It took Harper a minute to speak. "I didn't mean for it to be this way."

"Me neither."

All at once, Harper felt a crashing wave of love for Adri. Years ago, Harper had kissed her. On the mouth like a lover instead of a friend. They were side by side on Harper's bed in their dorm room, and Adri had said something that caused them both to dissolve into giggles. It was nothing, really, an unremarkable comment that held little meaning. But it made Harper feel as if her life could be beautiful after all. Normal. And she had forgotten for just a moment who she was and where she was and all the rules of the world she had known. Harper leaned over and kissed Adri as she laughed, felt the soft press of her lips and the smooth plane of her cheek, and knew that she had never in all her life loved anyone as much as she loved Adrienne Vogt.

When Adri jerked away, there was a second of confusion, a moment when they looked at each other and everything, everything hung in the balance. Harper could have wept for agony at what she had done, but before she could even take a breath to apologize, to try to explain, Adri gave a little shake of her head. It cleared the air. Erased all but the faintest imprint of what had happened.

"I love you," Adri said, one corner of her mouth quirking. But her eyes said the rest: Not that way.

And Harper didn't either. It was just an overflow, an un-guarded instant when she had tried to embrace the life before her with every ounce of her being. To let Adri know that she was accomplishing the impossible: singlehandedly convincing Harper that she deserved to be loved.

Harper wanted to tell Adri that now. Maybe even tell her again that she adored her still. Loved her like a sister. She had tried to convince her, in the way that she braided her hair and made her pancakes on test mornings and listened to every late-night whispered wish as they fell asleep across the room. They had shared so much. A life. A dream. A lover. Harper stifled a shiver.

"What in the world did you ever see in me?" Adri asked. It was an odd question, something that took Harper completely by surprise.

"What do you mean?"

"Exactly what I said. Why did you chose me? Those first days at ATU, I felt like you picked me out of a crowd."

"I did."

"Why?"

Harper sat up straighter, let her feet slide to the floor of the car. "I liked you."

"That's not enough." Adri was gripping the steering wheel, her hands white-knuckled as if Harper's answer mattered much. "I was a wallflower. A timid little farm girl. What in the world did you see in me?"

"You were kind," Harper began, searching for specifics, for the details that had inexorably drawn her to Adri. "You were smart and determined and serious. I think I was drawn to those things because I didn't understand them. I liked them in you."

Adri gave a small nod, but she wouldn't look at Harper.

"And you weren't a wallflower. You were an observer. Not the kind of girl who would run off at the mouth for no reason or make a spectacle of herself. Not like me. That's a good thing, Adri. You weren't flashy because you didn't have to be. Your character spoke for itself."

"Those are all nice things to say," Adri said.

"But you don't believe them?"

Adri shrugged. "I don't know. Sometimes I wonder how we ended up together at all." She looked quickly at Harper, apparently gauging if her words had stung. But Harper had thought the same thing herself many, many times.

And yet, her attraction to Adri was the most obvious thing in the world. Adri was quiet, but that didn't mean she wasn't confident. She was settled, perfectly comfortable in her own skin and the life that she had been given. Adri didn't know it, but she wore serenity like an aura. Peace like that was something you couldn't fake. Someone had to love it into you, and Adri had been loved well. Harper admired her.

No, she realized, as she studied her friend in the early-morning light, she didn't admire or esteem or even love her. She wanted to be her. And she always had.

～

It was spring, a month before graduation, and The Five had come down to the estate to get off campus. Harper's grand parties were a thing of the past, little more than a collection of fond memories, because they simply couldn't stand the thought of sharing each other anymore. Their days together were numbered.

Of course, things had been different since David and Adri's engagement, but that didn't stop any of them from jostling for time together, moments that would recapture the magic of what they once had. So they stayed up way too late, and drove to the estate when they should have been on campus, studying. Even Adri.

They were changing. In bursts and spurts and stops and starts they were becoming the people that they had to be. David was formidable and dark-humored, Adri pale and serious and withdrawn. Will and Jackson just tried to keep everyone laughing, surprising them all with sudden extravagances in the form of fresh lobster flown in on a Tuesday night (David, of course, footed the bill) or a screening of *The Rocky Horror Picture Show* on a bedsheet that they'd draped across the outside wall of David's apartment. And Harper was a girl on fire. She loathed herself, and David, too. But there was more than enough angst left for Adri.

David had said, It should have been you. Harper believed him. And yet, he didn't break off the engagement. He didn't do anything at all. Except screw Harper when Adri wasn't around.

Harper lived in a perpetual state of fear and regret, and every time she walked away from David, she promised herself, never again. But there was always another time.

Sometimes it was a game. It made her feel powerful and in control and alive. And sometimes it scared her so much that she cried herself to sleep like a child, tears hot and silent as they fell down her temples and collected in her ears. She was in love. She was in lust. She was miserable, and she was torn, because the person she loved more than anyone she had ever known was the same person she was hurting the most.

Once, she said to David, "We're sick. You know that, right?" He was buttoning his shirt, his back turned to her, and he laughed a little.

"I guess that means we deserve one another."

He was her weakness, her very own kryptonite, yet she hated to hear those words from his mouth. She wanted to be a better person. A stronger one. But before she could bite back somehow, David turned and took her in his arms. He folded her close and laid a kiss on the crown of her head, the place where her hair curved along the line of her high forehead.

"You're not just another notch in my belt," he whispered.

Maybe he thought it was what she wanted to hear, but he couldn't have been more wrong. Although Harper wanted him and always had, she loved Adri more. She wanted to erase what they did, what continued to do. She wanted to give Adri back what she had taken from her. And assurances that David loved her more than a one-night stand were not helpful in strengthening her resolve. Harper didn't want to wonder "what if ?" She just wanted it all to stop.

But not really. Not enough. Because it didn't stop.

"Well . . ." Harper pushed hard against David's chest and his arms fell away. "Maybe I'm not a notch in your belt, but what if you're just another in mine?"

She didn't stick around to see if her words had achieved the desired effect.

The weekend that Harper began to think of as the beginning of the end was the same weekend that Adri came down with a sinus infection. Their plan had been to relax at the estate with some horseback riding and a dip in the recently filled hot tub. It was an unseasonably warm spring, and the tulips were already six inches out of the ground by the beginning of April. But their retreat had been doomed from the start. David insisted on driving to Piperhall, even though he had already been drinking—an incontrovertible offense in Adri's books. She refused to get in the car and instead drove Betty on her own. Even Will and Jackson were out of sorts, uninterested in making the effort to be witty and jovial, mere shadows of their usually spirited selves.

They skipped riding and grazed in the kitchen until they were overfull and too tired to study. Victoria didn't exactly stock her fridge, but Elena, the woman who had catered for the Galloways for years, still came once a week and dropped off fresh produce, a dozen free-range eggs, and a handful of pre-made or easy-to-assemble meals. Victoria rarely touched them, and they were free game for David and his friends. Harper was delighted to find a baking tray with six individual quiches in lemon-yellow ramekins, each one slightly different—feta and spinach, tomato and bacon, a cheesy confection that tasted strongly of Gruyère. Will halved the grapefruits he'd discovered in the crisper, then buttered them and sprinkled brown sugar on top. He baked them with a fat loaf of French bread, which they spread with peanut butter and Elena's homemade strawberry-rhubarb jam.

Adri didn't have a single bite.

"What's wrong with you?" Will asked, shoving the last corner of bread in his mouth and licking peanut butter off his fingers.

"I have a headache," Adri said quietly.

"It's more than a headache." Jackson was sitting next to her and he put his wrist against the back of her neck. "She's burning up."

"I am not."

"Are too." Jackson gave her cheek a gentle rub with his thumb, then turned his attention to David. "Would you like some help escorting your fiancée to her bed?"

"Nope." David slid back his stool and went to gather Adri at the end of the long bar. Instead of helping her stand, he simply picked her up. She looked like a little girl in his arms, slight and pale, her eyes damp and shiny with fever.

"Don't carry me," she protested. "I'm still angry at you."

David hushed her. "I promise I won't drop you down the stairs."

Adri looked for a moment like she would struggle, but then she gave up and closed her eyes. Harper wondered if she was sleeping before David even tucked her into bed.

It was an early night for everyone, and long before midnight rolled around, the house was still but for the sound of the heater moaning through the old air ducts. Harper couldn't sleep. She wasn't much of a sleeper to begin with, but her unraveling life had made rest little more than a memory. Nights were spent pacing or drinking. Sometimes scribbling poetry on whatever slip of paper she could find. Of course, she usually tipped over the edge into a fitful sleep at some point in the long night, and when she woke in the morning she was often surrounded by evidence of her nocturnal wrestlings. Phrases and fragments that revealed a soul at war. Then she would gather them hastily, crumple them into tiny balls, and stuff them into the very bottom of the garbage can. Adri could never see them. Never.

But tonight, in David's house, with secrets and lies and a painfully unclear future before her, Harper was sick with insomnia. She couldn't write or pace. She couldn't even drink—her stomach was too bloated with guilt. Wakefulness throbbed beneath her skin, ached and burned dull. It made her want to scratch herself raw just so that she could release a little of the anguish that made every pore tingle like a bruise.

Harper didn't know where to go, so she went to the only place where she felt relatively safe from prying eyes: the tower. She climbed the stairs in the dark and emerged in the lookout to a sky so clouded that it was blackness itself. There was no moon, no stars, and the small, enclosed balcony was dense and close, so that Harper felt as if she was underground instead of standing at the highest point in the county. She had hoped to fill her lungs with air, but there was nothing for her to breathe here.

There was nowhere else for her to go.

Harper was in the tower less than five minutes when she heard footsteps on the spiral staircase below her. It wasn't Adri; she had been passed out for hours. Will? Jackson? Of course, David. She knew him by the way he walked, climbing the steps as if he had already conquered them, as if the tower itself, and the woman inside it, bored him half to death.

"Shouldn't you be nursing your wife back to health?" Harper didn't mean to sound bitter, but her words were razor-edged.

"She's not my wife."

"Yet."

Harper whirled on him, on the place where she thought he would be, but he was invisible in the thick shadows. "Are you really doing this? Are you going to play this game?"

"What game?"

Backing up until her shoulder blades touched the cool glass wall of the tower, Harper said, "I'm not letting you touch me with Adri sleeping somewhere below us."

"So now you have a conscience?" David laughed.

"That's a horrible thing to say."

"Come on, Harper." His voice was as smooth as cream, but it snagged at the end. Caught on some emotion that Harper couldn't determine. "You know we're both going to hell."

She was cold, but she pressed her palms to the glass behind her all the same. It was invigorating somehow. It woke her up, even though she wasn't tired and she was as sober as she had been in a long time. "We don't have to," she said. "We can make this right."

Harper didn't even know that she had been formulating a plan until that moment, but the second the words were out of her mouth, she could almost see the path laid out before her. They would do the only thing they could do. They would tell the truth. Because they loved Adri too much not to. At least, Harper did.

But David was having none of it. "How in the world can we make this right? You want to tell Adri? You think that would help?"

"Yes." Harper could feel him moving toward her, his steps shuffling, unsure.

"You're completely insane. We aren't telling Adrienne a thing."

"Adrienne?" Harper repeated softly. She hated how lately David insisted on calling Adri by her given name. It felt like he was already grooming her, turning her into a woman befitting the Galloway title. Harper stopped. "That's it, isn't it?" she said. "I mean, I've always guessed that you chose Adri because she was a more suitable wife, but that really is the reason, isn't it?"

He had found her, and though his hand fumbled as he reached, when he caught her wrist he held it tight. "You think you know me, don't you?" David leaned in close and drew his cheek along Harper's, his breath warm against her neck.

"I do know you." Harper stiffened beneath him, trying to resist the temptation to melt into his touch. She didn't want to love him, but when he held her close like this, when he revealed just the tiniest bit of how very truly messed up he was, she couldn't help herself. There was hurt buried deep inside him, the kind of damage that called out to what was broken in her. She understood him. He just didn't know it yet. Or maybe he refused to accept it.

"Listen," Harper said, rising on her tiptoes so that she could press herself against him. "You're not right for Adri." It was the truth. It was the honest-to-God truest thing she had said in a very long time.

"Thank you for imparting that nugget of wisdom."

She ignored him, and allowed herself the forbidden luxury of brushing her mouth over the place where his heart beat a steady rhythm beneath his jawline. It was just a second of contact, anything more and she knew that she would forget what she was saying and why. But it was enough to make David shut up.

"You will make her miserable for the rest of her life. And you know it. She'll make you miserable, too." Harper could feel David take a breath to say something, but she didn't let him. "We have to tell her about us. It'll be hard, but it won't destroy her, David. She's a strong girl. Someday, she might even forgive us."

"Us?"

Yes. Us. But Harper didn't say that. She said, "I love you."

It wisped out of her so faintly, the words barely existed at all. But David had heard, and she couldn't take it back. Harper was tangled up in him, body and heart and soul, her face buried against his shoulder where she could taste the salty sweet of his skin, and she knew that she had never been more naked, more vulnerable with another person in her entire life. Not even Adri. She wished she could evaporate. But she was flesh and blood, and when David let go of her wrist, she trembled.

He didn't say a word.

Harper didn't know there was anything left of her heart to break. But when she reached the bottom of the stairs—a desperate, staggering tumble that was anything but stealthy—she was choking on sobs. She pressed both of her hands over her mouth, shocked and furious at herself, but too wrecked to worry about the scene she was making. The people she might wake.

David caught her the moment before she fled to her room, and wrestled her into his arms, even though she fought him like a wildcat. "Come on," he said into her hair. "Don't do this. Please don't do this. I love you, too." But it was too late.

"You do not love me," she gasped, pushing against his arms, his chest. They were steel. He held her fast. "You use me."

"Harper—"

"You sleep with me."

"Please."

"I'm your whore," she all but shrieked.

"You are not my whore."

"And Adri's going to be your miserable wife. Why, David? Do you love her?"

"Of course, I—"

"Then what am I to you?"

But he never got a chance to answer. In the shadows there was a shuffling, the slightest scuff of slippered feet. David straightened and stepped away from Harper.

"Mother. Let me help you back to your room."

22

<img - decorative swash ornament>

They picked up doughnuts and coffee from the gas station. The pastries were fresh from the oven, warm icing dripping down the sides. Harper licked the sweetness from her fingers as Adri wove through Blackhawk, the only place where Harper had ever been happy.

When they cleared the city limits, Adri drove to Piperhall and they finished their coffee by the pool. The air was crisp but pleasant, and Harper chattered endlessly about every safe memory that popped into her head. She put on a good show, laughing and remembering, even though her heart was shriveling inside her chest. She longed to run.

"Would you like a tour?" Adri asked when it was obvious that every last drop of coffee was gone—and Harper's lighthearted anecdotes had run dry. "I think we missed that part the other day. Will interrupted us."

Harper had been swallowing Piperhall in greedy gulps as they walked from the front entrance to the back veranda. It looked exactly as she liked to paint it in her dreams. Bright and lovely. Perfect. But the thought of a full-fledged tour was somewhat terrifying. Betrayal and lies and regrets hovered like ghosts around every corner. What could she say?

"I'd love a tour," Harper said.

As they deposited their empty coffee cups in the garbage, a shiver ran up Harper's spine.

Someone was in the mansion. Harper could hear voices coming from the hall, and from the way Adri's head whipped toward the main living space, it was apparent that she could hear them, too.

"Were you expecting company?" Harper asked. Her hand floated to her throat of its own accord. She swallowed beneath her fingertips, then forced herself to hold her arms at her sides. She picked at her jeans.

"No." But Adri wasn't afraid. There was no reason for her to be. She started toward the entry with her shoulders thrown back, and called before she was halfway there. "Hello? Dad?"

Sam. Who else could it be? Will and Jackson were undoubtedly working. It was mid-morning on a Wednesday. In Blackhawk, of all places. It could be a plumber, an electrician, the pool boy. Elena? Did she still deliver food to the estate? Of course not. Harper jogged a few steps to catch up with Adri, and prayed that her friend couldn't hear the irregular pounding of her panicked heart.

"Dad?" Still no answer, and they were only steps away from the arch that opened onto the back half of the house. Once they were seen, there would be nowhere to go. Nowhere to hide.

Then Sam stepped into view, with a smile on his face that Harper could tell from half a room away was uncertain. Someone was with him.

"Hey," Sam called. "I figured you girls would be here. Hope you don't mind that we just let ourselves in. We knocked, but no one answered."

"We?" Adri flushed the tiniest bit. It made her look lush somehow, expectant, and Harper knew in that moment that she made the perfect foil for her lovely friend. She could feel the blood drain out of her face. It was pooling somewhere in her feet, and she fought hard to stop herself from folding to the floor.

Sam noticed at once. "Harper, honey. Are you okay?" He took a few steps toward her, but before he could reach out a steadying hand, Adri gasped.

"Caleb?"

Caleb. Harper caught sight of him around one of the pillars that held up the sixteen-foot ceiling in the grand entryway. He was taller than she had expected, broad-shouldered and visibly comfortable in his own skin. The colorful arc of a bright tattoo peeked out from beneath the collar of his Henley, and trailed down the exposed skin of his forearm all the way to his wrist. Harper hadn't expected a full-sleeve tattoo, or the square jaw of a man who looked like he belonged in military fatigues rather than a pair of secondhand board shorts on a beach in some forgotten third-world country. But for all his tough exterior, Caleb was undeniably handsome, and the kindness in his eyes betrayed a heart that Harper couldn't help but love. Instantly. She nearly melted from relief, and then joy at the understanding that this was the man Adri was falling for. He couldn't possibly be more different from David.

"What are you doing here?" Adri didn't seem quite as happy as Harper was that the man before them was none other than her coworker.

But Caleb was undeterred. A grin spread across his face and he eliminated the space between them in a couple of long strides. Adri's subtle protests were completely ignored when he swept her up in a hug that made her feet dangle off the floor. He buried his face in her neck, breathed deeply of her hair and her ivory smooth skin, and then lowered her as gently as if she was made of porcelain.

"I'm here to see you," Caleb told her, and though there was no way he could miss Adri's lukewarm reception, it appeared he didn't expect her to jump up and down at his surprise arrival. His smile was soft for her, but determination shadowed his eyes.

If Harper knew anything at all about men, she'd bet Maple Acres and Piperhall, too, that Caleb was going to do anything and everything in his power to win the woman before him.

Adri just stared at him. She looked a little mystified. A lot scared.

For a moment, it was as if Sam and Harper didn't even exist, and they exchanged a knowing smile behind Adri's back. Sam raised his eyebrows at Harper, and she shrugged to let him know that she had no insight to add into Caleb's sudden appearance in Blackhawk.

"I told you not to come," Adri finally managed. But her hand had trailed down his arm when he released her, and she held it there lightly against the intricate design of a tattoo that Harper couldn't quite make out. Adri's words were accusatory, but her eyes were wide, her lips slightly parted, as if she couldn't believe that Caleb was before her, in the flesh. "You can't just leave. That's not how it works . . ."

"I didn't just leave." He tipped her chin with his finger and searched her eyes. Broke contact before she had a chance to rebuff him. "The board trip this year included a GP and his three kids: a nurse, a hand surgeon, and a dentist. A high-achieving family, I'd say. I think they wanted us out of the way for a week or two."

"But—"

"No buts. My leave was scheduled months ago. They sent me home, and I told you I'd come. La Crosse is less than five hours from Blackhawk, by the way. I left at six this morning."

Adri seemed poised to argue even more, but Harper couldn't stand to see her disappoint him. There was too much hope in his eyes. "Hi," she said, stepping forward. "I'm Harper. It's nice to meet you."

Caleb turned his startling gaze to her, and a shy smile nipped at the corners of her mouth. Harper felt distinctly unbalanced, and fear was still leaching out of her bones in slow motion. But he was not only beautiful, he was warmth itself, and when

Caleb took her hand, she felt the last vestiges of panic slip away.

"It's nice to meet you, too," he said.

"Harper is an old friend," Adri finally said, jumping into the conversation a couple of seconds late. A confused look flitted across her features as she struggled with what to say next. All the regular niceties were beyond her reach. She couldn't say exactly where Harper was from or what she did. Or even why she was in Blackhawk. She settled for "We go way back."

"I surprised Adri, too," Harper said to Caleb conspiratorially. But she didn't want even a hint of impropriety to bloom between them, so she extracted her hand from his and took a step back. Not that she had to worry. Caleb only had eyes for Adri. "I'm afraid I have something I need to do, so I guess I'll leave you two alone."

Sam gave her a funny look, but quickly jumped on the bandwagon. "Me, too," he said. "I'll drive you, Harper. Caleb, can we count on you for dinner?"

His smile was dazzling for Sam. "That sounds great."

They left Adri standing beside Caleb, a bewildered look on her face. But Caleb didn't seem to mind. He put his arm around her shoulder, and instead of pulling away from him, Adri leaned slightly into his easy embrace and watched her father and Harper leave.

~

Sam and Harper climbed into his rusted pickup truck, Beckett between them. The huge dog seemed to take up most of the cab, but it was cold outside and he was stiff in the mornings. Harper didn't blame Sam for letting Beckett ride shotgun, and she took his graying head and pulled it down onto her lap. "So that's Caleb," Sam mused as he put the truck in drive and took off down the lane.

"Guess so," Harper said, and though there were a dozen

reasons for her not to smile, she couldn't keep the grin out of her voice. "I like him."

Sam shot her a sideways look. "Me, too."

"You do? You never really liked David." It was out of Harper's mouth before she could censor herself. What an impossible thing to say. Senseless. Callous. Too close to the heart of the problem that had plagued them all for half a decade. But Sam wasn't ruffled by her outburst.

"I didn't much care for him," he agreed.

The lid had been cracked, and there seemed no point in pretending that they weren't already talking about it, so Harper asked, "Why?"

"Lots of little reasons," Sam said without pause. He was focused on the road, his attention on the intersection at the end of the drive, but Harper could tell that whatever he was about to say, it would not be flippant. "Don't get me wrong. He was a smart kid. Handsome and friendly. He had a lot of potential. But there was one big thing that always bugged me about him."

"What was that?"

Sam turned onto the road, and when the truck was perfectly balanced in the center of his lane, he stared Harper straight in the eye for a moment. "He didn't love Adri."

"Did you ever tell her that?"

"Did you?"

He had her there. As much as she loved Adri, apparently, as much as they both did, summoning the courage to have that sort of agonizing conversation was something that neither of them had been able to do. Who could blame them? What were they supposed to say? Adrienne, sweetheart, your fiancé doesn't love you and never has? It was a conversation doomed from the start, coming from her father (the man who had never liked David) or Harper (the woman who had always loved him).

Even so, Harper could tell that Sam regretted his own cowardice. They both did.

"Well," Sam said after a moment. "You have plans for the day?"

"I need to get online. Does the library have computers?"

"Believe it or not, Harper, I have a computer. It's probably a clunker, but it works. Maple Acres even has Wi-Fi."

"Well, aren't you tech-savvy?" Harper reached over Beckett and gave Sam's sleeve a little tug. "Thanks for the offer," she demurred, "but I'd actually like some privacy."

"Of course. Feel free to use my truck."

Sam dropped himself off at the farm and left the engine running. It took a bit of convincing to coax Beckett off the bench seat, but when he finally lumbered down, Harper slid behind the wheel. "Thanks," she said, holding Sam's sweet gaze for just a moment too long. Her gratitude was boundless, deeper than it should have been, and it seemed Sam could tell, because he stayed wedged in the open door.

"You're coming back, right?" he asked, searching her face.

"Of course." She made a dismissive sound in the back of her throat, but it was weak and ineffectual.

"You don't have to run away from us." It was a bold thing to say, but instead of feeling affronted, Harper found herself wanting to hug Sam and never let go.

"I'm not running from you," Harper whispered.

"I know. But let me tell you something, Harper. It's obvious you're running, and if there's anything I'm sure of, it's that you can only run for so long. Eventually you have to stop, and when you do, we sure would love to be there for you."

Harper couldn't look at him anymore. She put her forehead on the steering wheel, over the peaks and ridges of her knuckles, as she held on for dear life. "What if I'm getting exactly what I deserve?"

Sam put a hand on her back. "Come on, Harper. You're forgiven."

"And what if I can't forgive myself?"

"I suppose you could spend the rest of your life running."

"I'm a masochist." She laughed dryly. "I intended to spend the rest of my life punishing myself."

"Doesn't sound like much fun to me," Sam said.

"You don't know what I've done."

"I don't need to know." Sam stepped back, but before he did, he kissed Harper on the head. It was such a gentle, fatherly gesture. She held her breath, tried to capture the moment and fold it away so she could keep it with her always. But it was a fleeting emotion, and even as she tried to hold it close, she felt it slip right through her fingers.

Sam said, "Doesn't matter what you did. Or what you try to do to fix it. The debt's already been paid, Harper." And then he shut the truck door quietly.

Alone in the cab, Harper breathed. In and out. Nothing fancy. But even that felt like too much, almost more than she could handle. How many times had she tried to drive away from this farm? These people? Twice in this morning alone. And each time she was turned back, drawn in by a family that seemed determined not to let her go. A family? She didn't dare to call them that. She couldn't.

Because Harper couldn't bring herself to drive away, she did exactly what she'd told Sam she was going to do: go to the library.

The library in Blackhawk was a small, unremarkable building, but the parking lot was packed. Harper almost turned around, but she didn't know where else to go. Weaving through the aisles, she found an empty spot near the back and parked, then walked through the tall double doors amid a horde of small children and their mothers headed in the opposite direction. Some library program had just ended, and though Harper was grateful that they were all exiting instead of entering, something about the crush of people made her feel exposed.

The feeling was exacerbated when someone said her name. "Harper? Harper Penny?"

Harper turned hesitantly and found herself face-to-face with a sophisticated, elderly woman.

"I thought it was you." She gave Harper a brief, earnest hug, then stood back a little to observe her. "First Adri and now you. I feel like my world is spinning backwards."

"Mrs. Holt?" The name came to Harper's lips involuntarily. She was shocked that she still remembered a woman whom she had only seen a handful of times.

"I wondered if you'd remember me." Katherine smiled demurely.

"Of course I do." The lie came easily, even though she was casting around for some memory, some telling moment that she could latch on to. "Do you work here?"

"Oh, no." Katherine shook her head as she touched the hair of a boy who walked past. "I'm retired, but I volunteer at story hour on Monday, Wednesday, and Friday mornings." She waved to a little girl in pigtails. "See you next week, Anna."

Harper was trying to think of a polite way to extract herself from the awkward reunion, but Katherine seemed to pick up on her subtle cues before Harper was forced to be rude. "Is there something you're looking for?"

"A computer, actually."

"We have several," she said. "Though you need a library card and a computer pass. I suppose you don't have either one?"

Harper shook her head.

"You may use mine."

"Thank you," Harper said sincerely, grateful for the first time that she had bumped into an old acquaintance.

It was obvious that Katherine was too decorous to pepper Harper with questions, but that didn't erase the obvious tension in the air. After Katherine had her settled at a discreet terminal, she asked, "So what are you doing in Blackhawk, Harper? Visiting ATU?"

Of course, Harper hadn't stepped foot on campus since arriving in Blackhawk. Maple Acres and Piperhall were enough of an emotional snare. No need to dredge up even more bittersweet memories. "I'm visiting Adri," Harper said.

"Well, it's nice to have you back for any reason. Blackhawk has changed a lot since the last time you were here."

"Blackhawk will always have a special place in my heart," Harper mumbled, though it felt like a stupid thing to say. She was discovering that she wasn't very good at small talk.

"I'm glad to hear that," Mrs. Holt said, patting her arm. "In spite of everything, I hope the Galloway estate has a special place in your heart, too."

"I have many fond memories of it." Harper felt mildly defensive, and Katherine stepped back as if reprimanded.

For a moment, Katherine looked as if she was about to leave. She leaned back on her heels, inclined her head to say goodbye. But then she seemed to think better of it and stalled. "Blackhawk has changed a lot," she said again. "And I can't help wondering if things might have turned out differently if the change had come sooner."

"What do you mean?" Harper asked, almost against her own will.

Katherine leaned in. Said quietly, as if it was a secret, "New stores, new people, new ideas. There's even a crisis center. It's called the Safe House."

Harper didn't know what to say. Was it that obvious? Could Katherine Holt see abuse like a tattoo on her skin? Or was she just alluding to everything that had happened with Victoria?

Mrs. Holt melted away without saying goodbye, and Harper tried to pretend that they hadn't bumped into each other at all. She had forgotten the intimacy of a small town, the way everyone seemed to know everyone else, and she hadn't expected to see a single familiar face in her little quest for information. It had thrown her off her game. Shaking off the vestiges of her odd conversation, Harper tried to focus on the task at hand.

She didn't really care about her fake Facebook account, but she clicked through to her home page all the same. There were updates, new photos, things that would have piqued her interest a couple of days ago. But Harper was dizzy with exhaustion. And though she had labored to distract herself with the events of the last several hours, Sawyer's morning wake-up call was a bass line that drummed through her veins.

The Facebook check took all of two minutes. It wasn't why Harper had come to the library. But it was a place to start. A way to ease herself into the main event. When she finally gave up the pretense and tapped in the username and password to her email account, she found exactly what she was looking for. A message.

Just one. An innocent-looking subject line: "Hi." That was it.

So innocuous, but Harper was downright terrified to open it. She took her hands off the keypad and wrung them in her lap. Considered logging off and walking away. But the lure was set. She had to know.

A click. And then . . .

Photos.

Not even a single written line. Just a nauseating cache of pictures that made Harper lurch out of her seat. She didn't simply close out her email or log off the computer. She flicked off the system unit and the monitor, and yanked the cord from the floor. As if that would do anything. As if she could erase what Sawyer had done.

On her way out of the library, Harper grabbed the phone book and looked up Safe House. Committed the address to memory.

～

23

"What can I help you with, sweetie?" Jenna Hudson, the executive director of the Safe House tipped forward in her chair and crossed her arms on the top of her desk. Harper guessed she was in her late thirties, but she looked younger. Her hair was a chaotic cloud of dark corkscrew curls, and there were happy little laugh lines around her bright eyes. Though a gentle smile graced her lips, a certain gravity lent a serious aspect to her countenance. Harper had intended to play it cool, but something about Jenna inspired trust.

"Actually,"—Harper tucked a strand of hair behind her ear and tried to act nonchalant—"I just have a few questions."

"I'm listening." Jenna seemed to settle, to focus all of her earnest attention on Harper. It was a little unnerving, but Harper found herself wanting to talk all the same. After holding everything in for so long, she felt almost giddy at the thought of letting even a few details slip. Giddy, and scared.

"I'm in a bit of a difficult situation," she said. "I guess I was just wondering what my options are."

"May I ask what kind of a difficult situation?"

Harper's mouth went dry. She squeezed her eyes shut for just a second, but the small action betrayed her. Jenna took the reins.

"Let's back up a little bit," she said kindly. "May I ask you a few questions?"

Harper nodded.

"Are you here for your own reasons, or on behalf of a friend or family member?"

It was a simple enough inquiry, but Harper found she couldn't form the words. She didn't even try to open her mouth, she just touched her fingertips to her chest.

Jenna went on. "Do you feel unsafe or threatened?"

Harper didn't have to answer. The look on her face was evidence enough.

"Do you believe that your life is in danger?"

She did. For the first time ever, she really did. Harper knew that Sawyer was unpredictable from the very first moment she met him, but she hadn't realized just how deeply the depraved vein of his selfishness carved into his wicked soul. The photos were meant to torture her. And the phone calls. What else would he do? It was clear he wasn't about to let her go without a fight.

"It's complicated," Harper finally managed. "I don't think he'd hurt me, but . . ."

"He doesn't have to hit you to harm you." Jenna put her hands palm down on her desk and searched Harper's eyes. She was grave now, deadly serious when she asked, "Is he controlling? Manipulative?"

Harper didn't answer.

"Does he isolate you from family and friends?"

She isolated herself from family and friends, but Sawyer cut her off from the rest of the world.

"Have you ever been forced to participate in sexual acts that you are uncomfortable with?"

It was too much. Harper regretted coming at all. Wished she had never parked in front of the inconspicuous home on a residential street in the heart of Blackhawk. When she pulled up to the address, she had wondered if she was even in the right place, because there was no sign, no indication at all that the humble blue house before her was anything other than some family's home. But then she had seen the heavy locks on the door, the windows hung with glass so opaque that she'd wondered if it was bulletproof. Harper had knocked on the door and Jenna had answered. She had been swept inside before she had a chance to think about what she was doing. What it would mean.

She had thought, for just a moment, that maybe she could do something. Fight back. But she had no option.

"You have options," Jenna was saying. She sat up pin straight in her chair and grabbed a folder off a nearby table. "One of our case managers can help assess the situation and decide on the most prudent course of action to keep you safe. If you have a paper trail, we can file for a restraining order against your abuser. Is anything documented?"

Harper shook her head.

"That's okay. I'll start a file now, and we can begin collecting the evidence that we'll need."

Evidence. Harper didn't want to share any evidence with anyone. And how could Sawyer be held responsible for something that she willingly and repeatedly allowed to happen? Okay, not willingly. Never willingly. But she had also never fought him. And he had never hit her, never held a gun to her head. Sure, he was manipulative and controlling and mean; sure, he had chased her through the parking lot of La Belle Vie, but did any of that make him an abuser?

"Do you have a place to stay?" Jenna continued.

Harper's thoughts were spinning out of control. "Yes," she stammered. "I do. I'm fine, actually. I'll be just fine. I need to go." She all but jumped out of her seat and turned toward the door, then felt a compulsion to say thank you or something and quickly spun back around to offer Jenna her hand.

The administrator of the Safe House stood, too, and took Harper's hand in both of her own. Held it tight. "I can't make you stay," she said, "but I wish that you would. I believe you, and I'd like to help you if you let me."

"Thank you," Harper said. "That's very kind. But I'm . . . overreacting. It's nothing."

"Please, come back anytime. Day or night. Someone is always here. We won't turn you away."

But the house was small and Harper had seen several women making lunch in the kitchen when she came in. "Looks like you've got your hands full," she said, pulling out of Jenna's grip.

"We always do." Jenna's eyes crinkled at the corners, a sad starburst of tiny wrinkles. "But we'll make room. We can always make more room."

Harper didn't want anyone to make room for her. She hurried out as quickly as she dared, carefully avoiding even the briefest glance into the kitchen at the women who were chatting away as they assembled sandwiches.

She didn't want to look at them. To see their faces and in them, see herself.

～～

The kitchen of Maple Acres was full of people when Harper finally returned. After leaving the Safe House, she had idled around Blackhawk for hours, stopping at every lookout and half-forgotten haunt, puttering through campus as she tried to gather the courage to drive away. She knew that Sam wouldn't chase her. He wouldn't call the cops or report his car stolen or do anything at all. She believed he would let her go. Still, she found that she couldn't bring herself to hit the open road. Not like this. Not quite yet.

But when she stepped into the kitchen amid the hustle and bustle of laughter and conversation, music and food, she felt like an outsider. Will and Jackson were shoulder to shoulder at the counter, their backs turned to Harper as they worked on something she couldn't quite see. Nora—it had to be her—was leaning against the buffet with one hand, absently stroking her enormous belly as she supervised the boys' handiwork. Adri and Caleb were across the table from each other, peeling and slicing green apples for a piecrust that had been draped over the edges of a deep-dish plate. The unbaked crust hadn't been trimmed or crimped, and Harper felt a sudden longing to take a pinch of it in her mouth. It looked so soft and sweet, so homey, dusted with pale flour and pleated in thick ridges.

She didn't reach out. The old Harper, the girl she had been, would have seized a fistful of the raw crust, stuffed it with fresh slices of the cinnamon-sprinkled apples, and dipped her mini pie into the open canister of sugar on the table. She would have grinned at the way Adri wrinkled her nose at Caleb, innocent and coy at once, her signature flirty move. And there was no doubt that she would have rubbed Nora's ripe belly, then squeezed between the men at the counter, one arm around them both. Maybe even dropped a kiss on each of their cheeks just so she could inhale all the warm, exotic layers of Will, so different and yet so familiar.

Harper didn't do any of those things. Instead, she battled the urge to flee. It was obvious that she didn't belong here.

Before she could slip out of the kitchen and into the orange dusk, the door opened behind her. Harper didn't even have a chance to turn around. She was less than a step away from the screen, and when Sam slipped through, the first thing he did was tuck an arm around her shoulder. Give her a quick hug.

"I'm glad you're here," he said, only for her ears. And then, louder, "You're destroying my kitchen!"

"We're doing no such thing," Will laughed, glancing over his shoulder. He caught sight of Harper and his face brightened. Or did she just imagine it? "Harper! I didn't even hear you come in."

"I'm sneaky that way," she said, mustering a faint smile.

"I'll say. How long have you been standing there?"

Every eye in the kitchen was on her, but she wasn't surprised that her quiet entrance had gone unnoticed. The music was loud. Everyone was consumed with the task at hand. Except for Adri and Caleb, who were obviously consumed with each other. Though Adri was trying to pretend not to be.

Harper felt sorrow swell inside her, regret at the realization that this would never be hers—could never be hers. But she forced herself to stand a little straighter. To smile, even if it was lopsided. "I've been here long enough to realize that you all need some help," she said.

Adri caught her eye and something passed between them. An understanding. A moment of almost girlish ebullience.

"Caleb is worthless at this," Adri said. "I wouldn't say *we* need help, but he certainly does."

Although it made her ache to do so, Harper joined in, and together they made free-form individual pizzas and apple pie. At one point, Nora gave her a mildly awkward one-armed hug and whispered what sounded like a heartfelt "Welcome home," and Harper nearly burst into tears. Who was this woman to welcome her? If Harper remembered correctly, and she was sure that she did, she had barely given Nora the time of day in college. She certainly didn't deserve her kindness now.

Instead of succumbing to her emotions, Harper gulped them down and teased everyone about the odd choice in dinner fare. Jackson informed her it was "anything goes" night. Caleb had confessed to a longing for pie, and Adri remembered the nights at ATU when Jackson hauled out his grandmother's recipe for homemade bread dough and made thick, bubbling pizzas for The Five.

"Anything for our guests," Will told her with a wink. "Is there something you'd like to add to the menu?"

Of course not. Though Harper had made fun of the hodge-podge meal, it sounded like pure perfection. They layered thin slices of tomato, peppers, and red onions from Sam's garden on the pizza, and finished it with crisp bacon and crumbled Italian sausage. Then, after they'd eaten every last bite and proclaimed themselves too full for another, Sam served the apple pie hot from the oven with vanilla ice cream and a drizzle of caramel sauce. They all somehow found room for more.

The table was a train wreck of plates stacked high and glasses half full of water and warm beer. Someone had tipped over the plastic container of shredded Parmesan cheese, and there was a little white hill of the dry, pungent slivers. Harper's heart caught at the comfort contained in the benign chaos, the way that each licked-clean fork told a story of plenty. Of laughter around the table. She cleared her throat and rose to clear it all away.

"Hey—" Will caught her wrist and ringed it lightly with his fingers. "You don't have to do that."

"I absolutely do," she managed, flashing him a crooked smile. "You cooked."

"You helped," Jackson reminded her.

"That's being generous. You all stay put, I've got this."

And because she sounded convincing, or because they were all full and sleepy and didn't feel like arguing, they let her. Jackson regaled Caleb with stories of Will's mishaps on the job (he rolled an excavator his very first week—butterflies filled Harper's chest at the thought). Caleb offered snippets of his experiences with Adri in Africa (she stepped on a sea urchin rescuing a nonswimmer from the riptide and Caleb had to painstakingly remove each spine with a tweezer). And Nora smiled faintly, glowing with life as if everything that had come before was irrelevant. Sam presided over it all with a look of pure euphoria on his face. It was lovely. It made Harper want to lay her cheek against the top of his head.

They chatted as she loaded the dishwasher and rinsed a cloth to wipe the table. As she leaned past them to mop up the crumbs, Jackson turned to Caleb and asked the obvious question that no one had thought to mention: "Where are you going to stay tonight, Caleb? I mean, I assume you are staying?"

"For sure," Caleb said, glancing at the clock on the wall. It was nearly ten o'clock. They had sat for hours. Nora was yawning against the back of her delicate hand. "Is there a hotel nearby? Something swanky?" He elbowed Adri with a grin.

"Blackhawk is all kinds of swanky," Will cut in. "But you're welcome to stay at my place. You can have my bed. I'll take the couch."

Nora nodded. "We have a couch, too."

"You're welcome to stay here," Sam said. "The girls are in the spare rooms, but I'm always up early and I happen to love my couch."

"So many couches! But I don't want to be a bother." Caleb said.

Harper put her hand on his shoulder. She had frozen at Jackson's question, and a plan was beginning to take shape in misty corners of her mind. "Let's stay at the mansion," she said quietly.

The laughter and conversation cooled and dimmed. Harper could feel every eye on her.

"For old times' sake." She knew it would take a lot to sell her idea, and she tried to muster the appropriate charm. Straightening up, she put her hands on her hips, damp washcloth and all. "Come on," she said, catching Will's eye. If she could get through to him, the rest would follow. "It'll be fun. We'll sit in the hot tub and play drinking games."

"Drinking games?" Will laughed. "We have to work tomorrow, Harper. We're grown-ups now, remember?"

"And I'm pregnant," Nora reminded them, though no one could forget.

"We'll be responsible," Harper assured everyone, but the twinkle in her eye said that they would be no such thing. She knew she could promise the world with a tweak of her perfect lips, and as she held Will's gaze, she made all sorts of vows she knew she could never keep. Not that she didn't necessarily want to.

"No," Adri said, but from her tone Harper could tell that she didn't quite mean it. Not fully. There might be ghosts in Piperhall, but they were their ghosts. Whether or not any of them would admit it, something felt distinctly right about going back.

About spending a night in the place that marked the advent of their nightmares. Harper knew it the second the thought entered her head.

"Please." Harper sought out Adri, but she was looking resolutely out the window, searching the dark night beyond the glass. "Just once," she cajoled, though Adri seemed to be ignoring her. "One night. I don't know why, but I feel like we should. If you're going to sell it or give it away or board it up . . ."

"Go ahead," Nora said, nudging Jackson and surprising them all. "One last hurrah. Besides, that means I'll get the bed to myself." She heaved herself to her feet and gave Jackson a kiss on the cheek, then held out her hand for the cloth that Harper had forgotten about. Harper handed it to Nora, and the visibly exhausted woman finished wiping the table.

"It might be good for us to spend one last night," Jackson said, watching his wife. It was obvious that he adored her. And that she deserved his devotion. Harper felt her chest tighten a little, watching them. But then Jackson tore his gaze away from Nora and shrugged. "We can say goodbye." He didn't say it, but they all heard it: And move on.

Harper loved him for it. And Nora, too. But not for the reasons that the others might have expected. She didn't want to stroll down memory lane or put anything at all to rest. She just wanted to get away from Maple Acres and the only known address that Sawyer had for her.

"I'm in, too." Will stood up and draped an arm around Harper's shoulders. "I think it's a great idea. And the house is just sitting there, Adri. One last time. Come on."

"Come on," Caleb echoed, leaning his forearms on the table and trying to catch Adri's eye. "It'll be fun." He looked around the table and mimed a shrug as if to say, Am I doing it right? Is this okay?

Adri put her face in her hands, but Harper could see her friend was fighting a smile beneath her twined fingers. "Fine," she said. "Whatever. You all win."

"We'll spend the night at Piperhall?" Harper shaded a bit of girlish delight into her voice and was rewarded when Will grabbed her hand and squeezed it. She squeezed back, aching.

"Sure."

"You won't regret it. *We* won't regret it," Harper said. But she didn't believe that for a second. When they woke in the morning and Caleb's car was gone—or Jackson's or Will's or Adri's, it didn't matter whose—they'd know that they had been tricked and they would have all sorts of regrets. But Harper couldn't worry about any of that. All she cared about was keeping Sawyer far away from the only family she had ever known.

Far away from the opportunity to make good on the threat that he held over her head like a guillotine. It wasn't just about the pictures, and it never had been. Shame she could deal with—Harper had endured more than her fair share of it. But there was no statute of limitations on murder. And if Sawyer couldn't have her, she knew that he would do nothing less than destroy her.

~~

Harper heard Caleb say it as she mounted the steps to pack her Goodwill clothes into a grocery bag: "She's very convincing, you know."

Harper could just imagine how Adri would roll her eyes. "I know. She could talk a fish into buying a piece of the ocean."

And it was true. All those years ago, after she discovered that David didn't love her and never had, after she understood that the moment of her college graduation would mark the beginning of the end of what was her pathetic, lonely life, she had done a lot of convincing.

"A trip," she said, making it sound like the most appealing, magical thing in all the world. "Just the five of us. Right after graduation. A grand finale, a climax, the zenith of our years together."

"You're laying it on a bit thick, don't you think?" David

asked. His words were a little slurry, but his eyes were trained on her. Adri was curled in his lap, looking as small and pretty as a doll. They seemed to be doing better since the night at Piperhall when Victoria had discovered Harper in David's arms. He was more attentive, more present. He kissed her slowly, even when other people were in the room. Sometimes, it seemed like he did it particularly when other people were in the room. Especially Harper.

But, in spite of David's attention, every once in a while, Adri wasn't quite herself. A trio of small bruises on her upper arm, a swollen lip that she tried to cover with pink lip gloss. Harper wondered, but she didn't dare ask. Adri seemed happy, and Harper wanted to believe that if Adri had told her the truth once, she would again. Besides, David was a passionate man. A hard kiss, a consuming embrace. It wasn't out of the realm of possibility. And Harper wanted to believe.

It wasn't quite enough. Harper longed for the chance to be alone. Ask questions. Learn the truth. She was downright obsessed with knowing. "If you're not convinced, I'm not laying it on thick enough," Harper said. "What do I have to do to persuade you? A PowerPoint presentation? A speech? 'Cause I could deliver a three-point sermon if that's what you're waiting for."

"Where would we go?" Will asked.

"I don't know." Harper threw up her hands as if it didn't matter. And in a way, it didn't. She was after one thing: time together. Enough time to figure it all out. To convince herself, and David, to tell Adri the truth before they ruined themselves. "The Maldives."

"I doubt you even know where that is." David brushed his lips against the fine line of Adri's jaw, but his eyes were trained on Harper.

She tried not to glare at him. Not to infuse her look with all the hatred that she felt in that moment. You're a pig, she wanted to say. A lying, conniving pig. But it hurt to even think those things, because as much as she wanted to hate him, she couldn't help but love him, too. He was still David. Broken, beautiful David. "The Canary Islands, Indonesia, Chicago? Does it matter?"

"British Columbia," Jackson offered as if coming out of a trance. Jackson was always quiet and unassuming and temperate, and it surprised Harper that he was speaking up at all. But, of course, he was offering the perfect solution. "My dad took me bush camping all the time when I was a kid. We'll fly into Vancouver, borrow my grandma's car, and I'll take you all to my favorite spot in the interior. You don't mind logging roads, do you?"

They didn't even know what logging roads were, but the promise of isolation, of a place where they could be utterly and completely alone in the world was too good to pass up.

"Done," Harper said, sealing a deal that would change their lives forever. "We're backpacking BC."

"Well"—Jackson shrugged—"not really. We'll find the perfect spot and park. Of course, we can hike as much as we want from there."

Everyone was quiet for a moment, but Harper marched up to Jackson and kissed him full on the mouth. "I love you," she said. "We'll park in BC."

"And camp," Jackson offered, seemingly unruffled by Harper's sudden, dizzying affection. "And fish if we want to or swim or free-climb. Whatever."

"I don't even know what free-climbing is," Harper said, but it didn't matter anyway.

It was done. They graduated, and the day after The Five flung their mortarboards into the air and celebrated their entrance into the "real world," they boarded a plane for Vancouver.

In some ways, Harper regretted stepping foot on that airplane almost more than everything that came after. If only, she had thought a hundred times. A thousand.

If only.

24

~

They were teenagers at a coed sleepover. At least, that was the vibe that Harper was going for. When they arrived at Piperhall carrying duffel bags (the guys) and plastic grocery bags (the girls) filled with toiletries and a change of clothes, Harper danced up the stone stairs and across the wide veranda as if there was a live band playing just out of sight. She shimmied a little and laughed while Adri struggled with her keys in the dark.

"We could break a window," Harper suggested, though the instant the words were out of her mouth she felt like an idiot. It was a stupid thing to say, the sort of inane filler that used to fall from her lips all the time. And though she knew she had once been brilliant, that she could understand people and motivations and situations that others couldn't begin to process, she hated herself for letting her mind atrophy. For playing a part that she was loath to play, simply because it was easier. She wondered if anyone could see that she wasn't who she wanted to be.

"I've got it," Adri said, unhooking the padlock and palming it. "No need to shatter any windows."

The mansion was dense with shadows when they stepped inside. Darkness seemed to shroud the quiet rooms, the air thick and heavy as a mausoleum. It was a cloudy, moonless night, and

Harper should have expected the stranglehold of blackness, but it took her by surprise. She must have made an unconscious noise because suddenly Will was at her side, his hand cupping her elbow as if he intended to help her stand.

"You okay?"

"Fine," she said brightly, trying to dispel the dark with the tone of her voice. She used to be able to do that. To shift the mood in a room simply by pressing into it, willing it to bend a certain way as if she was leaning on a whip of willow. "I just forgot how dark it is out here. No streetlamps, no moon . . ."

"Let there be light," Adri said from somewhere to the right, and without warning the chandelier in the grand entryway burst to life.

Caleb whistled low. "Magic," he said, looking around. "You know, this place is almost as nice as your bungalow."

That elicited a laugh from Adri, and the two of them exchanged a knowing glance over their private joke. "My entire bungalow would fit into the entryway."

No one talked about sleeping arrangements. Now that they were standing in the sparkling light of the cut-glass chandelier, the topic seemed almost off-limits. The mansion might be Adri's now, but it was still the Galloway estate. Harper could feel Victoria above her, drifting through the hallways of the place she had called home for the most significant years of her life. And there was David, echoed in the parody of the five of them standing in the entryway as if they had just arrived from ATU. Even Liam lingered, though Harper had never known him and was glad that she hadn't.

Maybe coming here had been a bad idea.

But all she needed to do was endure a couple of hours. Just long enough to lull everyone into a sense of companionship and peace, and then send them off to sleep. Harper knew she had to disappear, and fast. She could feel the clock ticking beneath her skin. She just hadn't decided yet if she was running to Sawyer or away from him.

"Drinks?" Harper pulled away from Will and all but skipped deeper into the house as she tried to recapture the cheerful nonchalance she was trying so hard to portray. "I can't imagine that Victoria burned through all of that Scotch." She was halfway to the back of the house when she remembered that it wasn't Victoria's Scotch anymore. It was Adri's. But the rest of their small party was following her, and Adri didn't seem put out by Harper's presumption.

"I think the Scotch is all still in the basement," Adri said. "Liam kept it on display in the billiards room."

"The liquor cabinet is above the refrigerator," Will offered. "And I noticed earlier that the wine rack has a few bottles left."

"I don't like Scotch anyway," Caleb said, slinging his duffel bag onto the counter and settling himself on one of the bar stools. "In fact, I'll take a glass of water, please."

"Water?" Harper sounded offended. "It's not that kind of party, Caleb."

He shrugged.

But Harper didn't have to cajole anyone else. Jackson had already opened the liquor cabinet and was lifting down a couple of bottles. Hennessy cognac and Bombay Sapphire and Chambord raspberry liqueur. He poured a shot for everyone, and Harper almost sighed. It wasn't them. This almost aggressive posturing wasn't any of them anymore, and yet, she didn't know any other way to blunt the edges, to dull senses enough to render everyone anesthetized. She had to be the party planner who would keep everyone happy and distracted. Drinking.

"To reunions," Harper exclaimed, raising her shot glass.

Adri's mouth was a narrow line, but she lifted her tiny glass in a toast, and everyone else followed suit.

The raspberry Chambord was warm and heavy on Harper's tongue, and she allowed herself to enjoy it slipping down. But that was it. One drink, she had decided. Just one, and when

Jackson poured again, she tipped hers down the sink when no one was looking.

It was cold outside, and though Harper tried to rally the group around the hot tub, Adri wouldn't hear of it. She took a small glass of a drink that Jackson had mixed for her and settled herself in front of the fireplace. It was wide, white marble with veins of charcoal and pale gray, a piece of art that had once been the real deal but now could be turned on with a switch. Adri tapped a couple of buttons on a remote control and the flames leaped beneath the stately hearth, a blue-hearted inferno that spread six feet across the living room. They could have roasted marshmallows in it, and had on many occasions. S'mores with sliced strawberries and dark chocolate, or peanut butter cups because they were David's favorite.

When the rest of the group joined her—Will and Jackson on the floor, Caleb in the middle of the couch where Adri sat snug against one end—Harper felt a flutter of panic in her chest. They were supposed to laugh and drink and be merry, not cozy up in the living room so they could stare contemplatively at the fire. Adri nursed a wrinkle between her eyes while she ignored her drink, and Harper knew without asking that she was thinking about David.

Harper felt like a net was closing around her. It wasn't just Sawyer and the things he knew about her, it was David, too. And Adri and everyone. It was herself. A part of her wanted to walk into the middle of the half-circle her friends had created and say, I did it. I had an affair with David and then I killed him. And because I couldn't forgive myself, I allowed my life to become the worst kind of evil. Then what? Anger, heartbreak, hatred. Lawyers and a trial. She had no defense.

Run. Run fast.

It was all she could think to do.

But she curled up in a chair across from Adri because she couldn't run away just yet.

They had covered all sorts of ground over supper, the little things, small talk and surfacey introductions and the stories that elicited polite laughter. It was no surprise, really, when Caleb asked, "So, what's the deal here? How did you inherit this place, Adri?"

It was stop and start, the thinnest details only, but Adri told him about college. The Five. David. She barely grazed the man she had loved, painting him watercolor pale with words like *smart* and *handsome* and *rich*. Harper knew these were throwaway words, adjectives that meant nothing at all.

"And . . ." Caleb paused. "He died?"

When Adri didn't answer, Jackson did. "It was an accident. The week after we graduated from ATU."

An accident. Harper swallowed hard, chanced a glance at Adri. Was surprised to see that she looked as troubled as Harper felt. Maybe she did know. At least, something.

Caleb looked for a moment like he wanted to ask more, but he took a sip of his drink and held his tongue.

The night wasn't what Harper had in mind, and when the clock chimed midnight and Jackson announced it the witching hour, she wrapped her arms around herself to ward off the chill.

"Bed, I think," Jackson said, standing and stretching. "I want to stop home and see Nora before work, and the crew will be waiting at the shop by six." At this tidbit of information, he tipped his head at Will and gave him a look laced with meaning. It could have been merely a reminder that they had obligations, responsibilities, but Harper felt like it was more than that. She watched as Will nodded.

Jackson got up and walked to the kitchen to rinse out his glass. Harper thought about calling after him, trying to convince him to stick around—at least long enough for everyone to reach the same tired state that he conveyed with a jaw-cracking yawn. Adri was wide-eyed, searching the heart of the fire as if answers were contained in the iridescent flames. And Caleb was still watching Adri, his mouth soft as he admired the glow in her eyes. When Harper caught Will's gaze, she was startled to find that he was looking at her, and she knew that if Jackson left, he'd ask for a moment alone with her again. She couldn't let that happen.

"I'm exhausted," Harper said, standing suddenly. "Done. Can't keep my eyes open another second."

"You might have to keep them open another second or two." A strange, small smile tugged at Will's lips. "You have a lot of stairs to climb."

"This is your party," Adri reminded her. "Are you allowed to leave early?"

"It's not early," Harper insisted. "Jackson said it's the witching hour. Sounds like a good time to call it quits, wouldn't you say?"

"I think I'll watch the fire a little longer," Caleb said, stealing a glance at Adri. She wouldn't look at him, but she nodded all the same. "Me, too."

"In that case"—Will slapped his hands on his knees and rose—"I'll walk you to your room, Harper. You know, in case you find you can't keep your eyes open for another second and lose your way."

She opened her mouth to demur, but Will was already taking her empty glass from her, looking into it as if he could tell that she hadn't really had anything to drink at all.

Will wandered off to get rid of their glasses, and Jackson came up to Harper and pulled her into a hug. It was exactly the sort of odd, unexpected thing he was known for, but she was nearly undone when he murmured into her ear, "We love you, Harper. No matter what. You know that, right?"

It was a sweet sentiment, but Harper was well aware that it wasn't true. They wouldn't love her no matter what. They couldn't.

"Thanks, Jackson," she said. And though she could tell that he didn't believe her, he squeezed her arm and let her go. Headed toward the entryway and the stairs that would lead him to the garden basement and all the memories that waited there.

"Got your bag," Will said, holding up her plastic sack. "Do I need to carry you or do you think you'll be able to keep your eyes open?"

Harper gave him a little shove. "I employ hyperbole. So sue me." Turning to Adri and Caleb on the couch, she waved. "Good night, sleep tight."

"Don't let the bedbugs bite," Adri finished.

But Harper wasn't worried about bedbugs.

They mounted the back staircase, the narrow one behind the kitchen. It was dark and close, and though Harper wished at one point that she had talked Will into taking the long way around through the entry and past Victoria's rooms, she warmed to his hand on the small of her back as she climbed. She didn't want to feel this way. Didn't want the proximity of this kind, gentle man to muddy the waters that simply had to be crystal clear. She didn't want to love Will as anything other than an old friend, a fond memory, but everything about him called out to the longings she didn't even dare to admit. He was the anti-Sawyer. The anti-David. A man who asked for nothing more than her company, no strings attached. Though she could see the ache in his own eyes.

At the top of the stairs Harper fumbled for the switch and turned on the lights that illuminated the upstairs hall. Her bedroom—she still thought of it as hers—was open, and when she stepped inside and flicked on a lamp there was a dent in the comforter as if someone had lain there recently. She wanted to curl up in the spot. But Will was still behind her, holding the ridiculous grocery bag that contained all that she had in the world. It was too much. More than she could handle.

Before she could sob, Harper spun and flung herself at Will, arms twining up around his neck, fingers tangled in the ginger shock of his hair. She kissed him hungrily, her mouth and her body and every ounce of her being caught up in the simple perfection of the boy she had overlooked. What had she been thinking all those years ago? David—with all his jagged edges, with his daddy hurt and a mother who ignored him because she couldn't even care for herself—what in the world had made Harper think that they were perfect for one another? She and David had been deadweight, anchors that pulled each other down. But Will, sweet Will. He made her feel like she could float away. He tasted of raspberries and burnt sugar, vodka and pie. She wasn't the kind of girl who deserved a man like this. A man who had softly and privately loved her from a distance for years. Harper knew he had. She could feel it in the way that he kissed her.

And it was wrong of her to give him any hope.

As abruptly as she threw herself at him, Harper pulled away. "I'm sorry," she choked. "I'm so sorry, Will. I never should have . . ."

"Harper." Just her name, nothing more. Will said a thousand words with his silence, but Harper didn't have the heart to translate.

"You should go," she said, and when he took a hesitant step toward her, she took one back.

"Okay," he said. There was uncertainty in his voice, and Harper wanted to cave, but she thrust her feelings down and grabbed the bag that Will still clutched in his hand.

"Thanks for walking me upstairs," she said.

"Look, Harper, I want you to know that—"

"I can't," Harper interrupted before he could say something that ruined her resolve. "I can't do this right now. You really have to go."

Will looked for a moment like he was going to walk away, and Harper finally let go of the breath that she held. But he didn't turn. Something came over his features, and Harper had no choice but to stand there and let him come. Will closed the space between them in a stride, his chest brushing hers as he looked down and took her chin in his hand. He kissed her once, gently, his lips so full and soft that she felt herself leaning into him almost against her will. Then he backed away and held her gaze long enough to say, "That should have been our first kiss."

Harper watched him go. He didn't look back, and when he hit the stairs, the lights in the hallway went off. Harper was left alone in the faint, cold glow of the lamp that she had switched on.

If she was a different woman, Harper might have collapsed on the bed behind her. Cried or laughed or maybe stared at the ceiling, her heart spinning in her chest like a top. But she was a fighter, she had to be, and her mouth was still swollen from Will's kisses when she sliced those minutes out of the fabric of her life. It was a ragged cut, dirty and uneven, but it accomplished the job. Harper sniffed once, swallowed her tears, and dropped the bag of her belongings on the bed.

Then she switched off the lamp and crept across the darkened hall, feeling her way along the once-familiar path.

~

25

The back staircase led to a hallway behind the kitchen, and since Harper felt sure that Caleb and Adri would still be contemplating the fire in the great room just beyond, she decided to take the main staircase instead. All was dark as she made her way through the house, and as she went, she felt herself let it go for the very last time. She and Adri had promised themselves and each other that they would never come back here, and yet for years she had longed for exactly that. Not to relive old memories or visit a place that made her smile, but to atone somehow. To find a way to wind back the clock, make things right, start over. Well, there would be no new beginning for her, she knew that now, but Adrienne Vogt was a different story altogether.

Harper never intended to be a martyr, but as she pulled open the front door and whispered a goodbye, she found that she was more than a match for the weight of the cross she felt destined to bear.

Three cars were parked in the gravel drive, Will and Jackson's work truck, Caleb's mother's sleek silver Honda, and Betty. It had to be Betty. Harper raced down the steps and crossed the parking lot, her head ducked against the cool breeze, chin to her chest as if that would somehow camouflage her in the night. As if someone would be watching out for her, waiting to stop her if she attempted to go. Not likely.

Her hand was on the car door when she felt him.

A shift in the air, a shiver of understanding, and Harper's throat closed tight beneath the iron fist of her panic. "Will?" she tried to say his name, to summon him with a wish, a word. But no sound came out of her open mouth save a tiny, breathless moan.

"I thought you'd never come." Sawyer's voice split the air, hard and cold as a knife.

She didn't know where he was, cloaked in night and watching her like a predator, but before she could even flinch he was behind her. Sawyer pressed himself along the length of her body, as close as a lover against her skin. One arm snaked possessively around her waist and held her shackle-tight. "Did you miss me?" he asked, and though the question dripped affection, it was poisoned with malice.

Harper went numb. "I've been waiting out here in the dark for hours." His mouth was against her ear, his breath hot and harsh on her skin. She tried not to tremble. Not to vomit from the overwhelming wave of revulsion that washed over her at his proximity, the sound of his voice. It was better not to speak, to hold her tongue and let Sawyer talk himself out of the mood he was in. He did that. Talked and talked and talked, threatened sometimes and alluded to the fact that the well of his unusual appetites, his depraved ambition, went deeper than Harper had ever dared to guess. She was used to waiting him out. To letting him intimidate her, menacing, terrifyingly calm, until his anger ran dry.

"I watched you leave that old farmhouse with an entire entourage," Sawyer accused. "Did you think they'd protect you? Did you assume that I'd leave you alone if you shacked up with some rich guy?" He whistled low at the silhouette of the mansion before them, the sweeping grounds, the scent of money in the air. "I'd threaten to expose you to him, but a guy like that would probably love to keep a girl like you. Maybe he already has a room with chains. Maybe he'd hold you there. What do you think? Would you like that?"

When she didn't respond, Sawyer took the top curve of her ear—the place where she had pierced a half-moon of tiny, diamond studs—between his teeth. He bit her, and though he had done so before, there was a new brutality in it. He was scarring her. Harper knew it even as her knees gave way at the burst of pain in her head, and she finally found enough voice to groan. She would have screamed, but Sawyer cut off the sound with the thick palm of his other hand, and reined his arm in even tighter around her waist so she wouldn't fall. It made her gasp and cough, her breath stolen in the moment that he crushed her closer still.

"I was on my way back." The confession seeped out of Harper as the last of the air in her lungs wisped away. Her head fell back against his shoulder, and a single tear slipped down her cheek and joined the thin stream of blood that ran into her loose hair.

She had been wrong. Nothing could be worse than this. Nothing.

"Oh, Stacey," Sawyer tsked. "Don't play with me. You don't mind if I call you Stacey, do you? I think it suits you better than Harper. I don't like Harper very much these days. Let's pretend she's dead, shall we?"

Harper wished that she was. She wished that she hadn't been so stupid, that she had calculated the cost long before she set out for Iowa and drew Adri and everyone she loved into this incomprehensible situation. What did it matter if Adri, if the whole world knew what she had done to David? She would take whatever she deserved, and gladly, if only Sawyer would dissolve like the nightmare he was. He was going to make her pay. She could feel it her bones. And she had never been so scared in her life.

"Stacey wouldn't run away," Sawyer continued. "She knows her place." As he talked he began to move, dragging her backward down the gravel drive of the Galloway estate.

Harper would have dug in her heels if she thought that

would help, but Sawyer was strong and he had lifted her entirely off her feet. Only her toes grazed the ground, small and insignificant in the secondhand Chucks she had loved only days ago. Useless. And she couldn't cry out, his hand was still smashed against her mouth and nose, smothering her.

Suffocating. Harper was out of air. Her lungs began to burn, her need for air eclipsing even the sheer terror she felt with Sawyer's arms so immovable around her. It was a desperation, a compulsion, and for the first time since he'd stepped out of the darkness, Harper began to fight. She squirmed, clutched at his muscled forearms, clawed all the way back to his shoulders and neck with her suddenly animate hands.

"You little bitch," he spat when her fingernails dug into his skin. Sawyer dropped her, and because Harper hadn't been expecting it, she collapsed to her knees and fell forward with her hands on the sharp gravel. She knelt there, gasping for air while Sawyer breathed heavy behind her. "You made me bleed," he said.

Her lungs were still on fire, the little nips of oxygen she managed to swallow weren't nearly enough to ease the ache in her chest. But Harper started to crawl away. She made it a foot, two, then attempted to push herself up so she could run. Or at least try to.

Sawyer began to laugh. "You think you can run away? You think I'd just let you go?" He caught her from behind, before she could stand, and threw her to the ground on her stomach. The gravel cut Harper's cheek, but that didn't hurt nearly as much as her arms when Sawyer climbed onto her back and dug his knees into her shoulders. "There are so many ways I could destroy you," Sawyer said. "I could call the police right now. Tell them I've caught a murderer. Solved a cold case that they didn't even know existed." He hummed a little, savagely happy, thinking. He loved to play with her, a mouse that he had caught in his claws. He delighted in it. "But I'm not done with you yet, Stacey. I hope you can understand that. That I own you. It won't go well for you if you keep trying to run."

Harper was weeping, tears muddying the dust beneath her face, making her eyes sting. Her soul was a winged thing, flapping wildly in her chest and head, beating itself against the walls of her ruined body as if she was her very own prison. There was no way out. Sawyer had her, no escape. He'd deface her in every way that he knew possible, punish her until she wished for death. And then he'd throw her away. Let her kill herself or turn her loose on the streets a raving addict. Harper could feel the hatred, the sadistic cruelty wafting off of him like cheap cologne.

"Are you crying?" Sawyer asked. "Did I make you cry?" His voice seethed with false sympathy. "Don't bother. I don't care if you sob like a baby."

All at once his weight was off her back, and Sawyer yanked Harper to her feet. She was dizzy, disoriented, tiny stones and a thin film of damp dust still clinging to her scraped cheek. "Don't fight me," Sawyer warned. "Your face means nothing to me anymore. I won't touch your body, but I won't hesitate to break your nose, your jaw, your perfect cheekbones . . ."

He let go of her, and Harper stood shuddering, round-shouldered before him. She didn't try to run.

"Good girl," Sawyer snarled. "Now, come."

The lane was dark, but the trees were ink drawings above them, their branches smudged sable like fingers dipped in coal. Harper felt like they were reaching for her, plucking at her skin, stealing tiny pieces of her with each step she took farther away from the mansion. She hoped that when she reached Sawyer's car there would be nothing left of her for him to take. But she had never been more aware of herself, of all the places he could touch, all the ways she could be hurt. The closer they drew to the shadow of his Lexus, the more alive and whole and vulnerable Harper felt.

Sawyer took keys out of his pocket and unlocked the car doors. "Get in," he told Harper. "Passenger seat. Oh, and put these on."

His hand on hers in the dark, the sharp, cold tang of metal between them. Handcuffs.

Harper was rooted to the ground. She couldn't do it. Wouldn't.

And then, from the heart of the night, from the road between Sawyer's car and the Galloway mansion, a sound.

Her name.

"Harper?"

She opened her mouth to cry out, but Sawyer's hand found the back of her neck. Pinched tight. "You are mine. I'm bringing you back."

A wind licked Harper's skin, and at that moment the clouds feathered away from the moon. Not much, just enough to reveal the world in relief, a landscape of shadows and darkness and ghosts.

"Harper?" Will was jogging down the lane, his pace light but his fists clenched as if he could feel the strain in the air around him, in the way the trees bowed over them, threatening. She could tell the instant that he caught sight of her, the stumble in his pace. And though she couldn't see his expression, his features seemed unaccountably pale to her.

Harper lifted her fingers. She had intended to wave, to say hello or something equally inane, but her hand pressed against the night, perfectly still. A warning.

Will stopped as if he had hit a brick wall. He was still twenty paces away from the place where Sawyer and Harper stood in front of the car, the interior lights glowing faint because he had unlocked the doors.

"Harper, what's going on?" But she couldn't speak. Discovered, at the moment that mattered most, that she couldn't utter a single intelligible word.

"I'm Harper's boyfriend," Sawyer said. "I'm bringing her home."

Will took a few steps forward. Jerked a thumb over his

shoulder in the direction of the mansion. "Why don't you come in? It's the middle of the night."

Sawyer dropped his hand to the small of Harper's back and gave her a shove toward the car. "Let's go," he said, ignoring Will. But Harper couldn't move. She couldn't talk and she couldn't move. She couldn't do anything but exist in the terror and the hope of the moment, every cell in her body calling out to Will with a despair that sank into the earth beneath her. Save me. She thought. Please.

"Come on," Sawyer hissed and pushed her again. This time, he tipped her off balance. Harper stumbled, almost fell, but Sawyer caught her beneath the arm and jerked her up harshly.

"Hey!" Will called and started toward them. "Let go of her."

Sawyer did exactly that. He let go, and Harper could feel him reach into the waistband of his pants, remove the gun that he always carried there.

"No," Harper whispered, finding her voice. And then she shouted, "No!"

"What's going on?" Will had crossed half the distance between them when Sawyer lifted the gun and pointed it in his direction. "Oh." His hands floated a little at his sides, palms at the ground as if he was patting it down, down. "Let's just back up a bit here, shall we?"

"Go home," Sawyer said. "Just turn around and walk back to the house. Pretend that you never saw us."

"Let's talk about this," Will reasoned. He sounded so calm. Harper's heart sank, and rose, as she watched him chance another step closer.

"I don't think so." Sawyer kept the gun trained on Will, but he nudged Harper. "Get in the car. Now."

"No." Harper said it so softly she wondered if anyone had heard her. They both had.

Sawyer made a sound of disbelief, and Will extended a hand to her. Nodded encouragingly. Just once. It was enough. Harper took a step toward him.

"I'll tell him," Sawyer growled. "I'll tell the whole world. You'll go to jail for the rest of your life, you worthless piece of shit."

"I don't care," Harper whispered. She took another step toward Will.

A soft click. Sawyer had cocked his gun.

The rage that rose in Harper was blinding. So red it was black, so thick it choked her, stole the last shred of reason that she had been clinging to so fiercely. When Harper flew at Sawyer, it was the last thing he expected. He stumbled back when she hit him, her fists whipping against his face with all the fury she had bottled for years. Her childhood, her unrequited love, the things he had done to her. It was all contained in the arc of her arms. And Sawyer couldn't do anything at all because there was still a gun in his hand and she was too close to shoot. To take aim at Harper would be like turning the gun on himself. Not that Harper realized any of this. Not that she cared.

They scuffled for what felt like hours, Harper trying to land punches that would maim, but she knew she was small compared to him. Just a girl.

When Sawyer's free fist found her jaw, Harper's head nearly spun off her neck. She fell back, but not before clutching at a handful of his shirt. He came with her, plummeting, the sound of a seam being ripped.

And then, a shot. The gun went off, echoed across the throbbing night, sent a scattering of leaves twining down from the bent trees.

From somewhere in the darkness, an exhalation. So soft it hardly existed at all.

"What have you done?" Harper was shrieking, hysterical, kicking and writhing beneath the bulk of Sawyer, who was still deadweight above her. "Get off me! Get off!"

He did, rolling to the side and then bursting up like a sprinter. Harper heard him wrench open the car door and ignite the engine. When he thrust the Lexus into reverse, he kicked up a cloud of gravel, pelting Harper with rocks that forced her to cover her head with her arms.

It was a couple of seconds before the air stilled and Harper could get a hold of herself, but it felt like an eternity. Somewhere between her and the Galloway mansion, Will had crumpled to the earth, shot. And it was all her fault.

"Please," Harper moaned, scrambling on hands and knees, half running, stumbling, falling to the spot where she had last seen Will. "Please, God . . ."

He was there, on his back, eyes open and blinking at the veiled moon. Harper didn't dare to touch him, but crouched over his dark form, hands hovering, trembling over his body as if she could discern where the wound was by divining it through her fingertips.

Will didn't say anything. His mouth opened and closed, opened and closed. Eyes fluttered at the spilled-ink sky. It frightened Harper how he couldn't focus on anything, didn't seem to really see what was above him or register that Harper was there at all. She had seen a thousand movies, a thousand scenes where the hero fell. Weren't there last words? Passionate kisses? Moments of such cognizance and clarity that the world was set right with just a couple of perfect phrases?

Harper finally reached out, took Will's face in her hands gently, feeling the fine hairs along his temples, his clammy brow. "Will," she said, clearing her throat, making herself sound as present and calm as she could muster. "Will, look at me."

He did, for just an instant, his gaze skipping away as soon as he made eye contact with Harper. If he recognized her, if he knew where he was and what had happened, she couldn't tell.

"Help!" Harper screamed it at the top of her lungs, shouted so loud her throat burned. "Help! Somebody help me!"

Will didn't flinch.

"Help!" Harper was on her feet, running down the road toward the mansion.

PART IV

~

THE BEAUTIFUL DAUGHTERS

26

~

ADRIENNE

After Harper, Will, and Jackson disappeared into the dark recesses of Piperhall, Adri settled into the role she knew best: she picked up the pieces. Glasses were scattered around the grand living room, pillows abandoned on the floor. She straightened corners, turned off the fireplace, gathered the empty tumblers. And Caleb fell into step beside her.

They cleaned in amiable silence until Will made one last haphazard appearance. He looked confused and disheveled, and barely glanced at Adri when he announced that he was going for a walk.

"It's the middle of the night." Adri looked up from the sink of water where she was up to her elbows in suds. "It's pitch dark."

Will seemed not to hear her.

"Be careful!" she called after him, and Caleb gave a low laugh.

"He's a big boy," Caleb said.

"Yeah, well, he's in love with Harper Penny. He'd better be careful."

"I like her." Caleb took a shot glass out of Adri's soapy, dripping hand, and toweled it off with deliberate gentleness. The expensive glassware looked like a toy in his large hands, and Adri found herself smiling in spite of her better judgment. He was getting under her skin. She wanted to lean against his shoulder, to press her face into the smooth line of his neck. But maybe that was the alcohol dulling her senses. Harper had made her drink and Piperhall had forced her to remember. But everything seemed soft and blurred with Caleb doing dishes beside her.

Caleb was a mystery. Even his aftershave was so subtle that she kept mistaking the fragrance. Sandalwood? Musk? Maybe it was all just Caleb. She wished she didn't love his scent, but she did.

"You like Harper?" The question was so belated that it was almost comical, and Adri felt herself blush all the way to her ears. If Caleb noticed, he didn't embarrass her by saying so.

"Yes, Harper." There was a smile in his voice. "She's a fire-cracker."

"That's a nice way to put it."

"You don't sound amused."

Adri ran her hands through the water in the sink and pulled the plug in the drain. It hadn't seemed worth it to run the dishwasher for five shot glasses and a few tumblers, and Caleb had insisted on drying. Even though she tried to send him to bed. Not because she didn't want him around. Because she was starting not to trust herself around him.

"I'm not amused," Adri sighed. She reached for the towel and Caleb held it for her while she dried her hands. "I love Harper, but she's hiding something from me."

Caleb laughed, his eyes sparkling as he studied Adri. "Now that's the pot calling the kettle black."

"What's that supposed to mean?"

"You're the queen of secrets and hiding, Adrienne Vogt. I've never met another woman with as tight a lid on herself as you. Do you know how hard I've had to work to get to know you? One-word answers can only carry a man so far."

"Why are you interested in me?" Adri asked suddenly. She surprised herself with the question and quickly busied her hands with the tumblers and shot glasses that Caleb had lined up neatly in a row on the counter.

But Caleb grabbed her wrists before she could turn away, and Adri was forced to let go of the dishes. They were only inches apart, but Caleb lessened the distance even more by lowering his head to meet hers. He brushed the tip of her nose with his lips.

"You're fascinating, Adri."

"Medical advances in developing nations are fascinating," Caleb didn't laugh.

"That was a joke," Adri protested weakly. Her heart was beating wildly and she could hardly breathe.

"You're gorgeous," Caleb continued.

"Harper's gorgeous."

Caleb ignored her and instead kissed each of her eyes in turn. It was so tender, so intimate, Adri couldn't stop the little moan that escaped.

"I love your heart." Then Caleb did the last thing Adri expected and pulled her into a hug. Her chin tucked against his broad shoulder, and when his arms circled her waist and pulled her feet off the ground, she found she fit perfectly in his embrace. "I want to know everything about you. Why you hate Blackhawk so much. How you ended up in Africa. What you're hiding from."

Although Adri had melted into him only moments before, she stiffened and pushed herself away. "I'm not sure that's any of your business. And I don't hate Blackhawk."

Caleb set her down and took a step back so that he could look at her properly. His eyes revealed hurt, but he didn't turn and leave. Even though Adri wouldn't have blamed him if he did. "I'd like to make it my business," Caleb said levelly.

Adri felt tears prick her eyes. She grabbed Caleb by the shirt, bunching the fabric in her fists so that she could push him away or pull him close, she couldn't tell. "Why are you doing this to me?" she asked, and was surprised at the tremor in her voice. "I've been doing fine. I'm trying to honor Victoria and forget the past and move on."

"You're not moving on," Caleb said.

"Maybe I don't deserve to."

"Come on, Adri. Everyone deserves a second chance. And a third and a fourth." The corner of Caleb's mouth tweaked as he bit back a grin. "I think I'm on my seventy-seventh."

Adri felt a giggle at the back of her throat. It was absurd and unexpected, and she wondered at the way that Caleb could bring her outside of herself. Make her forget all the serious things that weighed her down. "I think that's it for you," she said.

Caleb shrugged. "Maybe." Then he cupped her face in his hands and lowered his mouth to hers. Slowly, slowly he kissed her, giving her the time and space to shove him away. To say no. But Adri didn't want to. Nothing was fixed, but it felt like Caleb was knee-deep in the thick of it with her. For the moment, it was enough. Enough to savor the press of his lips, the way his body fit against hers. One hand cupped her jaw and the other found the back of her head, his fingers deep in the tangle of her dark hair. Adri was swept away. She wanted to be.

"Adri!"

The shout came from the front of the house. The entryway.

A bolt of adrenaline shot through Adri at the sound of her name. Maybe it was the fear of being caught all wrapped up in Caleb. Maybe she knew deep in her soul that something was not right. Either way, Adri was out of Caleb's arms and jogging fast toward the sound, as if they had never kissed at all. A part of her resented whoever had torn them apart, but she also realized it was for the best. Caleb was too good to be true. She didn't deserve him anyway. But he was on her heels when she found Jackson standing with his hand on the front door.

"Something's wrong," Jackson said.

She didn't even ask what.

Adri flipped on the porch light and threw herself into the night. There was movement and sound from below, but the gravel drive was all smoke and shadows in the darkness.

"Harper?" Adri called, addressing the form that took shape at the foot of the stairs. What was she doing outside? Why wasn't she in her room? But none of that mattered now.

"Will," Harper managed, gasping. "Please, help. It's Will."

There was no mistaking the raw panic in her voice. Adri and Caleb were down the steps and racing past her before Harper could say anything more. Vaguely, Adri was aware of Jackson rushing to Harper, but she was behind them and in the end, Adri didn't much care. He was out there somewhere. Her brother. Her Will.

They raced down the road, kicking up dust as they sprinted in the dark. Adri wasn't a runner, she never had been, but she pulled ahead of Caleb anyway. In the middle of the lane, less than halfway between the blacktop and the place where the drive curved into the roundabout, they found him.

Will was on his back in the gravel. One leg was cocked awkwardly, a caricature of a man mid-jump. His hands were fanned at his sides, palms up, fingers curled into his palms like an infant's. It was wrong. All wrong. Adri knew it the second she saw him.

She hit the ground too early and had to scramble on her hands and knees the last few feet to her brother. "Will?" Adri took his face in her hands, her heart so high in her throat she could hardly form the word. She swallowed. "Will? Look at me. It's Adri."

He didn't respond.

"Will!"

"He's bleeding." Caleb said it almost calmly.

Adri hadn't realized Caleb was there. But he was, and as he peeled off his shirt to stanch the flow of blood that was coursing unchecked from Will's wounded arm, Adri was filled with a gratitude close to elation.

"What happened?" The question was ragged, ripped from her throat.

"I don't know," Caleb said. "But this looks like a gunshot wound."

"Gunshot?"

"I'm going to need your help, Adri. You've got to press here. I'm going to make a tourniquet."

"I've been drinking." Adri choked on a sob.

"I haven't. You'll be fine. Just do as I say."

Headlights washed over them as Caleb finished cinching his belt around Will's shoulder. He pulled it tight, too tight if Will's anguished cry could be trusted. Adri was sickened at the sound of her brother's pain, but he wasn't aware enough even to register that she was there.

"I'm going to need you to help me lift him," Caleb said. "This isn't your brother, Adri. It's just another patient."

"But—"

"But nothing." Caleb's tone brooked no argument. "You've got to pull yourself together. I need you."

Adri wanted to scream. To throw back her head and bawl like a baby. But Caleb was right. Will's life might depend on it. She took a long, shuddering breath and squeezed her eyes shut. When she opened them, she looked straight at Caleb. "What do you need me to do?"

"Lift," he said. "On the count of three. We're going to lift him into the backseat of Jackson's truck."

"Jackson's here?"

"Adri, focus."

She nodded vehemently.

"Okay. One, two, three."

They lifted Will between them in one smooth, calculated movement and began to sidestep toward the pickup. Jackson leaped down from the driver's seat and opened the back door, helped them ease Will onto the long bench as carefully as they could.

Harper was in the front seat, cowering against the door and hyperventilating hard; the sound of her wheezing filled the cab. But Adri only registered this on a clinical level, in the same way that she could assess a patient in one calculated glance. She didn't have time or head space for Harper. Not now.

"He's in shock," Adri said, and knew that it was true. She wasn't Will's sister now. She was his nurse. "We need blankets. Tell me you have blankets in here."

"I don't know." Jackson was already speeding down the long drive, toward the main road and a hospital. "Open the sliding window." He gestured toward the window at the back of the truck, behind Caleb and Adri's heads. It was black beyond the glass, the space obscured by a large canopy that undoubtedly housed some of their construction tools. "I think we have some canvases or tarps or something back there."

Caleb was crouched on the floor of the backseat, one hand still pressing his shirt against the injury and the other holding Will's wrist, checking his pulse. "His heart rate is climbing," Caleb told Adri.

She thrust herself up from the place where she hovered over Will's bent legs and yanked open the sliding window. It was a wild, claustrophobic ride, but Adri, lithe as a dancer, plunged half of her body through the narrow opening and emerged seconds later with an armful of dirty canvases. They sent a fragrant cloud of sawdust into the air of the cab, and Adri's lungs constricted. But she didn't care. She was already tucking the stiff fabric around Will, talking to him all the while.

"We'll be there soon," she told him. "And if you're good they might assign a pretty nurse to you. A brunette." Adri's eyes snapped to Harper as she stared wide-eyed over the back of the headrest. There was fury in Adri's gaze. She could feel it in herself, this billowing anger at the injustice of what had happened. At the sight of Will before her, limp, unmoving. There would be a reckoning—she would see to it herself.

"Blood pressure is dropping," Caleb said quietly. "His pulse is faint. Systolic is below eighty for sure."

"Can you drive faster?" Adri asked Jackson. The speedometer was already hovering around 90, but Jackson pushed the pedal down more.

"The closest hospital is Fairfield," Adri reminded him. "Skip Blackhawk altogether. Take the highway."

It wasn't far to Fairfield, a fifteen-minute drive under normal circumstances, but it felt like Jackson made it in five. The town was all but deserted, the streets empty of people in the middle of the night, but as they screeched to a halt beneath the neon red sign of the hospital emergency room, a police cruiser pulled up behind them, lights flashing even though he hadn't engaged the siren. Or had he? Adri's head felt stuffed with cotton.

Adri fell out of the truck, screaming for a gurney, a trauma team, a surgeon. They came in seconds, nurses in scrubs and a doctor who was already wearing a surgical gown, looking as if he had been waiting for them to arrive. Maybe he had been. Maybe Jackson had called ahead on his cell phone. Adri couldn't remember.

Then, a whirlwind of activity, of bodies and shouts and a palpable urgency that echoed through the truck as they extracted Will's limp body. Just as quickly as they came, everyone was gone: Will was whisked away, Jackson bent in conversation with the officer, who had abandoned his cruiser with the lights still flashing. Adri and Caleb were left standing at the emergency bay door.

Adri wrapped her arms around herself and shivered so hard her teeth chattered. But then she realized that Caleb was naked from the waist up, his eyes frantic and trained on the red emergency room sign. The sight of him looking so vulnerable filled her with an emotion she couldn't explain, and she went to fit her arms around his waist. He was warm, his chest heaving, and she put her cheek against the place where his heart was a staccato of muted sound. After a second he held her back, his embrace so tight that she struggled to breathe. But it was exactly what she needed. A reminder. His strong, stable body around her.

Caleb's arms engulfed the whole of her narrow back. Adri felt tiny in his embrace. Protected. He bent his head and kissed her hair, again and again until she turned her face into his chest.

Adri felt like she could have stayed there forever, hidden in Caleb's arms, where the real world and all the horror it contained could be held at bay. She couldn't help but catch a few grave words passed between Jackson and the police officer. She looked over at them, assuming that she would find the middle-aged man in uniform studying Jackson's truck intently. But when she followed the line of his gaze, she discovered he wasn't looking at the truck at all. He was staring at Harper.

27

HARPER

Harper had forgotten that she had injuries, too. When the police officer rapped on her window with his knuckles and helped her out of the vehicle, the first thing he did was escort her into the hospital. A nurse took her to a small trauma room and made her lie on her side beneath a bright light that gave Harper an instant, blinding headache.

"Can you tell me what happened?" the nurse asked kindly. She probed the helix of Harper's wounded ear with gloved hands, and Harper shuddered from the sudden burst of pain. "Is this a bite wound?"

Harper didn't respond, but her silence must have spoken volumes.

"I'm going to have to start an IV. There's a lot of bacteria in the mouth. You'll need a round of prophylactic antibiotics. Are you up-to-date on your tetanus vaccine?"

Harper couldn't remember the last time she'd seen a doctor, much less gotten an immunization. But still, she didn't speak.

"Tetanus it is." The nurse turned to write something on a chart. "Do you have insurance, Miss . . . ?"

"Harper Penny." The police officer supplied from where he stood quietly in the corner of the room. Jackson must have given him her name.

"Do you have insurance, Ms. Penny?"

"No." It was the first thing Harper had said since she screamed for help. She half expected the nurse to throw her out immediately, but the older woman remained perfectly collected. Harper didn't know whether to be grateful or upset. She glanced at the nurse's shirt and saw that her name was Gayle.

"You're going to need a couple stitches," Gayle told her. "And an IV, though we might be able to manage the antibiotics with a series of injections instead. We'll have to see. Some wound irrigation, maybe an X-ray . . . Were you struck in the jaw?" Reaching out one hand, the other still clutching a clipboard, the nurse delicately explored the place where Sawyer had hit Harper. It stung, but Harper suspected it wasn't broken. "The doctor will have to decide," the nurse said, as if she could hear Harper's thoughts. Then she picked up Harper's hand and examined her fingers and the fine spiderweb of abrasions that had split across Harper's skin when she attacked Sawyer.

"Eventually, you're going to want to consult a plastic surgeon about your ear. Cartilage can be tricky. Unfortunately, we don't have a plastic surgeon on staff, but there's a center for reconstructive surgery in Sioux Falls. We can give you a referral."

Harper could hardly comprehend what the nurse was saying, never mind tuck away information for later reference. Besides, she didn't have insurance.

"Do you have any other injuries?"

"No." Harper squeezed her eyes shut again. At least, none that you can see.

"Well, sweetheart, you're lucky we're a nonprofit," Gayle told Harper. "It complicates things, I'll have to make a few calls, but we'll get you patched up one way or another." Turning to the officer who still stood in the corner of the room, she asked, "Do you want me to document?"

"Yes, please."

Gayle left the room quietly and returned minutes later with a camera. She didn't ask Harper if she wanted to have her wounds photographed, but Harper would have done whatever they asked of her anyway. She sat up on the bed, the paper crinkling beneath her, and offered up her cheek, her ear, her hands, her face for the camera. Her eyes were closed in every picture.

When Gayle was done, she had a quick, whispered conversation with the police officer. As soon as the nurse was gone, he made his way over to Harper's bed.

"I assume you're well enough to answer a couple of questions?"

Harper put her hand over her eyes, but she nodded as best she could. What else was there for her to do? What was the point of hiding now? None of it mattered. None of it. Not with Will shot. In shock? Undergoing surgery? Harper thrust such thoughts from her mind and took a deep, shuddering breath. One thing at a time. That was all she could handle. She shifted a little on the paper-lined bed.

"I'll tell you everything," she said, looking the officer—McNeil, according to the engraved tag on his shirt—straight in the eye. "Anything you want to hear."

And she did. The entire story, starting from the moment she first saw Sawyer across the bar. She paused once, when Gayle came in to start her IV, but after the line had been set and the antibiotic was drip-drip-dripping down the plastic tube, Officer McNeil asked for privacy. Gayle gave Harper a searching look, and Harper nodded, giving the nurse wordless permission to go. Harper's injuries were far from life-threatening. They could be dealt with later.

When Harper told Officer McNeil about the pornography, about the things that Sawyer had made her do, he asked her to hang on for a moment while he made a few phone calls. Within twenty minutes there was another police officer in the room, as well as a social worker. Jenna Hudson.

They listened, documenting, interrupting with the occasional question or point of clarification, and when Harper had finally recounted the last hour of her life (was that all the time that had passed since she stepped out of the mansion?), the two men stared at her with indiscernible expressions. Jenna only smiled faintly, a look of pity mixed with sorrow, and gave Harper's arm a comforting little pat.

Did they believe her? Would she care if they didn't? Were they judging her? Did it matter if they were?

After a few silent moments, Officer McNeil finally stepped forward and offered Harper his hand. She reached out hesitantly, but as soon as their fingers touched he pressed her hand between both of his palms. He looked sad. He looked like he believed her.

Harper felt tears burn hot in her eyes. She had held on to it all for so long, had pushed her fears, her revulsion, her hatred and self-loathing down so deep that she doubted she would ever be free of it. Her heart was cemented in her chest, walled off and cold, yet Officer McNeil's touch, the look in his eyes, sent a hairline crack through the hardest part of her. But she couldn't afford to fall to pieces here. She didn't deserve to. Harper fought to maintain her composure and won. She coaxed a faint half-smile.

"We'll get him," Officer McNeil told her. "You've given us more than enough information to nail this guy."

She had. Full name, address, license plate, places he frequented. Agency 21. Where he banked and worked out and bought coffee every morning. Physical description, down to the small birthmark on his upper arm. Harper had also given them her stage name, though it was bitter on her tongue and she nearly gagged. Worst of all, she had no doubt that a team of people would soon be scouring the internet for evidence. For pictures of her. Did they have a task force for this sort of thing? A Special Victims Unit? Would the FBI get involved? Harper had no idea, and she didn't much care.

"Is Will okay?" she asked, for now that she had done her part, he was the only thing she cared about.

Officer McNeil exchanged a look with Jenna. "Last I heard he was still in surgery."

"But is it serious?"

He shook his head. "I don't know."

"Your friends are in the waiting room," Jenna said. "Would you like to see them?"

Harper didn't know how to respond. Could she face Adri and Jackson? She felt like even Caleb, a relative stranger, was a better friend to Will than she had proved to be. But she had no choice. She nodded.

"I'll send them in," Officer McNeil said. "And I'll let Gayle know that you're ready to see a doctor."

The two officers started to leave, but at the last second Officer McNeil turned and said, "I'm going to need you to stick around for a while, okay? We'll put out an APB on Sawyer, but you're going to have to give a full statement, testify if this thing goes to trial. We can contact you at the Vogt farm?"

Harper didn't know if she'd be welcome there anymore. She shrugged. "I don't know. But I promise I won't go anywhere without telling you first."

"Thanks."

The door fell shut behind the men, but Jenna hovered near Harper's knees for a moment longer. "I'm sorry," she eventually said, searching Harper's eyes. "I'm so very sorry."

Harper knew how a heart could hurt for another person, could hold all the regret in the world on behalf of someone who had been wounded.

But Harper didn't deserve Jenna's sympathy.

She had told them most of the story. But not all of it. She hadn't included the one in her tawdry life story that would have changed Officer McNeil's compassion to revulsion. That would have made Jenna consider her anything but a victim.

Harper hadn't told them about David.

⌒

Adri didn't come. Instead, Gayle bustled in with another, younger nurse, and a doctor who attended to Harper's injuries with dispassionate calm. It turned Harper's stomach to hear him discuss her ear and the perforations that had torn right through the cartilage in places. It hadn't felt quite so violent at the time, but hearing him discuss it now was downright grisly. And she almost fainted when he painstakingly removed the half dozen earrings that ringed the uppermost curve of her ruined ear. But he assured her he would use small stitches, try to keep the scarring minimal, and handed her a printed referral sheet for a reconstructive plastic surgery center before he took his leave. Not that she ever intended to use it.

The doctor had determined that Harper didn't need X-rays for her jaw, and after washing her gravel-scraped cheek, the nurses smoothed it with salve and called her good to go. Only the IV remained, but Gayle removed it neatly and efficiently, lecturing Harper about finishing the oral antibiotics she had been prescribed and watching closely for signs of infection.

"Cross my heart," Harper assured her, but she felt completely anesthetized. Well past the point of listening. Or caring. It had been hours, and she had yet to hear a single word about Will.

When Harper emerged from the trauma room, it was almost six o'clock in the morning. She hadn't slept for a single second throughout the entire torment of the night, but she was throbbing with restlessness.

The waiting room was almost empty, but Caleb sat hunched alone in a chair beside the water cooler. He was wearing an ill-fitting sweatshirt bearing the hospital logo; the too-tight sleeves reached only halfway down his forearms. At first Harper thought he was asleep, but as she hovered uncertain in the doorway, Adri's would-be boyfriend looked up.

"Hey," Caleb said. It was a noncommittal greeting, casual. She couldn't tell if he was being purposefully short with her or if he was just tired.

"How is he?" Harper asked, not moving from where she stood. Not daring to.

"He's going to be okay."

It was such a benign statement, but all the air whooshed out of Harper's lungs at the news.

Caleb seemed to notice how fragile Harper was, and he put his hands on his knees and stood up. Walked over to where she was barely clinging to composure and gave her elbow a fortifying squeeze. "Gunshot wound to the outer left shoulder. Missed the brachial artery and the joint. Long story short, humerus fracture, nerve damage, muscle damage, and the tissue surrounding the exit wound is the consistency of soup, but our boy is going to live."

Harper buckled. Caleb caught her by the arm before she could hit the floor, and steered her over to one of the waiting room seats. It was smooth, blue plastic. Cold and uncomfortable.

Caleb sat down beside her, and touched her knee briefly, kindly. Harper was still reeling from his words, "Our boy is going to live." It was all she cared about. Almost.

"It could have been a lot worse, Harper." Caleb sounded grim.

"Will his arm be okay?" she whispered, staring at the wall unseeing.

Harper felt Caleb shrug rather than saw him do it. "It'll never be the same, that's for sure. TV has convinced the world that there is such a thing as a flesh wound, but that's just not true. A gunshot is a major traumatic event, no matter where the injury occurs. Of course there is blood loss and shock, the risk of sepsis due to the junk brought in with the cavitation wave . . ." Caleb trailed off and gave Harper a sidelong glance. "Sorry. Nurse talk."

"No," she shook her head. "I want to hear it all."

Caleb nodded. "He's out of surgery, for what it's worth. And when he woke up from the anesthesia, he asked about you."

"I'm fine," she said.

Caleb gave her a quick once-over. Seemed to assess the thick bandages on her ear, her scratched cheek and undoubtedly bruised jaw. Her palms were scratched, her jeans torn. Harper hadn't seen herself in a mirror, but she assumed she looked terrible. For a moment, Caleb seemed like he wanted to ask her how she was, maybe what had happened, but he refrained. He said, "We told Will exactly that. That you'd be just fine."

Harper looked around. There was no we, only Caleb, alone in the waiting room. And now her. The outsiders.

Caleb guessed her question before she asked it. "Sam and Adri are with Will. And Jackson is getting some things for him from Will's house. After asking about you, Will asked for his toothbrush."

Harper grinned in spite of herself, then buried her face in her hands because she was afraid that she'd laugh or scream or throw up all over Caleb. She had forgotten how vain Will was about his perfect teeth. How they had to be, at all times, pristinely clean. It made her unaccountably happy to think of him bending over the sink, scrubbing his teeth.

Sighing, Harper turned to Caleb. "May I . . . Do you think I could see him?"

But Caleb wasn't looking at her anymore. His attention was fixed on the entrance to the waiting room, at the place where Adri stood rumpled and gorgeous and vengeful. And, though she was a good six inches shorter than Harper, looking for all the world like a diminutive, dark-eyed Amazon.

28

ADRIENNE

Caleb excused himself quietly, but as he walked past Adri he ran his fingertips along her cheek. She closed her eyes for just a second, tolerating his touch. No, she savored it, turning her face toward him in the moment before he broke contact. She kissed the palm of his hand.

Everything had changed. And whether or not she could forgive herself for all that had happened, Adri needed Caleb now. She couldn't deny the depth of her longing for him. No matter what happened, Adri knew that a part of her would love Caleb forever. He had helped her save Will's life.

"Thank you," she whispered.

Caleb shook his head a little, but his gaze told Adri everything she needed to know. Later, he said silently. And then his eyes flicked toward Harper. She was curled up in one of the plastic waiting room chairs, as limp as a rag doll and just as worn and patched. One side of her head was swaddled in thick, white bandages, and the other bore the purpling stain of a wicked bruise.

Adri crumbled a little as she studied Harper. She was furious, so insanely angry that someone would dare to shoot her brother, so she could hardly see straight. Some of that anger was directed at Harper—of course, her former best friend was wrapped up in all of this. She would have to bear some of the blame. But seeing Harper so fragile, as small and scared as an abandoned child, Adri felt her fury leaching away.

Caleb caught her hand and gave it a fortifying squeeze. Then he disappeared behind her down the long hallway. Adri and Harper were alone.

"I'm sorry," Harper croaked before Adri could think of a single thing to say.

"You should be." There was a quiver in Adri's voice, but she got it under control. She hadn't meant to say that. To sound so judgmental and harsh. But she was sick of lies and half-truths; she could taste bile on her tongue. Adri wanted to vilify Harper, but she couldn't. She still loved her too much. And yet, she wouldn't stand for anything less than the truth. Not anymore. "I want to know what happened out there, Harper. I want to know everything."

Harper nodded. "Okay."

"And I mean everything. You've been hiding something since the day you showed up at Piperhall, and though I have done my level best to be your friend, to be there for you no matter what, you have lied to me again and again."

Harper didn't deny it. She didn't say anything at all.

"I need a change of clothes." Adri held out her arms to show Harper that her shirt was stiff with dried blood. Her hair, too, though she had pulled it back in a sticky ponytail. The scent of her brother's blood in her hair had almost sent her to her knees in the hospital bathroom. A part of Adri couldn't shake the feeling that this was all a nightmare and she'd wake up feverish and sweaty in her little bungalow, Caleb knocking on her bedroom door to make sure she was okay. But she couldn't bury her head in the sand anymore. She couldn't hide.

"You're coming with me, Harper." Adri said. "You're not leaving my sight until I know exactly what is going on, and how Will got tangled up in it."

"Okay." Harper nodded, looking contrite.

"Wait. Before we go . . ." Adri held up her hand, stopping

Harper before she could edge her way out of the waiting room. "I need to know: are we safe?"

It was a loaded question, and Adri wasn't sure that Harper would know the answer.

"He's on the run," Harper finally said, and Adri could tell that it was the truth as far as Harper understood it. "I saw his face after . . ." She stalled. Tried again. "He's afraid. I don't think he meant to shoot Will."

Adri's heart clenched, but she believed that at least they wouldn't be facing a deranged gunman in the parking lot. She spun on her heel and led Harper out of the hospital without another word.

The sky was milk and honey, pale with the promise of a brilliant sunrise. It was changing by the second, honey deepening to butter and then to the warm, rich tones of a ripe pumpkin. The prelude to a spectacular autumn day. Adri would have turned her face to the hint of sunshine, the softening horizon line, but her chest was too tight to take in such beauty.

Sam's old truck was parked crooked between two spaces near the front of the visitor lot, but no one had bothered to give him a ticket. Whoever monitored such things was probably well versed in the middle-of-the-night, emergency parking job, in the way that people in crisis might leave lights on or doors open or engines running. Sam had barely managed to park his car, but the lights were off and Adri held the keys. No matter that the doors were unlocked and the spare tucked in a magnetic holder beneath the driver's side wheel well. Sam had thrust the ring of keys into her hands in the emergency room hours ago. He had been pacing frantically, one fist pressed to his mouth and his eyes wild with fear and worry. It hurt Adri to see her characteristically calm, immovable father anchorless, and when the jangle of the keys at his waist seemed to drive him momentarily insane, she happily accepted them.

The girls didn't speak all the way back to Blackhawk, but when Adri pulled down the road toward Piperhall instead of turning in the direction of Maple Acres, Harper opened her mouth to ask why. "Do you really want to go back here?" She sounded fearful.

"It's closer than the farm," Adri said. "Will is sleeping, but I want to be there when he wakes up."

The estate was only four miles closer, but Adri wanted to bring Harper to Piperhall. She hoped the harsh reality of all that had happened there would work as a catalyst. Besides, they each had a change of clothes and toiletries at the estate, and she did want to be back before Will woke up.

But when they turned off the main road and down the gravel drive, it became obvious that they might not make it to the mansion at all. Three police cruisers were parked along the lane, and a handful of officers milled around snapping pictures, taking notes, and talking into cell phones.

Adri shook her head to clear it. "I forgot that they'd be here. Piperhall is a crime scene, isn't it?"

One of the policemen was already breaking away from the group, heading toward Sam's truck. It was Officer McNeil. Adri had met him outside the emergency room when Will was in surgery.

"Good morning," he said when Adri rolled down her window. "Sorry about this. We're almost done here."

Adri pressed her lips together for a second and nodded once. "Do whatever you need to do. We'll help in any way we can."

"You already have," he said kindly. "We've got all your statements, and Ms. Penny here has set us up well to snag this guy before he goes underground. We'll get him, Ms. Vogt. I trust your brother is doing okay?"

"Sleeping," Adri said. "The surgeon had to stabilize the arm with external fixation because it was a comminuted fracture and that was the only way to keep all the fragments secure . . ." She sighed a little, realizing that she was talking way over their heads. "What I mean to say is, Will's going to be livid when he wakes up and discovers that he has metal rods sticking out of his arm."

"We like livid." Officer McNeil smiled. "Livid is good. He can be as mad as he wants to be. It'll fuel his recovery."

"I hope so."

"You're remembering that we'll need to speak with him as soon as he wakes up?"

"Of course." Adri pointed through the windshield at the police cars. "Are you finding anything?"

"Everything we expected to find. It's not a murder scene," Officer McNeil said, gravely, gratefully, "so it doesn't require quite the same vigilance. But I'm still going to have you do a little off-roading. I take it you're headed to the house?"

"I'd like to clean up," Adri said, tugging the blood-stiffened collar of her shirt.

"Of course. I'll show you where you can drive."

Officer McNeil walked in front of the truck, leading the way into the shallow ditch beside the road and then indicating that they should take it all the way to the mansion. Adri drove slowly past the police cruisers and the yellow tape, and though she tried to keep her eyes trained in front of her, she couldn't stop herself from searching the gravel for evidence of all that had happened there. Deep gouges in the dust, a wide swath of tire tracks from a hasty departure, a dark pool of blood where Will had fallen. Or was she just imagining it all? There were red tags scattered across the ground, sprinkled in a haphazard pattern that indicated there was much to read in the clues left behind.

Rather than going all the way around the circular drive and parking beside Betty and Caleb's borrowed car, Adri pulled up beside the stables and cut the engine. She breathed heavily for a few seconds, her hands still clutched tight to the steering wheel, and then swiveled to face Harper.

"I'm ready," she said without preamble. She didn't dare to say anything more. Didn't trust herself to. Adri knew that if she opened her mouth, she'd be the one apologizing, dragging Harper into the past and forcing her to relive every mistake they had made. But this wasn't about that. It was about Will. And as much as Adri ached to come clean about David and everything that happened five years ago, before she could focus on the sins she had to atone for, she needed to know who shot Will. And why.

Apparently Harper was just as ready to confess as Adri was. She started to talk. About the guilt she felt after David's death and all the ways she tried to punish herself. Drugs, the bite of a razor, men who treated her as if she was disposable. It sounded like a bad after-school special to Adri, but this wasn't fiction. It was Harper. Her Harper. And Adri didn't have to wonder if her former best friend was spinning a story. The thin white lines on her wrists and the hollow look in her eyes were evidence enough.

And then, Sawyer Donovan.

Adri found that she had tears rolling down her cheeks when one slipped off the edge of her jaw and dropped on her folded hands. She was weeping without making a sound, and though she wished Harper would reach out and wipe all those tears away, fold Adri in a hug that would erase everything that had come between them, Harper simply looked away. Kept going.

It was the right thing to do, and Adri palmed away her tears. Forced herself to give Harper her full, deliberate attention.

By the time Harper made it to the night before and Sawyer's unexpected appearance at the mansion, Adri had gotten hold of herself enough to speak.

"Will was collateral damage," she whispered, interrupting Harper's account. Adri shook her head. "I don't want to hear anymore. I know what happened next. Will tried to stop Sawyer and got shot."

"More or less," Harper admitted. "But I can't figure out how Will knew I was outside instead of asleep in my bedroom."

"I don't think he knew you were outside. Will came downstairs after escorting you to your room." Adri looked her friend full in the face. "I don't know what happened between the two of you, but my brother thinks he's in love with you. You're breaking his heart. Again."

"I don't want to break his heart." Harper's voice was so faint that it hardly existed at all.

"Yeah, well, you're breaking mine, too." Adri rubbed her cheeks again, wiping the tears away so harshly it was as if she was trying to erase them altogether. "I just don't understand. Why, Harper? How did you ever end up with a man like Sawyer? It's not you."

Harper looked as if she had asked herself the same question a hundred times. A thousand. "I hated myself. I believed I deserved him."

"That's a terrible answer." But it wasn't as awful as Adri claimed. She understood. She hated herself, too. Adri believed she deserved the exile she had forced upon herself, the hiding and the pretending. It was easy to convince the world that she loathed Blackhawk and everything about her past, but it was much harder to convince herself.

"I don't know what else to tell you," Harper said. "It's the truth. After college I was sad and vulnerable and more or less homeless. You know my family life has always sucked, and everyone disappeared after David died. It wasn't always . . . like that with Sawyer. It wasn't always as bad as it got to be in the end."

Adri could tell that Harper was just scratching the surface. But she didn't make her friend say any more. She was all too aware of her own warning signs. Signposts along the way that pointed to the ruin where she now sat trying to piece back together all that had been broken. How many times had she tried to erase herself? In how many ways? But she couldn't say all that. She wouldn't. It was too self-serving.

Adri sighed a little, but decided to let it go for now. There was another question burning on her tongue. "Why didn't you tell me? I could have helped you, Harper. We could have stopped Sawyer before he ever showed up here."

Harper swallowed hard. Then squeezed her eyes shut and plunged forward. "He was blackmailing me. He knew something that would have ruined my life, that would have made me lose everything and everyone I ever loved."

Adri didn't know what to say, so she didn't say anything at all.

Harper sucked in a shaky breath, and before she even said the words Adri knew that she would exhale the truth. "He knew I killed David."

~

29

HARPER

Bush camping wasn't at all what Harper had pictured. She'd had visions of serene mountain vistas and meandering hikes through flower-studded meadows. Time together and long conversations that would eventually unravel the heart of the lovers' knot that was their intertwined relationships. But in some ways the trip was doomed from the get-go, because everyone had a different idea of how their last hurrah together should play out.

Will was eager for fun, anxious to sign The Five up for sky-diving lessons in the valley or a river rafting expedition that cut through the core of the coastal mountain range. David was distant and moody, drunk before they even got on the plane and bent on keeping himself in an inebriated state nearly every waking hour. As for Harper and Adri, they were, for one of the very first times in their relationship, at odds. When Harper said black, Adri was already whispering white, and although they didn't try to annoy one another, it was clear before they ever made it out of the Fraser Valley that their fun excursion was going to be anything but. By the time they finally found a place to set up camp, they were at each other's throats. Only Jackson seemed unperturbed.

As Harper pitched the tent she was supposed to share with Adri, she duly noted the exquisite beauty of the little pocket they had found. The arch of the mountains, still snowcapped in the cool spring air, and the narrow river that carved between, bubbling green and frothy before the pebbled beach that Jackson had led them to. He acted as if getting to their site was as simple as driving to the nearest McDonald's, but they had wound their way down unmapped logging roads, parked in the dirt beside one of a million identical trees, and then hauled their gear in four separate loads down an indistinguishable path that Jackson eventually had to mark with strands of yellow twine. They were off the edge of the known world, and while in some ways it was exactly what Harper had been hoping for, she felt distinctly isolated. Cut off and alone. And it wasn't just the rugged terrain.

"We're in the middle of nowhere," Harper said, holding up her cell phone as if raising it two feet would help her get better reception. Still zero bars.

"I thought that was the point." Jackson flashed her an almost impish grin as he took a tent stake and mallet from her limp hand. She was too focused on her cell phone to notice, but he was in his element as he pounded the metal peg into the rocky beach. Straightening up, he leaned close and half whispered, "I brought everyone here on purpose. I think we have some things to work out. Don't you?"

And then he walked away.

Harper didn't know what to make of his strange comment. Did he know more than he let on? Or did he just feel the tension between them all as keenly as she did? It was hard to know with Jackson. He was usually quiet, often unreadable, but it went without saying that he loved them all. Jackson was forever putting every member of The Five before himself. And this trip was no different. He had taken them here for the peace. For the quiet. For the chance to make everything right before they set off into the world on their own.

But now that they were here, Harper didn't know how to fix anything at all.

Jackson, however, seemed to know exactly what to do, and

he wasted no time once their camp was set up. He recruited Will to help him haul fat stones the size of basketballs from the shallow edge of the river to create a ring for the coolers they had brought along. It was chilly outside, and Will screamed like a little girl when he first stepped into the slow current. But he wasn't about to be shown up, and the two men worked until their bare feet and hands were blue.

"What in the world are you doing?" David asked after a while from his spot in a lawn chair near the water.

"The ice in the coolers will melt," Jackson explained, "but the river is so cold it's as good as a refrigerator. We'll submerge the coolers halfway in the water and voilà—fresh food for a week. We just have to make sure the coolers don't float away. Hence, the rocks."

David was only half listening. "We're staying here for a week?" he complained.

"That was the plan." Harper tried not to sound bitchy. "I think it's a great idea," she told Jackson. "And I love this spot. Could we walk across to the other side?"

Jackson laughed. "It doesn't look deep," he said, "but it drops off fast."

Adri pushed herself up from the rock she had been sitting on and joined Harper as she watched the guys work. "But I can see the bottom all the way across."

"That doesn't mean it's not deep. Those rocks?" Jackson motioned out toward the center of the bottle green river. "They're boulders."

"Shut up." Harper stepped forward, craned her neck to see better.

"This is glacier-fed water, baby. We're standing in snowmelt." Jackson seemed proud, as if he had designed the river himself. "Clear as glass and cold as ice. I'd bet it's twenty feet to the bottom in the center. You could cliff jump if you wanted to."

Harper looked up at the rock face that flanked their makeshift camp. The layers of ancient gray stone and blue moss, the odd, small evergreens that poked from between tiny crevices. Just looking up gave her a rush. "I'm totally doing it," she announced.

"You'd have to clear the shallows," Jackson warned. "I'm not sure I'd recommend it. I said you *could* cliff jump, not that you should."

"You'll teach me," Harper instructed. "You'll show me exactly what to do and I'll do it."

"My older brother is the cliff jumper in our family, not me."

"Oh, come on. It's like, what? Twenty feet to the top? That's not much." Harper didn't really know anything about heights and distances and how to measure danger in feet and inches. She didn't much care. For the first time since she'd stepped foot in British Columbia, she found there was something she actually wanted to do.

But they didn't cliff jump. Instead they got on each other's nerves for a couple of days, fished a bit—ate the rainbow trout they caught for breakfast—and then lolled around much as they always had back at ATU. Conversations went nowhere. Adri and Harper circled each other warily instead of confiding in one another like the best friends they had always been. David drank.

On the third day of their so-called fantastic vacation, their escape from civilization, Jackson woke up and announced, "I'm going for a hike."

"There aren't any trails," Adri said. Like he needed to be reminded. He was the only one of The Five who seemed to be totally in his element.

Jackson produced a compass from his pocket. "Believe it or not, I can orienteer. I guarantee we won't get lost. For long. We'll find our way back. Eventually." He smiled at his own joke, but only Will offered to join him.

"No thanks." Adri shook her head. "I'm reading."

This was the first anyone had heard of a book, but Adri did emerge a few minutes later from the tent she shared with Harper, clutching a worn paperback novel. Harper had never seen Adri read anything other than nursing textbooks.

"I think I'm out, too," Harper said. Her mind was already spinning, devising a way that she could sweet-talk David into a little alone time, if Jackson and Will were heading out and Adri would be buried in a book. She didn't much want to be alone with David, she didn't trust herself around him, but talking to him was the only way she could think of to convince him that his life, and everything he planned to do with it, was a giant mistake.

Harper gave herself fifteen minutes after Jackson and Will had left, and then she announced to no one in particular, "I'm bored."

Adri didn't respond. Neither did David. The two lovebirds were sitting on opposite ends of the campsite.

"Adri . . ." Harper cajoled, putting just enough supplication in her voice to sound eager, not needy. "Come cliff jumping with me. Or, at least, come check it out with me."

"I'm not into rock climbing or cliff jumping," Adri said. She glanced up from her book and gave Harper an inscrutable look. "Take David."

Harper tried to keep her expression neutral. "Are you sure?"

For just a moment, something in Adri's eyes shimmered raw. There was hurt in her gaze, and hope, too, but Harper could only guess at the reasons behind her friend's inscrutable emotions. Was Adri longing for Harper to free her from the prison of her engagement? Or was she praying that Harper would refuse even a couple of minutes alone with David? Did Adri understand just how warped all their relationships had become?

As much as she wanted to make things right with Adri, Harper knew that she couldn't do it until she and David came clean. And there was only one way to make that happen. "Guess it's you and me," Harper said over her shoulder to David. But before she turned away, she tried to wish her way into Adri's mind and heart. I'm doing this for you, she thought. Please know that.

Harper took David by the hands and pulled him to his feet.

His protestations were mild, and by the time they were hiking away from their camp toward the bluff that overlooked the water, he was following more or less willingly. They didn't talk at all. The river burbled noisily, a breeze rustled through the trees, birdcalls, sounds in the underbrush of animals that went unnoticed, unseen.

David and Harper wove through a copse of trees separating the beach from the rocky ledge that climbed toward the distant peak of whatever mountain they were perched upon. When they reached the craggy rock face, Harper began to free-climb, hand over foot on thick outcroppings and wide ledges of the huge, jagged stone. It wasn't necessarily hard work, but it required her to focus all the same, and by the time she crested the very top of the cliff, Harper was a little breathless, but triumphant. David followed slowly, his own path apparently more laborious. He was panting when he finally reached the relatively flat, uppermost surface.

"Why the hell did you drag me up here?" he grumbled, not pausing to admire the view. They were much higher than Harper had thought they would be. At least, it felt that way.

"Why did you come?" she shot back. "You didn't have to follow me."

"You yanked me out of my chair."

"Because you've been sitting on your ass since the moment we got here. It's pathetic, David. What happened to you?"

He gave her a dark look, and though she was so frustrated with him she could hardly stand it, his deep, brooding eyes still made her shiver. "I was born," he said.

"What's that supposed to mean?" Harper couldn't tell if he was drunk or not, but she was shaken by how unbalanced he seemed. How angry.

"I'm a recent college graduate," he told her, sweeping his hand grandly as if inviting her to study his diploma. "Not that that means anything. But I am also a soon-to-be husband and the proud new partner and powerless co-CEO of Galloway

Enterprises. I have decades of living my father's recycled dream before me. I have life by the tail. Lucky me."

"Wow," Harper whistled low. "Bitter much?"

"You have no idea."

"I don't know what your problem is"—Harper took a step forward and poked a finger at him—"but this has got to end. I know you've got unresolved daddy issues and you think your silver spoon life is crap, but you're not dragging the rest of us down with you. You're not dragging Adri down with you. It's not fair."

"And the truth comes out." David leaned forward a bit until Harper's finger made contact with his chest. "That's why we're here, isn't it? You want to fix me."

"No, I want to fix you and Adri. I'm not sure David Galloway is fixable."

"He isn't."

Harper wondered in that instant if there were things that David had never said. If Liam had allowed a stallion—and his fists—to raise his son. She tried to imagine what it would be like to be so rich, to have so many expectations thrust upon her shoulders that she could barely stand beneath the weight of it all. Maybe David's life was harder than she could have ever guessed. Maybe she'd drink herself to oblivion and be bitter and angry, too.

But Harper would never take Adri down with her.

"Why do you insist on clinging to her?" Harper didn't mean to beg, but there was an edge of desperation in her voice. There was still a part of her that loved him, that wished he loved her, too, but she had seen too much of what David Galloway was capable of to harbor any fantasies that he'd come to his senses and sweep her off her feet.

"Why do I cling to Adrienne?" he mused, but of course he knew exactly what Harper was talking about. He seemed almost happy to answer. "Because she's sweet and soft and pliable. Adrienne will make the perfect Galloway, and when we're old and ugly and have nothing but money to comfort us, I'll turn around and she'll still be there. She's faithful, that one."

It was out of her mouth before she could realize what she was saying. "You hit her, don't you? It wasn't just the one time."

David wouldn't look at her. "What do you know about love?"

Harper was stunned speechless. Her blood ran cold, her heart thumped painfully in her chest. It sounded to her like a door closing, her faith splitting open on the rough fringe of a reality she didn't want to accept.

"That's not love," she managed. "Hurting Adri has nothing to do with love."

"And yet, you hurt her all the time, don't you? She just doesn't know it."

"She will soon enough," Harper said. She wasn't sure if she meant it or was bluffing. "I'm surprised Victoria hasn't enlightened her already."

"My mother? You're kidding, right? Victoria never says anything about anything. Least of all anything of importance." David winked at her. "We Galloways are good at turning a blind eye."

"You're sick," Harper whispered.

David seemed to wake at her proclamation. He grabbed her chin in his hand. "And you wanted this. I think you still do."

"I did," Harper said. "Up until this very moment." And she jerked her head out of his grasp.

David shrugged. "We're ripe fruit, you and me. Perfect and stunning and desirable. But we don't last long, do we? Eventually, we rot."

"I have no idea what you're talking about." Harper took a tiny step back, a tremor of fear raising the hair on her bare arms. David seemed beyond himself, angry and contemplative and yet somehow deeply sad. Depressed even. She didn't know who he was or how to reach him. Suddenly, her only objective was to bring him back. To get him off the cliff. Harper steeled herself and reached out a trembling hand to him. "Come on.

You're hungover. Are you still drunk? I shouldn't have taken you up here at all."

"I'm not drunk."

"Whatever. Just come. Please?"

David studied her outstretched hand for a moment. "Are you afraid of me?"

"Should I be?"

"Yes," he said after a long moment. "Yes, I think you should be."

Harper had been in some awful situations, had felt scared and alone and at risk, but nothing compared to that terrible moment on the top of a rock in BC with David Galloway before her. She had thought that she knew him, that she could pinpoint the things that had made him such a bad boy. An enchanting, excusable rebel who just needed the right kind of love to bring him back from the edge. She had believed herself the woman for the job, the perfect counterweight to his unique brand of instability. But she was so far out of her depth, it was downright terrifying.

"Please," she whispered.

But David ignored her. "I should just end it all. Stop inflicting myself on other people."

"David—"

He had already turned away from her. He was walking to the lip of the outcropping rock, looking over the edge as if the answer to every mystery was contained in the shifting water below.

"Don't be an idiot." Harper took a few hurried steps after him, but there was a fine gravel over the surface, a million tiny pebbles that made her feet slip precariously. She caught herself, pulse pounding in her ears, and slowed down. Crept to the side where David stood, leaning over the precipice as if it was the most inviting thing in the world. "Back up," she commanded, taking him by the hand.

"Or what?" David's arm slid around her waist, pulled her close. "Maybe I'll just ruin everything right now. Destroy both our lives. What if I blew this whole thing sky-high and took you while Adri was watching? Right here."

Over his shoulder, Harper spotted her. Adri was far away, but not so far that Harper couldn't see her friend's face turned toward them. The book was abandoned in her lap, the sunshine highlighting her cheeks as if nature itself had deigned to blush her. Even at a distance, Adri looked exquisite. Eyes wide, lips slightly parted in what Harper interpreted as shock.

David's hands were on her. His fingers clawing beneath the hem of her T-shirt and scraping against the warm skin beneath. She burned in the places he touched her, but it wasn't from desire.

"No!" Harper grabbed his wrist, but David was stronger. He twisted out of her grip and lunged for her again, yanking her tightly to him; she could feel his hot, ragged breath against her cheek. He snagged a handful of the waistband of her jeans and the button strained against the stiff fabric as he struggled with it.

"You wanted to tell her," David hissed, warm and wet against her neck. "Let's show her."

The thought skittered through Harper's mind that David didn't just want sex. In fact, she doubted this had anything to do with sex at all. It was an act of violence that would destroy everything once and for all. The games they played, the illusions they clung to. David was going to burn them all to ash.

When David leaned in again, his lips parted to kiss her or bite her or whisper more things that Harper didn't want to hear, she didn't think. She just gathered every ounce of strength she had left.

She pushed him away.

～

The silence was absolute. Adri stared at Harper, eyes round and unblinking, for several long moments, and then, impossibly, she laughed. It was a cold, mirthless sound. She said, "You did not push David."

Harper didn't know how to respond. "Yes," she stammered, "yes, I did."

"I watched the whole thing." Adri was getting louder by the second, her entire body facing Harper now as she tried to make her friend understand. "I wasn't reading that stupid book, and I watched you two from the very first second you climbed onto the top of that rock. I could tell you and David were fighting, and I was terrified when you went so close to the edge. But, Harper, I saw David hug you. And then I saw him step backwards."

Harper was shaking her head. "No," she whispered. "I pushed him. I pushed him away because he was going to . . . kiss me."

Adri sat back suddenly, her face frozen. She seemed paralyzed for a few heartbeats, but she managed to squeeze her eyes shut before she said, "You were having an affair with him, weren't you."

It wasn't a question, and Harper didn't answer it. She didn't have to. "Adri," she breathed. "I'm sorry. I'm so very sorry."

Of course, a five-years-late apology was nowhere near enough, and Harper wasn't the least bit surprised when Adri threw open the truck door and slid out. Slammed it shut behind her before she took off toward the stable.

But Harper had come too far to play shy now. She hopped out of the truck and jogged after Adri's narrow form. "I've never been more sorry for anything in my life!" she called, anxious to make Adri listen, to make her understand. "I've spent the last five years hating myself for what I did to you—to us. Everything that has happened from the moment I kissed David until now has been a downward spiral that—"

Adri whirled around and caught Harper by the shoulders. Harper hadn't realized she was following so closely, and she was both surprised by the strength in Adri's slender hands and a little scared of what the smaller woman might do. "I knew about the affair," Adri admitted, pinching Harper's upper arms until numbness seeped into her elbows and beyond. "Or at least, I guessed. It's one of the reasons I suggested you take David on your little hike to the top of the cliff."

"One of the reasons?" Harper parroted, lamely.

"I wanted him to go. I wanted you both to go. I needed a minute to breathe."

"But—"

"Look, Harper, I'll be the first to admit I was naive." Adri let her hands fall to her sides. Searched Harper's face helplessly. "And I was blinded by what I thought was love. But I knew things were going sour. I knew that David had feelings for you."

Harper shook her head. "He loved you, Adri."

"No, he didn't."

"Yes, he—"

"Just stop." Adri put up both of her hands as if she could physically prevent Harper from saying another word. "I was engaged to him, remember? I knew him. David Galloway didn't love me." She turned around and walked away. Several long strides and she was at the pasture fence, her fingers wrapped around the uppermost board as she called the horses to her with a soft click of her tongue.

Harper was rooted to the earth. She didn't know whether to be depressed or encouraged that Adri had known the truth all along. Did that make things easier? Did it nullify all the angst, the myriad of worries that she had once associated with confronting Adri about her relationship with David?

"In a way, it didn't matter," Adri said when Harper finally found her feet and made her way to the fence. "I was caught up in it all. The wedding, the improbable marriage, the perfect life. I wanted David Galloway before I even knew who he was. I wanted a fairy tale."

"Don't we all," Harper murmured, but Adri acted as if she hadn't said anything.

"I hate myself for pretending when I could have changed everything—everything—by just admitting that I had fallen out of love, too." Adri paused for a moment, gathering herself, it seemed. "I hated him," she finally admitted, an edge of defiance in her voice. "I hated him for what he did to me. When he fell, I was free."

And there it was between them, the truth that they had tried so hard to ignore. The realization that his hand against her, his fist, his mouth, his words, were more than sticks and stones. It hurt, all of it. But even more, it changed her and fractured love and shifted things deep inside so that the person she had been was buried beneath the weight of all that happened. Harper didn't know how to comfort her sister, how to admit, "I know." But she understood that purpled skin or photos that betrayed in the most irrevocable, elemental way, were wounds inflicted by bitter weapons. Adri and Harper were soldiers. They had seen war.

Harper sighed. "Oh, Adri." She had been wrung dry by the events of the last twelve hours—maybe the last nine years—and at the end of all of her fears, she found that she wasn't so much scared as she was exhausted. Coming clean felt like letting go, and though it pained her to know that Adri was hurting, in a way Harper felt freer, lighter than she had in years. Never mind the horrible muck of the place where they found themselves, the telling and the regret and the blame, or the fact that if (when?) Sawyer was caught he'd take his revenge and shout the truth to the whole wide world. Because whether or not Adri was willing to admit it, Harper knew what she knew. She had felt David's chest beneath her hands. Its gaping absence when he fell.

"You don't believe me, do you?" Adri was saying.

Harper blinked, came to. She had heard every word, but all at once she wasn't sure that she had been listening. "What do you mean?" she asked.

"I'm telling you that it's my fault." Adri's voice cracked on the last two words, and although it didn't seem she had any tears left to cry, she was blanched white, and Harper put out a hand to steady her.

"What are you talking about?" Harper asked. "None of this is your fault. None of it."

"You're wrong," Adri whimpered, shaking her head from side to side, looking as if she was trying to dislodge the thoughts that plagued her. "You're so wrong, Harper. It's all my fault because I knew that he was suicidal. I knew, and I didn't stop him. I didn't save him."

Harper shushed her friend. "Don't be silly. David wasn't suicidal."

"Yes, he was."

"Fine. He was. But he didn't jump."

"Yes, he did. And when he hit the water, I let him drown." Adri was staring at the fence post blindly, and as Harper came closer she clutched at her clothes, her hands. A blind woman feeling for sight. "I could have saved him," she said. "But he hurt me. And I was so, so angry at him. I let him drown."

Harper stroked Adri's blood-stiffened hair. "That's not true," she said, lacing her voice with as much calm, as much comfort as she could muster. "David didn't drown, Adri. He was dead the instant he hit the water. The force of the fall, the way he landed . . . No one could have survived it."

But Adri wouldn't hear it. "I just sat there. I watched it all happen."

"That's not how—"

"I was a registered nurse. I could have done something. But you were there for him," Adri broke in. "You climbed down from the cliff while I sat paralyzed in the lawn chair. You waded into the water and pulled him out. You held him for hours. Until the helicopter came."

Dazed, Harper floundered for words. Tried to speak but couldn't, then tried again. It was no use. Nothing she could say would set things right. The earth was hung askew. She didn't know where to begin.

They sat in silence for a minute or two until Harper finally gathered her wits. She summoned the fortitude to take Adri's chin in her hand. "Look at me," she commanded with far more authority than she felt. "Adri, honey, look at me."

She did. For several long seconds, the two former best friends locked eyes. Everything they had loved and lost, all the hope they had forfeited and the years that came between were contained in the breadth and depth and width of their gaze. "Adri," Harper said, "I need you to listen to me. You're remembering it wrong."

"No," she argued, "I'm not . . ."

"Ask Will or Jackson or the emergency medics that lifted us all out of that godforsaken valley," Harper pressed, because she had to make Adri understand, and it was probably one of the most important things she would ever communicate. "You were in the water with David. You held him for hours. And when the helicopter finally came, they had to pry David Galloway out of your bloodstained hands."

～

It was a shower, nothing but a run-of-the-mill, everyday shower, but as Harper watched the foamy water slip down the drain, she couldn't help but wonder if she was washing away more than just the dirt on her skin.

Surreal, Harper decided. The events of the last day were beyond her comprehension. There were so many ifs. If Sawyer was caught. If Will got better. If Adri was right. What if David had stepped over the edge, had meant to do exactly the thing that she blamed herself for? That had tormented her for so long? What if everything she'd believed to be true was a lie? What then?

Harper's world had been upended, shaken and thrown like dice that would land wherever fate or chance or circumstance dictated. And she was mid-spin, twirling over possibilities so quickly she hardly had time to consider what each outcome would mean.

But Harper wasn't the only one dealing with the fallout.

Somewhere else in the mansion, Adri was taking her own puri-
fying shower. Confronting her own demons. As Harper toweled
off and wriggled into a fresh outfit from her small Goodwill
wardrobe, she ached for her friend and the harsh reality of the
truth that she was facing.

How could Adri possibly have believed that Harper was the
one who'd stayed in the river with David? If Adri had watched
Harper and David together before his fall, Harper was the one
with a gruesome front-row seat for all that happened after. The
truth was, Adri was in the water almost before David broke
the surface. She had tried to save him, even though he tried to
destroy her.

David had fallen all wrong. That much was painfully obvious,
even to a pair of women who knew nothing at all about cliff
jumping. Maybe it wasn't far to fall, and maybe he would have
been just fine if he landed feet first. But David tumbled backward, then rolled over halfway down and hit the water on his
side. The sound was what surprised Harper the most. The dull,
flat thud of his body breaking against the surface. It seemed
there was no splash. And then, before Harper could even form
a scream, there was a crimson cloud spreading beneath and
around him, as if someone had poured out a bucket of paint.
Harper fell to her knees, disbelieving, horror-stricken, but Adri
was already in the shallows, dragging his limp body into her
arms. Cradling David's head in her quivering hands.

Had Adri repressed the truth? Endured a minor psychotic
break? Lived the lie of a false memory? Or maybe it was the
simple burden of guilt. She had fallen out of love with David
before he plummeted from the cliff. Maybe she hadn't wanted
to go to him, to rescue her fiancé from the water where he died,
and had spent the next five years hating herself for the betrayal
of her own brittle emotions.

But maybe Harper had done exactly the same thing. Had she
pushed David? Or had he jumped?

When Harper descended the main staircase, Adri was on the

phone. Her dark hair was still damp and she wasn't wearing a stitch of makeup, yet Harper found her almost agonizingly beautiful. She wanted to hold her friend, tuck her chin against her shoulder, and weep over the years that they had lost, the lies that they had believed, the hurt they had endured. And the very next moment, she wanted to laugh. Because sometimes life was not at all what you expected it to be.

Sunshine was streaming through the tall windows of the entryway as Adri clicked off the cell phone and stuck it in her pocket. She turned to face Harper, and suddenly the light from all the tall entryway windows haloed her dark head, blessing her shoulders with all the expectation of a new day.

"You clean up nicely," Harper said, and though she felt stupid for saying it, Adri gave her a tentative smile.

"So do you."

There was an awkward pause, a few beats of silence as the two of them studied one another. Harper couldn't pretend to guess Adri's thoughts, but it seemed to her they were both trying to come to terms with what had happened and all that they had learned. About each other. About themselves.

"I'm not lying to you," Harper finally offered, wishing there was a way to convince Adri that she was only interested in the truth. After all this time, all the exaggerations, falsehoods, and lies, only the truth remained.

Adri looked at her feet. "It's going to take some time," she said slowly. "I hated him in the moment before he died." She looked up and caught Harper's gaze. "And you."

Harper nodded, accepting.

"And in a way, I think we are both to blame. Whether he jumped or you pushed him or I drove him to the brink, we all made this mess." Her voice caught at the end, and Harper watched as Adri swallowed hard. "But this changes everything."

Harper knew exactly what she meant. She was having a hard time dealing with it too, but suddenly the world was a very different place. "Why didn't we ever talk about it?" she wondered out loud. "Before our lives spun out of control. Before it was too late."

"We didn't have a chance," Adri said, and just the mention of those long hours after David fell took a visible toll on her. She crossed her arms against her chest, as if warding off the memories. "As soon as we were airlifted out of there, we were separated."

"I told them David fell."

"Me, too."

"Again and again and again. I think the police asked me the same question a dozen different times. And as many different ways." Harper bit her bottom lip, remembering.

"Our stories matched even though we both walked away blaming ourselves." Adri shook her head.

"Do you believe me?"

Adri thought about it for a second. Nodded slowly. Gravely. "I think I do. Do you believe me?"

Harper closed her eyes, pictured again the moment that David leaned in to kiss her, felt again the fabric of his shirt beneath her hands. His fingers rough and hungry against the flat plane of her stomach. She didn't know exactly what had happened, but those long minutes on the ledge had been a nightmare. He had been so mad at the world, at his own prearranged life and the way he had wrecked it beyond redemption. Though Harper couldn't understand it at the time, she knew now what it was like to have someone else call the shots. To grapple at some small power because it was the only expression of self she had left. It was a kind of oppression. And maybe that's what David had been doing all along. Wrestling Adri into submission because his own life was out of control.

By the end, David wasn't the man she once loved.

Would he have raped her in front of Adri? Harper wasn't so sure now. Perhaps his final moments weren't about sex or control or lies after all. They were about making a decision. Putting himself in a place where the answer seemed very black-and-white.

Maybe Harper could believe. She gave Adri a sad little smile. It was the best she could do. For now.

It seemed to be enough for Adri. She smiled a bit. And then she took a stuttering breath. Appeared to set their conversation aside as she recalled something. "Hey," she said, patting the phone in the front pocket of her jeans. "I have something to tell you."

"Will?" His name was faint on Harper's lips.

"No." Adri shook her head. "I was just talking to Officer McNeil. My dad gave me his phone so we could stay in contact when I left the hospital, and apparently he gave his number to the police."

"Okay . . ." Harper said slowly. She steeled herself for bad news, for a new development that would shake the tenuous calm that had settled over her.

Adri seemed to sense her friend's disquiet, and drew close so she could take both of Harper's hands in her own. "Harper," she said, "they got him. A state patrolman picked Sawyer up just outside of Kansas City. About an hour ago."

Harper's ears buzzed with static and her skin began to crawl. She pulled her hands out of Adri's grip to clutch at the noose that had settled around her neck. Panic was the wrong emotion, she could see that much reflected in the confusion that muddied the water of Adri's dark eyes, but Harper didn't know what else to feel. She had feared Sawyer for so long, had been so utterly convinced that he held her life in his cruel hands, that knowing he would do everything in his power to retaliate against her was a horrifying thought. But Adri was already pulling Harper into an embrace. She had to stand on tiptoes to fling her arms around Harper's shoulders, but she held her tightly, like she might never let go. "He has no power over you," Adri whispered. "You didn't kill David. I was there."

"But . . ."

"I don't care about any of the rest of it," Adri cut in fiercely. "It doesn't matter. None of it."

She didn't say I love you, and Harper didn't expect her to. It was something that they had professed all the time when they were younger, but it felt strange to admit such precious emotion now. So much had happened. They weren't the same people anymore. But they were together. They were here and they were hoping, fumbling toward a togetherness that would be entirely different than anything they had known before. It was more than Harper could have ever wished for.

When they left the mansion, Adri didn't bother to lock the door behind them.

"Aren't you worried about somebody breaking in?" Harper asked.

The way Adri cocked her eyebrow was answer enough. Harper had to agree—there wasn't much that could happen at Piperhall that would trump what had already transpired.

"It's haunted," Adri said, but Harper could tell that she didn't mean it. Adri paused at the edge of the wide staircase and leaned back against the railing to take it all in. The high, white face of the mansion that had been their very own princess castle, the glittering windows, the scrolled edges and sharp angles and audacious air. She shook her head. "Nah. It's just a house."

"What are you going to do with it?"

"I still don't know. I guess I'm waiting for inspiration." Adri took each step slowly, tracing her hand along the stone balustrade as she went. "I'd like to figure out what Victoria would have wanted me to do with it."

⟶

They drove back to the hospital in silence. All but one of the police cars were gone from the lane leading to the Galloway estate, but yellow tape still marked the gravel road a crime scene. Adri waved at the lone cop in the driver's seat of his squad car, and took the ditch just like Officer McNeil had instructed her to when they first arrived seeking showers and time alone. And clarity. Harper couldn't help thinking they had gotten far more than they'd bargained for.

She felt like she had lived a lifetime in the span of a couple of days. And yet, for the first time in more years than she dared to guess, Harper also felt like herself. Almost. Like the girl that she had been. Or, more accurately, the woman she had always hoped to be. It was an exhilarating feeling, and she found herself staring at her own hands, the half-moon where her bare fingernails peeked from beneath the scarlet polish that Sawyer preferred. The real Harper was in there somewhere, she could feel it. Beneath the coiffed hair and the manicured nails and the humiliation that had grown like moss over her stagnant life. A woman who laughed hard and loved fiercely and embraced the days that she had been given with an abandon that some would undoubtedly call reckless. But Harper knew she wasn't reckless. She never had been. She'd just been unapologetically, gloriously in love with life. And she would be again.

When they made it to the doorway of Will's hospital room, Adri stepped in front of Harper and whispered something to Sam and Jackson. The two men were standing with their backs against the closed door, looking for all the world like body-guards hired to protect William Vogt. Harper wondered if they thought they needed to protect him from her. But they nodded at Adri's words, while Sam motioned Harper closer. He hugged her wordlessly and patted her back. Then he opened the door to Will's room and led Adri and Jackson away.

Will was asleep, or at least, his eyes were closed. His left arm was suspended in a sling from a system of pulleys above the bed, and there was so much metal sticking out of his wounded limb that he looked like a character in a science fiction movie. The poor guy who got abducted by aliens and became the lab rat for their barbaric experiments.

Harper didn't know that it would crush her to see Will so broken, so vulnerable. Or that the hollow place where her heart was supposed to be would fill to overflowing in the instant he opened his eyes. It was irrepressible. Complete.

"Harper?" Will said. His voice was thick and pebbly. He cleared his throat.

"Shhh." Harper put her finger to her lips and navigated the tiny room until she was standing beside the bed. She looked down at Will's handsome face, the features she knew so well that suddenly seemed so very different. His eyes were indigo in the dim light, framed by the laugh lines that made him look happy even when he wasn't smiling. His hair, just a bit too long, fanned out on the white pillow like a flame. She couldn't stop herself from touching it, from taking a strand of it between her fingertips and rolling it against her skin.

"Harper, I—"

But she didn't let him finish. Harper leaned down and kissed his open mouth. He tasted of peppermint. Of her future.

She said, "I'm going to count that as our first kiss."

Epilogue

~

Adri could see the wave coming for a full minute before it was upon her. It was perfect: wide and high, but not more than she could handle. If she had a board, she would have waited for the next set, for the waves that were already crashing on the rocks far beyond the breakers—the ones that would form again and slap the shore with a power that left her breathless. But this was exactly the way to end the day. A long, slow ride up the beach on a wave that would carry her effortlessly.

A few hard strokes, a strong scissor kick, and Adri was a part of the ocean, if only for a few wild seconds. Before she could run out of breath, the wave broke and thundered gallons of water over her head. Up her nose and in her ears. Then all at once she was deposited on the orange sand beach, laughing like a little girl.

Robert was dancing over her, laughing too, because he loved to watch her body-surf. Sometimes she took him into the ocean with her, it was good for his joints, but he could never quite get used to it. He clung to her for dear life, and on nights like tonight, when the moon was already full and the sea had a mind of its own, it was safer for him to play in the sand while she swam. To watch. To giggle at the crazy white lady and her incomprehensible love of water.

"You did it!" Robert shouted as Adri picked herself up. There was sand in her swimsuit and her hair had washed over her face, but she ignored those details and wrapped the boy in a wet hug.

"You'll do it someday, too," she told him, using one hand to flip her hair back in the right direction. "You're going to be a great swimmer."

"And a great doctor," he said proudly. It was something he often claimed, a litany that required her to smile, kiss his head, give the expected answer.

"The best," she assured him, squeezing even tighter. She dropped a kiss on the top of his warm, dark head. Just like she was supposed to do. Just like she loved to do.

Adri could tell that his legs were bothering him, so she toweled off quickly and bent down so Robert could climb onto her back. She didn't mind carrying him, and sometimes felt that she would do it forever if only he would let her. But Robert was eleven, past the years of cuddles and coddling, even though he was more affectionate than most of the boys. The piggyback rides were the ideal compromise.

In fact, the entire setup was the ideal compromise. If Adri could have her way, she'd adopt every kid in the series of orphanages where she worked, but there were more than two hundred of them. Two hundred children she loved as dearly as if they were her own. She had to settle for house dates, for days and weeks, sometimes months when she got to plug in with an individual child or two who needed special attention. Robert had sickle cell anemia, and after a particularly bad flare-up he had come to live in the bungalow on the beach. He had been hers for over six weeks. Well, theirs.

Caleb was walking down the beach toward them, a dishcloth slung over his shoulder and a cell phone in his hand. "It's Harper!" he called, waving the phone at her. "Do you want to take it?"

Adri ran the rest of the way, Robert jostling on her back and snickering all the while. "You take the boy," she said, breathless, "and I'll take the phone."

Caleb laughed and lifted Robert off her back. "Bedtime, young man," he said, settling Robert onto the ground. The boy slipped his hand into Caleb's. Looked up at him adoringly. "And there's some banana cake on the table for you," Caleb told Adri. "I saved you the last piece."

She stood on tiptoe to kiss him full on the mouth, a passionate moment that stretched and evolved until Robert slapped them both on the hands and laughed.

"Okay, okay." Adri ran her fingers over the boy's shaved head, stole one last kiss from Caleb.

"And don't talk too long," Caleb said, finally handing her the phone. "We have to be up early tomorrow."

"I know." Adri took the phone with a wink, and held it against her shoulder as she watched Caleb and Robert walk hand in hand up the grassy slope to the road and the little bungalow that glowed bright in the deepening twilight. Then she spread her towel on the sand and laid back to watch the stars as they began to prick tiny holes in the black canvas of the night. "Hey, Harper," she said, pressing the phone to her ear.

"Is Robert still living with you?" Harper asked without preamble. "He's been with you guys for a while now, hasn't he?"

"A month and a half," Adri admitted. "I'm having a hard time letting go."

"I'll say. Is this the longest?"

"Yeah, I think so." But Adri knew so. She knew that Robert had found a special place in their hearts, a place that would only ever be occupied by him.

"Maybe you can adopt him . . ."

"Maybe someday," Adri agreed, but it wasn't a possibility. Not yet. "How are things going at Piper's House?"

Harper's voice took on a lustrous quality that was evident even from even six thousand miles away. "We have another girl."

"You do?" Adri didn't know whether to be sad or excited. When the Safe House approached Harper about becoming a case worker several months after Sawyer Donovan's trial and conviction, neither of the women could have guessed how the relationship would unfold. And a year after that, when it became obvious that the Safe House was outgrowing its narrow walls, everyone was surprised when the perfect solution presented itself. Piperhall had sat empty for nearly two years. Adri's inspiration finally hit. A home for lost girls, girls exactly like the Piper of Piperhall fame. And Victoria and Adri and Harper.

"She's fourteen, Adri." Harper sounded heartsick. "Fourteen."

"I love you," Adri said suddenly. "I love what you're doing. You take good care of her, okay? You love the life back into that sweet thing."

"We're working on it," Harper said.

There was a scuffle and some words that Adri couldn't make out, then Harper said, "Will's here. He wants to talk to you."

"Put him on."

"Okay. Take good care of Caleb, Adri. And Robert, too. See you guys soon."

" 'Bye."

"Adri?" Will always seemed to feel the need to shout, as if the greater the distance between them, the louder he had to be.

"I'm here, Will. Take it down a notch or two."

More shuffling. A door being shut. "Gotcha. Say, I gotta skip all the hi and how are you stuff and get right down to it. Did you mean what you said in your email?"

"Every word," Adri said, a smile in her voice. "It's yours. She's going to love it."

"But David gave Mom's ring to you. I don't want to—"

"Will," Adri interrupted. "Shut up. It's yours. Give it to Harper so that she can plan a wedding before we come out at Christmas. We're expecting a Christmas wedding, you know. Trees and tinsel and lights and everything that goes with it. Eggnog. Tell me you'll serve eggnog at your wedding."

"Sure," Will laughed. "Whatever you want, little sis."

Adri's throat suddenly felt tight, and though she tried to squeeze back the tears that threatened at the corners of her eyes, it was no use. They spilled down her temples, adding salt to the ocean water already in her hair. Maybe Caleb wouldn't notice that she had been crying. Or maybe he would smooth the faint trails of her tears, kissing the twin paths that curled away from her eyes. She hoped for the latter.

They hung up quickly after that, Will afraid of being caught by Harper, and Adri well aware that morning would come altogether too quickly. She clicked off the call and held the phone against her forehead, saying a breathless, wordless prayer for Harper and Will. And Sam. Jackson, Nora, and little Emma. Caleb and Robert and herself.

Adri stood up and grabbed the towel that was scented with her suntanned skin and shook it out hard before folding it over her arm. She picked her way through the night to the bungalow and the man she called home.

To the place where in the morning, all that was darkness would be made light.

Acknowledgments

I loved writing *The Beautiful Daughters*. It was so fresh and exciting; I often felt like a debut novelist instead of the author of seven previous books. Much of my delight in the process was fueled by friends, critique partners, and family members, who championed this particular work and encouraged me along the way. I owe them all a debt of gratitude (as well as wine and goodies and my undivided attention the next time we meet). I hope to mention everyone here, but if I overlook someone, please forgive me. You know who you are. I adore you.

A big hug to the ladies of my local writing group. Kelly Youngblood, Jen Sandbulte, Susan Stanley, Nikolyn Kredit, Lila Sybesma, and Ashlee Koedam never cease to amaze me with their insight and enthusiasm. They are wise and gifted and so much fun. I hope we are together for years as we take turns celebrating one another's victories.

Kellie Coates Gilbert, Roberta Gately, and Andrea Lochen read early editions of the manuscript and offered sage advice when it was desperately needed. I am so grateful they were willing to take time out of their own busy schedules to help me find my way.

The talented Elizabeth Blackwell has also been an early reader, cheerleader, sounding board, and friend. I wish we lived closer so our phone dates could be face-to-face with coffee, but near or far, I couldn't ask for a better publishing sister to help me navigate the waters.

Kate Brauning is my writing partner and unofficial social media guru. I'm so thankful for her advice and expertise, but her friendship has trumped even my appreciation of her keen assessment of plots and character motivation.

Josh and Jessica Louwerse are the kind of people that Aaron and I want to be when we grow up. Josh didn't know it at the time, but our first long conversation about his work at Covenant House sowed the seed that became Harper's story line in *The Beautiful Daughters*. I so admire who you are and what you do. Your lives are a testimony and an inspiration.

My agent, Danielle Egan Miller, and the entire team at Browne & Miller (Joanna MacKenzie, Abby Saul, and Molly Foltyn) are brilliant, tenacious, and so supportive of my work it's humbling. They are also excellent editors and offered much needed guidance at every stage as the book unfolded.

A special thank you to Sarah Branham and the entire team at Atria for taking me on and bringing such energy and excitement to the table.

Finally, my family put up with a lot as I wrote and rewrote *The Beautiful Daughters*. Never mind that we were in the process of adopting our own (and only) daughter during the months I put pen to paper. We don't just survive chaos, we thrive on it. Aaron, Isaac, Judah, Eve, and Matthias, thank you. I love you and this crazy life we lead.